Three Lives of Eliza

Three Lives

of

ELIZABETH

by

Shirley Seifert

J. B. LIPPINCOTT COMPANY
PHILADELPHIA AND NEW YORK

Library of Congress Catalog Card Number 52–5087

To

BOONSLICK
Heart of Missouri

CONTENTS

Part 1

A Young Man Named Wilcox

Part 2

The Fascinating Mrs. Ashley

Part 3

Lady Crittenden

Author's Note

Part One

A Young Man Named Wilcox

CHAPTER ONE

Boonslick, Land of Opportunity

IN 1820, A TRAVELER, wishing to cross from the so-called city of Franklin, Missouri Territory, to the newer settlement of Boonville on the opposite and southern shore of the Missouri River, was entirely at the mercy of that rolling, yellow stream and Captain William Porter's strictly one-horsepower ferry. On a chill March morning of that year, a young man stood well forward on the snub-nosed boat to make this observation. At the same time he thought, whimsically, that, if the boat struck a snag, or the jaded horse, weary of its treadmill, took a notion to kick the clumsy craft apart, sending all on board to the bottom of the river, his chance of ultimate survival might not be less than if he should reach the far shore without mishap. Things were that desperate with him.

Nothing about the young man externally betrayed this inward discouragement. Wrapped in a caped coat against a raw wind—straight off a glacial ice cap, he was sure—his posture was something between Napoleonic majesty and the dauntlessness of a Crusader. His well-shaped mouth was set in a firm line. His nose was a bit white with cold and, he could have added, some recent malnutrition; but, under dark brows meeting at the bridge of it, gray eyes of unquenchable warmth looked steadily at the high shore ahead. It was a noble shoreline, rising from water level in graduated heights to a long, crescent-shaped parade of hills and headlands, all well forested, none craggy or forbidding, several high points so symmetrically rounded as to suggest that the hand of man had helped the hand of God in smoothing and sodding and planting. Behind him spread the broad, fertile flood plain of the river. He found no fault with the scenery except that it seemed increasingly barren of prospects of a livelihood for him. At twenty-two, he very much wanted to live and he had hoped to turn his abilities and his education into good living. That was what had brought him to the Boonslick country. A mistake, he began to suspect.

His luggage, a worn leather portmanteau and an oblong black case suitable for surgical instruments or dueling pistols, the two articles holding all his earthly goods, rested on the deck at his feet. In one hand he held the folded sheet of a small newspaper, the ink on it hardly dry. It was, in fact, because of this edition of *The Missouri Intelligencer* that Captain Porter was making this crossing. His handful of passengers, including the brave young man, wasn't worth the effort; but the population of Boonville, while small, was, if it could read at all, of a high grade of literacy and avid for its news the day and the hour when it was ready. Every man on the boat carried a similar sheet; and, about midstream, one of them walked forward to address the stranger.

He was a middle-aged man, short but wide. Decisive action, a purposeful gait and an even more purposeful gleam in his eye suggested one with special interests to promote. His approach, while courteous, was direct. One thumb marked an advertisement in the first column of the paper.

"Mornin'," he said. "Pardon the liberty, but would this be you, sir?"

The advertisement announced that one Daniel P. Wilcox, an accredited physician, was opening an office in Boonville, where he intended to practise medicine and surgery.

"I am Dr. Wilcox," the young man acknowledged.

That in the paper was a bolder announcement; considering that he had not as yet set foot in the town of his choice; but ordering the notice, then seeing it in type, had been the one thing, he felt, that had kept him from turning in his tracks and beating a retreat—an act wholly unworthy of a Wilcox, or a Pinchbeck, for that matter, which was what the *P* in his name stood for.

"My name's Harris," the older man said. "I make my home in Boonville yonder. Reason I was interested. We've been getting a right smart supply of doctors lately."

"So I was told," Daniel answered, bitterness burning his throat, "after I had paid fifty cents for the notice."

"Oh, it's not that bad," Mr. Harris consoled, then added, "Hard money?"

Only Daniel could say how hard. He shuddered to think how near that silver piece had come to being his last coin. But he knew what the Boonslick man meant. Familiar as he had been all his life with barter, he had never seen it practised as extensively as it was on this frontier. Almost anything here went for money except money—a scrap of paper, smudged and tattered from being passed from hand to hand, a bundle of deerhides, a pig, a bushel of corn. His cheekbones stood out more sharply than before. His mouth hardened.

"I am a professional man and a stranger," he said tightly. "I have no produce." Certainly he would not yield his few scalpels and lancets.

Then he was sorry he had spoken discourteously to one obviously kindly disposed. He could do with a friend or two in this new land. "I beg your pardon, sir. It is just that I— A person wonders how people live out here. On what?"

Mr. Harris was not offended.

"Credit," he said briskly. "Expectations."

Daniel Wilcox opened his mouth to groan; but, before the sound came out, the absurdity of the situation struck him and he laughed, instead. He laughed helplessly and hard. The pain of it racked his chest. Before the spasm was over, he took out a clean linen handkerchief and wiped his eyes.

"I do beg your pardon," he said again. "I . . . I mean no offense."

Mr. Harris beamed on him paternally and pursued his questioning. "Virginia?" he guessed.

"No, sir. K-Kentucky." Daniel choked and asked pardon for that.

"Same thing," Mr. Harris suggested.

"I suppose. My father was a Virginian. My mother's people are from North Carolina."

Laughter fled. Perhaps this was the reason he had not beat a cowardly retreat. Empty as the horizon ahead looked, the rearward view was still more empty—with known loss.

"Good mixture," Mr. Harris commented. "Ought to feel at home here."

Ought to, maybe. Might some day. Right now . . .

"Could you," Daniel asked, his throat hurting again, "recommend me to a lodging house?"

Mr. Harris looked him over thoughtfully.

"No," he said conclusively, "I couldn't."

"I assure you, I've seen all kinds lately."

"I'm dead sure you have, son, gettin' here. It's a long two hundred miles up river from St. Louis and the country's new. Only been opened for settlement a half-dozen years. I—" obviously he hated to admit a flaw in this land of his adoption. "To tell the truth, we have nothing to offer in the way of a proper tavern as yet." He hesitated again and then his sympathy overcame his last reserve. "Our house, like most in town, is small for our needs. Just at present we have other guests; but, if you'd not mind a pallet somewhere, Mrs. Harris and I would be glad to accommodate you."

This extreme and unexpected kindness struck Daniel so suddenly and so hard that he scarcely knew what he answered. Something purely defensive.

13

"Thank you, Mr. Harris. Thank you, indeed. I would not think of discommoding you or your lady. I will make some arrangement."

Blinking, he gave his full attention again to the shore. Did God's ravens by chance inhabit this wilderness?

The boat was now near to the landing. He could see people waiting there. An astonishing number of people, when he was sure the houses on the rising ground could not count up to more than twenty or thirty. White people, with a trimming of black. Men and several women. Well, naturally; but, again, it was not reasonable to expect to find any such as the two on whom his eyes, drawn by irresistible magnetism, came to rest.

They were two young women, so wrapped in shawls against the wind that their body contours were fairly obliterated; but their faces, framed by snug, quilted hoods, one of bright red and the other sky blue, were not. They were rosy, charming girl faces and plainly to the liking of a tight circle of men surrounding the two.

No ravens probably. Girls. Beautiful girls, sweet . . . Daniel swallowed hard and turned back to his interrogator.

"Mr. Harris, you've been very good. There is a favor I might ask. These other doctors—the ones who got here ahead of me—would you care to tell me something about them?"

"Glad to," Mr. Harris said. "Only one has located right in Boonville so far. Name's Bohannon. Ambrose Bohannon. Big feller. Young. Foreigner of sorts. Good man, I hear, when he's sober."

"Oh?" Daniel murmured, and waited to hear more; but Mr. Harris, perversely, had nothing further to communicate about this potential rival.

"Most of them," Mr. Harris continued, "have settled on the other side. For some reason people take to that land more commonly." Yes, Daniel could see now that the north bank of the river, which he was leaving, had a more settled, populated look than the high southern shore. "The best doctor of them all, I've no doubt, is a Virginia-Kentucky gentleman by the name of Moss—Dr. James Moss. Has a half-brother in St. Louis who is a big name down there, I hear; but Dr. Moss is interested in farming as well as doctoring. He took up several thousand acres down on Two-Mile Prairie twenty miles east of here a while back—in Boone County. Built himself a fine house and has great plans for developing the land and the community. Twenty miles . . . it's a good piece to go; but, pshaw, we think nothing of riding that far for a good doctor if we need one."

Mr. Harris paused to let this sink in. It sank, like a lead plummet. Boonslick folk would ride twenty miles for anything they needed and wanted. A sturdy lot, no doubt. Few ailments probably. An occasional broken bone. Babies. Twenty miles was a distance to go with a baby coming.

"Dr. Moss has the right idea about the land, I think," Mr. Harris resumed. "Very good land hereabouts, Dr. Wilcox. Boonslick, as I said, has been open to settlement only a few years and we've made three counties out of it already—Howard and Boone on the other side of the river, and Cooper over here. Hills over here bother some, but don't let them scare you off. Pockets of fine land between them, water, pasture—available in any quantity from a New Madrid survey of one hundred and sixty acres to a quarter section. Ah . . . speaking as one with official connections . . ."

With a jerk Daniel recovered his balance. So, that was the secret of Mr. Harris's kindness. He had land to dispose of. Daniel shook his head. He had no idea what a New Madrid survey was, but he knew exactly how flat his pockets were.

"Later," he said. "Later, perhaps; but, thank you."

"Certainly," Mr. Harris agreed. "Want to get your bearings, of course; but keep it in mind. Sorry I didn't make your acquaintance on the other side. You might have liked to talk things over with Dr. Moss. He's up here checking boundaries with the land office in Franklin. Meantime his daughter's staying with us, visiting my girl Barcie. They're of an age. The two of them are over yonder. See them? H'lo there, my honeys!"

He raised his hat and waved it. Handkerchiefs came out of the shawls and waved in response. The ferryboat made its landing with a bump and a jolt, and an oath from the captain, who vowed piles weren't made to stand the orneriness of that river. Resolutely Daniel shouldered his portmanteau and picked up his instrument case.

"Mrs. Harris must be somewhere about," Mr. Harris was saying. "Come over and meet the family. You'll have a bite to eat with us. . . ."

He was still waving to the girls and holding out other temptations in speech to Daniel, when the latter leaped ashore and began to force his way through the small mob of citizenry.

This was cowardly flight certainly; but, if Mr. Harris had wanted to send him running, he could have chosen no better way than his offer to take Daniel over and present him to the two girls. Haste, even more than penury, made him brush aside the dark hands reaching for his luggage. He was a third of the way up Wharf Hill before he realized what a spectacle he must appear to anyone watching him from below, and checked his gait to what he hoped was a more decorous and dignified stride.

Girls . . . now, God knew he had no natural aversion to them. Almost the last advice his mother had given him, when she knew she would not live to see him well launched into manhood, had been to marry young.

"Marry young, my son," she had said, "while life is sweet and full of zest"; and he had hoped to do just that. For one thing, he knew that the void left in his heart by the passing of the proud, gentle woman who had ruled it up to then could be filled in no other way. But hard circumstance had arranged things otherwise. His father, a colonel in General Washington's Revolutionary Army, had left the war with honor, a chest ailment, and a bounty of land in Kentucky. Grief over the early loss of his wife and the chest ailment had combated against proper development of the land; and, when he, too, died, Daniel's combined inheritance from the two parents was barely enough to enable him to complete his study of medicine in the small but excellent school in Lexington, and then make his way to a new land, where he had hoped to make his start in life among people generally of the same restricted means. He began now to have his doubts even about that. Most of the people in Boonslick seemed in one way or another to be doing very well.

However that might or might not be, here he was; and one thing was absolutely certain. Women, except as patients, were not for him. He must avoid their society as much as possible, must not indulge even in a small flirtation. He straightened his back, pulled his face into its most forbidding expression of sternness and trudged on.

A few steps later he came to a dragging stop. It actually was as if something were trying to pull him downhill when he meant to go up. It was the girls, of course. How he could have seen them really, as he hurried off, even he couldn't say; but the picture was clear in his mind and growing clearer by the minute.

Two girls—both, he was sure, eminently desirable. One was a plump, blond pigeon. That would be Mr. Harris's girl, Barcie. Barcie, hmm! Sweet as honey, no doubt. But the other was even more of a temptress. She was dark. He was pretty certain of that. The red hood suggested dark eyes. Medium tall. All slender grace under the disguising shawl. Now, how could he know that? She was a hallucination. The two were a double hallucination, sent by the Devil. He gathered himself together again, shifted his portmanteau and in a final burst of energetic speed, disregarding appearances, he made it to the top of the hill.

The main result of his hurry was to land him on a deserted town-site. The rutted lane he had climbed continued on up and over a gentler rise, cutting at right angles several so-called streets paralleling the river. There was no suspicion of paving or sidewalks. The center of the streets had been beaten into some smoothness; and the straggling houses, mostly log cabins, with here and there a clapboard front, were set more or less in a line; but that was the extent of planned development. The clapboarded cabin on his left bore a sign, saying it was a store belonging to one Jacob Wyan; so he entered, but found it as empty of people as the town. He came out to find that the gathering at the river's edge was just beginning to break up and a few, with more pressing duties above, were now coming back up the hill. Happily, the girls and Mr. Harris were not among them.

Reassured, Daniel stepped out boldly to meet the returning procession and to address a question to its leader, a workman in canvas apron, armed with a hammer.

"Good morning. Can you direct me to the office of Dr. Bohannon?"

Until the words were out, he had no idea of what he was going to say; but perhaps it was as good an answer to his many perplexities as any. The name Bohannon seemed to have stuck to his memory. A Scottish name, he thought. In North Carolina, where he had visited often, there were many Scots. He liked them.

The man in the apron looked Daniel over—a prevailing custom apparently—smiled with some secret knowledge and motioned indefinitely to his right.

With no better directions to work on than that, it was a groaning, deep and repeated, which brought Daniel up finally before a one-room log house a square and a half away from the first crossroads. The house had a tight door and two glazed windows fronting the street; and, when he came right up to it, he saw in the corner of one window a card reading, "Ambrose Bohannon, Physician. Knock and enter." Sighing, Daniel set down his portmanteau and, having no idea whether the groaning came from the doctor in a spirituous state or from a patient, obeyed instructions.

Inside, of course, he found the answer. He stepped into a room, sparsely furnished but unlittered and clean, smelling agreeably of whitewash and disagreeably of people—two bearded, bloody, disheveled and nearly disabled men, placed strategically on a cot and a chair at opposite sides of the room, with a third man, the doctor, presumably, ministering to the wounds of one and keeping the bulk of his body athwart the other.

17

"Just a minute," this man said, his back still to the door. "Can you not see I am busy?"

"I can, indeed," Daniel said. "Would you like me to lend a hand? My name is Wilcox, Dr. Wilcox at your service."

The other Doctor fastened a bandage, straightened his back and turned. He was a big man with broad, slightly stooped shoulders, the peering eyes of a scholar, a massive forehead from which dark hair had begun to retreat, and a nose that had been smashed beyond re-pair in some disaster. Daniel had never seen a homelier or a more likable face.

"Ye don't mean it?" Bohannon said incredulously. "Yes, I see you do. Put down your duffle and give us the hand then. I've only two of me own and both overworked at present."

Without further palaver, Daniel peeled his coat, rolled up his sleeves and went to work, helping Ambrose Bohannon clean and bandage sundry deep and jagged cuts on the arms and chest of the man on the cot. The man's head was already done up in torn sheeting. He, however, was not the one who groaned. That was the man on the chair across the room.

"Multiple fracture of the bones of the forearm," Bohannon explained between his teeth as he and Daniel worked. "But this one was bleeding. There now. Finish him if you will. I'll just step out for some medicine I lack before taking hold o' the other. Keep them apart —that's the main thing—till I come back."

"He come at me with his huntin' knife," the fellow on the cot said hoarsely to Daniel as Ambrose went out the door. "Lucky I had on boots."

Boonville, Daniel thought, breathing easily for the first time in hours, seemed a more fertile field for experimentation than he had hoped a while back.

When Bohannon returned, his copy of *The Intelligencer* stuck up from his coat pocket and his medicine was in a jug. He measured out a dosage in a cup for the man on the bed, reserved an equal portion for the one with the broken arm, then set out a clean glass from a wall cupboard for Daniel. Daniel refused the drink for the present. Absolutely hollow inside by this time, he mistrusted the effect of neat whiskey on his hand and eye. The second patient, he observed, was also wearing boots; and it looked as if setting his injured arm might be a task.

It was all of that, and made no easier by the acute pleasure that the too suddenly revived man on the cot took in his mate's sufferings.

18

This time Bohannon held the patient down while Daniel put the damaged bones in line, bound the arm and adjusted splints. Twice the patient howled and called Daniel, Bohannon and the man on the cot names that smoked up the air; but Daniel's hands remained steady and sure. He worked fast, exulting in the almost involuntary skill of his fingers. When the job was done, the last trace of depression was lifted from his spirit by the respect in the eyes of the banged-up ruffians and of Ambrose Bohannon.

A half-hour later, with the room cleared of combatants and swept and aired, he sat at the pine table in the center of it, trying not to wolf down a slab of nutritious, well-cured venison between thick slices of wheat bread, and discussed professional partnership with his host.

"Ye could do worse," Bohannon said diffidently.

Much worse, Daniel thought. He liked Bohannon. He suspected in him a great and tender heart, as lonely as his own or lonelier, scarred by ten years more of living. They had exchanged credentials, Daniel's diploma from the College of Medicine in Lexington, Kentucky, seeming small now beside Bohannon's from Edinburgh. The rest of his story the latter did not give to everyone. Upon his graduation he had been pressed into military service, Great Britain being harassed by Napoleonic wars and even by a small one with her former colonies in America, and had been shipped finally with his regiment to Canada. Simultaneously he had conceived a great dislike for the bloody butchery of even a small war and an equally great attachment for the freedom of the New World. Manifestly he could not enjoy that freedom in Canada; so at his first opportunity he had slipped over the border into the United States. The irony of that was, of course, that he had needed then to put himself as far as possible from the reach of the King's officers and legal niceties. So he had come to this place, where he had occasionally more than he could well stomach still of blood, fighting it out being a frontiersman's way of settling most disputes. The whiskey, Daniel was to understand, was to steady his stomach and for the lonelies. He made a ceremony of stowing the jug now on the top shelf of the wall cupboard.

"I have the small advantage of two years on the spot," he pleaded, seeming really anxious to achieve the suggested partnership. "I know the lay o' the land and a' that. Ye wouldna need to bother about lodgings. There is room here for a cot, which ye can procure from the trader, and blankets, too."

19

"I have almost no money," Daniel reminded him.

"Your credit is by now well established, man, with two living witnesses telling a' and sundry aboot you, and this in the paper."

The Intelligencer was spread on the table. Embarrassed by sudden emotion, Daniel dropped his eyes to it.

"You really think," he said, "there is work enough here to keep the two of us?"

"Man, there is work and a great need wherever people gather to live," Bohannon assured him. "As to keep, are you a fair shot?"

"Fair," Daniel allowed.

"There is meat then in plenty, running wild in the forest, wi' a quarter of beef for variety to be had handily at the shootin' matches. We hae them most every Saturday. It is a way of keeping a man's gun oiled and his eye true."

And his hand and his heart steady, because of the challenge to heroism, which abides in every young man's bosom. Ambrose Bohannon painted a more appealing picture than the bustling, overeager Mr. Harris. Still there was a flaw.

"You do not hold out much hope," Daniel remarked, "of a rapid rise from poverty to wealth."

"No," Ambrose admitted, "and I'm hard pressed to know why. It is a rich and bountiful land and a' much as the redmen left it a short time back. Sweet springs for drinking water. Salt licks for cattle, if you can keep the painters at bay. Some springs, they say, have medicinal value, but we'll go into that later. Little and big rivers full o' fish. Prairie land deep and fertile and loose to the plow, though subject now and again to inundation. Nature's sugar where the bees have stored it in a handy hollow tree— Now, laugh if ye will but it's the truth. For our need, perhaps, the population is still scarce. This town and Franklin over the river are a' of consequence in the whole wide region, but it could be an advantage to have arrived at the beginning of growth rather than at the end of it, for growth there will be. I'm sure o' that." He leaned back in his chair and closed his eyes, the better to dream. "A man could take a thousand acres, clear it, cultivate it, build himself a house, and live like a king, tipping his hat to nobody."

Dr. Moss? Daniel pricked up his ears. The father of that exquisite . . .

"Or," Ambrose continued, "he could look into those medicinal springs."

"For either purpose," Daniel prodded, "he'd need a little something to lay down on the table when he closed the bargain."

"Aye," Ambrose agreed somberly. "Aye."

They considered that obstacle and how likely it was to thwart the ambitions of a young man with nothing in his pockets, all his fortune still to be made. They observed that those who came with capital to invest, enough to tide them over the first lean years, were the most likely to take wealth from the country. Ambrose named two—a Mr. Taylor Berry with enterprises in land on the north side of the river in Howard and Boone counties, and a William Ashley of St. Louis, who had worked on the original survey of public lands in central Missouri and had purchased likely pieces wherever he could. Daniel conceived a distaste for both these fortunate men, but especially for Mr. Ashley, who seemed to be able to put a finger into all sorts of pies in search of plums. In the very copy of *The Intelligencer* spread out on the pine table he announced himself as candidate for the office of Lieutenant Governor of Missouri in elections projected to follow the admission of the territory into the Union as a state, the terms of that admission being now a leading subject for debate in the national Congress.

"If I were so situated that I could buy land," Daniel said bitterly, "I should probably be adding to the profits of one or both of those men."

No doubt, Ambrose agreed. The world, they concluded, was grievously unkind to young men of no inheritance. Occasionally one so handicapped made a name for himself, but it was not often. Ambrose uncorked the brown jug, and the simple act gave him an inspiration.

"There is just one thing," he observed, "that a young man can do better than an older one. He can marry the daughter of a rich man."

It was the one remark needed to plunge Daniel back into despair and he said so.

"Na, na," Ambrose chided. "You cannot hold it against a girrul that her father is prosperous."

"It adds nothing to her charm," Daniel insisted. Also, it put her farther out of reach.

"I do not agree entirely," Ambrose said. "I ken a sonsie lass lives right here in Boonville who seems well fixed; and right now she has a friend visiting her who some think is even lovelier. The second beautiful creature is the daughter of a physician, if that means aught to you."

A Dr. Moss, a Virginia gentleman, who had bought not one but several thousand acres of land. Lovely, indeed, the daughter; but . . .

"They're planning a dancing and barbecue party for a housewarming," Ambrose informed him. "I've had the honor of an invitation for myself and such friends as I choose to take along. These are always community gatherings."

Daniel could imagine no prospect more heart-warming than that of attending this party, though not, he thought, under a general community invitation. He would prefer to establish his own identity in advance, say with a proper call upon the young lady's parents. That was manifestly not possible; so he smothered his warm desire under a cold stiffness of denial.

"By that time," he said, "I shall hope to be too busy to ride twenty miles to a dancing party. Besides, I lack a horse."

For the second time Ambrose Bohannon set down the jug untapped.

"Dr. Wilcox," he observed, "you have shown the first taint of dishonesty in dealing with me. A horse is to be had as easily as bed or blankets; but who gave you the distance to Dr. Moss's place in miles and where have you seen the young lady?"

CHAPTER TWO

A Double, Hewed Log House

IN AFTER YEARS, when life in the Boonslick country was both sweet and sour in the remembering, Elizabeth Moss returned always in thought to the house her father had built there, and not to the externals of that house, though they made their own pretensions. A double, hewed log house, its specifications read; and that was pretentious for the time and the place; but her fondest recollections were of what was styled the great room in that house.

The great room—it ran from front wall to rear, filling the space to the left of the wide central hall. It was a room designed for general living. The chairs were deep seated and sturdy, lined with pillows for those whose bones wanted such padding; and there were stools for very tired feet or for the young and quick to light upon. The larger furniture was a mixture of elegant mahogany from Virginia and of Missouri walnut, fashioned by local craftsmen, overshadowing chairs and stools of hickory. The pieces were or were not treasures according to the age of those who possessed them. At sixteen, Elizabeth knew that furniture was just wood put to good use; and yet, always the bright picture remained.

Entrance from the hall—it would have been a dogtrot in a homelier house—was through an open arch, so that one came immediately from out of doors into the glow of the fire in the deep hearth midway of the long wall. Always, except in the heat of summer, someone had a chair drawn up to that fire; and on this chill, wet late afternoon in March, one week to the day after Elizabeth's return from Boonville, there were two—Miss Mary, her bright-eyed, sharp-spoken mother, and an auburn-haired, modishly attired young matron whom she rather absurdly called Aunt Farrar, born Anne Clark Thruston of Louisville, Kentucky, the new wife now of Dr. Moss's half-brother, the illustrious Dr. Bernard Farrar of St. Louis. The women at the hearth were comparing patchwork quilt blocks; but their talk was chiefly advice to the young and unmarried, slanted sideways at Elizabeth. It was a way, Elizabeth had observed, that women, securely settled in life, had of talking when such an audience offered. One wondered alternately whether they were boasting or sounding a warning.

"I agree with all you say about position, Sister Mary," Anne Farrar was saying. "A girl should marry in her own station and continue to enjoy the refined associations among which she has been reared; but, you know, I shouldn't fret too much about the remoteness of this region. If they ever succeed in bringing steamboats up the Missouri or even in making a good stage road, there will be a constant coming and going. Now, take my journey up from St. Louis for an example. Our steamboat ran aground at St. Charles, I know; and we had to come the rest of the way by whatever conveyance the men in our party could secure; but here I am, safe and sound. To be sure, I had the protection of my half-brothers, the O'Fallons, who make the journey upriver often by keelboat. In addition, there was this brave young man I've mentioned to you, who did so much for the comfort of the women in the party—at the expense, I'm sure, of his own."

Elizabeth sharpened her ears. If mention had been made before this of a young man, it must have been when she was away. Could he be the same young man whom she had noted—just noted—at the ferry landing in Boonville? The time was right. But how could she ask without seeming more interested than she really was?

"I'm sure he contemplated settling," Anne Farrar continued, "and he's an example of what I think you might expect. Young men of good breeding and education, fired with the spirit of adventure . . ."

Mrs. Moss sniffed delicately, but with emphasis. The last thing, she implied, in the way of a marital opportunity for a child of hers would be an adventurous young man, such as young Mrs. Farrar mentioned. Vagabonds, vagrants, no matter how you sized them up.

Dear Miss Mary. A person had to make allowances for her. Born a Woodson of Virginia and a Randolph, too, great-granddaughter in direct line of Isham Randolph of Dungeness, second cousin to Thomas Jefferson and other illustrious folk, she had a very burden of halos to keep bright. One sprang from a legend concerning her own small part in the nation's history. She had been, the story went, a baby in her cradle when Lord Cornwallis on his way to Yorktown had quartered himself and his staff at Dover, the Woodson home on the James River. Nobody knew that he was marching to his downfall and the family had been in a natural state of tremble. Noticing this, Lord Cornwallis, to reassure them all, had picked up the baby, held it a moment in his arms, then kissed its cheek and laid it back in the cradle. A woman who had felt the salute of such lordly lips was likely to have a touch of the hoity-toity forever after.

"Probably without a cent to his name," Miss Mary said of Anne Farrar's brave young man. "Most of them have nothing. Some of them marry before they leave home—girls delicately bred, used to comforts —and bring them out here, to settle them in mean little log cabins, with no comforts, the nearest neighbor an hour's hard riding away; and they—" she leaned toward Anne Farrar and whispered—"have babies under those circumstances. Really," she settled back in her chair and rocked hard, "it should be a lesson."

It was a lesson. Elizabeth's father had taken her to visit such a forest cabin where there was a new baby. The cabin was bare, but it was not mean. The baby, a boy with fuzzy black hair, was so sweet, the mother so proud, the father so solemn that meanness could not endure in their presence.

"A person wonders," Mrs. Moss said, "what such girls' people are thinking of—to let them go."

As if a girl's people could come between her and her true wishing! They probably fussed, as Anne Clark Thruston's people had fussed when she married, as Mrs. Moss fussed now, with only vague apprehensions for a reason.

"If young folks would only listen to their elders!" she said. "They have no way of knowing otherwise what lies ahead."

"Ah, but they think they know," Anne Farrar said.

Perhaps they did know, Elizabeth would have added, if it had been her place to enter the conversation. Older folk might be surprised at what went on in the heads they thought so empty of wisdom. A girl had her own ideas. Elizabeth had. At sixteen she found life so sweet to the taste just as it was that she was in no hurry to change it. She and Barcie Harris had talked the whole matter out under a shared bed quilt in Boonville. They had decided that the one thing was not to be in too great a hurry. Play parties and husking bees and housewarmings were fun, and young men's eyes were warm and their words breathless and breath-taking; but, if you chose one before another, very soon you found yourself, plunk, in a low chair by the fire with a cap on your head and a piece of sewing in your hand and babies pulling at your skirts; and those things were all good and part of living, but being sixteen and pretty and sought after were part of living, too; and one could wait quite safely for several years if one were an Elizabeth Moss or a Barcie Harris.

So, if her mother was worried about anything that might have happened in Elizabeth's three days in Boonville—and plainly something about that did worry her—she could just dismiss the matter from her mind. Nothing really had happened.

Heigho, nothing! Her toes still curled under, remembering the cold ground that morning at the foot of Wharf Hill. She had come down with Barcie and Mrs. Harris to meet the ferryboat, expecting her father to cross on it with Mr. Harris, which would be a sign that she must get her things together for the return journey and home. They stood there hours, it seemed to her, watching the monotonous roll of the river, then watching that ugly little chip of a boat stagger across. When it was halfway over, she knew that the man talking to Mr. Harris was not her father. A minute later Barcie Harris clutched her arm.

"Look!" she said tensely.

Pretending only a mild interest, Elizabeth looked. The arrival of a boat, it seemed, carried the same power of excitement in the wilds of Missouri as it did at Louisville or Maysville, Kentucky, possibly more because boats were rarer. In spite of her cold toes, she felt a strong thrill run through her at the moment of landing. Neither at Louisville nor Maysville, nor even in St. Louis, had she seen a more personable young man than this stranger. There was a distinguished look about him. He rose up like King Saul—and then abruptly he disappeared, to emerge again, carrying his own luggage and hustling up the hill as if somebody were shooting at his heels.

"Well, did you ever?" Barcie gasped.

No, Elizabeth had never. It was the first time since she had put up her hair that a man, young or old, within sight of her—and he could see her just as clearly as she saw him—had moved away instead of toward her. That alone was enough to claim her attention.

Mr. Harris was still fuming when he came up to the girls.

"Young popinjay! And he seemed such a nice fellow. Right in the middle of my asking him— Barcie, girl . . . Miss Libby, how are you? Sorry to disappoint you, child, if you were looking for your pa on that boat. He finds that business will keep him in Franklin the rest of the day. I'm to have the pleasure of taking you across to meet him there tomorrow mornin'."

"Oh, good!" Barcie cried. "We'll have another day and a night to talk about the housewarming. And now, Pa, who was he?"

"Who was who?" Mr. Harris growled.

"You know. The young man on the boat. Look, there he goes yonder! Now, don't say, Pa, that he's just another young man and the woods are full of them. He looks . . . well . . . different."

One of the nicest things about Barcie Harris, Elizabeth had decided early in their brief acquaintance, was that she could be relied upon to say right out what another person thought but kept decently covered. Everybody else's eyes were now following the young man up the hill; so she, Elizabeth, felt that she could do the same.

"No," Mr. Harris said thoughtfully in answer to Barcie's remark. "No, because this time I'm inclined to agree with your judgment. Just the same . . ."

"But who is he?" Barcie demanded.

"It's all here in the paper. You two can read it," he put the sheet defensively into his coattail pocket, "after I'm through. Where's your ma, pet? Surely she didn't let you two pretties come down Wharf Hill alone."

And that was everything there was to the episode. All about him in the paper, indeed! His name and his profession and that, disappointingly, he was settling in Boonville. Of course, even in Boonville, there were other young men. A Mr. Claiborne Jackson, for example, had come clear across the river that evening to call at the Harrises. A taking young man, light of foot and pleasant company. He was clerking, temporarily, he said, in Hickman and Lamb's store in Franklin. She saw him again the next day, but had felt in no exceptional peril of losing her head or her heart over him.

Back in Boonville there was that odd character, Dr. Ambrose Bohannon—older than Mr. Jackson. Didn't she like men to be a little older, Barcie had interrogated. What . . . what did she think of Dr. Bohannon? Elizabeth had smiled in reply. With Barcie that was safest.

"What do you find so amusing, daughter?" Mrs. Moss asked suddenly.

"Nothing," Elizabeth answered. "Just something silly Barcie Harris said when I was there."

"I know it was silly if that featherhead thought it up."

Miss Mary did not appear to like Barcie Harris. That was too bad, for Elizabeth had never been so fond of a friend as she was of Barcie. The newness of their acquaintance made the flowing together of their really quite different personalities only the more remarkable. Having no sisters so far in her own house, only a couple of boisterous, though precious, younger brothers, Elizabeth especially appreciated Barcie's warm, unspoiled sweetness and absolute generosity of deed and impulse. They would be friends forever, she was sure.

However, the whys and wherefores were not likely to be understood by older folk; and the profundities of their reasoning would be misinterpreted. So she must keep her own counsel about the confidences she and Barcie shared. It might be best to turn her back on the two women by the fire even while she was only thinking of Barcie.

This was easy for her to do. At the lower end of the room a table had been spread for supper. She was moving about it now, adding finishing touches—a dish of pickle here, a dish of jelly there, small brother Oliver's bib, napkins for the rest, the silver sugar bowl and creamer. Their servants in the new country still were few, their hands occupied with heavier duties. Anyhow, it was an accepted fact that a house where the ladies of the family did not add their refinements to the essentials of living lacked both grace and elegance. This was her opportunity to demonstrate the completeness of her education along those lines and, she happily suspected, a certain aptitude. She had spent most of the afternoon in the kitchen to the rear of the house, "messing about" with sugar and spice, raising finally what Pomegranate, the cook, called a powerful rich smell, some of which had even penetrated the walls of the main house. The mouth-watering fragrance took nothing from the bright picture of the room and the waiting table. Elizabeth drew a deep breath of utter satisfaction, feeling the walls about her, the security, the peace, the tranquility, the genuine richness of the great room—feeling herself light, buoyant, triumphantly young, holding the present, looking back no more than a week into the past and very little farther into the future. The housewarming had been set definitely now for the first week in April, to let March blow itself out.

"Libby!" Her mother's tartness pierced her dreaming. "Where do you think you are, child? I've spoken to you three times and you haven't answered. Can't we have some light?"

"Oh!" Libby said. "Yes. I suppose so."

The day was finishing in a tempest of rain. That brought the dark of evening down early and the dark drew the heavy beams of the ceiling closer to the floor and the firelight seemed twice as ruddy against the shadows. However, older folk, it seemed, liked neither dark nor semi-dark. Reluctantly she took a taper from the mahogany sideboard; but, before she could carry it across the room for a light from the fire, someone knocked on the house door.

She put the taper down and looked toward the hall, then toward her mother. The three women were practically alone, small Oliver asleep across the hall, the doctor away and eight-year-old Josiah with him—not that Josiah could have protected them. The few servants were toasting themselves in the kitchen out back. After all, this was the wilderness. The nearest house was Colonel Richard Gentry's new tavern on the Boonslick Trace, six miles away.

The knock was repeated. It was not a demanding or a threatening knock, but it seemed emphatic.

"Pshaw!" Elizabeth said, and went to see who was there.

It was the young man from the Boonville boat landing.

"I was never more surprised," Elizabeth said afterward, though in real truth she was not surprised at all. It was as if her thoughts had conjured him into appearing.

"Well, I certainly was surprised," Daniel Wilcox said. "I mean, I didn't look for you to be the one to open the door."

So they both stood, gawking probably, each taking in the other. "She is not as dark as I thought," Daniel observed. Or was it the fire-light that touched her brown hair with red? He would never go on oath as to the color of her eyes. Gray? Brown? Both probably, a golden hazel, made more alluring by the shadow of dark lashes. Above them, dark brows made smooth arcs against her fair skin. She was so beautiful that the realization and her sudden nearness struck him hard, stealing his breath as well as speech. Beautiful, exquisitely slender, like a tall blade of grass supple to the wind . . .

And from Elizabeth's point of view, the firelight reached out to the stranger, painting him in dim outline against the dark canvas of the rain and early twilight—a tall, young man, in boots and caped coat, a riding crop and a hat in his hand.

"You . . . will you . . . ?" she said uncertainly.

"Am I right," he said in the same second, "in thinking this is the house of Dr. Moss—Dr. James Moss?"

She was mistress of herself on the instant.

"You are looking for my father? He is away at present."

"Libby!" Miss Mary called from the great room. "Who or what is it?"

"A gentleman asking for Papa," Elizabeth answered sweetly, and somewhere in the dark a horse whickered. The young man's eyes dilated, but his next move was forward, not rearward.

"Well, do come in out of the rain!" Mrs. Moss said sharply, as the horse whickered again.

"Why, thank you, ma'am, I will."

A spattered young man, seen in a better light, but still pleasing. And full of manners. He bowed to Elizabeth and more deeply to her mother. Miss Mary was a small woman, frail; but she had a certain imperiousness.

"My name is Wilcox," the young man said. "Dr. Wilcox, at your service, ma'am, and yours." A bow to Aunt Farrar and another—exaggerated?—to Libby. "I've lately settled in this region—at Boonville, west of here. From various sources I have heard such good word of Dr. Moss that, being new to the region and to my profession, I took the liberty . . ."

Obviously there was no reason for the exultation that tossed Elizabeth's heart about or for the equally foolish petulance that laid hold of her. He had not come to seek her out. It was her father.

"Yes, of course," Miss Mary said. "Do come in and lay aside your wet coat and hat. Oh, never mind the floor. It has been dripped on before this. My husband should be back presently, unless," more tartly, with an edge of anxiety, "he has drowned somewhere in the dark."

The young man gripped his hat and riding crop more firmly.

"Madame, if I thought there was any danger of that— I have my horse . . ."

Short of sacrificing Dr. Moss to his noble intention, he would have welcomed the opportunity for heroic action. Anything to make his presence in this house seem other than the bold intrusion which it really was. However, before he could back out of the door and before Miss Mary could explain that her words had been just a manner of speaking, a smaller door at the rear of the hall opened and Dr. Moss himself had arrived.

He was the mildest of men at heart, but he had a great way of sputtering, designed perhaps to conceal his gentleness.

"Miss Mary—Betsy—where are you all? What a night! What a night!" He slid out of his coat and gave it to the black boy who had followed him into the house, and a slap sounded flat and wet on the seat of his son's breeches. "Upstairs with you, J'siah! Change from the skin out, mind! Take those things out to the kitchen to dry, Poke. I can't abide the smell of wet woolen in a warm house. No, wait a minute till I ask about that young man. Miss Mary, where are you? I passed Colonel Gentry's tavern just now and he hailed me to say a young man named Wilcox had stopped there asking directions to our place. Said he was a stranger, and on a night like this— J'siah, what's holding you? I said, 'Upstairs!' And what's the front door doing standing wide open? I— Well, bless my soul! You, sir, are the young man named Wilcox?"

All evening exultation fought with rising petulance for possession of Elizabeth's heart. Oh, Barcie, he came! He just came! Of his own will and wishing, he came! And then she would think she might as well not have been present. Everyone else seemed to have an equal, if not a prior claim to the young man's attention. There was her father.

"You'll have supper with us, sir? Of course, you will. And stay the night if the storm keeps on. Nonsense! It's a poor house that cannot shelter a stranger. Poke, take Dr. Wilcox's hat and coat with mine to the kitchen. Then stable the horse. Rub him down and feed him."

The stableboy was probably the only one unhappy about that. He hated a wetting worse than the barn cats.

Then, of course, it was natural that Dr. Moss should play the genial host and elder counsellor, which he did always to perfection, bless him. He loved a bountiful table and as many to partake of the feast as possible. He drew the young man out in friendly questioning. How had he happened to come to this part of the country?

"A man from the land office in Frankfort told in Lexington about a flurry of speculation in land newly opened for settlement in Missouri. It was touted as rich prairie land to be had cheaply. A number of people bought, some meaning to settle here, others speculating on the country's future. Everybody in Kentucky was talking Missouri."

Dr. Moss nodded. In Maysville he had heard the same talk and that was what had induced him to move westward.

"Did you invest in land?" he asked.

"No, sir. I was hardly in a position to do so, being still in school. I did make up my mind, however, that Missouri seemed a good place in which to set myself up professionally."

His eyebrows went up quizzically. Oh? It didn't look just that way to him now? What a pity!

"Ah!" Dr. Moss said. "And why did you pick on Boonville?"

"I hardly know, sir. A town seemed the thing."

"Penniless," Mrs. Moss said afterward. "Not two coins to rub against each other. And somehow you knew he never would have much. Too easygoing."

Not just that, perhaps. He could be firm to the point of obstinacy.

"Hungry," Mrs. Moss added. "The way he went for his supper!"

But she as much as anyone else pressed food upon him. The meal was simple but hearty—roast prairie chicken with rice balls, roast young porker with hominy and gravy, baked winter squash, fresh Sally Lunn and hot cornbread with wild grape jelly and honey, sweet watermelon pickle and sour relish. Finally Pomegranate herself carried in the dessert, the pan wrapped in a clean kitchen towel. Bless Pommie! She fussed about folks messing around in her kitchen, but she wanted Elizabeth to have full credit now.

"Mercy on us!" Mrs. Moss said, and Josiah's eyes bulged. "Is that

31

what I've been smelling? A small portion for me, Libby. It is good, I know, but very rich."

Elizabeth stood to cut the pie. For the first time since the door had opened to let him in, the young man looked at her, forgetting the others. Or . . . was he looking at the pie? It seemed a pity, truly, to break into the fluff of the filling. She plunged the knife down, to cut her mother's small portion, releasing incense into the already well-flavored air.

Now it was Anne Farrar's turn. Dr. Wilcox, of course, was the young man who had traveled up from St. Louis in her boatload, and had done so much to make the journey endurable. This was her claim to his attention now. She had known him longest.

"In Missouri, Dr. Wilcox," she said, smiling with condescension on Libby, "I find that, as in Kentucky, a lady with a reputation made or still to achieve as mistress of a house, must pin her banner to some particular delicacy. I think at this early age our Libby has probably found hers. Do taste it, but I repeat her mother's warning. It is rich."

"You didn't?" Dr. Wilcox said to Elizabeth. "Did you?"

Elizabeth nodded, and he sighed. Or was it Josiah?

"You're supposed," Josiah prompted, "to say how big a piece you want. Don't let 'em scare you off. It's mighty good." He did some calculation and finished hopefully, "After Aunt Farrar . . . and Libby—I reckon she'll want a piece—there's just three of us left."

He sighed again. Or was that Dr. Wilcox?

"What do you call it?" Dr. Wilcox asked, his tone reverent. "I mean, if it is to be a reason for fame, the delicacy must have a title."

Libby's eyes met his for a breathless moment and fell. Whether his worship was for her or the pastry, it was still worship.

"Vinegar pie," she told him, dimpling, and cut him a fair portion.

This was a sample of their first meeting—the exchange of a half-dozen commonplace remarks; but she knew. There would never in this life be another who could by a mere glance reach the deepest part of her. And this was falling in love? How pleasant, how alarming, how miraculous! Of what use was it for settled matrons to rock and speak sage words to a young heart bent on doing its own exploring? Their words passed through one's consciousness and left, perhaps, a little sediment as they passed, as a light breeze picks up dust and drops some in blowing over. No more. It was as if God in Heaven had planned the meeting, saying, "These two I have made for each other. It is time now that they should come together. I will so direct it."

32

Why did she love Daniel Wilcox as she might never love another? For one thing, he was young, as she was young, splendidly young, in the first vigor of manhood. She could never picture him otherwise than young and strong and eager. He was not meant to know the feebleness of years and illness and crushing sorrow. So far, he had endured enough in life to challenge his strength and courage, not to beat them down. He could laugh heartily at his own discomfitures and bring others to laugh with him. His description of his housekeeping with Ambrose Bohannon, his curious fees for medical services in Cooper County, his accounts at Jacob Wyan's trading store, involving two-way credit and no cash, had them all in stitches after supper. Deep, rich laughter, with the sting of tears hidden somewhere, to make it memorable.

"Penniless," Miss Mary would still insist, having laughed with the others. "Not a copper cent to his name, certainly not a silver dollar."

He was a stranger who had stepped suddenly into Elizabeth's life. And yet, he was not strange, really. He had so many Kentucky associations to share with the Moss family and with Anne Thruston Farrar that the wonder was they had not met there instead of here. He answered with assured frankness Miss Mary's questions about the Pinchbecks of North Carolina, the Wilcoxes of Virginia. She could find no fault in his parentage and made that a matter for argument. His excellent birth made his poverty the more regrettable. Heavens, how it worried her that Daniel Wilcox was poor!

He was a man easy to know. Small intimacies, each insignificant by itself, but all taken together seeming quite important, came naturally when one was with him. After supper, without presuming on the welcome given to him, a stranger, he fitted perfectly into the bright family scene. Josiah, though filled to bursting, cracked river-bottom pecans with a hand-sized stone on the hearth and passed the dish of tasty kernels.

"J'siah, have mercy!" Miss Mary begged, but took some, as did everyone else, including Dr. Wilcox.

He was most respectful of the information the boy had gathered about nut trees and bee trees and paw paws and persimmons, and said, next fall, when the time was right, Josiah must show him. Then, with the same grave courtesy he submitted to Dr. Moss's professional examination.

This turned out to be a thorough questioning, involving lancets, leeches, feverfuges and what not.

"Hear it rain!" Miss Mary said, half-smothering a yawn, to warn her husband that he was being tiresome.

"Eh?" the good Doctor jumped; then his eyes twinkled. "Well, you must call again, sir, when you have time to look over my library. I have a considerable collection for these parts. Please feel free to consult the books at any time—or me, for that matter."

It was his way of bestowing a *cum laude*. Elizabeth had never loved her father more warmly. She studied the faint marks of crow's-feet around his eyes, the lines beside his mouth, his broad forehead and the dark hair growing thinly above it. "Papa," she thought happily, "likes Dr. Wilcox very much."

Her own part in the picture was what it had been through supper—everything and nothing. Suddenly discomfited by her plain dress—linsey, made Empire style, with a white fichu—she had found time to slip upstairs and fasten a length of bright green ribbon in her hair. She sat now on a low chair near her father's and gathered everything into her heart for keeping—the wind howling in gusts about the house, the rain hissing down the chimney against the hot logs, the talk rising and falling against the cadences of the storm, Josiah nodding and being ordered to bed, the stranger who was not a stranger —a young man with noble dark head and warm gray eyes staring moodily at the flames, watchful lest he turn those eyes and reveal to all the true reason for his presence. Ah, beautiful . . .

"I'm sorry," Dr. Moss said, "that you have settled yourself so absolutely in Cooper County. Bohannon is a good man, I am sure; but I like this end of the region—perhaps only because I saw it first, perhaps because its ups and downs remind me of the eastern slope of the Blue Ridge. Boone County is new and sparsely settled so far, but we have plans. We, too, are plotting a town. Must have a county seat if we have a county. I hope you'll bear us in mind when you are in a position to acquire property." He stretched his legs to the fire. "It is good land," he said, as everyone did.

"Paradise," the young man agreed.

Silence fell on the room—a full, potent silence. A rocking chair creaked as Miss Mary leaned forward.

"Listen!" she said in her sharp way. "The rain has stopped."

Sure enough, it had. The wind still blew but there was no slap or hiss of water. Dr. Wilcox stood up.

"I must be going," he said. "Bohannon now will think I'm lost. I must be in Franklin for Captain Porter's first crossing tomorrow."

Dr. Moss protested. There was a comfortable cot in his study. Surely Wilcox did not mean to ride on to Franklin that night. The journey was long, especially to one not too familiar with what passed for roads. The creeks would be running full.

34

"I will stop at Colonel Gentry's tavern again," Dr. Wilcox promised. "If he advises against my going on, I will rest there until morning and daylight."

"Good!" Dr. Moss agreed. "I'll send a boy that far with you. And now, while we wait for the horses, will you take some refreshment with me? What do we have, Betsy?"

It was his name for Elizabeth. No other used it. No other ever would. She smiled at her father again happily.

"Cider?" she suggested. "New cider, from our own winter apples?"

"I hope not too new," Dr. Moss objected.

"Three days old. Just right for you," she said. "How do you like your cider, Dr. Wilcox? Papa prefers his warm."

"Any way," the young man said. Their eyes met again and held. "Any way you bring it, Miss . . . Libby."

CHAPTER THREE

Colonel William Ashley

EVERYTHING, EVEN THE SUN, smiled on the day of the housewarming. The entire Moss household turned out bright and early.

"Oh, Barcie, look! It's a wonderful morning. Oh, Barcie, I'm glad you could come ahead, so's not to miss any of it." Elizabeth sat up in bed, smiled down at her dearest friend, then giggled with pure, spontaneous exuberance. "Oh, Barcie, do I look as funny as you do in rag curlers?"

"No," Barcie said, with typical, even self-sacrificing honesty. "You're prettier than I am all around the clock and you know it."

"But not half as sweet and you know that," Elizabeth answered. "Get up, sleepy. Folks'll be coming."

Nobody wanted to stop for breakfast.

"Now, you all eat a little somethin'," Pomegranate ordered, producing hot cornmeal mush and syrup and biscuits and fried eggs and platters of sliced ham and chicken. "You all eat somethin' now. You won't have time later on. You got time now. Folks ain' gonna git yere dat soon. Dey got to git up and git goin' deyselves fust, 'member. You all eat now. Wha's yore pa, Miss Libby?"

"At the roasting pits, I reckon," Libby said. "Did he go to bed at all last night?"

"Yas, ma'am, he did. Miss Mary tuk keer o' dat and I'll take keer he gits his coffee and mush now—soon ez I kin ketch um."

He was difficult to catch at any time that day. If he ate, it must have been samples of the meat roasting over the deep trenches.

"Perfect," he said of the weather. "A week sooner and the ground would have been mush. A week later and everybody would be plowing."

Nobody in Boonslick stayed home to plow that day. From the farthest boundaries they came—the Coopers, the Coles, the Maupins, the Stevenses, the Gentrys, the Williamses, the Callaways, the Kingsburys and the rest. A clerk could have made a counting of the first families and their immediate progeny. Leaving Boonville, Doctors Bohannon and Wilcox had no qualms over an abandoned practice.

36

Anyone who could walk or ride a horse or endure a wagon was either ahead of them on the road or just behind. By midmorning, when they reached the grove where Poke, the Mosses' stableboy, directed the placing of mounts and vehicles, the crowd looked like the gathering for a sale. Daniel had now progressed enough in his acquaintance to recognize a number of the people, among them a family whose youngest child he had treated for a spell of croup. He went over to ask about his patient; and the mother proudly lifted the baby, rosy now with health, from the wagon bed to show him.

"Well, hurrah for you, James!" Daniel said, and then, "Can I help you to the house, ma'am? Which is heavier, I wonder, the boy or the basket?"

"I'd sooner trust ye to tote the baby," the mother answered.

Daniel's crest fell. He had counted on her saying that, with the help of the rest of her family, she could manage. There was nothing for him to do now but take the child and set off with the mother for the house. Thank Fortune, she was bound for the kitchen entrance, for this was not the manner of arrival that Daniel had planned. He carried the baby in the crook of his right arm, well away from a new and elegant shirt front. He and Bohannon had been to considerable pains to locate a woman who could sew up a shirt according to their directions, they furnishing the linen, thread and buttons; and he did not purpose to have that glory spoiled before festivities ever began.

Contrarily, Elizabeth Moss's duties took her, too, with the arrival of each new party, around to the kitchen, where she presented proud donors of cakes and pies and pickles to Pomegranate and helped her decide which dishes were to be carried at once to the plank tables under the trees and which were to be held in reserve. So there she stood.

"Dr. Wilcox!" she said. "How nice of you to come; and, my, what a beautiful baby!"

Now, why, Daniel thought, with the longest eyelashes west of the Alleghenies, should she have a dimple also at the corner of her mouth? Because his heart filled his throat, his response to her greeting was stiffish.

"This," he informed her, "is Mrs. Milroy of Cooper County. She had, as you see, more than she could well manage, so I offered . . . this young man is Jimmie Milroy."

Wanting worse than anything to dump the child into a handy bush, he bounced him on his bent arm. The baby laughed aloud, then, seeing Elizabeth, reached for her and said, "Coo!"

Elizabeth drew back. She had gone to as much trouble over her

37

frock as Daniel had over his shirt. In red and white gingham, suitable for an all-day picnic, she had copied every detail of Anne Farrar's russet silk. The beauty of the dress was its crisp perfection. If that should be marred, all would be lost.

"Good morning, Mrs. Milroy," she said sweetly. Her heart, too, was skipping about. This was the third time she had seen Daniel Wilcox. Once had been on a gray, cold day, once against the wet black of night, with flames painting a ruddy glow all around him like a nebula. Now in broad sunlight he was handsomer than ever. It was almost too much. "I am Libby Moss. Mercy, that is a heavy basket. I'll help you into the kitchen with it."

Mrs. Milroy was a woman of divination.

"Now don't you bother, miss. I'll take it in myself. I'll be back in two winks for the baby, Doctor, so that you— I'll be back."

Her two winks, Daniel was afraid, might prove a hazardous length of time. Then he had what he thought was an inspiration. As the mother turned toward the house, Jimmie reached after her with a little cry, but, seeing Elizabeth again in her bright gingham, switched the direction of his desires to her. This time Daniel gave her no chance to draw back.

"He wants you," he said, "and I don't blame him." And threw the child at her.

At least, Elizabeth said he threw the baby. She was furious, but caught the boy, to save him from being dashed to his death, and covered her discomfiture by pretending to tug his garments into proper order. So, the young man was smart as well as handsome? She'd show him.

She showed him only what had been in his heart since the moment when he had first seen her. After considerable searching of his soul and some discreet consultation of his partner, Ambrose Bohannon, he had decided that, while he was in no position to declare himself as a suitor or to ask a girl to think of him that way, it was flying the face of nature not to enjoy company of approximately his own age and of his own choosing. He must simply guard his tongue and his behavior. Now, seeing this girl, lovelier, because she was real, then any Madonna ever painted, handling a baby with an expertness which was only the result of having a delicate mother and two younger brothers, but which he thought was nature triumphant, his guard crumbled to nothing.

"You . . . angel!" he said prayerfully.

She peeped up at him from under her long lashes.

"Why, Dr. Wilcox!"

"Have you any idea how wonderful you are?"

She had a faint idea, but was willing to hear more about it.

"I love you," he said helplessly, hoarsely. "I have ever since I first laid eyes on you. I love you. I shall love you . . . till I die."

Shaken to her shoes by the declaration, Elizabeth fought for her own control.

"Dr. Wilcox, considering that this is only our second meeting—"

"Third!" he corrected.

"Oh! So, you did see me that day in Boonville?"

"See you? Of course, I saw you. I've seen nothing or nobody else ever since. Waking or sleeping, I . . ." Belatedly he realized how he had emptied his heart before her. "Miss Libby, I—I beg your pardon. I had no right. I didn't mean . . ."

"No, of course not," she cooed. "You couldn't, naturally. I'll just forget all about it."

Good Lord, that was not what he wanted.

"No!" he said, first in a hot sweat, then a cold one. "I meant every word. It is just that I have no right at present— Ah-h-h! I'll speak to your father at once—today."

"Papa," she said, "will be more astonished than I am."

"But you're not offended?"

Offended? She wanted to laugh, she wanted to cry. If older women from their rocking chairs wanted to give a girl advice, why didn't they tell her what to do at a time like this? When she knew she must not throw herself into a young man's arms and still did not want to send him away—possibly forever?

They would have said probably that a girl needed only to look about her to find a refuge. Here came Mrs. Milroy for the baby; and from another direction here came Mr. Harris, escorting a group of gentlemen, strangers, and her father away off at the barbecue pit!

The trench was not that far away, Daniel said afterward. Anyhow, she need not have run, as if she were escaping a fire or the plague. He always insisted that she knew the identity of the gentleman on Mr. Harris's right hand. If she didn't know, she could have guessed from Mr. Harris's strutting. He carried his stomach out front like a bass drum on parade. No man, Dr. Daniel Wilcox said, had ever fathomed a girl's or a woman's conniving; and no man ever would.

But he was wrong in this instance. Elizabeth did not know the gentleman with Mr. Harris or those who trailed behind. When she heard his name it meant nothing to her. She did not habitually pore over the front page of *The Intelligencer* or read its notices.

Of course, before the day was over, she had heard about all there was to know about him, but was still not too deeply impressed.

Mr. Ashley of St. Louis and a lot of other places, the rich Mr. Ashley, his wealth in mines and bank stock and land. A girl of sixteen, pleasantly occupied with other thoughts, was not likely to dwell too long on those points. Colonel William Ashley of the Missouri militia, aspiring to be elected Lieutenant Governor of the new state. Yes, but her ears were filled daily with diverse opinions of Missouri. To Dr. Moss and Mr. Harris it was the land of all promise. Miss Mary said it was the jumping-off place. Dr. Moss, she declared, had buried his family in the raw wilderness. Daniel Wilcox, looking at Elizabeth, said it was Paradise. Which opinion was one to accept?

"There's my girl!" Mr. Harris greeted her. "How are you, sweetheart? How's Barcie behaving?"

"Barcie's wonderful," Elizabeth told him. "I think it was precious of you to let her come and stay."

"Didn't have a word to say about it once she'd made up her own mind. Libby, I've taken the liberty of adding a few folks to the gathering. When I got to Franklin this morning, I found these gentlemen wandering about, asking where everybody was. So I told them. Said if they'd come to Boonslick to do business or hold a meeting or just to see somebody, they'd best follow me. So— Well, here we are. Libby, allow me to present . . ."

The other men of the party did not matter. It was Colonel Ashley to whom Mr. Harris gave his special attention and he expected her to do the same. A person just naturally would do that, though it was hard to say why. At first glance, he was anything but a dazzling person—a man medium tall, excruciatingly thin, compared to Barcie's father, and, to Elizabeth's youth, in the same general age classification. When he removed his hat to bow, she was surprised to find his hair still abundant and of a solid dark color. It was dressed closely to his head, as if in recognition of the fact that the molding of that head, a breadth and a height to his forehead, and his very alive dark eyes were all his claim to comeliness. He had a very eagle's beak for a nose, a thin, tight mouth and an excessively pointed chin. His complexion was sallow, and darkened by the shadow of a well-scraped beard that no amount of attention ever made entirely invisible. But there was that noble brow and there were his eyes—dark, alive, questing. They rested now on Elizabeth with an intensity that made her blush, but she managed a pretty speech of welcome.

"We are very happy to have you attend our barbecue, gentlemen. Papa will be so pleased, Mr. Harris." Then, to the latter's inquiry, "He's at the pits, of course. If he did not dig them himself, he watched every time a spade went in or out. So far, nobody has been able to draw him away; but, if you don't mind going where he is, he just may look up and say you are welcome. This way, gentlemen."

She walked over the new grass between Mr. Ashley and Mr. Harris.

"You surely stepped proudly," Barcie said later, having watched the meeting with Daniel Wilcox from afar. "I saw you, too; and even more than Papa you looked like something special had happened."

Nonsense! If she looked like that, it was only because Mr. Ashley had paid her a compliment.

"It is a privilege to accompany so charming a guide," he said.

She looked at him in surprise—not at his words but his voice. It was a deep, resonant voice. Words and tone lingered in a person's ears. She remembered other things he said in those few minutes.

"You've a beautiful place here," for example. His bright eyes took in rounded hillock and level greensward and the sparkling water of a chattering creek. "It is beautiful country generally, but this is a gem."

"You must say that to Papa," Elizabeth told him. "He is very fond of this farm."

"Is he really? And you?"

Bedazzled with a dozen kinds of happiness, she had only one answer.

"Of course, I like it, too. Very, very much."

"Do you really? You surprise me."

But why?

"I think I won't explain!" His eyes flashed past her at Mr. Harris.

"I believe I get your meaning," Barcie's father said.

But Elizabeth did not, and that vexed her. To say something that a person didn't understand, and not to explain, to leave the thought there to worry a body at odd times forever afterward—that was a horrid way.

"But I do like it here," she pouted. "I really do."

And she really did. On this day to her, too, Missouri was Paradise.

Feasting and fun went on all day; but dinner proper, in the sense of gathering to eat at the long board tables, began when the first person took two slabs of bread with hot roasted meat between them from the trench over to where ladies had set out pickles and custards and cakes and pies and other such trimmings. Then there was a stuffing beyond calculation or description, everybody being happy and curious and bent on showing appreciation. That went on until the first sleepy child howled and its mother took it away to put it to bed either in the family wagon or in the house. The other women followed soon after, the elder ones to rest in the bedroom downstairs, the younger ones to share the girls' room above. Small fry were laid out in the boys' room across the hall. By the time Barcie and Elizabeth were ready for their beauty naps, every bed in the house had people laid across it like sticks of wood and the two girls cheerfully took to a pallet and a blanket on the floor.

"I'm not the least bit sleepy," Barcie yawned. "I'd much rather be dancing. How long do you think they'll speechify out there, Libby?"

"The good Lord only knows," Libby answered. "Clear till dark, maybe. I didn't count how many men there are, but each one will have to have his say."

She was very right in her estimate. Such gatherings as this were men's only opportunity for direct intercommunication in sparsely settled regions. Dr. Moss would have displayed ignorance of custom and neglected his duty as a host if, after the tables were cleared— only so far as the kitchen, from which light refreshments could be had from then on—he had not called the complete roll of his guests and invited each one to say a little something. "Toasts were drunk," the next copy of *The Intelligencer* would report, and truthfully. Whiskey—Monongahela, Kentucky and Boonslick distillations —was set out, with pitchers of cider and bottles of wine. All throats being well lubricated, everyone responded briskly to the summons, the only hesitation being over a topic which would serve as a springboard from which to leap into full oratory. However, by covering all the national holidays, each member of the Moss household, other heroes national and local, all the branches of the government and leaders of rival political parties, there were subjects, and some over, to go around.

Daniel Wilcox, reared in Kentucky, knew well what to expect; and most of what was said he didn't hear. His mood since his reckless declaration of the morning had alternated between deep depression and wild exhilaration, according to whether a realization of his folly weighed him down or his privilege of knowing a girl like Elizabeth Moss raised him up. He had had no opportunity to speak to Dr. Moss and didn't know what he would say when he did speak to him. He must confess his utter lack of resources, and what would he offer as a surety of a more prosperous future? There was just one possibility—a mad idea of Bohannon's. He turned to address a question to his partner, just in time to hear Ambrose's name called and to see his friend struggle to his feet, all of a sweat, and then give out a toast which for many a day could lift him out of despair into laughter:

"The ladies! In war our arms their protection; in peace their arms our refuge."

"Be still, you ass!" he growled at Daniel, taking his seat to polite clapping and some present merriment. "I could think o' naught but that bit. I heard it in barracks somewhere! Let's hear you do better."

It was Daniel's turn to prove he could; and he, having given all his mind to other matters, could think of absolutely nothing to say. He stood a full minute, looking at the faces about the long table, all of them older than his, most of them marked by weather and toil, none unmarked by some trial; and he found his answer in simple remembrance of what had brought him into their midst.

"Mr. Toastmaster and our host!" He swallowed hard. "I am grateful for the opportunity to address these, my new-found friends. I give you, sir and gentlemen, the people—men, women and children—who call Boonslick home. For it is people, more than springs and streams and hills and prairies, that make this a good land. I want to thank all for the welcome given me here. I am humbly grateful to those who have placed their trust in my professional abilities. To all, friends, clients and compatriots, I pledge my best service."

"Hear, hear!" Ambrose Bohannon said when he took his seat. "I did not know you had it in you. If medicine does not reward ye, ye can take up politics."

Daniel was a little surprised at himself. It seemed to be his day for making pledges. However, a stir of comment along the boards did indicate friendliness and new interest and Daniel would have taken full comfort from that except for the attitude of one man and he an outsider—Colonel William Ashley. His speech finished, Daniel looked naturally in the direction of his host but met instead the sharp scrutiny of this gentleman, who sat on Dr. Moss's right. By now Daniel also had received a full account of Colonel Ashley's accomplishments—his wealth, his popularity, his enterprise. It was an overwhelming record. Certainly Daniel had not expected Colonel Ashley to take notice of him; but that was just what Ashley was doing now. His mouth was puckered into an expression of thoughtfulness and his eyes were alight with interest and, Daniel thought, some amusement. Daniel blushed hotly—and furiously, and his hands were hard fists on his knees as Ashley rose in response to a call from Dr. Moss to say a few words about his candidacy.

The speech—the final one of the afternoon—was simple and brief.

"Fellow-citizens: My name is announced as candidate for the office of Lieutenant Governor of the State of Missouri. My long residence and general acquaintance in the country gives you an opportunity of judging my abilities." That for the upstart newcomer who made an appeal of his strangeness! "I flatter myself that those who are well acquainted with me entertain the belief that my political course will be independent and, as far as I am capable of judging, directed to the general good of our country. I submit the subject for your disposal without further remarks."

A short speech and fairly insolent, Daniel thought, in its self-assurance. Daniel's hands were still fists as he rose, with the others, from the table. Animosity, due only in part to Ashley's superior attainments and more to the fact that he had walked across the grass that morning with Elizabeth Moss, murmuring compliments into her receptive ear, burned like a hot coal in Daniel's heart. Alongside was a cold area of fear. If Colonel Ashley had domestic ties, no mention had been made of them. If he had not, and his eye was as keen for beauty as it was for riches—well!

"Where are ye off to now?" Bohannon said. "Do you not hear the fiddles making ready for a reel? The girruls are waiting."

"Make my excuses, Bo," Daniel begged. "Say I'll be along presently. I've something to say to Dr. Moss now. Tonight on the way home I want a serious talk with you. Go along now. I'll see you later."

This lull, this change in activities, was his best opportunity for cornering Dr. Moss; and he felt he must do so, though he had no idea—any more than he had known what he was going to say when he stood up to speak just now—of how to approach Elizabeth's father. As it happened, however, he caught the good doctor at just the right moment. Earlier in the day he would have been too occupied to give Daniel his best attention. Later he would be weary to the point of testiness. Now, just past four in the afternoon, he was mellow with gratification, good company, good food and good wine.

"Ah, Wilcox!" He put a hand cordially on Daniel's shoulder. "That was a neat speech of yours, and well received. In fact, I've been hearing only good reports on you generally. How are you making out in Boonville?"

"Very well, in a sense," Daniel reported honestly, "but not just in the way I had hoped."

He was no richer in pocket than when he had come, he confessed. He had even added a small burden of debt, certain purchases seeming to him necessary. Incurring a judicious amount of debt, Dr. Moss encouraged, was characteristic in a new country, its prosperity largely a matter of future reckoning. Well?

Daniel plunged. He could not, he must not wait any longer.

"You are very kind, Dr. Moss. You may not feel that way when you know what I've come to tell you. I, sir, have had the presumption to fall in love with your daughter."

The Doctor, as Elizabeth had foretold, was astonished.

"What? Our Betsy? You can't mean it. You've seen each other only—"

"Three times," Daniel said. "I saw her the day I landed in Boonville. I had no wish, certainly no intention, but—"

"Why, confound it, sir," Dr. Moss rubbed his head helplessly, "she's a child still."

"No, sir, I can't agree with you on that. To me she is everything fair and desirable."

"Do you mean," the Doctor said, "that you are asking . . ."

"No, sir. I am in no position to ask a promise from you or her. God knows when I shall be. Still, I had to speak to you because . . . you see, I've already spoken to her."

"The devil you have!"

"It was unintentional, but it happened. It will again, I am afraid."

"Then, why— Young man, your reasoning is hard to follow."

"I'm afraid I'm not saying it very well. Dr. Moss, I abhor anything clandestine or underhanded. I was brought up that way and it's my nature, too. You've been so kind and hospitable, that it must seem an abuse of confidence; but . . . I love her very much. I do, sir, believe me."

How was a man not to believe him? Dr. Moss struggled hard to achieve and maintain an attitude of offended parental dignity, and failed miserably.

"What you are trying to say is that you're in no position to ask a young woman to marry you—my child, in particular; and yet, you intend to pay court to her. Is that it?"

"I— Yes, sir, I reckon that's how it is, sir."

"I could forbid you to see her again."

"I hope you won't do that, sir."

"What does the young lady say to your impudence? Did she offer you any encouragement?"

"No, sir. Still . . ."

"No discouragement? Good Lord, she has grown up. In which case . . . mind you, no promise is to be asked for or given."

"No sir. At least, not without further warning."

"What?" The Doctor's eyebrows shot up and his mouth turned down. Then he laughed and finally Daniel with him.

"The damnedest thing!" Dr. Moss allowed afterward, telling his wife. "I couldn't say no to him. I didn't want to. I thought, here's a fine young man and I'd no right to rule him out of Betsy's future. I asked him if he had any plans for improving his fortunes. He said he had several, all pretty far in the future, I gathered; but I don't agree with you, Miss Mary, that he will never amount to anything much. He will amount to a great deal some day—in his own way. It will be a hard way, no doubt, hedged on every side by points of honor. If he doesn't impale himself on one of those points, I'll be surprised. But after all, it's for Betsy to say, I reckon."

"The idea!" Miss Mary said. "What does a girl that age know?"

"Nothing," the Doctor admitted. "Nothing, and everything."

Nothing and everything. His step was light in the dance, perhaps because his heart, unburdened, was light now. Having made his tempestuous declaration to her and a more troubled one to her father, he said no more of love that day in words; but there were other ways. He would woo her now, to win her when the time was right.

"Miss Libby, may I have the honor?"

"Dr. Wilcox, we have just left the floor. There are other guests to whom I must show some courtesy."

"Then let them step forward quickly. I am late to the dancing."

And she was in the center of a square again, curtseying to his bow. His step was light, his arm was strong, there was a pleasurable thrill in his nearness. She forgot the others, even those who watched outside the area of the dancing.

"Dr. Wilcox, my mother bids me say that Mr. Harris and his party will stay for supper. If you and Dr. Bohannon care to join us, you are welcome."

"Miss Libby, how sweet of you and your mother! Bo and I are delighted. Will there be some of your special pie?"

"No, indeed. I am full young to compete just yet with the best cooks of Boonslick. Your Mrs. Milroy's pies will have to do."

"My Mrs. Milroy?"

"Your patient, I believe. Have you so many that you can disregard one?"

46

Her heart sang like a tight fiddle string. In the quiet hour after supper it still vibrated to a word, a glance, a sigh.

A quiet time. A fire burned low, with no fuss, in the great chimney. Everybody sat about pleasantly exhausted, replete with food, musing, quiescent. As Elizabeth remembered it afterward, Colonel Ashley did most of the talking, perhaps because someone had touched him off with a question on a favorite enthusiasm—the Missouri River.

It seemed to Elizabeth a strange enthusiasm for a gentleman who looked more suited to a life of business or politics than a life of rough adventure. To be sure, her acquaintance with Colonel Ashley was slight and with the river not much more extensive. She knew it as a brawling, turbulent stream more terrifying than advantageous to anybody. Boats of any size had trouble making their way against the current for the comparatively short distance of two hundred miles between St. Louis and Boonville, let alone any farther; and Colonel Ashley had in mind going clear to the source of the river in the Rocky Mountains.

Plainly the river had no terrors for him. To him the one great fault of Two-Mile Prairie and the land thereabouts was its distance from the river. Dr. Moss, of course, was of those who believed a stage road from St. Louis would come long before successful navigation of the Missouri; but Colonel Ashley said no, the river could be navigated successfully and he was going to prove it.

In person? It seemed incredible. He meant to use keelboats—those long, oversized dugouts with shanty cabins built amidships, which, for their wild crews, were a scandal of the inland waterways. He meant to take a fleet of those boats up the river in an expedition organized on a grand scale to bring out the riches of the mountain country. Incidentally there would be some exploration of the nation's frontiers, but profit was the thing. The riches were in furs, much in demand over the world. It was a hazardous undertaking certainly, but a man in one successful year could make his fortune.

A strange undertaking for a man like Colonel Ashley; and yet, one had to believe he would do it if he tried. Josiah Moss stretched out on his stomach, propping his chin on his hands, drinking in every word.

"How will you man your expedition, Colonel?" Dr. Moss asked. "Will you rely on hired, professional voyageurs?"

The fighting, drinking, gouging keelboatmen of the waterfronts?

"Not entirely, Doctor. I must have experienced boatmen and hunters and trappers, of course. Guides, too. For the rest, I have in mind engaging a number, almost any number I can, of hardy young men, eager for adventure, who will work for a share in the glory and the profit. Such men as—" his bright, searching eyes went directly to Daniel Wilcox—"say, young Wilcox here. Of adventurous spirit and few home ties. How about it, sir? If I do organize such an expedition in the near future, will you honor us by joining? In your profession you would be a welcome addition."

Elizabeth jumped and almost cried out. No! Not Daniel Wilcox! For a minute the river in flood boiled through the room. The Rocky Mountain country, bleak and cold and peopled with savages, blotted out warmth and peace and security. Not that, for Heaven's sake! Her eyes, too, went to Daniel. He met their appeal and smiled. His answer was to her, not Colonel Ashley.

"Thank you, sir. I believe not. I feel sufficiently challenged in my present situation."

Ashley shrugged his shoulders.

"You have time to change your mind," he said. "It will be a year or two before I am ready. I will put a notice in the papers when the time comes, and my offer still will stand."

"Thank you," Daniel said again. "I will watch for it, but I think my answer will be the same—for reasons which I hope will be more comprehensible by then. I, too, have plans in the making."

"Are you sorry," he asked Libby, as he took his leave, "that I declined Colonel Ashley's dazzling offer?"

"I am glad you are to remain among us, Dr. Wilcox."

"Bless you! But it may have been a mistake. I might have come home with a sack of gold."

"You might drown or be murdered by the Indians and not come back at all."

Yes, there was that to be considered. Still, he could have used a small sack of gold.

Then it was Colonel Ashley saying his good-bye. Apparently he had overheard what Daniel had said.

"If I promise not to take your young man away, Miss Libby, will you send me an invitation to the wedding?"

"He is not my young man," Libby said. "I mean . . . I have no plans for a wedding to anybody."

He laughed at her confusion.

"Put it this way," he said. "If I hear in time, wherever I am I'll turn about and come."

"But, Colonel Ashley, why?"

"I'll be there," he promised.

48

But it remained for Barcie Harris to finish off the day.

"Oh, Libby, how does it feel to have every man who looks at you fall in love with you? First Dr. Wilcox, then Colonel Ashley . . ."

"Barcie! You scandalize me. Colonel Ashley has a wife. You heard Mamma ask him."

They broke off the discussion to laugh at Miss Mary. She had asked the distinguished man whether or not he had a family. She had wanted to know, she said.

"But I think from the way he spoke, she's not long for this world," Barcie said when she could stop laughing. "He said she was delicate. Libby, a rich widower with a fine house probably . . ."

"Barcie, you are a scandal! What would Dr. Bohannon say?"

"Him?" Barcie gave minute attention to rolling a next day's curl. "He's much more interested in persuading your father to set up a distillery than— Anyhow, that's what I mean." Her blue eyes filled with tears and she let curl and its accompanying rag fall from her hands. "Every man who lays eyes on you . . ."

"Barcie, darling!" Libby threw her arms around her friend and rubbed her hot cheek against Barcie's wet one. "They don't, really."

"But they do!" Barcie declared.

CHAPTER FOUR

A Wedding

"SHE COULD have done better for herself," Miss Mary maintained to the last.

Now, how could she have done better? Even featherheaded Barcie, caught herself in love's entanglements, saw how right everything was for Elizabeth.

"Libby, your first love!" she sighed. "And he has eyes for nobody but you. It's like a dream."

It was, indeed. Sometimes Elizabeth had to pinch herself, to be sure that her good fortune was real. That her heart's love should have set his course for Boonslick as if he had known she waited there for him! It was past believing. A day was a flower to be plucked, a month was a mere shadow over the face of time. A-tingle from top to toe with happiness, and, at the same time, as nearly humble as she was ever likely to be, she alternately forgot Barcie's very existence and then was all sympathy for Barcie's difficulties. Poor Barcie! She had given her heart away also, willy-nilly, whether or no, but to that big bear Ambrose Bohannon—to tell the truth with slight encouragement. Bo, as Daniel called him, was a man given to moods, now boisterous, now gloomy and self-depreciating; but Elizabeth would have no part in Barcie's insistence that he preferred her to Barcie. That couldn't be what ailed him.

"Dear Barcie," she said generously, "it's you, I'm sure; only, being poor, he hesitates to declare himself. Couldn't you prod him along a little?"

"No," Barcie said. "I wouldn't dare. Besides, it would do no good. You've never had to prod Dr. Wilcox . . . I hope."

Elizabeth was not saying. There was a night in June—could it be another summer, the second of their knowing each other? Again Elizabeth was visiting in Boonville. She and Daniel and Bo and Barcie that night rode out by pairs to a dancing party. They had planned to go in the Harris Dearborn; but that day Mr. Harris had broken a wheel on a rocky road. Then it was a case of stay at home and pull taffy, or join an already overfull wagon taking other young folk from town, or ride pillions behind their escorts. The last promised to be the most fun.

"When I was young I never went anywhere any other way," Mrs. Harris said.

The night was warm, the air sweet with flower scent and the richer fragrance of garden soil turned up to catch sun and rain. A shower had caused the young people several tremors that afternoon but now a moon shone through tattered clouds. Riding halfway up the sky, it made dark razor-back ridges of some of the hills and illuminated the slopes of others. Every streamlet was puddled silver.

"Are you comfortable?" Daniel asked.

"Yes, thank you—except when I think of the poor horse."

"Rosinante doesn't mind."

She laughed, as she always did, at the horse's name, and sighed. It was nice to be beaued by a man who read the books she had read. And it was possible that a horse used to carrying near two hundred pounds would not mind another hundred.

"Still, I am glad we are not going far." She was not as glad as she should have been. "Are you sure this is the right road? How do you tell?"

"Bo and I come out this way often. It's the road to Chouteau Springs. You've heard of them?"

Dozens of times. They seemed a fruitless subject for conversation now.

"Mineral springs," she said, wrinkling her nose. "Horrid to taste or even smell."

"Depends," he said. "You've heard of Saratoga or White Sulphur? They're famous for their evil-smelling waters. That's why Bo and I think we could build a spa right here in Missouri on the Chouteau Tract if—oh, a thousand ifs. Just one of our mad, impossible dreams."

"Truly impossible? Why?"

"Money," he said grimly, as was his way of treating that subject. "To begin with, we should have to buy the land. I doubt that we could manage even the small part we need. Certainly we can't take it all—thirty thousand acres."

Land. Already Elizabeth was inclined to close her ears when men talked of it, as almost everyone in Boonslick did. The land of which Daniel spoke now was a near legend in these parts—a gift of the Osage Indians, when Spain ruled this territory, to a Mr. Pierre Chouteau, a wealthy fur trader of St. Louis—one of those. Apparently Mr. Chouteau cared nothing for the land, only his name being attached to it now, except to sell it; but the mad Americans who came in following the Louisiana Purchase viewed it, now for one reason, now for another, with longing, although nobody could buy it, the title still being in litigation. She had heard her father and Mr. Harris and others talk about it; but did a young man with the lady of his choice on a pillion behind him have to do so?

"Dr. Wilcox, why do you want to make a fortune?"

"I think you know," he said, waiting a full minute before he answered and sending delicious shivers through her with his weighty silence and now his solemn tone of speaking. "Sweet as it is to have you riding this way with me—for myself I'd be content forever so—for your sake I hope . . . I . . . Libby, it's been over a year since I first told you I loved you."

She held her breath.

"I still do, you know. More and more and more."

"I began to wonder, Dr. Wilcox."

"Say Daniel," he begged.

"I couldn't!" She was truly horrified. Had she ever heard her mother call her father by his given name? Never! It was always, "Dr. Moss."

"Say Daniel," Dr. Wilcox insisted. A stubbornly persistent young man.

"Daniel," she murmured finally at his back.

Lord! The horse stopped. Time stopped. For a wild minute she thought Daniel was going to whirl about in the saddle and he might have done so, had not the halt come with Rosinante's forefeet in a creek they had been about to ford. And so, as always, putting another's safety and well-being ahead of his own desire, he managed, just managed, to hold himself as he was. Even Rosinante seemed disappointed. She blew out a great sigh as she dropped her head to drink.

"Libby," Daniel said finally, "what do you think of Colonel Gentry's new town in Boone County?"

Real estate again? What ever possessed men?

"Columbia?" she said. "Papa thinks it promises well."

"I'm glad," Daniel said. "A year ago it was only a plan on paper. Now they have begun to lay out streets and to build."

The streets were still mostly surveyors' stakes. The houses were six.

"No doubt," she said, "it will be a city when I return from St. Louis."

"You're not . . . ?" Daniel said. "I mean, are you going to St. Louis?"

"Very probably," she told him. "Uncle and Aunt Farrar have written, inviting me to spend the coming winter with them. Mamma feels I should go. I have had no instruction of any sort since we settled in Missouri."

"Instruction?" he cried. What in Heaven's name did she not already know?

"Lessons in French, perhaps," she amplified, "or music—the pianoforte."

The moonlight went right out for Daniel Wilcox.

"You have no pianoforte," he said glumly.

"I might have some day."

So she might, St. Louis being full of people of wealth, many of them eligible for marriage. Daniel stiffened and counter-attacked.

"I saw," he told her, "General Ashley's"—it was General Ashley now, the Lieutenant Governor holding top command of the state militia—"first advertisement calling for a hundred enterprising young men to accompany him up the Missouri."

Oh, dear! She had seen it, too. "To be employed for one, two or three years," it read.

"You were saying something about Columbia, Missouri," she murmured.

"Yes. I'm not advancing very much in Boonville, Libby. It's either throw in my lot with General Ashley or— I've been offered the district clerkship of Boone County, if I will take up my residence in Columbia."

"Oh!" Her heart sang again. "Will you do that?"

"It depends," he said. "The office carries a salary of three hundred dollars a year—specie or negotiable drafts. It would finance a small house in the town—a very small one, I'm afraid, a saltbox affair, with no possible room for a piano."

"A piano," she said, gloating, "is a frivolity, not a necessity."

"Libby, can I take that for an answer?" She could feel gladness surge back into him now.

"But you've not asked me anything."

"Then I do. If I take this clerkship and establish myself in Columbia, and all promises well, will you marry me?"

"I prefer not so many ifs, please."

"Libby, sweetheart, will you marry me?"

"I might . . . some day," she said.

That fall Daniel Wilcox was named district clerk of Boone County, with all the honors and emoluments thereunto pertaining; and he made ready to move his practice the coming spring from Boonville

53

to Columbia, where now two public squares and six lanes, to serve as future streets and running both ways, had been cleared of brush, and one deep well had been dug to supply town water. There were fifteen houses of mud-daubed logs and one had been projected of brick. Columbia was considered well on its way toward being a town.

Elizabeth did not go to St. Louis to visit or take lessons on the pianoforte. She busied herself at home perfecting her knowledge of the domestic arts—sewing, cooking and generally maintaining a home. From the kitchen behind the Moss house almost daily a new variety of fragrance arose, including that of scorched flour or fat, and seasoned frequently with argument.

"Trouble wid you, Miss Libby," Pomegranate scolded, "yo're set on fancy cookin'. You got to feed a man bread and meat."

"I know," Libby sighed. "To tell the truth, I would rather make a pie than cook a kettle of soup."

"You got to make de soup fust," Pommie insisted.

"All right, all right, Pommie. I will," she said, so quiescently that the cook looked her over anxiously for signs of failing health.

But found none. It was just the way Libby felt those days—gentle and sweet and wanting to please. All selfish waywardness was, for a time, dormant. There was a new toddler in the Moss house now, a small sister at last, a little Miss Mary—to distinguish her from Miss Mary. One day Mrs. Moss found Elizabeth tying a bib on the baby and feeding her candied watermelon rind.

"Libby," she scolded, "you'll ruin that child's stomach if you don't stop poking sweets into her hands."

"Such a little piece," Elizabeth objected, "and she's so fond of it!" In this full hour to help another to a bit of sweet!

"You wait . . ." Mrs. Moss began, looked at Elizabeth, bit her lip and left the room. Behind closed doors Elizabeth heard her sobbing and went for her father.

"Mamma's having a fit over me," she said. "Try to help her."

Dr. Moss tried, without much success.

"She's so young, so beautiful," Miss Mary wailed. "Have you noticed how she gets prettier every day?"

"Isn't that as it should be?"

"But she doesn't know," Miss Mary insisted. "She doesn't know."

"She will learn," the Doctor said.

"I don't want her to learn. I can't bear the thought of it."

"Now, Miss Mary, that's ridiculous. You can't keep her as she is. It isn't possible in life and you wouldn't have it that way if you could."

"She could have done better for herself," Mrs. Moss insisted. "If we had only given her other opportunities, she could have done better."

"With all the world to choose from," Dr. Moss said positively, "I don't see how she could do better than Daniel Wilcox."

He thought he knew whom his wife had in mind. It was that man Ashley. The Farrars had gone out of their way, it seemed to him, to send the Mosses a copy of the St. Louis paper announcing the death of Mrs. Ashley. Some vague hope had been behind the abortive plan to send Elizabeth to St. Louis for a visit. The whole idea was fairly abhorrent to him and he could not understand his wife's insistence. General Ashley, whatever his rank and fortune, was twice his Betsy's years. He thanked God that he had taken up land away from the river. In the spring of 1822, when the flagship of the Ashley fleet, a long keelboat named *Enterprise,* tied up at the Boonville landing, every town in Boonslick that touched the river buzzed with talk; but Two-Mile Prairie and the new town of Columbia heard only echoes.

Certainly William Ashley was far from Elizabeth's musings when she stood before a preacher with Daniel on that hot, bright day in July of 1822 and gave her final promise. She remembered the drone of a bee, the hush that fell on the chattering crowd as she and Daniel took their places. Again it was a goodly crowd, the time having been chosen to follow the wheat harvest and the first cutting of hay, so that people could leave their farms and come.

She remembered Daniel's face when he saw her in her bridal frock of feather-light muslin over an underdress of thin China silk. A sewing woman had cut and fitted the dress, following a chart sent from St. Louis; but Elizabeth herself had hemmed and gathered yards of narrow ruffling to trim the skirt hem and the bodice. Her fingers had fashioned four dozen miniature white silk rosebuds, with tiny, pale green leaves, to set off the short, puffed sleeves and nestle in the folds of the full, flowing skirt. Sashes were being tied two inches lower this year but still well above the normal waistline, the short, snug bodice being as charming on a slender figure as it was cruel to a plump one. Elizabeth, her bright hair up in a soft bun on the crown of her head, with only a few curls at her ears, looked half-sprite, half-angel; and Daniel's face was a study in worship. For that matter, the awe on Ambrose Bohannon's rugged features was as great.

"Man," he stammered to Daniel, "ye hae taken on a g-great responsibility!"

"What would you not give for the privilege?" Daniel challenged.

"Man, dinna speak of it!" Bo answered, in the brogue which he had all but lost in four years among people who spoke otherwise.

There was that to remember. And she remembered the dry, flat tones of the preacher. In those days in Boonslick, for burials or weddings or baptisms, one availed one's self of whatever itinerant preacher happened along, with small regard for sect or creed. This man was a Baptist, a stranger; and he felt impelled to add a sermon to the wedding service. Mrs. Moss was outraged at what she called his performance, but she needn't have been. Elizabeth heard no clear word of his exhortings. There was the sleeve of Daniel's new blue coat just at her eye level; and later, while those still young and footloose were clapping and dancing to the measures of "Old Sister Phoebe" and "Come, my Love, and Go with Me," there were Daniel's arms closing about her.

"My Libby. Mine—to keep."

What could a preacher add or take away?

It was on the day of the infare, the second day, that William Ashley kept his promise, lightly given, she had thought, and so lightly forgotten, to dance at her wedding.

Gray clouds hung from the sky that day; and, in a sense, that was a blessing. Elizabeth's second-day dress was of rich silk, a becoming green-blue in color and not diaphanous. With it went a coal-scuttle bonnet set with ostrich tips, elegant French kid gloves, and a cashmere shawl even more superfluous than bonnet or gloves, since the house for which she and Daniel would be leaving presently was just six miles away. However, immediately after the wedding breakfast she went upstairs and put on bonnet, gloves and shawl before she reappeared on the steps with Daniel, the two of them waiting to take their places at the head of the procession that would escort them to their new home.

And there, at the foot of the steps, beside her father, stood this man. Moccasins, leggings, gingham shirt, belt and leg knife, a French headkerchief over long, dark hair, were not unrecognizable details to anyone present; but the deep curing of his swarthy skin, eyes narrowed from squinting into the sun or searching thickets and distance for game or enemy, lines of endurance deep at the corners of the thin-lipped mouth, a stoop to the broad shoulders, a bow to the squat, sturdy legs, and, above all, a restrained wonder and impatience to find himself standing in this house reeking of spice and cookery and flowers and gaiety, said he was a woodsman who had made a long journey to be here. His eyes—a wild creature's bright, black eyes—fastened themselves on Elizabeth descending the stairs, so that she stopped even before her father spoke.

"For you, Betsy." His gentle voice seemed loud in the general silence. "From General Ashley's camp on the Upper Missouri. A message and a gift, I take it."

Everyone twittered then with wonder and curiosity. Elizabeth turned to Daniel.

"He said he would come to my wedding," she told Daniel. "Two years ago when he was here. You remember. I thought he was joking. How do you suppose he knew?"

But the woodsman now had taken from his shirt a flat packet of deerhide and was untying the strings. Inside were a sealed letter and a scrap of newspaper.

"An express messenger, following me up the Missouri," General Ashley wrote, "carrying for our camp's entertainment such news matter from our other world as he could manage, brought, I feel by some design and not mere chance, the issue of *The Missouri Intelligencer* giving notice of your coming marriage.

"It called to my mind a promise I made—was it so long as two years ago? Present circumstances making it impossible for me to keep the promise literally, I made haste to get together a sort of apology or earnest of my intentions. I hope you will so construe the small bundle of peltries the bearer has instructions to lay before you.

"I can think of no fairer use for peltries than that they should help to adorn one so young and beautiful. If I were in or near St. Louis, I should ask some lady of taste to guide me in having them sewn into somewhat suitable for your wearing; but perhaps you would prefer to direct that operation for yourself at your convenience and to your desire. The pelts, I believe, are whole and without blemish. They were cured by Indians who are masters at that sort of thing, and with care will remain in good condition for a long while. I hope that I shall have the pleasure at some not too distant date of expressing my felicitations in person. And so, not being there to dance at your wedding, I take the liberty of drinking a toast here to your long life and happiness. Please believe me always

Your obedient servant,
Wm. H. Ashley"

Shivers ran over Libby as she read. It was so unexpected and done with such a flourish. It was the sort of thing one read in high romance—an extravagance which pleased one's fancy and yet was not meant to be believed wholly. But now it had happened. She handed the letter and the bit of newspaper to Daniel and met on his face a frown of perplexity to match her own, also a trace of displeasure. Oh, of course, not at her. He could see as well as anybody else how astounded she was.

But no woman could have been entirely proof against the beauty of those skins when she saw them and felt them. The courier's impassivity vanished as he laid open the outer wrappings of deerhide and lifted the top pelt, holding it over his brown hands for her to see and then to touch with her fingers, and finally to take into her own grasp. Soft as the finest Lyons velvet, softer than that. Light—she could crush it in her hands like a handkerchief, open her hand to release it; and there it would lie in feather-soft and feather-light, dun-hued smoothness . . . and richness.

"Beautiful!" she said, half in a whisper.

"*Oui, madame!*" the courier agreed, with enthusiasm.

"Tell Mr. Ashley— No, I must do better than that. Are you returning to the camp?"

"*Oui, madame.* To St. Louis first *vite, vite,* then back all at once." He made motions that spelled running or flying, if possible. His urgency led Dr. Moss to put in a question.

"I hope all is going well at the camp?"

The courier drew up his shoulders, expressing doubt. In halting French, mixed with English, he explained that winter would come too soon, too soon. There were unfriendly Indians. Too many. As for the Missouri . . .

"Eet is one hell of a river, god damn!" he finished.

Shivers ran over Elizabeth again. That had always been her opinion.

"Will you carry a letter back with you?" she asked. "I think," she appealed to her father and Daniel, "I should write."

"By all means," her father said at once.

"Yes," Daniel agreed, more slowly. "It is a princely gift."

His level, honest eyes, studying her and not the pieces of fur, were troubled. She put her hand on his arm coaxingly.

"If I can find a piece of writing paper in this house," she said. "Come with me and tell me what to say."

But Daniel went instead to see that the courier had food and drink; and Elizabeth sat down alone before a sheet of paper at the desk in her father's study.

"You will know what to say," Daniel had assured her, but she did not. She thought she knew what troubled Daniel. Elsewhere in the house, and outside, the halted wedding procession buzzed over the gift and its manner of arrival, most of the argument rising from attempts to appraise its value. Beaver pelts in 1822 were equal to banknotes, running from three to five dollars a pound. The value of the courier's pack might compare favorably with the annual rent Daniel must pay for the saltbox house in Columbia.

The Honorable William H. Ashley
Lieutenant Governor of Missouri
Dear Sir:
   I have no words with which to thank you for your princely wedding gift, which arrived in the hands of your messenger just this morning, the day following my marriage to Dr. Daniel P. Wilcox.

Should she refuse to accept the pelts? No, that suggestion had not been made, even by her mother. Somehow, to do that would be as exaggerated in its way as Mr. Ashley's gift seemed on his part. Valuable as the pelts were, to one of Mr. Ashley's wealth the sum was a trifle. Her heart ached with sudden fierce tenderness over Daniel. She wished—she almost wished that the gift had not been made.

The pelts are beautiful. I have never seen their equal.

That was the truth. Her finger tips remembered the softness, her eyes the pale forest-brown of a beaver skin against the green of her dress. Unbidden, fashion charts paraded before her—a muff, a stole. . . .

My young brother Josiah professes to be a master hand at curing and preserving skins. He has promised to keep them for me until I can make use of them as you suggest. That may be some time away. My husband has newly set up practice in Columbia, the seat of government in Boone County; and we have much to accomplish here before we can contemplate any traveling.
   Meanwhile, if in your journeyings you should chance to pass near, my father and my husband beg me to say that we hope you will visit us again, so that we may extend the acquaintance begun so agreeably two years ago, of which you have now so graciously reminded us.
   Also, my father and my husband beg me to extend their heartiest wishes for the successful completion of your journey to the Rocky Mountains. May I add that this is my wish, as well?

There! That would have to do. She would not read what she had written for fear that it would not satisfy and she must make another start. She would give the letter to Daniel to read before she sealed it. If it was not right, he must say. She signed her name: "Yours obediently, E. Wilcox." Smiling over that, thinking only of Daniel, she looked up, not into his adoring eyes but into bright, searching ones of William Ashley. For a minute his presence in the room was so real that it frightened her.

"Daniel!" She rose up with a fluttering cry, just as the door opened and Daniel came in.

"Through?" he asked cheerfully, whatever had troubled him now gone.

"Sweetheart, yes," she said, wild with relief. "Close the door, will you? And . . . kiss me, quick! Where have you been? I miss you so when you're away! Did you know that?"

CHAPTER FIVE

Two Houses

THE FIRST HOME in Columbia was truly a saltbox; and, since it had to do double duty as residence and surgery, life in it was cozy to a degree.

It was on Broadway at Sixth, not just because Broadway was expected to be the main thoroughfare. It was at present the only thoroughfare.

"Excellent location," Daniel said. "Everything that passes must pass here."

There was not too much passing. The house had two rooms. One of them was furnished with plain, stout chairs, not too comfortable, a long table and hanging bookshelves, occupied for the time being by one volume which was Daniel's own and six of his father-in-law's. There was a desk here, too, for the keeping of accounts and such records as he made at home of county business. That, he reported ruefully, still exceeded his private bookkeeping.

The other room, of the same size and uncompromising, square lines, was graced by dimity curtains at the two windows, by a cherry four-poster bed with a silk and velvet log cabin counterpane, two corner cupboards, one for glass and queensware, the other for groceries and kitchen tools, a curtained wardrobe in a third corner for Elizabeth's other dresses and Daniel's wedding suit, a walnut chest of drawers with a mirror, a walnut table with candlesticks, Daniel's riding crop and hunting rifle on the wall above the chimney, and two deep chairs by the hearth, but most of all by the presence of the mistress of the house.

Where the queen was, Daniel said, there was the throne room of the palace; and a dozen times a day he looked in to make sure she was about. She usually was present, because a person wouldn't believe how many things she found to do—all those jobs for which Daniel formerly had hired a sewing woman or which he had let go unheeded until—well, really, it was time he took a wife. He was a terrible man for popping off buttons and bursting out his socks. Then there were her own clothes to keep fresh and alluring, her wedding pretties to shine, and three meals a day to prepare, all of them with bread and meat and one, at least, with a surprise. Occasionally, but only that, she was away—visiting in town, shopping at Mr. Kearny's grocery or Mr. Williams's general store, or perhaps spending the day at her former home, helping with the preserving of fruit, for hers and Daniel's share. She had the impression that Daniel paced the floor during such absences, though he had sanctioned them in advance.

It was wonderful to be wanted like that. Every late afternoon when she was at home, Daniel would open the door between the two rooms, put his head through like a boy gone suddenly hungry, and beseech her to join him in his office.

"It's much too early to abandon my pretense of business," he would coax, "but it's pretty cheerless sitting here alone."

And she, hiding as best she could the fact that she had been a half-hour waiting for this invitation, would put up her sewing, take a peek at whatever simmered or baked at the fire, and yield to his entreaty. He would set a chair for her by his fire or preferably one chair for the two of them. They would sit there together going over things or just dreaming, sometimes until a kettle boiled over or a crust scorched. A patient, entering without knocking, would have been scandalized. Even servants underfoot would have been a nuisance.

The two they had were seldom underfoot. A twelve-year-old daughter of Pomegranate, named Susan, came every day to do scrubbing or other heavy cleaning, to see that Elizabeth had water in the house and generally do other toting; but she was gone at the latest by early afternoon, being required to report to her mother before daylight declined and to spend the night under her mother's guardianship. Poke, the stable hand, Dr. Moss had given to them outright, along with his main wedding present of a light gig and a horse suitable for driving or riding. The horse was from a small stud of thoroughbreds the Doctor had grazing now on his good grass. Poke cared for the gig and the horse and slept in the stable, unless, by rare chance, Daniel was called away at night. Then Poke slept on the floor of the office, guarding Elizabeth. He kept up the wood supply for both fires, and showed up promptly for food, but was otherwise pretty scarce.

Days danced and drifted by. A gentleman by the name of Ashley and his gifts were again forgotten. Or nearly. His first magnificent voyage of exploration and trade up the big Missouri ended in disaster. He barely escaped with his life and one bullet-riddled boat. Elizabeth, hearing wild tales of ruin, wondered whether this might not be the time to return the beaver skins, but again did not yield to the impulse. If Ashley's losses were as great as rumor said, a few dollars would not mend the breach in his fortunes; and it was perhaps unkind to remark on his defeat. As it happened, it was also unnecessary. In the way of men of property, he re-established his credit and went right back, with better knowledge of the odds against him and better plans and a greater force, and, by sending his men in separate parties overland through river valleys and mountain passes, instead of trusting too long to the vagaries of a turbulent river, achieved victory. He came back from his second expedition enormously rich in pocket; and not only he, but even more the men under him—James Bridger, Thomas Fitzpatrick, Jedediah Smith, the Sublettes, Robert Campbell —were famous forever on the western frontier.

In 1824, his term as Lieutenant Governor expiring, he offered himself as a candidate for Governor of the state; and Daniel Wilcox did what he could to keep him from being elected. Oh, Daniel did not mention Ashley in his orations, prearranged or spontaneous. His war cry was "John Quincy Adams for President"; but his enthusiastic support of the upright New Englander in opposition to the rising popularity of General Andrew Jackson of Tennessee, and his satisfaction in the nation-wide victory of Adams and his party, were too warm to seem impersonal.

"Poor Mr. Ashley!" Elizabeth teased. "What have you against him?"

"Once," Daniel growled, "he had the effrontery to look at you."

Well, the man had effrontery, sure enough. Not content with the fortune he had amassed, on his return from the Rocky Mountains he had married wealth, his second wife being a Miss Christy, the daughter of a man of great property in St. Louis. Miss Christy, now Mrs. Ashley, was also the younger sister of the first wife of Uncle Bernard Farrar, the predecessor of Anne Thruston Farrar. On top of that, through her mother, a Taylor of Kentucky and Virginia, she was a distant cousin of Elizabeth's. Mrs. Moss could unravel the relationship if Elizabeth would only listen, but she would not. She was sure the new wife's charms were her dowry—and her father's sense of real estate values. Again she thought of sending back the beaver pelts, and again chose to wait. It would be more satisfactory to return them in person should an opportunity develop. It seemed just possible, because of the relationship, that one might.

Meanwhile, other events and other people touched more vitally the lives of Elizabeth and Daniel. For example, the abrupt disappearance of Ambrose Bohannon. Barcie Harris was visiting in Boone County—not at the Wilcox house, where there was no room for visitors. She slept in the Moss home and was very welcome, the Doctor said, sighing. Part of every day she spent with Elizabeth; and once Bo was there, too, for supper. It was autumn. Supper was roast duck and ribs of young pork with baked apples, and Libby made a pie. Bo ate to repletion and was never more entertaining. There had been another duel at Boonville. Did Daniel recall the one over which they had sworn partnership? The duel with knives and boots? Well, this had been with shotguns. Two mortal enemies had met by accident in the same house and on sight had been possessed with the idea of making way with each other. Both had run to their horses for their weapons, then had come back along the sides of the house, each determined to shoot first and so— Ah, well, they had again met with such suddenness and raised their guns so exactly on the same instant that the charge of one went directly down the barrel of the other, which so stupefied the two duelers that their friends were able to cool them down with a douse of cold water apiece; and hostilities ended, for the time, at least.

The story achieved its purpose. It produced merry laughter over the rough, tough ways of Boonslick's hardiest settlers. Humor dragged at the corners of Bo's big mouth as he told it; but pain, they could see later, simultaneously clouded his honest eyes. A crunching grip that nearly spoiled Daniel's shoulder was Ambrose's good night and goodbye. He rode off alone, and darkness held him from then on.

"Daniel, why?" Elizabeth said, thinking it better that Daniel should talk than be so grimly silent about the affair. "Have you any idea why?"

Daniel smiled at her, but sadly. Belatedly he knew very well why. All the time that he had courted Elizabeth he had been beset by so many difficulties of his own that he had been blind to the fact that Bohannon had loved her as well and even more hopelessly. He had had his first suspicion of the truth on the day of the wedding; and now he was sure that seeing Elizabeth happy in her own home, married to another, was just more than the big, sentimental fellow could endure. So he had packed his kit and gone away. They'd never see him again.

"Oh, Daniel, you don't think that, too? Barcie always said, but— Oh, what can I do to help her now?"

"Nothing," Daniel said. "Barcie's all right. She'll find her own way out of this."

Barcie's way was to marry a stranger, a newcomer to Boonslick, a Mr. Harvey Freeman, who worked in the land office in Franklin.

"Now I've lost Barcie," Libby mourned.

It was not that she disapproved of Barcie's husband. Mr. Freeman, while not exciting to know, seemed a worthy man. Being interested in land, he would make a good son-in-law and partner for Mr. Harris. It was the manner of the marriage and a previous gesture of repudiation on Barcie's part that made a cleavage between her and Elizabeth.

The repudiation grew out of another circumstance. The little town of Columbia was growing. People settled there with children, who needed instruction; and Elizabeth asked Barcie how she would like to be mistress of a school if one was organized. She made the offer in all kindness, but Barcie refused it emphatically.

"I'll have my own children," she said. "I won't have you or anybody else feeling sorry for me, Libby Moss, making up your minds what I'm to be."

So she married Harvey Freeman and the twenty miles between the two households might as well have been a hundred.

Ah, well, times changed and people with them, Elizabeth said. Columbia grew to recognizable proportions as a town; all of Boonslick prospered. The nation was expanding to the westward. Every year travel increased—to the Northwest, where the mountain streams yielded fortunes in furs, to the Southwest, where the Spaniards' mines yielded silver and gold. Steamboats traveled the Missouri River—to the Osage, the Kaw, the Platte, the Yellowstone. A mail stage route went through Columbia overland. Specie, coined money, jingled in men's pockets; and Daniel Wilcox became a man of consequence in Boonslick. His practice outgrew the one small room in the first house; and he built a brick residence on Cherry Street a block away from Broadway and moved his family there. It was a family now. What Mrs. Moss had foretold with a shudder had come to pass. Elizabeth had a daughter of her own. She named her Mary, to keep the string going. In the family she was called Mary Jane, to set her apart from the others.

"A grandchild," Mrs. Moss wailed, "and I not through with my own family."

"Isn't it fun?" Elizabeth said, content to sit before the fire in the great room of her father's house, with this exquisite small creature on her lap.

"You are more beautiful than ever," Daniel groaned.

He spoke a truth that must have been evident to anyone. Barcie Freeman plumped up a few pounds with each child that she bore, but motherhood added grace to Elizabeth. Daniel's groan was self-reproach.

"I've done nothing I promised," he said to Dr. Moss. "Nothing."

"You've done wonderfully well," his father-in-law said. "Betsy couldn't be happier. What do you want?"

"I want deep carpets under her feet wherever she steps, silk dresses for her to wear, gold chains, a carriage and pair, a coachman and butler. . . ."

"Pshaw! Worst thing that could happen!"

But that was what Daniel wanted. He had done well. He was a man of prestige and influence, in great demand at Fourth of July celebrations and political rallies. At thirty he had more than ever that look of a Crusader carrying a banner. Everybody respected him and almost everybody liked him; but he was not a man of wealth.

"And never will be," Mrs. Moss still insisted.

In 1830 he was elected a Representative of Boone County in the Missouri State Assembly. He would be Governor some day, his friends said. Elizabeth smiled, fun dancing in her eyes. Wouldn't that be a joke on somebody?

Daniel wondered. Elizabeth was twenty-six now to his thirty-two. They had a second daughter, named Anna Marie, a sturdy, healthy baby this time; but Libby, he thought, was much too thin. Exquisitely slender a stranger would have pronounced her; but Daniel traced shadows under her eyes and was troubled.

"Sweetheart," he said on impulse, "this new capital of Missouri—the City of Jefferson as they call it—it's not a very civilized town as yet, I hear; and I'm not sure of the boarding accommodations, but there must be some. When the Assembly opens, surely there will be some sort of doings. Would you like to attend—with me? I'd be proud to have you. We could leave the babies at your mother's, with Susan to take care of them. It's not far—thirty miles."

Libby's face pinked up at once. Was she twenty-six, really?

"That would be fun, except," more soberly, "I've nothing to wear."

Daniel shouted with relief. An earthbound remark, if he had ever heard one, coming from the cleverest needlewoman in Boonslick, with no end of ideas about style and ornament. Always putting other women's noses out of joint. This might be the medicine she needed. Madness seized him.

"Very well," he said, "we'll go to St. Louis first and buy some finery. Seems to me I owe you a visit to that town. How would you like that?"

Even more than the projected visit to Jefferson City, he thought; but madness persisted. When she protested against the expense, he informed her that, strange as it might seem, he could afford the journey. Besides, he had some business in St. Louis that might go along better for his personal attention. He wouldn't say what it was. It might come to nothing, but . . .

It was that old scheme of his and Bohannon's to build a spa in Cooper County. He had heard recently that the title to the Chouteau Grant was again up for argument in the courts. If he could get an option on the mineral springs, and a few men to go in with him on the buildings—that was how fortunes were made.

Libby sang and planned and he scratched on paper.

"You had some beaver skins," Daniel said to Elizabeth one evening. "Ashley beaver. Have they gone bad?"

"No," she said. "I have them still. They're as good as new."

"Know exactly, I suppose, what you're going to do with them."

"Exactly," she agreed; but now she wouldn't say.

It was a bright September noon when the steamer *Liberty* from up the Missouri, Captain Crooks commanding, dropped her stage on the St. Louis levee, and Libby covered one ear against the hullabaloo but kept the other one and both eyes open, to miss none of it. Anyhow, Daniel had her left arm tightly under his.

"I'm thinking," he said to a question in her eyes, "of that day I landed here ten years ago—on my way to Boonslick."

His spirits were as high today as they had been low then. How things had changed! Lest she miss some of them, he catalogued the improvements for Elizabeth—the handsome cobblestone pavement replacing the ragged bluff and sand-bank that he remembered, the row of steamboats, reducing the surviving keelboats to mere skiffs, the solid front of stores and warehouses facing the water, all but obliterating the few steep-roofed log huts of the original French merchants, the market house and City Hall. How the city had grown! He had heard that its population had passed five thousand, years ago. It must be well on the way to ten thousand now.

While he was absorbed in stone and brick evidences of growth, Elizabeth's excitement was over people. So many people, so handsomely attired! The women in silks and laces, the men in fine broadcloth and brass buttons and tall hats. If they looked like this at a steamboat landing in the morning, how would they appear at a reception or a ball? The width of the new sleeves! That redingote opening all down the front of a street dress! When it came to choosing a hat, would it be one of those broad-brimmed affairs with feathers, or a turban? She favored the broad-brimmed hat as having more grace. The turbans were a bit pillowy, Turkish, but practical, no doubt, on

67

a windy day. Mercy, she had lived apart from the main stream of life! She felt, well, not dowdy but slightly rustic, akin to that shawled woman selling apples.

"City Hotel! Kerridge an' baggage wagon fo' City Hotel! Anybuddy yere fo' City Hotel?"

"That's ours," Daniel said. "Here, boy. You say you have a baggage wagon? This trunk and small bag and bandbox—"

"Please," Elizabeth interrupted, "I'll keep the bandbox with me, if I may."

She was a little disappointed at finding nobody on the landing to meet her and Daniel. It had been Daniel's idea to take a room at the hotel, rather than visit the Farrars. Having business to attend to, and people to see, he said, he would feel more independent. But Elizabeth had written her uncle and aunt of their coming and she did think someone might have come to the boat. However, this way she would have time to do this and that to her wardrobe before inspection.

"Something special in that bandbox?" Daniel asked in the hotel hack.

"Very special."

The beaver skins and one of his old hats. Before she saw dressmaker or milliner for herself, she meant to locate the best hatter in St. Louis. Daniel Wilcox of Boone County was going to have the finest hat in Jefferson City that winter, she would make certain. As handsome as he was, if he wore a fine hat, his other accoutrements could borrow enough glory to pass. Out of the fur remaining she contemplated ordering one of those new pillow muffs for herself; but the hat came first.

"Happy?" Daniel asked next.

"Enchanted," she answered.

Happier still to be met at the hotel by Mr. Town, the manager, and a message from the Farrars. The Doctor was occupied with a serious case some miles out of town, so that Mrs. Farrar lacked a conveyance and could not meet the boat. She hoped to call that afternoon and make amends for a seeming lack of cordiality.

"Good!" Daniel said. "You can visit with her and I can get my business started."

Elizabeth was disappointed. She had hoped to show off her handsome husband at her first meeting with her city relatives. Aunt Farrar alone had seen him before, and that ten years ago. He had changed—all for the better Elizabeth was sure.

"I'll see them another time," he promised. "We'll be here several

68

days, at least." The thought struck him that he might obtain some practical advice from Dr. Farrar about that health resort. Several were in operation in and around St. Louis.

So Elizabeth was alone, with a dress spread over the bed for examination, when her Aunt Farrar, taking advantage of seniority and position, followed a second messenger directly to the hotel room. Elizabeth's pique over being taken by surprise melted quickly under the warmth of the other's greeting. What a gracious lady the copper-haired Anne Thruston Farrar had come to be! She held Elizabeth at arm's length a while, then kissed her warmly.

"I am so glad to see you again!" she said. "I do wish you had come directly to our house to stay."

Elizabeth mentioned that Dr. Wilcox was occupied with some business.

"Then I shall have to reason with him," Aunt Farrar said. "My dear, how lovely you are—prettier by far than I remembered." And then, almost in the same breath, "There is someone who must see you. Did you know you had an admirer in St. Louis?"

Now, how could that be?

"A relative of ours by marriage in a roundabout way," Aunt Farrar said. "According to your mother, more directly related to you. There, I won't tease. It's General Ashley, darling, General William Ashley, no less."

There was no reason for Elizabeth's heart to beat faster, except that a woman would have to be older than twenty-six and insensible, not to be stirred by compliment.

"But," she said, "he saw me just once—one day, I mean."

"I know, and your home, too, just that once. Yet, both are the subject of extravagant tribute from him still. 'The prettiest girl I ever saw anywhere,' he says, 'walks an earthly Paradise known as Boone County, Missouri. She would grace a palace, but Fortune, wiser and kinder than man, perhaps, has placed her there.' But you will hear from him directly now, I think. I saw him yesterday and told him you were coming to St. Louis. You will hear."

Elizabeth, pleasantly confused, spoke more pertly than she felt.

"Whatever he thinks of Boonslick, I notice he lives here."

"For the present," Aunt Farrar agreed. "He has a beautiful home here and I hope you will see it. He is a rich man, as you know, and his business centers here. I wouldn't swear, however, that, when he is satisfied with his fortune, he would not choose your part of the state in preference."

Elizabeth recovered clearness of judgment. A rich man; and St.

Louis was his first choice, Boonslick second. So, in the matter of wives, his first choice was an heiress.

"What would you like best to do this afternoon?" Aunt Farrar asked. "I have the carriage. We can drive about."

Elizabeth, warming to this lively relative of earlier memories, confessed her misgivings about her clothes. There were not only those women at the boat that morning. She had noticed the dress of the ones in the hotel dining room at noon. She, who set the style in Boone County, was not a lady of fashion here.

"Don't ever be," her aunt advised. "Don't even aspire to it. I am sure those ladies were also quite aware of you and envious, in the bargain, of your eyes, your hair, your complexion.

"And your husband," she added, when she had seen Daniel again.

"However," she concluded now, "there's nothing I like better than buying pretties for a pretty person. So, we'll look in at a few stores, to see what can be had, then talk the matter over at our leisure—perhaps this evening."

And they would locate that hatter, Elizabeth thought.

When Daniel returned to the hotel late that afternoon, Elizabeth was lying back on pillows with a towel over her eyes. Not that they needed brightening. When she removed the towel, stars shone in their depths. It was just that she had seen so much that she needed to black everything out, to bring order out of bewildering confusion.

"Such houses!" she said. "The grounds are like small parks. Such treasures on display in the shops—jewelry, silks, laces—"

"And so much dust everywhere," Daniel added. "My eyes are full of grit and my throat more so."

And there was a lump in his throat that grew as he studied his wife's hand in his. Such a small hand to hold a man's heart so tightly! Impulsively he drew Elizabeth off the bed to his knee and held her in the chair in the way they had liked to sit when the wonder of their living together was new.

"Tell me," he said, "and tell me straight. Would you rather live here than in Boone County?"

"Yes," she said simply, and then in a spasm of premonitory fright, "No. I mean, if I could have everything I have at home and a little of this, perhaps?"

Daniel laughed and laughed, the lump disappearing for a while, at least. He told the story at the Farrars', where they had supper and spent the evening. Such a gay evening! If all the visit could have matched it! Uncle Farrar was a livelier copy of her father, much more

of a gallant. There was a turbulence of children, too, in the house—
young boys full of dreams and schemes and devices, enraptured by
her and Daniel's tales of frontier settlements.

"You must visit your uncle and aunt in Boone County next
summer," Elizabeth urged. "Your Uncle Moss has horses to ride and
there's a Cousin James about your age."

Brightly, but solemnly, too, they gave their promise. And they
would visit her also, and her little girls, and Cousin Wilcox? Elizabeth kissed them good night with special tenderness for this tribute.
Daniel was so without kinfolk in this part of the world!

Soon afterward, she and Daniel said their farewells. A full day had
been planned for the morrow. In the morning, Daniel was to accompany Dr. Farrar on his rounds while she and Aunt Farrar consulted
a sewing woman and made a few purchases. Then all were to take
two o'clock dinner with General and Mrs. Ashley. Elizabeth, her arm
in Daniel's, looked up to see how he would regard this invitation. He
smiled down at her, happy and confident in his full possession.

"And old admirer of my wife, did you know?" he said to the
Farrars.

At noon the next day, Elizabeth, returning to the hotel with her
arms full of bundles and her head full of matching vanities, and feeling equally pleased over her interview with a hatter, found Daniel
ahead of her. He stood at the window of their room, looking out over
the roofs between him and the river, and hardly seemed aware of her
entrance. She knew at once that something had gone wrong. She
studied the rigidity of his back, the willed erectness of his head. He
never looked so much that way as when his fortunes were in the dust.

She laid her bundles on the bed.

"Well!" she said, with determined sprightliness. "You back so soon?
I thought I should have a full hour to make my grand toilet."

But pretending was no good. Daniel turned; and she saw pain, distress, and, what was more foreign to him, confusion on his features.

"My darling," she said, "you are ill."

"No," he said, trying to clear his expression, but not succeeding.
Deceit was never part of him. "A slight headache, that's all. A rustic,
not used to a big town."

But he had been out all morning with Dr. Farrar, who would surely
have noticed had he looked ill then.

"Dr. Farrar dropped me in town a half-hour ago," Daniel said, "at
my request, at Mr. Chouteau's place of business. Mr. Pierre Chouteau
—you've heard of him?"

71

Elizabeth wrinkled her nose.

"Too much," she said. "The Indian trader. Aunt Farrar showed me his place yesterday as we drove past." That place and Mr. Ashley's, too, saying that she might call now with Libby but the owners might not be at home and she was sure each gentleman would prefer to do the honors of his estate in person. Men were like that if they took pride in their homes. "A full square," Libby continued now, "with a fence and spikes on top of it. Aunt Farrar said when his Indians came to town to see him they made camp on his grounds." She wrinkled her nose again. "Was he horrid?" She tried to remember something Daniel had said a long time ago about land Mr. Chouteau had in Boonslick—something about springs.

"No," Daniel said. "A noble, kindly gentleman. You could see why anyone—Indian or white—had respect for him." Then it was not Mr. Chouteau. "A rich man, of course. There is something about a man so rich. . . ."

Hmm?

"That's what Mamma always said," Elizabeth told him. "She claimed she could tell on the instant. Darling, had you rather not go to the Ashleys' for dinner? We can send a messenger with a note."

"Nonsense!" Daniel said. "Of course we'll go."

He would go to please her, if for no other reason. Elizabeth persuaded him to take off his coat and sit back with a wet cloth over his eyes while she attended to her costume. She had bought a frill of starched net to insert into the opening of her best dress. It was a plaid silk and to her present, changing viewpoint, it had seemed suddenly a little garish. The ruching, put in just as the sewing woman had instructed, lightened and smartened it wonderfully.

"You look very winsome," Daniel said, when she was ready for his inspection.

Elizabeth's face fell.

"I wanted to be irresistible," she said.

"I prefer you winsome," Daniel said.

"Winsome it shall be then, milord!"

The Ashley residence was between Second and Third streets, northward of the original city limits, but in the direct line of present growth, situated on the first of a series of Indian mounds, abandoned before the time of the white man by the aboriginal builders. Ah-h! More about Indians! Undeniably, however, a mound made a good eminence on which to build a proud house. Several St. Louisans of wealth were considering them for that purpose; but Mr. Ashley, as might have been expected, was the first.

A flight of steps with railings took one up from street level to the flat summit of the mound; and at the head of those steps Mr. Ashley waited, with his lady, to welcome the Wilcoxes, the first of the day's guests to arrive.

"This is," he said, his hands extended, "a surprise and a rare pleasure."

Elizabeth was amazed to find how well she remembered him. That deep, resonant voice, which, with his glowing, dark eyes, made a man of importance and impressiveness out of one not otherwise endowed with visible distinction. Ten years had passed since their other meeting; and, while she did not look at him now, she hoped, with the captiousness of a young girl, she thought his nose and chin seemed sharper than ever. Daniel rather towered above him. Daniel . . . but it was hardly fair to compare another man with Daniel.

And now Mr. Ashley was presenting Elizabeth to his lady.

"My dear, here she is, the fairy princess of the wilderness Paradise, of whom you've heard me speak."

The man had no abashment.

"Often," Mrs. Ashley agreed, her eyes flashing over Elizabeth but not revealing her opinion. "You are most welcome, Mrs. Wilcox—Dr. Wilcox. I understand that we are distantly related."

She was a dark, handsome young woman, but lacked, Elizabeth thought, some needed serenity of manner. Well, that was a quality hard to achieve, perhaps, in association with Mr. Ashley. He was the most restless man she had ever seen. And he forgot nothing that he'd ever said or that had ever been said to him.

"I hear you moved over to Boone County at the time of your marriage," he said to Daniel. "I've thought of you often and wondered if you ever regretted not joining my river ventures."

"There have been times," Daniel answered straightforwardly, "when I have at least wondered whether I had been wise to refuse your offer."

"Well, nobody can deny that you had cogent reasons for your choice." Ashley bowed to Elizabeth.

Then he must show them his grounds, of which, as Aunt Farrar had warned, he was extravagantly proud. Proudest, perhaps, of a fountain that threw jets of water into the air on one side of the walk, the water dropping then in sparkling drops into a basin where goldfish swam among trailing ends of water hyacinths. A very extravagance of water, even when one knew its source. Across the walk, a great stone basin—large enough for its walls to have made the foundations of a house—held water pumped up to it through pipes from the Mississippi River. So, of course . . .

"Ah?" Daniel said inquiringly.

"An arrangement I have with the city government," Mr. Ashley said proudly with satisfaction. "I allow them this eminence for locating a reservoir, from which water again is piped down to residences and manufactories below, able to command such service; and in return I have water for my own use."

"Ah?" Daniel said, still politely.

Elizabeth shook her head. It was not the arrangement of pipes that astounded her. She hardly comprehended the intricacies of that. It was the way Mr. Ashley looked, standing at the rim of the stone basin, his eyes passing over the roofs of houses and huts between him and the river, sparkling clear and handsome at this distance. One might have thought that he, compelling and indomitable, drew the water to his plateau by his own will. He could have been the original sachem or priest of the mound, receiving a visiting chieftain, and boasting of his domain. She must not think such wild thoughts, she knew, lest they show in her manner. She must think, instead, of the wonder of river water flowing directly into one's house, to be turned on or off as one willed. She had read of such wonders.

"You are amazed, are you not?" Ashley said to her suddenly. "Come. I will cut you a rose. You will understand that better."

What did he know of her understanding? But it was a beautiful rose, a delicate pink one, shaded to creamy gold at its heart, and fragrant as a spice jar. She thought ruefully of her plaid dress, which, for all its white frill, was still green and gold, splashed with crimson; and, along with her "thank you," she asked if she might have a glass of water, to hold the rose and keep it fresh.

"I would have it to wear this evening," she promised. "I would dress to suit its lovely color."

"But I would not be there to see," Ashley said.

"No, I'm afraid not." She smiled at him sweetly, as supreme in her domain as he was in his. "My husband has promised to take me to see a stage play at your theatre. Buried as we are—" she broke off, looked helplessly at Daniel, then smiled at him, seeing that he understood. What she would have said must have sounded like Miss Mary, rebelling against Boonslick.

"What is a rose?" Ashley said, not noticing. "You may have an armful when you leave."

And he went on to show them the rest of the garden, which was

74

almost too lavish to be taken in on one inspection, late roses and other flowers blooming richly in the mild September sunshine and with that extravagance of water for their thirsty roots. Here and there against beautifully kept and trimmed domestic greenery were giant ferns and lemon and orange trees from the sub-tropics, curious lilies from China, even a holly tree from England. It seemed there was a rivalry among St. Louisans in the way of gardens, encouraged by a young hardware merchant of the town named Shaw, English-born, who knew and was known in the world-famous Kew Gardens of his home land. He liked nothing better than to order for his friends such foreign specimens and see them planted and watch their growth. This time Elizabeth caught Daniel's eye before he said, "Ah?" What ailed Daniel? He loved flowers, could rhapsodize over a wood violet.

However, by then other guests were arriving and the Ashleys went to welcome them. To Elizabeth's surprise, Daniel hung back for another look at the maze of planting. He frowned; then his lips twisted in a smile.

"Daniel?"

"When he was a boy in Virginia," Daniel said, "he was poor; but he lived near people who were not and they had fine gardens and maybe he wasn't allowed in them. Or, if he was, he must be careful where he stepped."

"Daniel, what are you talking about?"

"Gardens," he told her. "I remember some fine ones, too; but it was different with me. I belonged in one of them. So, I was not so fiercely determined—not fiercely enough, I reckon." His smile now was a wicked one for him. "You can't wear the rose, can you? On account of the dress? So you made a pretty speech about a glass of water. Women!"

"Such a fuss about a flower!" she said. "Men!"

But the exquisite shading of the rose was gone. She left the garden, puzzling over Daniel's comments on William Ashley. If they were well founded, the two men had at least one thing in common. Both had known, at different times in their lives, the deprivations of poverty, and each had won a hard-fought victory over circumstance; but Daniel Wilcox, it would seem, was now measuring his new prosperity and prestige against Ashley's flamboyant wealth, and finding his attainments, by contrast, very small. It was a mood, of course; and it would pass. Meantime, it was likely to ruin a happy hour.

In the house—the tall, incredible house—with its polished dark stairs, with its gold-framed mirrors everywhere one turned, and its paintings and elaborate chandeliers and its curio cabinets and what-not, as she laid aside her shawl on a canopied bed in an upstairs room, she did ask for a glass of water for the rose, then smoothed her hair and, with high color on her cheeks went down the long stairs, determined, if Daniel's captious mood should turn off into something like cold dignity, to offset it by being her most charming.

Since over half the guests at dinner were men, she had a fair field to play in; and, she fancied, she did rather well. She could tell by a gleam in the eyes of the Farrars, by the somewhat blanker contemplation of Mrs. Ashley—afterward it was difficult to remember a dozen words that lady spoke during dinner—and by the more startled appreciation of the only other woman present, also a stranger to the scene, a bride of a year, on a visit to St. Louis with her husband, Mr. Hugh Campbell of Philadelphia.

Mrs. Campbell, a chestnut blonde, good-looking without being beautiful, a wholesome, amiable young thing, reminded Elizabeth strongly of the Barcie Harris of her girlhood, though, of course, she was more handsomely got up than poor Barcie had ever been. Poor Barcie—why did she think of Barcie now in that way? Why did she think of her at all in this glittering house?

Mr. Hugh Campbell, a man of wealth also, had made the long journey to St. Louis serve several purposes besides that of showing his bride and himself the country. He had wanted to look over various business projects of his own, but more particularly those of a younger brother, a Mr. Robert Campbell, who was also present at the Ashley mansion that day.

The younger Mr. Campbell was one of those "enterprising young men" who had taken employment under Mr. Ashley in his Rocky Mountain ventures. Together with a Mr. Sublette, also present, he had recently returned from a most successful season in the Far West; and there was business afoot about that, though, naturally, it was not taken up in detail at the table, before the ladies. More outspoken were felicitations on Mr. Robert Campbell's apparent, vigorous health. It seemed that he had been all but dead of consumption when he had first embarked on his western adventures.

He was a dark-featured young man, a Scotsman from the north of Ireland, about her own age, Elizabeth guessed, and grave as an officiating clergyman in manner—as one might expect a man to be who had once so nearly died. In lighter turns of the conversation he came under considerable fire for being what his brother Hugh called a settled bachelor. The latter, richly pleased himself just now with marriage, said he would feel more secure in his mind about Robert off here in St. Louis if Robert had a wife to watch over him. If he would go back now with the Hugh Campbells to Philadelphia, both of them would busy themselves to find him a proper mate.

"Speak a word for me, William," Mr. Robert begged his friend Sublette.

With the others, Elizabeth waited for Mr. Sublette's answer. Here, she thought, was the most diverting person of the party, and guessed him wrong at every turn. A backwoodsman? No, that was just a roughness showing through his plain but conventional city attire— frock coat, tight trousers, waistcoat and white shirt complete with stock collar and cravat. A Frenchman? No, just of French extraction. He had been born in Kentucky, he told Elizabeth, but revealed no more. A partner of Mr. Ashley? No, merely a hired hand, he insisted. Really, he and Robert Campbell were now in business independently. A rough man, but not uncouth, tough as rawhide, except that no human flesh can ever be that tough. He was so charmed with Elizabeth's attention that he minded none of her questions; and Ashley, laughing, had him placed next to her at the table, warning her that the man was as shy of women as some dogs were of guns.

"I don't believe that," Libby said.

"And it isn't so," Sublette told her. "I've just not had the time to cultivate my better instincts."

And now . . .

"It's this way, Mr. Campbell," he said to the Philadelphian. "Robert and I have an agreement. We will neither one take on the liability of a wife unless we should happen to attract a lady with fifty thousand dollars' cash on the side, to put into the business. If you've a mind to institute a matrimonial search, those are the specifications."

"Mr. Sublette," Aunt Farrar said, "you shock me beyond expression."

"I am sorry, ma'am. It's the lowest possible figure for Robert and me at present. The little we have we have gained in a hard and bloody fashion, and we've no mind to dissipate it by one rash promise."

"But," Mr. Hugh Campbell protested, "I am to find two brides so endowed, in order to redeem either of you? Beautiful, too, I suppose?"

"That's not so important," Mr. Sublette said. "The money's the thing. And, if you can scratch up only one wife, we can arrange that peaceably. Robert can have the lady and I'll take the money."

Friends, Libby thought, with sudden understanding. Deep, true, everlasting friends—like Daniel and Ambrose Bohannon. Did Daniel ever think of Bo regretfully?

Rich men, too, for all their pretense of impoverishment. They tossed a sum like fifty thousand dollars into the air as lightly as she might a ball of yarn. Could you tell by looking at a man that he had the Midas touch? There was one more at the table that day—a Mr. Sweringen. She could not define his business, but everyone deferred to his opinion on almost any matter. He was a rich man by the fineness of his broadcloth and his linen. He had a noble face, broad of brow, open, but with a rock-hard jawline. The Campbells had long jaws, set squarely. Mr. Sublette's jaw was not of the same solidity but he had bright, acquisitive eyes, like a squirrel's. He might have done better with a hard jaw as, take, for instance, Mr. Ashley, who had both the shrewd, bright eyes and the jaw. Mr. Ashley . . .

And now the talk, by design or accident, was of Boonslick. Mr. Sublette had looked humorously down his nose at a biscuit in a pool of gravy on his fine French plate; and Ashley, laughing, had ordered the servant, James, who waited on the table, to fetch a loaf of bread and cut Mr. Sublette a slice such as he could recognize for what it was.

"Do you dole out bread in such small measure where you live, ma'am?" the backwoodsman asked Elizabeth.

"They do not," Ashley answered for her. "The biggest slab of wheat bread I ever saw lined with good meat, I had hot from a barbecue spit on the Moss farm in Boone County."

"And all this time," Elizabeth said, "I thought it was me you remembered. Now it seems it was our roast pig. Mr. Sublette, you would not go hungry in Boonslick. We live simply, I think, but abundantly."

"Boonslick," young Mrs. Campbell said. "It has such a sound! Is it a town or a county or what?"

"It is a place," Ashley again answered. "A commonwealth within the commonwealth of Missouri, a kingdom, sufficient unto itself."

"It is a place, a region," Elizabeth said, "but my husband can tell you of it better than I. I should talk of quilting bees and picnics and a woman's gossip, generally; because I have lived close to our own fireside. Dr. Wilcox has been to all the far corners in one way or another."

She must get Daniel to talking. It was not like him to sit so quiet in such a provocative assemblage. The tightness with which he held himself began to hurt her. He must break the silence even if he said something unfortunate; but she had no idea that he would do that. Daniel cleared his throat.

"As my wife says, Boonslick is a region." He spoke thoughtfully, as if calling up the picture himself, rather than trying to show it to others. "It takes its name from a path old Daniel Boone and his sons beat through on their way to a salt spring, which lies now in Howard County on the north or left bank of the Missouri. It is a region many miles long, on both banks of the river. An old survey defines it as all that land lying west of Cedar Creek—a little stream not far below where we live now—and west and north of the Osage River, which flows into the Missouri from the south, to the territorial line. Perhaps General Ashley can say whether new lines have since been drawn. General Ashley," Daniel said to the table generally, "surveyed much of the land before it was opened for settlement following the War of 1812. And bought several pieces that took his fancy. Did you not, sir? I had heard something of this before, and was reminded of it again this morning."

The question was a sudden stab. Elizabeth felt the prick of it. When Daniel had first begun to speak of Boonslick, she had thrilled with tender pride in him, but now it seemed he had taken up her challenge with a purpose of his own. She looked at Ashley, and thought his eyes had narrowed, as if he had been put on his guard.

"Your purchases were all in Cooper County, I believe," Daniel said.

"Yes," Ashley said, almost angrily. He was not accustomed to being challenged, certainly not at his own table. "I have always thought that the town of Boonville, on the Missouri, but high, out of the way of floods, had the best prospects for development."

"Ah!" Daniel turned back to the others. "Now I must do some more explaining. The region known as Boonslick is large enough to be made into a half-dozen counties; and when it was thrown open to settlement, it was expected that this would come in a hurry, because all western migration must pass through the region. Unfortunately for us, that is what it did—pass through. Too little of it stopped and stayed. The development of the section has been steady, but not phenomenal. When I settled there ten years ago, three counties had been mapped out. There are still only the three. As you go west from St. Louis, the first is Boone County, on the north bank of the Missouri. My wife's people took up land there and we have our home in the principal town, Columbia, which is thirty miles away from the river, on Boone's old trace, now the mail stage route westward. On beyond, on the same side of the river, is Howard County. Its chief town was Franklin. I say was Franklin, because successive floods ate away that bank and four years ago swallowed the whole settlement. It probably will rebuild; but for the present we have most of its business, even its newspaper, and most of its people. Directly opposite, on the south bank of the river, high, as General Ashley says, is the town of Boonville, the county seat of Cooper County, named for the first settlers in the region to follow the Boones. General Ashley, how do you account for the fact that this county, with so much in its favor, should also seem a little stagnant in its growth?"

Again that sudden sharpness of question. Oh, Daniel, Daniel! Not here! Not now!

Ashley thought a minute before answering.

"Probably a matter of people," he said. "The leading citizens of Boonslick, who have given character to its development, are people who like comfortable living. Comfort is not always characteristic of growth. . . ."

"I beg to disagree with you," Daniel said, his color rising. "I think Cooper County has not developed because the best part of it—a vast acreage—has not been open to settlement."

Now a person could see the bones of Ashley's jaw harden.

"You refer to the Chouteau Tract?"

"I do, sir."

Elizabeth remembered now. She had sat on the broad back of a horse behind Daniel, clinging to him, and Daniel, who should have been talking about that, was going on about this grant of land the Osage Indians had made to Mr. Chouteau of St. Louis out of gratitude for his protection of their rights. She had been vexed then; she shivered with apprehension now, her consciousness curling up and away like one's toes trying not to touch the floor on a winter morning.

"The title has been a matter of dispute ever since the American occupation," Daniel was saying, "perhaps because the Land Commission felt that Mr. Chouteau, having taken considerable wealth in furs out of the country, had enjoyed his fair share of the profits of ownership. It amounts to between thirty and forty thousand acres of the best land in Cooper County, with noble highlands, including one plateau set with Indian burial mounds. Was it those that took your eye first, General Ashley?"

He did not wait to be answered.

"Also a rich and fertile valley, with its own small river—La Mine—and springs, some of which, being saline, are thought to have medicinal value."

Horrid-tasting, evil-smelling; and Daniel and Bo were going to have a spa and become rich. All that stood in their way was the lack of money to put down for the land and the fact that the title had not been cleared.

"Dr. Wilcox is especially interested in those springs," Uncle Farrar said now. "How did you come out in your interview with Mr. Chouteau this morning, Doctor? Did he receive you kindly? Yes, I know he did; but did he give you any encouragement about that disputed title?"

"I think," Daniel said, with fearsome quiet, "the dispute will be settled soon, and, of course, in Mr. Chouteau's favor. It would probably never be settled otherwise; but it is of no consequence to me now. Mr. Chouteau has, and has had for some time past, a purchaser for the entire tract. Naturally, in view of that, he is not interested in selling a small corner."

"But how is that possible? And who? Did he say?"

"No, and I didn't ask him. Why should I? A man with means and foresight to buy thirty thousand acres of land has his own plans for developing his purchase."

Mrs. Ashley, at a signal of some sort from her husband, took the ladies away to the front parlor—an exquisite white and green and gold parlor, with a pianoforte. Because light talk had been made impossible, Mrs. Campbell played on the piano. Every note was like somebody shaking a rattle in Elizabeth's ears to torment a headache that was already torture. She was in the parlor with the ladies only a short while, but it seemed eternity. It was another eternity before she was alone with Daniel, still quiet, dangerously contained, bitter through and through with disappointment, in their hotel room.

"Daniel?"

"Libby, I hope I did not behave too boorishly. I . . ."

Not boorishly. Never that. A little accusatory, stiff . . .

"That horrid land," she said. "Are you sure Mr. Ashley even wants it?"

"He has it. Yes, I am quite sure. It was for you and the girls I wanted it, Libby, not for myself."

She repressed a shudder.

"Daniel, why did we go to his house today? We needn't have done that."

"I wanted you to see . . . I wanted to take a good look myself at a man who wants everything and always gets what he wants."

A man so bitter, feeling himself defrauded, must vent his animosity on someone.

"Daniel, don't hold away from me now. Sweetheart, please!"

Then, with his arms around her, feeling his hurt still: "Daniel, I'm frightened."

"My sweet Libby! Your holiday spoiled."

If it were only the holiday!

CHAPTER SIX

The City of Jefferson

IT WAS GOOD to settle down at home after that. She would never willingly leave Boone County again, Elizabeth thought. Winter sharp in the air outside now, ice on the streams and the rutted roads, but her father's house as snug and warm and safe as ever. Pray God that she might always have this place of refuge.

Elizabeth was enjoying an hour alone with her father. She had many things to go over with him. Today it was a bill for a beaver hat, too long unpaid.

"Betsy," her father said, "Daniel would not have wanted you to do this."

"I didn't ask him, dear. I ordered the hat without his knowing it. Then it seemed important that the order should be filled, regardless of everything. He looked wonderful when he rode off in November, don't you think? He was pleased."

Daniel away at the state capital alone, after all. The town was a barnyard still, folks said who had been there. Pigs running loose in the streets. No place for a man to put up a wife. The one hotel not adequate for the visiting legislators. Every house, fit or unfit, was crowded.

"Darling, I'll wait until you are Governor," Elizabeth had told him.

And Daniel had turned the hat in his hands, examining its splendor.

"I'll have to be Governor now," he said. "Nothing less will do."

And then he had said— But now this hat business.

"After what happened at the Ashley house," Elizabeth said, "I wouldn't have it made of the Ashley pelts. I wouldn't deceive Daniel about that."

"I should hope not," her father said. "Not Daniel."

"Well, I had trouble with the hatter. He didn't want to surrender the skins and let me choose others. I had an awful time making him see my side without explaining everything. I suppose that added to the cost."

82

"Probably," Dr. Moss agreed. "Have you heard from Ashley since you returned the pelts to him?"

"I didn't expect to hear. What was there to say?"

"Nothing, I reckon. Nevertheless— Well, here's this bill. Hm! Since the pelts meant nothing to Ashley and you say they mean nothing to you, you might have tried selling them. You might have made the price of the hat."

Elizabeth gasped. Such a thought had not entered her head. Could she? Her father looked at her sharply, then rubbed his thinning hair helplessly. One of these days, she thought, he would be clear bald.

"Have you any money at all, Betsy?" he asked now.

"Hardly any," she answered. "Daniel left a little but I was to use it to settle our store accounts if he was kept away. Lucky he did that, isn't it?"

"Yes," her father said, "and don't you touch it for any other purpose. We must keep Daniel's record clean in his absence. Well, I'll settle with the hatter, Betsy. In the future, however— Sweetheart, I know you've had small experience in handling money, but now you may have to learn. As Daniel's fortunes improve—"

"Oh!" Elizabeth said. "You do think they will improve? You don't think just because he lost those springs . . . I still don't see what possessed him!"

"Only," Dr. Moss said, "what possesses every man who wants to lay the sun and the moon at the feet of the woman he loves. He'll get over this special madness. We all have to make our compromises with reality."

"I wish I could be as sure as you are that he will get over his disappointment," Elizabeth said. "Daniel believes in destiny. In St. Louis last September there was a Mr. Hugh Campbell of Philadelphia. He, too, had been educated to be a doctor; but just as he was about to begin practising medicine, he became involved in a business deal and did so well at it that he never went back to the field he thought he had chosen. Daniel would say that was the difference between him and Mr. Campbell. Before he left for Jefferson City, somebody prophesied a fine career for him in politics. Daniel just smiled—you know how—and said, 'All depends on whether in a time of crisis a sick call doesn't distract me.' "

"Daniel's a good doctor," her father said, "and a fine man. My dear, I never knew you to be so oppressed with fears and anxieties."

"It's having him away so long," Elizabeth said, "and not hearing."

"You will hear," Dr. Moss promised. "The river's been running so full of ice that a mail boat couldn't get through. It's frozen over now,

83

and you can be sure that the first man who crosses will carry mail for this side. Meantime, stay with us—at least for tonight. You and the babies. We love having you."

"No." Libby rose and began to gather her wraps. "I must go home. I must . . . chiefly because I don't want to. I never knew a house could be so empty, but I must not yield to that. There is nothing to be afraid of. Daniel is all right. He promised me he would take care of himself. And I'm all right, with Poke and Susanna."

"Who?" Dr. Moss said.

"I call Susan that now. She is such a child of nature. I thought if I gave her a fancy name she might try to live up to it."

Before Dr. Moss could comment, someone knocked on the house door. Elizabeth jumped visibly.

"Child!" her father said. "Do you always do that? There's probably no connection with you or Daniel."

"No!" Libby closed her eyes, sighed. For a week now she had had the strangest feeling; but she would not yield to that, either. She would think brighter thoughts. She . . . warm color suddenly overspread her face. "Once," she said wistfully, "someone knocked on the door like that, and it was Daniel."

On a cold, gray afternoon in mid-January in the City of Jefferson, Daniel Wilcox sat on his upended trunk in the privacy of a narrow bedroom on the upper floor of the Rising Sun Hotel with a writing case on his lap and began a letter home to Elizabeth. Open and facing him, was one from her, written in her fine, crowded script, expressing her disappointment that he had not found it possible to return home for Christmas. It was most inconsiderate of the legislature to continue in session over the holiday season and equally unreasonable of the river to be so packed with ice that a ferry couldn't operate. Would he stay forever if it didn't freeze tight or thaw? And what kept him so busy as a doctor? Was there sickness in the capital? How was he feeling?

"My own Lib," he wrote, and stuck. All he had said in his previous letter was that he had had the marvelous experience of finding his services in great demand. The town was full of people, and, so far, there were only two doctors besides himself to attend to their ailments —a Dr. Lane of St. Louis and a Dr. Linn of Ste. Genevieve. Ah, the precious ability of a woman to compress the affairs of the world into her own small sphere! Of course he was well. He had never felt better. How to reassure her?

He looked about the room for inspiration, finding little. It was a narrow room, crowded under the eaves, its one virtue the fact that through this long session he had maintained sole occupancy. The furniture was a crude bedstead and a combination washstand and chest. No chairs. No room for any. Hence the upended trunk. No fireplace. For that reason, and because presently he was going out to his supper, he wore his greatcoat and his fine hat. If his hands stiffened for writing, he would light a candle to warm them. He would have been warmer in the common room downstairs—drugged with warmth and other suffocating emanations. He would not take Libby even in thought into that assemblage.

A cheerless room in a cheerless town. It seemed to be his lot to know towns in their raw beginnings. Some day the City of Jefferson might be a proud capital. Some day a domed state house and a governor's mansion, in place of the brick barn which at present served both purposes, might crown the bluff overhanging the river—lifting marble and fretwork and statuary high above the effluvium of the waterfront; but the town now was still Lohman's Landing. The long brick state house, this hotel, two halfway-respectable taverns, a scattering of houses, mostly boarding houses, clung desperately to High Street and adjacent ridges, from which gullies in place of avenues ran down to what recently had been wild ravines but were now the abode of human squalor. Here the underlings and the hangers-on of government in session, people without aspirations or much hope, lived, both from need and from choice. "It's col' up yondah on de hilltop!"

Daniel had never dwelt much on this aspect of the town in his letters to Libby, and he would not now. Wagon teams were able at last to cross the river ice. In this iron cold that condition would hold and even improve. Surely in a week or two the last small business of the legislature must be finished. He would be home in Columbia long before the ice gave, to tell her all about everything. He could tell her everything then because, come next November and his second session, he would live more comfortably. He had already engaged a room at Major Ramsay's. The Major was a Kentuckian and kept a good house. Unfortunately, for this session it had been filled to capacity, but the Major was building an addition over summer and had promised to save Daniel a room. Daniel already took his meals there—along with seventy or eighty other legislators. When he had finished his letter, he'd have a nip of brandy—against the cold—and set out for that pleasanter haven.

As for the sickness, it was nothing but the usual round of grippe and winter fevers. Nothing like a virulent epidemic so far, thank

God—a possibility he and the other doctors had discussed gravely.

His thoughts neatly marshaled now, Daniel again dipped his pen, and dropped it. Seized, without warning, by a convulsive fit of shivering, he had just time to push the writing case over on the bed, to keep it from clattering to the floor.

In a minute the shivering eased off; and he stood up, rubbing his arms, slapping at them to quicken the flow of blood, stamping his feet. He stumbled to the dresser and found his brandy flask. A nip now was what he needed. The cold had penetrated his bones more deeply than he had realized. This room was all right for sleeping. Under blankets and a buffalo robe its frigidity had seemed a sort of antidote for other things; but it was no place for sitting.

The brandy warmed him. It even caused a light perspiration to dampen his forehead; but when he looked into the dim mirror over the dresser, he was appalled by his pallor and a distress in his eyes. Now, now! he thought, then turned to answer a knock at his door.

A Negro boy with a tattered woolen cap in his hand waited there. He was breathless, as if he had been running. His words tripped one another.

"Mist' Doctah, Aun' Susie . . . de man she got in her house . . . dat man f'om Lexin'ton . . . he wuss. He outen he haid. She . . . nobuddy cain' ha'dly hole him. You said . . ."

"Ts!" Daniel said now; and to himself he added, "Why did you come for me? Why not Dr. Lane? I'm sick, too. I would like to go to bed . . . get real warm. . . ."

All the time, with automatic motions he was tying a wool scarf around his neck and closing his medicine bag. The last thing he put into it was the brandy flask. The last thing he saw in the room was his letter home: "My own Lib . . ."

"Get along," he said to the boy. "I'm coming. Get going . . . fast."

Outside, the bitter cold took him in his chest and his stomach. He gritted his teeth and pushed forward. No good pulling back. No good shriveling. In cold as bitter as this, a man had better thrust out his chest and take it. And keep moving. Keep moving right along. Down the steep gully called a street to the colored section below. A quiet town tonight, the cold sealing doors and windows. That might be a good thing, if what he feared proved to be so.

That it was so he knew the minute the Negress known generally as Susie or Aunt Susie opened the door of her cabin. He did not need to go near the cot or the man on it picking at his ragged coverlet.

"He quieted some now, Mist' Doctah," Susie said, wiping her face on her apron. "Look lak he fixin' to break out wid somethin'. Soon ez dat comes . . ."

"Yes," Daniel said, fighting down nausea. "Yes. Shut the door, Rufe."

"Mist' Doctah, is it bad?"

"Afraid it is, Aunt Susie."

"Ketchin'?"

"Yes. Rufe, I said, shut the door. Bar it. Don't let anybody in, and don't let yourself out. No use in running now. It's too late. If you're going to be sick, you will be—wherever you are. You stay right here!"

"Mist' Doctah," Susie said, "man's jes' my sist'-in-law's cousin's boy."

Human driftwood, steeped in poison.

"It doesn't matter now, Susie. You've been nursing him and you might as well go on. You will, I am sure. Have you still some of that fever medicine I gave you? Good. If he wakes up, give him a dose. Otherwise let him alone. Keep yourself warm. Get your sleep. Rufe, see that your aunt has wood and water when she needs it. I'm going to get word to Dr. Lane now— No, not you, Rufe. I'll go. I'll be back soon, with something that may keep you from getting the sickness; but, if I don't find you here, I'll not do a thing for you, mind."

He had never felt more brutal in imposing his white man's will, except that he had no idea he would find the boy when he returned to the cabin. The woman might stay, but not the terrified boy.

"God," he prayed, stepping out into the night, "get me up the hill fast!"

It was a long climb. Twice he thought his strength would not be equal to the demand he made on it. Once he was on the point of abandoning the effort. He sagged with a great weight of weariness. He thought, "I can't move a leg. I can't!" But lights pricked the darkness up on the ridge now. One of them would be Major Ramsay's house. Warm, with friends. He must go on, must deliver his warning. The wind whipped his coat about him. He stumbled forward.

He made it. High Street at last! High Street . . . did every town on that black river have a High Street? He reeled, then steadied again.

The solid bulk of Major Ramsay's house rose up ahead of him, light in every window. A servant opened the door.

"Is Dr. Lane in?" Daniel asked. "Ask him, please, to step to the door."

Dr. Lane was right behind the servant.

87

"Wilcox? That you? Come in, man, come in."

"No. Can't come in. Listen! Down by the river, that woman called Susie—Aunt Susie, the laundress. Man sick in her house. Smallpox. What we talked about. Must quarantine . . . vaccinate . . . wish I could help . . . taken a chill somewhere. I—" He took one step toward the light and fell.

He had, of course, no sense of the time he spent in delirium. When he awoke, it was only to half-consciousness at first. A bed under him. Nice and flat and strong. Home? No, not soft enough. The hotel? No. Room too warm. It didn't matter. Safe in bed somewhere.

Somebody was caring for him. He heard voices presently. Not clearly. It was another space of time between sleep and waking before the words took shape.

"Young," somebody said. And another, "Ummm. Too bad. So much promise. Family? Ummm. Wife and two children. He talked about them constantly."

He struggled hard for wakefulness, but again he drowsed. Then suddenly his eyes were open—open on the plastered logs of a cabin. On the wall beyond the foot of his bed a set of deer antlers made a clothes rack. On a high horn perched a fine gentleman's hat—his hat. Below it a caped coat hung limply to the wall. Something about that hat, that bodiless coat. His eyes moved on. Not easily. They were hot and dry. Sick eyes. They came to a washstand, with a basin, a black bottle, a spoon, then, oddly, a writing case. Something about that writing case . . .

Later a man stood by his bed.

"Water," Daniel said from a parched throat. Horrible, croaking sound.

The man gave him water from a spoon. It must have evaporated in his mouth, because its coolness never reached the true burning.

"More," he said, and then out of a great wishing, "Bo?"

No, it wasn't Bo. He saw his mistake almost at once. Some other man but he couldn't say the name. A doctor, too, but not Bo.

"Shouldn't be here!" he croaked.

"I'm all right," the Doctor said. "Been vaccinated twice. Thought I told you. Two terms in the army, you know. And somebody had to care for you sick folks."

"Many of us?" Why couldn't he sound human?

"Not too many. Town's deserted, you see. Almost everybody who was able packed up and ran."

Almost everybody, but not a doctor. A good doctor like Bo or

88

this fellow. He groped again through a confusion of memories and shrank before a knife thrust of perception.

"Libby?"

"I've written to her. I waited until I was sure she would hear otherwise and perhaps act too rashly. I addressed a note to her and one to your father-in-law, I urged him, for her sake, not to come, not to let her come. I hope I did right."

"Exactly right." If he could only speak the words as clearly as he thought them! "Mustn't come. Sick town. Sick man. I'm very sick, Doctor?"

"Yes. Dr. Linn and I did everything we knew. It was the exposure probably. A person can never be just sure. Sometimes the weakest pull through and the strongest go down."

Then he knew. This was all of everything. His eyes moved again to the hat on its high perch.

"Tell Libby, very sorry about hat. Never wear it as Governor."

"It doesn't matter, does it, really?"

"No. Tell her doesn't matter. Only life and love . . . springtime . . ."

He closed his eyes and didn't open them again, though he thought he did, because he saw her so clearly. The shadowed brilliance of her eyes, her bright, soft hair, the grace, the ineffable sweetness that was his Libby.

"God bless you, sweetheart. Bless . . . and keep you . . . always!"

Part Two

The Fascinating Mrs. Ashley

CHAPTER ONE

A Marriage Contract

"No," ELIZABETH SAID. "I'm sorry. I can't see anybody. Not yet. Please make my excuses." To herself she added. "Not him—of all people!"

Her father did not press the point. All he said was, "Sweetheart, it's going on two years now."

She did not need to be told how long it had been—two years or eternity. Two years since Daniel had ridden away on his bright bay thoroughbred, the new hat high and proud on his head; and, if she had known she was never to see him again, she would have clung to the horse's tail, until, to save her from being kicked or dragged, Daniel must have turned and drawn her up behind him. They would have ridden off together then, to glory or death, as once they had ridden, laughing, excited, venturesome, when life had been at its glad beginning.

Together . . . oh, Daniel, my darling, my love, is there no end to sorrow? Sometimes she thought she must die of her loneliness.

She looked down at her black dress and saw that her father, too, was looking at it. How he hated the stuff! And, in her secret heart, so did she. When first she had seen widow's black laid out for her to wear, she had shrunk away. Then, in a kind of madness she had snatched the ugly garments to her and said she would wear black only, from that day on and forever. With her own hands she had put all her bright things away. Whose eyes would shine now to see her wearing them? Whose? To get up on the fairest morning into black, to wear it all day, to go to bed at night under the blackness of the lonely dark—this it was to be widowed.

Forever, she had said, and meant it; but life and youth were against her. The sun continued to shine, the seasons to change; and lately rebellion had stirred in her. Did her father know? This morning, on rising, she had turned from her black dress and dug, instead, an old frock of linsey from a locked chest. The linsey had sharp, painful associations; but that was true of anything else she might have chosen. She had put on the dress and stolen a frightened look at herself in the mirror of her old room and . . . shuddered, but looked again.

Shadows under her eyes, skinny, pale . . . an impulse toward flight added itself to rebellion. She did not reason with the impulse. Adding stout shoes and a shawl to her plain dress, she managed to slip down the stairs unseen and out of the house.

She walked—part of the time she ran—for miles. It was folly, she knew. She could escape neither her grief nor herself that way—the abject wraith that had once been the gay, light-hearted Elizabeth Moss and later the gentler, even happier Elizabeth Wilcox. She had no idea of how far she had gone until the chatter of water over stones told her she had reached Bonhomme Creek—the farthest limit of her father's land. A slab of rock put itself in the way of her stumbling feet and she sank down upon it, exhausted.

For a while she had respite. She threw the shawl from her head, then from her shoulders, and let the warmth of the September sun soak through her. "This feels good," she thought, and even drowsed a little, then roused sharply to a familiar acrid smell. Sour mash— she named it on the instant; and there went peace. She had come out of the woods at a turn of the creek just below her father's distillery; and there was no thinking of that without recalling that crowded day when Ambrose Bohannon had first suggested that Dr. Moss build one. Later, matching Scottish lore with Kentucky tradition, Bo and the Doctor had rigged the still, Daniel standing by, hilariously amused but finally the most intensely practical engineer of the three. Daniel . . .

She stood up, wild-eyed, clutching her shawl, poised again for flight. Then she dropped her arms and let the shawl trail. There was no escape for her here. Everywhere she turned a memory mocked her. She must get clear away, to some new place, where memory had nothing to feed on and so finally must die. But where? And how? She had two babies. Poor lost mites! Daniel had left a little property. She was afraid to think how little, in terms of dollars. Nevertheless, she must go away. She must consider how.

She turned and started back toward the house. She went more slowly now and the miles stretched out full length. At the end she dragged herself, looking, she had no doubt, like some disheveled Ophelia, up the stairs to her room and flung herself, dusty and bramble-tattered, across her bed and burst, without warning even to herself, into a tempest of tears.

"Let her alone," Miss Mary said, her sharp, lady tones rising above general commotion. "Let her cry. She has done too little of it. Let her cry her heart out. Mary, come away."

Whether the Mary in question was Mary Moss or her own little one, Elizabeth did not know. She cried as if there were no end to weeping; and, whether she dredged her heart or not in that fashion, she arrived at another sort of exhaustion. It was well past dinnertime when Pomegranate opened the door without knocking, and backed into the room, carrying a tray with a pitcher and a glass and a covered plate on it.

"Miss Libby, you 'wake? Dis yere's some fresh churned buttahmilk."

"I don't want—" Elizabeth began, from habit.

"How you know you don' wan' hit, till you take a swaller? Git up now an' wash yoreself wid col' watah whilst I shake out dis bed you done made a nes' of. Wait now. I'll pore de watah. Pitchah's heavy. Dar. Now you wash—good!"

There was a compulsion about Pomegranate. There was, even after she propped a window open, an earthy emanation, compounded of woodsmoke, kitchen condiments, clean calico, uninhibited human sweat, and general human kindliness. She was, moreover, Pomegranate—complete unto herself. She had the room to rights in short order; and by the time Libby was ready to put a comb and brush to her tangled hair, she had poured out a glassful of the nearly solid buttermilk.

"You drink hit," she ordered and there was no refusing. "Hit'll set good even ef yore stummick is addled. An' dis yere's fresh gingercake. Won' hurt a flea. Give de buttahmilk suthin' to wuk on. Eat now, lak I say. Ef you don' eat, Miss Libby, one o' dese mo'nin's you gonna ben' ovah to tie a slippah an' break in two. Else you gonna lay yorself up in bed an' cain't move."

Relentlessly she poured two glasses of the milk down Libby, augmented by two cuts of the warm spice cake. Miraculously the second helping of each tasted better than the first. Elizabeth ate with an approach to avidity. Then Pommie helped her with her hair and into the black dress of her widowhood.

"I gonna iron you a len'th o' white frill," Pommie said. "High time . . ."

"No, Pommie."

"Knew dat's what you'd say. Gonna iron a piece, anyhow." And finally the announcement which had brought Pommie upstairs in the first place: "We got comp'ny, Miss Libby. Gemmun— I'll tell yore pa yo're up now."

Even Pomegranate had lacked the courage to say who the gentleman was—Mr. William Henry Ashley of St. Louis—General Ashley, as many still called him. He was in Boonslick on business, political probably, because the year before he had been named to fill out the term of Missouri's one Representative in the lower House of Congress, a Mr. Spencer Pettis, well-known throughout the state, who had died in a duel on St. Louis's own field of honor—Bloody Island in the Mississippi. The sensational news had reached even Elizabeth in her retirement, also that in August of this year Mr. Ashley had been re-elected, to serve a full term. His business in Boonslick now might be canvassing in connection with the imminent presidential elections.

"... *take a good look ... at a man who wants everything* ..."

If her father had insisted on her seeing Ashley, Elizabeth would have abided by her first refusal, but Dr. Moss knew better than to do it that way. Coming upstairs right after Pommie's descent, he had made the simple announcement that Mr. Ashley had called and had asked for Elizabeth; then he had left Elizabeth's action to her, suggesting only that two years were enough for pining and that she couldn't go on forever, refusing to see people.

"Darling, I'm sorry—"

She stopped, remembering another bit of news about Ashley. He was again a widower. The dark, quiet lady of the glittering St. Louis mansion, her distant cousin, had died that spring of some sudden, unnamed illness. Now, if Mr. Ashley thought, if anyone thought ...

"Miss Mary sent you," she accused her father, her lips twitching, in spite of her repulsion, over her mother's willful persistence.

Dr. Moss was enchanted by this pale imitation of a smile. His own mouth drooped humorously.

"I did say I'd speak to you," he admitted. "But see here, Betsy, don't think for a minute that I—"

Then he stopped. He was thinking just what she was thinking: "This could be a way." She shuddered. No, not that. Nobody could ask that of her. She couldn't ever— But it might be the only way. What then? Controlling herself again, she went over and cuddled her head against her father's shoulder.

"Darling, I am sorry," she repeated. "I've been a miserable wretch. It's not right—to you or Miss Mary or anybody."

"Child," her father petted her helplessly, "anything you do is right with me always. I do want to see you get well. I want to see you happy again, but ..."

"There!" she said, and kissed him. "I'll try—for you. Go back now where you came from. Say I'll be along presently. Just ... give me a minute."

She spent the minute before the dim mirror. Helplessly her hands flew to her hair, bright still perhaps only in contrast to her pallor and the black stuff of her dress. It had been a long time since she had fussed with curls or puffs. Severely plain for her, but bright. It would have to do. She dabbed a square of chamois skin over her nose and chin and raised her head. That was better. Carry her head high and proud. . . .

Her dress made a whisper about her as she descended the steps and crossed into the great room, her head as high as she could hold it. Ashley heard her coming and stood to receive her, but it was a minute before he could speak. She could feel the force of the shock her appearance gave him.

"My dear girl!" He held out both his hands in a gesture of compassion.

She recoiled. He pitied her? But anyone might. With what dignity she could command she gave him her hand, then was astounded to find how his strong fingers and wrists buoyed her, strengthened her. She thought wildly, "I don't dislike Mr. Ashley. I never have, really. I don't like him especially, but certainly I don't dislike him. There are things about him. . . ."

"It was good of you to see me," he said. His voice filled her ears. His dark eyes held hers. She drew her hand away.

"It was good of you to come," she answered. "Out of your way, I know."

And where were the others, she wondered. Someone, it seemed, had called to consult her father; and Miss Mary was attending to a child.

"Miss Libby," Ashley said, "this is my first opportunity to say to you in person what has been heavy on my heart for a long time. I hope you do not hold me to blame for what has happened. Please believe that I have never wished for anything but your happiness and well-being. I would do anything, I would have done almost anything to remove the suspicion and animosity your husband held toward me. . . ."

Almost anything but relinquish his claim to that piece of land! Afterward Elizabeth could realize that not once did Ashley mention doing that. Not he. Now she was too stunned and too bruised still to reason sharply, and she never matched his keenness in such matters. Few people did.

"You had nothing to do with my husband's death," she said. Except that, when Daniel had left for Jefferson City, he was still depressed, still angry over a legal sleight of hand that had deprived him of his dream of a quick fortune.

"Mr. Ashley, I'm sorry," she said. "I hope you will understand. This is a thing I can't talk about to anyone. I just can't. It's wrong, perhaps. It's selfish. Everyone has sorrow. I have heard of your loss, too."

Ashley bowed, his eyes still searching; then Dr. Moss returned, and soon afterward Miss Mary with the elder of Elizabeth's children —six-year-old Mary Jane, a child so delicately proportioned that she still looked more like a fairy that one might have taken down from a sugarplum tree than a creature of earthly origin. Except for a bright overtone on her brown ringlets, she bore no resemblance to either of her parents. "All Randolph," Miss Mary pronounced her. "I was small like that, I am told." Elizabeth put out her hand to the child, who nestled against her, looking shyly at the stranger, but very soon went over to sit on a stool at her fond grandmamma's knee.

"It's this black dress," Elizabeth thought, "and I've not paid much attention to my babies. They'll grow away from me entirely at this rate."

The conversation, with the return of the others, was on more general topics, both Dr. and Mrs. Moss leading Ashley on to talk of Washington and the representation of Missouri there, the popularity and the unpopularity of President Andrew Jackson, and the likelihood or the reverse of his being elected to a second term against the valiant strivings of Mr. Clay of Kentucky. From Washington the talk veered to the development of national roads, the opening of new lands for settlement, and arrived then at the scene of Ashley's greatest ventures—the Rocky Mountains. He spoke sadly of the death the year before of one of the brave young men who had first followed him out that way—a Mr. Jedediah Smith, murdered by Comanche Indians at the Cimarron Crossing on the Santa Fe Trail.

"He was with us," Ashley said in tribute, "when we opened the South Pass through the mountains. He was at the rendezvous in 1825 at the Great Salt Lake. A force of men in himself."

Intentionally or otherwise, the tribute called to mind the range of his own activities. Listening not so much to words as to implications, Elizabeth thought, "I have lived in a very small area. The world is wide outside."

The world was very wide. After Ashley had left, Elizabeth sat on before the fire, lost in thought, remembering. She remembered his first visit, his one other visit, to this house. For some reason she saw him more clearly now than she had then—a restless, burning-eyed man, driven by one or more great ambitions, but missing nothing of what went on around him even while he spoke of his dreams, aware of her, as she, deep in her consciousness, had been aware of him, as anyone in his presence must be aware of him.

And now he was a man of wealth, as she had seen, possessed of all or most of what he had dreamed of attaining. Still there was a restlessness of wanting upon him. What was it he wanted now? Could it be her? This time she did not put the thought away quite so abruptly. She did not welcome the suggestion. She did not even accept it. But she did not put it away.

Another day she was able to consider what her life might be if she married again; and she was astonished to find that, while marriage in general seemed abhorrent, marriage to William Ashley seemed not quite so impossible. Why? Was it because of what he could give her? As the wife of Daniel Wilcox, everything worldly or selfish in her had been submerged in love and devotion. She had been content with a narrow sphere of living, narrow horizons, because all were so radiantly bright. Now Daniel was gone. Irretrievably, hopelessly lost to her. And she lived on. She might live on many years. How would she live those years? For her parents' sake, her babies', for her own sake, she must think of that.

Ashley's business kept him in Boonslick for a week. On his second call at the Moss house he broke impatiently through the barriers of painful memories between him and Elizabeth and almost harshly told her what had brought him to the area. He wanted her to marry him. Would she do him the great honor of becoming his wife?

Something in Elizabeth still held back. She looked down at her hands, fast in the strong, nervous grasp of his.

"Mr. Ashley," she said, "I would not want to deceive you. I like you. I share the respect of others for you. Anything more than that seems to me impossible."

But his grasp of her hands only tightened.

"My dear, ghosts walk in both our houses, remember. Is that any reason why we should go lonely all our days? We can have a good life together. Let me show you."

She took refuge then behind another barrier. "I have not only myself to consider. I have two children."

"And I have none," he answered. "Do I need to say that, if you marry me, you and all who are dear to you shall live softly forever? I am counted a wealthy man. You shall have it all to enjoy."

It was an offer magnificent in its implications. Afterward, when Elizabeth could analyze it more deliberately, if not more calmly, she saw that it was just that—an offer meant to dazzle. No passionate declaration of love, no insistent demand for what she was not ready to give. Just the world in exchange if she would honor William Ashley by becoming his wife; and yet, Ashley's eyes glowed with a softer light than she had ever seen in them when she asked,

"Will it make you truly happy if I say yes?"

"Happier than you can know," he answered, "and you will be happy, too, I swear."

It was a simple bargain, to hear it said. It might not prove so simple in the fulfillment, but the chance seemed worth the taking. She asked still for delay, but knew finally what her answer would be. There seemed no reason in this world for Elizabeth Wilcox to go on being. Elizabeth Ashley might tell another story.

CHAPTER TWO

The Ashley Mansion

THE LESSON on the pianoforte went badly. Mr. Seidensticher, who guaranteed for a modest monthly fee to give anyone, with or without special ability, mastery of the instrument in a minimum of time, with a minimum of tedious practice, threatened to mark a visible footpath on the Brussels carpet. His hands, clasped behind his back, opened and closed, opened and closed. His breath suggested strangulation. How should he say it? How should he tell this charming, this exquisite lady, who made him even a little giddy if he sat on a chair close beside her, whose name could have attracted other pupils by the dozen if things had gone as he had been sure they would . . . how should he tell her that apparently she was the one person whom he could teach nothing? Nothing, whatever! She had no aptitude, no ear, she paid no attention— Why did she vex herself—and him— this way?

"Madame Ashley . . ."

Elizabeth smiled at him mistily. If he had not been such a funny little man, so anguished himself at her defeat by this mocking parade of ivory keys, which could make more unpleasant noises than she would have believed possible, she would have had her own frenzy. As it was—

"Dear Mr. Seidensticher," she said, "I am sorry. What ever do you suppose ails me?"

"Madame," he clawed his hair. No wonder it stood every which way! "Your mind is not on what you are doing."

"Oh, but it is," she insisted. "It is my fingers that are at fault."

She looked at her hands. Supple, white hands. Very idle these days.

"Madame, why do you wish to play the forte piano?"

She couldn't tell him. What would he make of an old fragment of talk:

But you haven't got a pianoforte. . . . I know, but I might have some day.

What did he mean by saying her mind was not on what she was

doing? Everything she undertook these days was designed to keep her mind busy.

"It's such a lovely accomplishment," she pleaded.

"Madame," Mr. Seidensticher said helplessly, "there is no need. For you God has accomplished all."

Elizabeth smiled at him sweetly. Mr. Ashley would be greatly amused, she was sure, at this new conquest; but—

"Why, Mr. Seidensticher," she said, ignoring Ashley's pleasure, "how charming of you to say so! I wish everyone were as kindly disposed."

Everyone decidedly was not so. The ladies of St. Louis had adopted an attitude of stiff resistance to the new Mrs. Ashley's charms. A few, impelled by curiosity or their husbands' insistence, the husbands being business associates of Mr. Ashley, had called. The Farrars had given a reception. The rector of Christ Church, where Mr. Ashley rented a pew at one hundred and fifty dollars a year, had brought his wife to pay their respects. The Ashleys had returned the calls and in turn had entertained; but Elizabeth had not lived twelve years in Boone County without learning to distinguish between true cordiality and such lackadaisical, if not frigid, welcome.

It helped a little, though not much, to understand the reason. Mr. Ashley's first wife had come from somewhere down the Mississippi and was fairly unknown in St. Louis. His second had been the daughter of a prominent family here. When she died, moreover, Mr. Ashley at once became the most desirable prospective matrimonial *parti* in town; but, before speculation as to his next choice could decently begin, with typical self-sufficiency he had gone outside again and married another stranger. To be sure, her connections were of the best. And she was beautiful. Even the disappointed ladies could not deny their senses. But it had all happened too suddenly. Eliza Christy hardly cold in her grave! It looked almost as if the man had been waiting for this opportunity.

It did, indeed. Elizabeth had her own thoughts on that score. And she did not mind the coolness of the St. Louis ladies so much, though the rebuff stung, because the town and this tall, glittering house, too, had other associations for her which were even more painful; but she thought, suppose the ladies in Washington did not take to her? That was the goal of her hopes now, St. Louis an interlude. She did want to be a success in Washington, for her own sake and Mr. Ashley's; but St. Louis had taught her that being new and young and beautiful was not enough. It could even work to one's disadvantage that at a party most of the men gathered about one and left other ladies unattended. She must know how to win ladies, too, and quickly, in case her opportunity was brief. She thought, if she could only cultivate an accomplishment which would make her good company among just ladies. Something new. Boonslick accomplishments would not do. Mrs. Ashley could not go into the kitchen and bake a cake or a feather-light meringue pie. Or sit in public sewing up her own frocks, no matter how clever she was with the needle.

But here was the pianoforte. Sometimes, for one reason or another, conversation among ladies fell off. Sometimes it was desirable that it should. Music then filled the void and . . . it was a pretty thing to do.

"Your advertisement made it sound so easy," she said wistfully, to the grotesque little teacher. "Like playing the guitar."

"You play the guitar, madame?" He did want to succeed with this pupil. There was the prestige, and the fee helped pay the rent on his Main Street studio. He could not afford a failure.

"Simple chords," Elizabeth said, "to sing by."

"As, for example, please?"

He took his place at the keyboard. Laughing, a little diffident, she sang a few bars of "Lady Margaret." Before she reached the end of a line, light notes on the piano had found the pitch of her low contralto, were steadying her rhythm and tempo and leading her on. She sang two more lines and stopped, enchanted with her own and the music teacher's performance.

"Mr. Seidensticher, that's wonderful. Do you know the song?"

"I have heard it, perhaps. No, I do not know it, as you say."

"But it seems so easy, really. Or, is it difficult?"

"No," he confessed, studying his hands now. "It is very simple—a musical trick."

"Could you show me?"

"I could perhaps, but—"

With sudden decision Elizabeth snatched the manual from the music rack, closed it and handed it to the teacher.

"But not out of this book," she said. "We must start all over."

"Madame!" With word and gesture Mr. Seidensticher protested that she must learn a few rudiments. The pianoforte was strange to her. She must know the value of the keys, something about fingering. Reluctantly she kept the manual.

"I will do a little, with each lesson," she conceded, "if we can spend the rest of the time on something interesting. Come, show me now what you did. There's a song my babies like: 'The Cat Fell into the Cream Jar.'"

After that, the lesson went better. Only because this willful, charming lady was pursuing her own course. She became at once docile and receptive. Where there had been no aptitude, now there were perception and response. She herself was radiant over her progress and the professor was at least bemused. A servant, appearing at the parlor door, was an interruption.

Elizabeth looked up and caught her breath, as she was likely to do these days whenever she saw Dr. Moss's boy, Poke. She had brought both Poke and Susan with her to St. Louis, the girl to care for the children and to train as a lady's maid; Poke— Well, the truth was that both servants represented her inability to sever all ties with the past. When the time had approached for her actual departure and they had begged to be taken to the new home, she could not refuse; and now she would have hated to confess how their presence steadied her in what had turned out to be more a testing of her own quality than of theirs. She had warned both servants that life in St. Louis would be different from anything they had ever known and they might not like it; but so far she had heard no murmur of homesickness from either. Pomegranate's daughter, in starched apron and cap, was now Susanna for keeps. With her mother's training in the domestic arts and her pride in her relationship to Elizabeth to fortify her, she took no impudence from anybody and yielded precedence to none.

As for Poke, it had seemed at first that there would be no place for him in the new home. Mr. Ashley had a servant, a sort of major-domo, named James, who seemed to fill to capacity every niche that would have fitted Dr. Moss's boy.

"Miss Libby, I ain' fixin' to take anybody's wo'k f'om him," the young Negro said. "I'll fin' plenty to do—jes' holpin' out. You'll see."

And he had been right. He now "holped out" in particular Mr. Ashley, whom he called "de Gin'ral," and studied the ways and duties of James, the major-domo. Both busy and happy, he had informed Elizabeth that, if she had in mind any more new clothes for him, she had best get them a size larger. He was busting off the buttons of those he had—from lazy good living. However, in spite of this well-being, in spite of his new house servant's livery—striped coat and waistcoat and bright blue breeches—he was still and forever Poke. There was nothing anybody could do about that. He did not put on airs like Susanna and would submit to no suggestion about changing his name. The suggestions in themselves were feeble. The name could be spelled out differently, when written; but, spoken, it was irretrievably and fittingly Poke. Right now—

"Time to go, Miss Libby," he said.

She could have been wrong in keeping this one.

"Is the carriage ready so soon?" she asked, reminding him of what he should have said.

"Ready an' waitin', Miss Libby. Hosses stompin' . . . and hit ain't soon. Hit's late. Kin I fotch yore bonnet an' cloak?"

"No. No, thank you, Poke. You can serve Mr. Seidensticher some wine. Oh, indeed yes, Mr. Seidensticher. This has been a hard half-hour, I am sure. And you can take the time because I shall be driving you back to town. Nonsense! I am going, anyhow. I do every afternoon that's fine, to pick up my little girl at school and then Mr. Ashley. Will it be sherry or port?"

"Miss Libby—" Poke said.

"Poke, the wine from the sideboard, please."

Ten minutes later, with the more than ever bemused music teacher beside her in the open barouche, she was bouncing over the rutted, dusty thoroughfare known as Broadway toward town. Poke perched up front beside James. Supposedly he was learning the map of the city, the way the streets followed or crossed one another. When he had accomplished this, he was to be Elizabeth's coachman, giving her more use of the carriage because James then would not be taken from his duties at the house. Had the preceding Mrs. Ashley been a recluse? It was possible that she had not been as light-footed or as socially minded as Elizabeth; but Elizabeth would never know, because she would not bother to find out. Eliza Christy was not the ghost that walked in Mr. Ashley's memory.

"When you come to Locust Street," she said to James, "turn down there, if you will. I can't remember that I've ever been that way."

There was a house at Second and Locust that she wanted to see. James touched his hat to indicate that he had heard her and would drive as directed; and Elizabeth, for want of a better target, smiled her satisfaction at Mr. Seidensticher. In her dress of rich *gros de Naples* silk, wine-red striped with silver, so modish of design that the accompanying dolman wrap, of the same shade of red, but plain in color and edged with fur, had had to be fitted carefully to accommodate the high, full sleeves, and against the sleek black and silver of the open carriage, she knew she made a picture that even the moth-eaten music teacher could not mar. Plainly he thought so, too.

"Madame," he said—his first spoken word since they had left the Ashley mansion—as the carriage turned into Locust and drew up to the curb, "with your permission, I shall alight here."

Elizabeth's bow and words of dismissal were almost as absent as his request. She forgot him completely before he disappeared, her whole attention being occupied by a narrow stone house behind a prim iron fence on the same corner. So, this was the place! With nobody now to impress, color drained out of her. She felt herself as she was—pale, thin, wistful—under the bright dress, the broad-brimmed velvet hat. The fine feathers were not all vanity. Her behavior over music lessons was not pure willfulness. She had hoped to borrow color for her paleness from her dress, and by a pretense of lightsomeness to learn again the way of gaiety. Such an emptiness persisted still!

"Dis yere's Ashley proputty, ma'am," James said respectfully, knowing what she wanted to see. "We lived yere," he selected his words with care, "befo' we built de big house on de moun'. We rents dis place now."

Elizabeth knew. She had heard Mr. Ashley mention a lease to that square-jawed gentleman whose financial advice he so respected—Mr. Sweringen. So this was the place—the house where Ashley's ghost walked. The first Ashley mansion in St. Louis. Here the comparatively unknown colonel, then brigadier general, of militia, then Lieutenant Governor of Missouri, had lived with his first wife—the comparative unknown Mary Able, of Cape Girardeau. Her obscurity was due only to the fact that she came from downstate. Her people were of substance there, Elizabeth had learned. Mr. Ashley still maintained cordial relations with certain steamboat captains of the same name—Able. More than that Elizabeth could not know, because who could persuade Mr. Ashley to talk of a past love if he were not himself inclined to do so? And why did she concern herself with Mary Able, so long dead? Chiefly, perhaps, because of her own memories, which were fresher. The thing was, where did she herself stand now in Mr. Ashley's affections? It tormented her not to know because to be anything but first with him under the circumstances would seem intolerable.

"Thank you, James," she said. "It is a handsome house."

"Yes, ma'am. It's a right nice town place."

"Shall we drive on now? Go past the school first. It's about time."

Not her enameled chatelaine watch suggested haste, but a passionate longing for the touch of her own flesh. When they arrived at Mrs. Lucinda Snow's Select Academy for Young Ladies and Mary Jane Wilcox was not the first through the door, Elizabeth fretted. Then, when the child did appear, she was impatient with Poke's ritual play of snatching off Mary Jane's button nose and proving it by the pink tip of his thumb showing between brown index and middle finger.

"You, Poke!" Mary Jane said. "Mamma . . ."

"Poke, stop it!" Elizabeth said, then blessed him for handing the child into the carriage and seeing her safe in the circle of Elizabeth's arm.

"Darling," Elizabeth began, and hushed. She must not ask her what kind of day she had had or was she happy now in this school. Mary Jane was a sweet, docile child, and always said everyone was kind, as everyone was to her; but she would be radiant when the time came for her to return to her grandparents' home in Boone County. The children, it was understood, would not accompany the Ashleys to Washington, in December.

Today Mary Jane herself provided conversation with a picture she had made out of yarn stitching on cardboard—a red house and a green bush and a green walk.

"What? No fountain?" Elizabeth said.

"I could do a fountain, maybe." Mary Jane studied her work so anxiously, that Elizabeth hugged her more tightly to her.

And that was the picture they made as they drove over Main Street. The Honorable William Henry Ashley, waiting in the store of his friend and protégé, Mr. Robert Campbell, of Sublette and Campbell, General Supplies and Merchandise, heard the clink of specially shod hoofs and stepped to the door in time to get a full view of the smart carriage and its team of matched blacks, of the liveried servants on the driver's seat, then the splash of color that was his wife and her winsome small daughter. He braced his shoulders, bowed for hours over business papers, and drew a deep breath of satisfaction. Who said that money could not buy happiness? His had bought him what he wanted most.

Movement in the store then warned him to leave off musing and step to the curb if he wanted to be the first to greet his wife. The new Mrs. Ashley might have to make her way in this town against a certain amount of adverse female opinion, but the male citizens made no attempt to conceal their devotion. When the carriage pulled up, Bob Campbell and Bill Sublette were right at Ashley's back and the redoubtable James Tower Sweringen was only six paces behind them.

When the Ashleys drove away, there were presents in the carriage —two boxes—a small, heavy one for Mary Jane and her sister, Anna Marie, and a long one, filling the whole seat opposite, for "your beautiful mamma," Ashley said.

"You spoil the children," Elizabeth told him, her eyes trying to make out the name on the big box, which was partly hidden by the small one, and all she could read was a piece of the word Philadelphia, and Ashley following her eyes and being pleased with his astuteness in seeing through her protest. "They look for something every day," she said; and he laughed aloud.

When they arrived at home and were met by Susanna with the rosy toddler, Anna Marie, he opened the children's present but had Poke take the large box into the house—to be delivered after supper. A little as if she were a child, too, Elizabeth thought, but carefully suppressed her small vexation and gave full attention to the children's gift.

It was a music box of Swiss manufacture. When wound up with a key, it played in succession three simple, tinkling waltzes. Anna Marie danced and clapped her hands. Mary Jane's wonder was more quiet. She said to Elizabeth, "Is it ours? Can we take it home to Grandmamma's with us when we go?"

Elizabeth, seated on a low stool, to be on the children's level, looked up quickly to see whether Ashley had heard the question. Apparently he had not. His sharp features, lighted by his deep eyes, wore the same expression that had greeted her on Main Street—satisfaction, gratification—something not simple to name.

"Cornelia and her jewels," he said to the inquiry on her face.

A man of little formal schooling, Elizabeth had discovered, he had tried as opportunity offered to supply the lack through reading. He forgot nothing, it seemed, so acquired.

"Her jewels were sons, weren't they?" she asked, to be saying something.

"I'm well pleased with daughters," he answered.

A trace of a frown she read to mean, "even if they are borrowed"; and pity stabbed her sharply. This, she had learned, was likely to happen unexpectedly, so that it had really been unnecessary for her mother to deliver the long homily which she had felt moved to offer before the marriage in October.

"Mr. Ashley is an older man," Miss Mary had said, wholly pleased with the turn of events, but overly anxious about a daughter, head-strong by nature and now fortified by ten years' independence of her parents. "He is a man of the world, different from anyone you have known. Your life so far has been very restricted."

Oh, sweet restraint! The barriers had been a flowering hedge, no more, until vandal hands had torn them down.

At supper Ashley said to her, a little testily, "You're very thin, my dear. Are you accommodating your tastes to my dyspepsia?"

Now, there was a thing of which nobody had warned her, because few people knew. Ashley himself made mock of it the first time when, alone like this, he had refused his food with such a green complexion that there could be only one answer.

"A devilish thing," he said, angry, ashamed, and angry about that. "No sense to it. When I'm out in the open, I can eat with the best of men—salt pork, anything that passes for bread, boiled seaweed for coffee—and sleep like a child. But, shut me up in town and the trouble begins. The answer, of course, is to live ruggedly and be well; but a man wearies of that. Besides, you can't make a fortune that way. I found that out. You can gather riches for somebody else; but, if you want to build your own fortune, you've got to live among the money-changers. You've got to be where you keep your eyes on your accounts and your ears open to what's going on. Now, don't look so appalled, my dear. I manage very well in spite of the nuisance."

Certainly he managed concealment, but Elizabeth was dismayed. This was truly a new experience.

"I had no idea," she said carefully. "I am so sorry. Why didn't you talk it over with Papa? Perhaps he could suggest—"

"My God!" He was really ill that evening. "And have him more dubious than ever about our marriage?"

"Oh, no!" she protested. "Papa? He was delighted."

"Papa was hopeful," Ashley corrected. "He told me too earnestly that your happiness was his one desire, for me not to perceive he reserved a doubt."

Such acidity was the way of dyspepsia. It could be a warning sign, her father said, when she wrote to him privately for such advice as he might be willing to offer, being careful to include in the letter a statement of her general well-being. Following his reply and even in anticipation of it, in so far as she could, she tried to have their private meals simple and tasty—delicate roast fowl, custard puddings, clear soups.

"Above all," her father advised, "keep a cheerful house."

So now she said, "Would you like it better if I were plump and cushiony?"

The picture she called up was so opposite to her supple slenderness that Ashley laughed heartily.

"I suppose there would be that much more of you for me to adore," he said. "Seriously, dearest, it is your health that concerns me. Are you well?"

He meant, "Are you happy?" She answered brightly that she was very well. Excess weight was not characteristic of her family. Besides, nowadays a slender waist was a requirement of fashion. Was it, indeed? He studied the wide puffs of the wine and silver silk frock. He would have said that some plump lady had designed the mode, to make everyone else look as large as she was.

"You mean these?" Elizabeth rested her finger tips on the sleeve puffs. "It is true everyone measures the same above and—" she stood up from the table to show the width of her skirt—"below." The striped silk had its panels cut three ways to exaggerate its fullness. She turned about to show it off. "But all that," she spread her hands, as if about to do a pirouette, "only serves to call attention to the waistline." Thank Fortune, she did not have to be tortured by steel stays! "Do you see?"

"I do," he said drily, and with such brightness in his glance that she sat down quickly, in confusion. "Thank you, dearest, for the pretty demonstration. I have never paid much attention to women's fashions before."

He might have added, "But now, having you, I do." Elizabeth's cheeks flamed. Under cover of the heavy damask cloth, she clasped her hands tightly together. For silks and ostrich feathers, for lessons on the pianoforte, for cushioned ease and safety, for change, she had sold herself. Was this deliverance?

Her present was a dress, complete to the last stitch. How had he dared?

"You don't like it," he said to her silence.

"It is the most beautiful dress I ever saw," she said finally. It would have been better for her pride had it been less exquisite.

The material was silk moiré, not ivory, not gold, something between the two, the color all but molten in the lamplight. This was the beauty of the dress—its richness, its color, its simple elegance of finish. It was a gown designed for an evening reception or a ball, its sleeves short puffs that must end well above the elbow, the décolletage low but softened by a touch of creamy lace. With the dress went a short cape of the same material finished with an upstanding ruche of the lace, tied with velvet ribbon.

The most beautiful dress she had ever seen. Her favorite striped silk was cheap, gaudy, in comparison.

"You don't like it," Ashley said again.

"It takes my breath away."

If only he had bought her a jewel or a fan! If he had said to her, "These St. Louis dressmakers are all very well as far as they go; but I know a designer named Rachel Bridport, of Philadelphia, who is in great demand among the fashionable ladies of the capital. You will want to appear at your best in Washington, I am sure. Wouldn't you like to order a gown or two from her—in addition to the pretty things you already have?"

No. Arbitrarily, as he bought or furnished a house, as he chose a wife, for that matter . . .

"In some way I have given you offense."

How should she answer? Something—perhaps everything—hung in the balance. She searched her mind, her heart. Surely no offense had been intended. It was just Ashley's way to act upon decision, wasting no time in considering. And yet, the hurt remained.

When she looked up, her eyes were bright with tears she would not release.

"You are the soul of generosity," she said. "I never know what to expect." She thought, "If I were wholly pleased, I would throw my arms around him and kiss him rapturously, because it is a lovely dress and very costly."

She touched the rich silk lightly, then put the box and the dress aside and stood up; but oh, this was a hard thing still for her to do— to offer a caress. It was the harder because, when she had the impulse, Ashley would wait until there could be no doubt of her intention. He waited now until she came quite close.

"Thank you for the lovely gift," she said, turning her face to his; but she could not lift her arms. "You are sweet to think of such a thing."

He kissed her once lightly, then hard. His arms about her tightened. She could feel a deep tremor inside him and was conscious of the beating of his heart.

"You do like it, then?" he asked—anxiously, still standoffishly.

Something in her clamored still for escape, but she stood quietly in his embrace. "Yes, oh, yes!" she said. "I will save it for the first grand occasion in Washington." In the next breath she demanded, drawing away a little, "Tell me about this Philadelphia dressmaker, Rachel Bridport."

Nothing she could have said would have delighted him more.

"You witch!" He laughed, buried his laughter in her bright hair, kissed her again—lovingly and tenderly now—and laughed some more. "You inexpressible witch! Made sure of the name, didn't you?"

She drew farther away. Here was an offense to which she could give expression.

"I thought only, since we planned to travel to Washington by way of Philadelphia, I would not buy anything more here."

"I know well what you are thinking." And, of course, he did. That, she could tell anybody now, was one secret of Ashley's success—an ability to see into the minds of others, to read their intent. Except for pride, which demanded that she maintain some personal dignity, and for defensive caution, she might as well have laid bare all her feelings on this and matters in general.

"My rashness," he concluded, still richly amused, "is likely to cost me a pretty penny now."

So it should, she made up her mind on the instant.

"Would you like me to try the dress, to make sure it fits?" she asked, pulling free of his arms, as she could now, because he was still laughing.

"By all means," he said, and then, watching her struggle with the large box and the dress hanging over its edges, "Hadn't you better call your maid?"

"Susanna is with the children. If I called, I'd waken them."

In spite of the awkward box and her full skirt, she managed, she felt, a dignified ascent of the staircase. Halfway to the floor above, an impulse made her stop and look down. Ashley stood in the door to the parlor, watching her. His eyes were very bright. He might still be laughing; but there was something about him, standing there under the flare of the crystal-shaded lamps. . . .

Years ago, when he was a child, he had little . . . but he knew people who were rich and proud . . . and they said, "Go away, little boy. . . ."

She thought, "He is lonely—as lonely in this fine house as I am." A proud, sensitive man, for all his attainments, scarred by early and too well remembered rebuffs, had he gone hearthungry all his days? It was possible. Two childless marriages would seem to argue that, while he could acquire riches and satisfy other ambitions, command the respect and even the devotion of his fellow men, he did not know how to win or hold a woman's heart. Was this another scar, never to have known the sweet, selfless, and complete tenderness of true love?

She all but set the box down on the turn of the stairs, meaning to run back and make complete, abject surrender; but she hesitated. Did he want this of her? He had not said so. "Do me the honor," he had said, asking her to be his wife. "Marry me and we shall have a good life together." A little about happiness, but very little about love. Since then he had been devotedly kind, proud of her on display, indulgent, sometimes in their hours alone showing something approaching ardor, but never just that. Too wary, too cautious, too ready to withdraw before a possible rejection.

And what of herself? Marrying him, she had told him in so many words that, while she could promise herself, she could not promise her heart. Not yet. Perhaps not ever. He had seemed to accept her terms, but it wasn't natural that he should be content with them. But there it was. If she went down to him now, it would be an act of pity. No more. He might even know it for that and turn aside her impulse with a sharp word, a brittle laugh; and she was no more anxious for a rebuff than he was.

Baffled, perplexed, willing and unwilling, as lonely in her way as he was in his—lonelier, perhaps—she smothered the impulse herself, and went on upstairs to try on the beautiful dress.

CHAPTER THREE

The Capital City

WASHINGTON WAS EVERYTHING that Elizabeth Ashley had hoped it might be—and more. After one season, life anywhere else seemed impoverished. If she had been asked to locate the city geographically, she would have looked at the dome of the sky. Surely it belonged to the realm of the stars.

There were some, William Ashley among them, who pretended to be amazed at her enthrallment. The streets were no better paved than in St. Louis and usually they were muddier because in Washington it rained more and longer and harder. Even so, hub-deep in mud, Pennsylvania Avenue, from the unfinished Capitol—she never saw it without scaffolding, sandpiles and a block and tackle somewhere—to the President's House and the President's Park, offered the vista of vistas. She did not see the mud.

"Drive more slowly, Poke. How can I tell who that gentleman is who bowed to me?" And how could the gentleman know to whom he bowed?

A gentleman on horseback usually, that being the accepted form of transportation for men; and he would be a senator or a secretary or a federal judge or an ambassador—at the very least, the attaché of an embassy—almost never plain Mr. Smith or Brown. The Honorable William Henry Ashley, Member of Congress from Missouri, kept a saddle horse and rode every day when he could spare an hour, for his health. The Honorable Mrs. Ashley went about in her own carriage here, as at home; and, from the beginning, since there were not many such equipages privately owned, she was a marked personage.

"What did you say the name is, dear? Ashley—from Missouri— money and influence. Made the money, I understand, on furs from the Rocky Mountains. Astor? No, indeed. The way I heard it is that John Jacob Astor subsidizes him, pays him to keep his trappers away from the American Fur Company's hunting grounds. Much money? Bags of it, my dear. That's real lace on her parasol. Well, who is she— I mean, really, besides being the Honorable Mrs. Moneybags? Hold your breath, pet, while I tell you. She's a Randolph. Down with the eyebrows. She's from a sound limb of that tree—second cousin to Martha Jefferson Randolph. Her mother was born at Dover on the James River. There is a story that when Lord Cornwallis marched south through Virginia . . ."

If there was a story about one's past, present, or likely future, Washington tongues soon spread it, or one was a person of no consequence. Even the gossip had for Elizabeth its special flavor and sparkle. She faced its inherent malice serenely from the cushions of her carriage, sometimes ordering Poke to slow the horses to a walk, giving her an opportunity for a word or two besides a nod of recognition, more often leaving the pace to his own excellent judgment.

For, in being transplanted here, Dr. Moss's boy Poke had come home. He was, by birth and heritage, an out and out James River man. His promotion to his present responsibilities had been Ashley's idea and nothing could have given better evidence of his sure judgment of character, however natural it might have been to leave the older James in St. Louis as caretaker for the abandoned mansion there. In two weeks Poke—Susanna, too, to some extent—had learned more about Washington's code than Elizabeth could have learned in a year. His field of exploration extended to areas where neither she nor Susanna could follow. Very soon he was a complete oral directory of the capital and the absolute authority in the Ashley household on protocol.

"But, Poke, that was the Eaton woman. Was it necessary to stop for her?"

"Won't hurt none to pass de time o' day, Miss Libby. Dose ladies what try to freeze her out ain' gittin' nuthin' but fros'bite fo' deyselves."

He was right. Best to smile and be pleasant to everyone alike, until one knew. Even then it was a good rule to follow.

"Poke, draw up to the curb. That's Mrs. Foxe on the sidewalk yonder."

Pennsylvania Avenue—the Avenue—boasted a brick walk on its north edge.

"Yas'm, sho is," Poke agreed. "She walkin' herse'f an' her dog fo' dey health."

His mimicry was perfect.

"Poke!" Elizabeth rebuked sharply, though it was her own observation that people in Washington who depended on hired hacks for distance walked themselves to death on shorter errands. "I'm sure she'd enjoy a ride. It's a lovely day—almost like spring."

"Miss Libby, we kin fill dis kerridge wid folks what knows jes' 'bout when you sets out f'om de hotel."

Home for the Ashleys in Washington being a suite at the National on Sixth and Pennsylvania.

"Poke, will you do as I say, please? I want to speak to Mrs. Foxe."

Lily Foxe. She was the first close friend Elizabeth had after life's complexities had come between her and Barcie Harris; and two women more widely different than Lily and Barcie God had never fashioned, if God had had anything to do with the fashioning of Lily Foxe.

Lily was a New Englander by birth. Vermont? New Hampshire? There was a vagueness about that. She was now the wife of an ambitious young New York attorney named Charles Foxe, who had some connection with Mr. Van Buren, Andrew Jackson's vice president during his second term. Charles Foxe, for the sake of what influence and prestige it might give him in future business, rather than for any money gain, held an obscure secretaryship in Mr. Van Buren's office; and this was so commonplace in Washington that the Foxes, without means and, as yet, without position, might never have crossed the path of the Ashleys, except that the Foxes were not that kind. In combination—or it could have been through Lily's wits alone—they had a make-do and a reach that called nothing impossible.

Lily and Elizabeth met at the President's House, during the New Year's Day reception. Elizabeth wore the Bridport moiré. She had thought, briefly, of saving it for the inaugural ball, but that was far-off March; and a Jackson inaugural, she was told, was more like a Kentucky burgoo than an affair of state. Even this most democratic President could not take away the formality attendant upon the New Year's Day levee, which regularly opened the Washington "season."

"The Honorable Mr. and Mrs. William Ashley of Missouri."

Not that anybody paid attention to the Mister, Ashley said afterward. Not an eye took in his new broadcloth tailed coat, with its velvet buttons and wide reveres, his brocaded waistcoat, his pleated linen shirt and acutely fashionable choker stock—all his vain efforts to justify himself in the eyes of this world in bright holiday mood. His statement was an exaggeration. Almost everyone gave him the second look, though Elizabeth did not deny that she received the first.

Their entrance made a perceptible stir. There was a hush, then a rustle of bright silks and broadcloth, both blue and black, of uniforms stiff with silver and gold lace, as the wearers turned for more direct observation and whispered comment.

116

Jeweled lights from prismed chandeliers seemed to shine with concentrated force on the Ashleys as they moved through the first parlor to the spot where the President waited, on his left his trusted secretary, Mr. Donelson, standing by to repeat the names of the guests into the presidential ear, on his right the ladies of his mansion—a matter of choice in the case of this lonely old man, whose personal history was a sad one. Of this group the first and prettiest was the auburn-haired Mrs. Donelson, the President's niece, who, to almost everyone's relief, had now with gentle obstinacy just about shouldered the Eaton woman out of the picture.

"My first grand *fête*," Elizabeth called it, writing the story home. Here, indeed, was an entire new world. Her color was high, her lips parted on pure excitement, her eyes reflected the light of the lamps— she looked and felt a fresh nineteen. It was a cold night. A sleety rain fell outside; and, disliking more than its misery the outward aspects of a cold, she kept the cape of her costume about her shoulders, tied loosely by its velvet ribbons. In a sea of extreme and chilly décolletage this lent her dress a deceptive simplicity and to only a few suggested the good sense that went with maturity. The most obvious sign of that was the poise with which she met the compliments murmured over her hand or into her ear. All evening she gathered them in as if they were flowers, smiling, murmuring an acknowledgment if there was time, never faltering or stammering, not even when the tall, silver-haired, aging but still soldierly President held her hand between his beyond the allotted second.

"My dear," he said, "you bless this house. I hope you shall—often." Ashley was not a perfervid Jackson man. "Emily . . ."

Mrs. Donelson said graciously, "Mrs. Ashley . . . Mr. Ashley"; and they moved on, and so came to the Vice President in office, Mr. Calhoun, and finally to the Vice President elect, Mr. Van Buren, in broadcloth as fine and well-tailored as Ashley's, and, shortly afterward, where the line began to disintegrate into a general mob, a Mrs. Foxe and her husband. Someone said, "You two ladies should meet, both being new to the capital," and made the introduction.

"St. Louis . . . Missouri?" a cool voice said—just that, not cold. "Are you sure you don't mean Charleston? Or Savannah?"

A shock of recognition, a warning, not unpleasant, ran through Elizabeth. Compliments were beginning to blur and run together, now this. A compliment, too, in a sense, but barbed. She took Mrs. Foxe's measure before answering.

What she saw was a woman of about her own years, more striking than handsome. Lily Foxe made no pretensions to beauty. She had fine eyes, large and dark brown—so dark that it was difficult to read any feeling from them, if feeling was ever there. Her black hair, amenable to no kind of curl or crimp, she wore severely plain in a style of its own, with a heavy, netted knot at the back of her neck. Her complexion was sallow, her mouth noticeably wide especially when she smiled, which was seldom, probably because it drew attention to her mouth. She was tall—about Elizabeth's height—not quite so slender. If she had carried as little flesh over her bones as Elizabeth had, she would have been craggy. It was evidence of her almost perfect control that she kept always just the right amount for covering. In defiance of her complexion but as a compliment to her eyes, her dress was a green velveteen, made severely plain, the only ornament a circlet of beaten gold about her neck and smaller ones to match on her arms—her own handiwork, Elizabeth learned later. There was little the brown hands could not accomplish, when directed by a brain restless beyond belief.

"The oddest person," Elizabeth thought, "but there's something about her. . . ."

And Lily, taking stock of Elizabeth, while being measured herself, decided just as promptly, "Sweet, so beautiful that it is a crime. Sinfully rich, everything made easy. Ordinarily I've no use for that kind or that kind for me; but this one may be different. And maybe I've been wrong."

Aloud Elizabeth said sweetly, "You don't know many people from Missouri?"

"Oh, yes." It was instinct with Mrs. Foxe to make much out of a little of anything. "The trouble is, it never seems to be Missouri. One reads and one keeps hoping—but hoping in vain—for someone in buckskin and porcupine quills."

"I have worn buckskin," Ashley said. "Will that cover the deficiency?"

"But there is no deficiency," Lily answered. "That is my complaint."

"Buckskin is still being worn in Missouri," Elizabeth said, as the press of people began to force them apart. "You must visit us before it goes entirely out of fashion."

"I hope that is an invitation."

It was not an invitation. Things didn't move that fast. And later, when Elizabeth and Lily were close friends, if never exactly true ones, while Elizabeth spent weeks and months in the other's company in New York or Saratoga, there was never any talk of Lily's making the long journey westward to Missouri. Happily, the place remained to her the utter, outer limbo.

As the evening went on and the reception broke into smaller parties, moving from house to house, Elizabeth found herself the center of another group in the residence of a Virginia connection, a Mrs. Pleasants. There was a parlor, with a piano.

"Do you play, Mrs. Ashley?" someone asked. It happened to be a Virginia judge, newly appointed to the Supreme Court.

Ashley turned to Elizabeth, startled, apprehensive, ready to defend her again if his help was needed; but it was not.

"A little," she said. "My music lessons were interrupted—to the great regret of my dear teacher." She smiled—a deep, dimpled smile. "Would you like to hear about my teacher, Mr. Justice? His name is Seidensticher."

The Judge said he would be charmed; and, with a wave of her hand to reassure Ashley, she launched at once into an imitation of the professor.

" 'Mrs. Ashley, madame, you must gif some attention to the foondamentals. The r-r-rudiments. You cannot master music without the r-r-rudiments.' "

Painfully she picked out a scale, worked it to a certain fluency one-handed, then brought the other one along. She walked the floor, clasping and unclasping her hands under imaginary coattails. It was an inspired performance. Bonds that had held her spirit prisoner burst. She had not been so gay since . . .

With laughter rising all about her, she untied her cape, handed it to the Judge, and sat down before the keyboard. She found a chord, struck it cautiously and sang. For safety, she chose a simple tune—the nursery ditty: *"The Cat Fell into the Cream Jar."* She sang over a swelling lump in her throat.

"I never heard a more affecting tremolo," Lily Foxe said afterward.

At the time she appeared suddenly out of the shadows, saying, "I still think it should be a harp. Don't you agree, Mr. Ashley?"

William Ashley, for once, was speechless. Elizabeth stood up and, with a gesture, asked for her cape.

"I trust you mean an earthly harp," she said, as the Virginia judge settled the silk bit reverently on her shoulders, "not a celestial one. Mrs. Foxe, we were planning on moving on now to the hotel for a simple supper and dancing. Will you and Mr. Foxe join us?"

"Thank you, Mrs. Ashley. I'm afraid we can't. We are in the Vice President's party. . . ."

"Perhaps Mr. Van Buren will honor us," Elizabeth answered, understanding at once which Vice President she meant.

It was two in the morning. Nothing was further from Elizabeth Ashley's desire or need than sleep. William Ashley considered speculatively the flush of color on her cheeks, the brilliance of her eyes.

"Only think . . ." she said breathlessly and did not finish, but he knew what she meant. Consider the people they had entertained at supper—a major general, a justice of the Supreme Court, the Vice President elect, two senators—and their ladies, when they had ladies, none nearly so lovely as his own.

"Was it bold of me to perform at the pianoforte?" she asked, anxious now.

"Charming," he said. "I didn't know you were so accomplished."

She breathed more easily.

"A little venturesome," Ashley suggested. "Have you a repertory? You will need to have now, I think."

"No," she said, frightened again. "I'd only begun to learn a little."

"Would you like a piano—to continue your studies?"

"You mean here?"

"I think it could be arranged."

"What I need more," she said, "is another Professor Seidensticher."

"That, too," Ashley said. "There must be any number who would be glad to oblige."

Perplexity dulled the bright edge of her mood.

"Now tell me," she coaxed. "What did you really think of the whole evening? Did I do badly or very well?"

"Is my opinion important?" he asked. "Among so many compliments?" It was inconceivable that he could be jealous; but he suggested something of the sort. "Didn't I say you were charming? You were, you know. It was what I believe is called a successful evening and you made it so. The bit at the piano was pretty. I, too, thought of a harp. A large golden harp and a fair lady." Abruptly his tone changed. His sharp face twisted with displeasure. "I don't like Mrs. Foxe."

"Poor thing!" Elizabeth said.

"What? Why should you pity her?"

"I don't know. She's very clever, don't you think?"

"Yes. That's what I don't like about her. I detest clever women."

Yes. He would. A man who had made his way to heights by his own endeavors would not care for women—or men, for that matter—with wits and ambitions as keen as his own.

Early in their marriage she had learned how truly self-made he was. When he first showed her through the big house in St. Louis, of which she was now to be the mistress, they had stopped in a room in the wing peculiarly Ashley's own. The room was half museum and half library. The museum part—an assortment of Indian trophies and rocks and other souvenirs of exploration—would have delighted Mrs. Foxe and been an acquisition for any collector; but what surprised, and briefly delighted, Elizabeth was the books. Most of them were on one subject, but there were shelves of them. The one she took down to examine was by the famous Captains Lewis and Clark—their *Travels to the Source of the Missouri and Across the American Continent to the Pacific Ocean*. She asked if she might take it back to the main house with her. It had been her custom, while still a girl at home, to read aloud to her father on evenings when they sat alone by the fire. It might be fun to read this one aloud.

With his usual politeness, Ashley had consented; and she had settled down happily to the task; but she hadn't read ten minutes before his restlessness communicated itself to her and she stopped. His restlessness did not mean lack of interest in the text. It was not that she stumbled in her reading. He would have been happier if she had stumbled. He fidgeted against the admission of her suggested intellectual superiority.

"You read well," he said, but edgily. "Evidently you have had good teaching. I was not so fortunate. Please, go on."

But she laid aside the book, saying another time, perhaps. Not everyone enjoyed being read to. Privately she had thought she would finish the book herself. Indirectly it might give her some information about one of the blank periods of Ashley's past; and she needed all the help she could gather if she was ever to understand this stranger who was now her husband. However, when she looked for the book where she had left it, it was gone. Ashley had returned it to its shelf in his library. The inference was plain to her. He was displeased by the incident and did not wish to be reminded of it. As with his dyspepsia, she had uncovered what he fancied was a deficiency in himself. A small occurrence, perhaps, painful only if she dwelt upon it; so she had put it out of her mind, filling the many empty hours with more trivial pursuits, the music lessons for one.

Now it all came back to her; but, she thought, surely here in Washington, where great events were always in the making, where everyone she met had some claim to significance, where even light talk had its own profundity, she might be allowed more depth. Only Lily Foxe earlier and Ashley now had suggested otherwise.

"We'll order a piano tomorrow," Ashley said, "and a teacher, if you want. Meanwhile, I've a simpler reward to offer, though one you'll hardly refuse."

In their absence from the hotel, mail from the West had arrived. Ashley had a bundle of letters; and there were two for her—from home. Washington, all her present adventure, was forgotten. She reached greedily for the letters, and in a rush of emotion she did not trouble to explain or to hide, carried them away to a chair near a lamp. In trembling haste she broke the seals of one addressed by her father.

"Dear papa!" she murmured; and then, as if she had worried about this, "They're all well. Mamma, the children— Oh! I am sorry."

Ashley's letters remained in a neat stack under his hand on the table.

"You haven't opened one," she said uncertainly. "Isn't there anything . . . I mean, important?"

"Nothing I'd clutch to my heart," he said drily. "Accounts due and payable. A communication from Mr. Sweringen in St. Louis— ominously long. Other communications from the good people who elected me to Congress and are now fearful lest I forget some of the issues that led them to do so."

And there it was again. The utter, indescribable loneliness of the man. And the unapproachable isolation of that loneliness. Not one to make intimates of even his closest friends, he seemed to have no family connections. Knowing that this was most improbable in the literal sense, she had dared to ask the brothers Campbell about it. They would know, if anyone did. Mr. Hugh Campbell said he believed there was a sister—one, if not more—in Virginia, to whose support Ashley contributed. But how could she show interest in them if he chose not to tell her of their existence?

"Papa and Mamma send you their affectionate regards," she said still uncertainly. "The children, too, ask to be remembered. There is a new colt."

This was a free rendition of the actual passages. The children were more fervent in their remembrances to Susanna and Poke. They had named the colt for Poke, calling it Pocahontas, because it was a filly. Would Ashley find this amusing if she told him? Or just trifling?

Ashley, watching her, smiled with sudden warmth at her perplexity. He got up then and crossed the room to where she sat. Taking her face between his hands, he studied her features minutely, searchingly. His own shoulders ached with fatigue, but she showed not a trace. The mistiness of her eyes, the droop to her mouth were not weariness. He kissed her gently. To be sure, she was only twenty-eight and he . . .

"Go to bed, my sweet," he said. "It's well on into the morning. I'll be along presently. Take your letters with you. I'm glad Missouri has still a secure place in your heart. I was afraid you might be willing to forget."

Missouri? What did he mean by that? She had been talking of her parents, her children, dear people, not a place.

Fondly, proudly, Ashley watched her walk out of the room. The rustle of stiff silk was still in his ears when he took the top letter from his pile. It was a statement—overprompt—from Rachel Bridport. He tossed it aside. His Libby was worth every penny of her cost. One of two great desires in his life, he had once thought her unattainable and now she was securely his. So, with the other . . .

He went through his stack of letters now, stopping to weigh again the one from the St. Louis broker, Mr. Sweringen, and another from a St. Louis attorney, but laid them both down unopened. Their business could wait for another day. Only one letter in the pile interested him now. It was from a land agent in Boonville, Cooper County, Missouri. He had asked for a new survey of the boundaries of the Chouteau Grant, an estimate of acreage in English measure, and an appraisal of its general value.

Its value on the market, not to him. There was no possible dollar estimate of that. With the opening paragraph of the letter, Washington—even, in a measure, his Libby—faded from his consciousness, too. He was a young man again, wearing the buckskins Lily Foxe had demanded, tramping the headlands along the Missouri, dragging surveyor's instruments as evidence of his right. He was a young man, open to dreams, standing on the summit of an Indian burial mound on one of these high hills, looking down at the great, coiling river, following it until it disappeared in the haze of distance. All his life's purpose had taken shape as he stood there.

Only the impetuosity of youth had given him the boldness to seek out Mr. Chouteau, to pay into his hand privately a sum of money—a legal option was not possible—to insure that, if the land where he had stood that day ever was put up for sale, he and he alone would own it. Seventy-five hundred dollars on an urge, a faint possibility. It had been every dollar he possessed and all he could borrow. Mr. Chouteau had been a hard bargainer. He had known what the magnificent land was worth to him and to this bemused young man; but when he had given his word, it stood. And now . . . very soon . . .

Before returning to the letter, Ashley opened his desk and took from it a sheaf of legal paper, copy of a land bill pending in Congress. Its text was a jargon of legal technicalities; the letter, with its rods and angles and landmarks, was another jargon. Ashley settled down to study both texts with an avidity that an epicure, with better digestion, would have brought to a feast. Nobody, seeing him, would have needed to ask what he did for Missouri in Congress. Internal improvements, a ruling on land titles in dispute, and so, through legislation, clear possession at last of the barony of his dreams.

CHAPTER FOUR

Portrait of Mrs. Ashley

IN THE ORIGINAL CAPITOL the special stairway leading to the Ladies' Gallery of the Senate chamber ascended from an elliptical enclosure separating the chamber and its colonnaded vestibule from the main rotunda of the building. Coming down that stairway, a lady of consequence or merely of some acquaintance with official Washington, if the time was right, was almost certain to meet or be met by one of several distinguished gentlemen emerging through the screen of columns; and the business of the nation or the world was seldom so engrossing that a senator, thus emerging, failed to glance toward the ladies' stairway.

On an afternoon in February, the year 1833, Lily Foxe laid her hand on Elizabeth's arm, signaling her to wait. With outward docility Elizabeth waited. She could see for herself that their departure from the gallery had been precipitate. As yet, nobody had appeared in the small rotunda. Really, one might think from Lily's manner that she owned this wing of the Capitol; but, since Elizabeth attended sessions of the Senate at Lily's invitation and in Lily's company, condescension was to be expected. Mrs. Foxe must score a few points now and again if the rivalry the two called friendship was to have any sort of balance. Obviously it was in Elizabeth's power to grant Lily more favors than Lily could offer her.

There was just one thing—the matter of companionship. In Washington, much more than in any other American city, a lady did not go about alone—and continue to be reckoned a lady. Elizabeth no longer took long drives in her carriage unattended except for what she knew to be the complete chaperonage of Poke. She lost considerable in backstairs gossip that way, but bowed to the hard fact of established convention.

It was a convention that took strange turns. A woman's natural preference would have been for a male escort and her first choice, presumably, her husband. If, however, one's husband was busy, the capital abounded in other gentlemen not so hard-pressed by duties. Some were men without family ties. More had families but, being present in the capital only for court sessions or the meetings of Congress, did not go to the trouble or expense of moving their households with them. It was considered not only permissible for a woman to accept attentions from these detached males, cheering their loneliness as a return; but it was quite the thing to collect as many of them as possible in a circle of admirers. Of course, if a man of prestige had a wife, or produced one unexpectedly, one hastened to make friends with her.

Elizabeth Ashley within a few weeks could have commanded a sizable entourage; but, being new to the scene, she chose to observe caution and the stricter proprieties, and to make her first friends among women.

"You're a sly one," Lily Foxe said. "The women will like you better and the men no less."

It was more instinct than slyness, a heritage of gentility. That, however, would not explain her developing friendship with Lily Foxe. To be sure, she did not dislike Lily, as Ashley did. Not ever. Lily's affected honesty of speech could be most amusing—if one were not the target of her wit. This outspokenness reminded Elizabeth faintly of Barcie Harris, though it was a far cry from Barcie's naïveté to Lily's sharp sophistication. Lily was clever and she was truly sly. Elizabeth never wholly trusted her and certainly Lily never confided completely in Elizabeth; but even this was a challenge—the way a brisk, cutting wind could set one's teeth on edge, but also enliven one's general circulation.

There was more to the friendship than that. Elizabeth would be fearfully angry at Lily, ready to scratch her off her visiting list for some underhanded trick; and suddenly she would think, "If I had come to Washington as she has come, if my husband were young and unknown and without means and needed desperately to get on, I would be just like her." She wouldn't have been that; but the situation would have been the same. She would have hated the favors she had to accept and even to court, but she wouldn't have put herself out of the way of receiving them. If the Honorable Mrs. William Ashley had been, say, the Honorable Mrs. Daniel Wilcox, Washington would have been a harder nut to crack. She knew that.

Pshaw! Why rub a hole in a good thing with so much pondering? Lily Foxe was an accident that time solidified into something of more moment.

Anyhow, here the two of them were on the steps to the Ladies' Gallery of the Senate and Lily's proprietary airs bothered Elizabeth less than they might have, because her ears were still filled with oratory. That she did not comprehend all of the periods disturbed her little. In fact, what she did comprehend bothered her more. The speaker had been Mr. Henry Clay of Kentucky, whose name was part of her earliest consciousness of public names and whose long face and lank hair were now included in her growing collection of portraits of the nation's great. By Washington's definitions she could now claim personal acquaintance with him, having enjoyed ten minutes of private conversation with him during a musical evening in January. In that ten minutes she had asked the great man whether he knew that his father, the Reverend John Clay of Virginia, had officiated at the marriage of the parents of Dr. James Moss, her father. Mr. Clay had not known this but he said it made him proud to hear that the good man had rendered such a service to future society.

"Mr. Clay," Lily Foxe said, that afternoon in the Senate as the Kentuckian rose from his desk.

Elizabeth smiled at her knowingly and, forgetting for a second where she was, put a finger to her lips. Over in the House, where she was a more frequent visitor, if one spoke above a whisper anywhere, an echo was likely to catch up what one said, carry it against a sounding board in the domed ceiling and fling it back, magnified into a ringing shout to be heard all over the place. At the same time the pronouncements of the Speaker or the reading of the clerks might not be audible at all, lost entirely somewhere in magnificent, columned space. The echoes of the House were a thirty-year-old scandal. Ashley excused himself from attendance much of the time, doing his work in committee rooms and appearing only when a vote on some measure important to him was anticipated. A secretive man in his public relations as in the privacy of his home. Over there, one did not go to listen to the proceedings; one went to see and to be seen: "The Honorable Mrs. William Ashley—Missouri."

Here Lily's indiscreet and superfluous murmur remained a murmur; and Mr. Clay's gentle, unhurried addressing of the chair was sonorous and undistorted. Elizabeth felt a thrill creep through her. Here was another Washington adventure to be reported at length in a letter home—one of many letters that traveled to Boonslick these days, letters so bright with activity that she could imagine their being read aloud in the family circle and even to chosen outsiders. Few people, hearing them, would think of raising a question as to her health and spirits. Even her father, to whom she would address this report, would say in his reply, "Did you, indeed, hear Mr. Clay's great speech on the tariff? What a privilege, daughter!"

As it truly was, she knew and thanked Heaven for it and other blessings.

The Senate was in full attendance that afternoon, all present deferential and respectful. In his place Daniel Webster rested his heavy head on his fists—so satisfactory when a man had a massive brain for him to have a great head, too—and listened. In another part of the room Senator Benton watched and waited. Another suitably leonine personality, he quite overshadowed the junior Senator from Missouri, a Dr. Linn from Ste. Genevieve, whom Ashley had known in his earlier days in the state and whom Elizabeth noted for another reason. He had been a member of the State Assembly at Jefferson City that terrible winter. He had written one of the letters a messenger had brought to the Moss home that January afternoon telling of Daniel's illness and death. Did he know who she was? Several times in social gatherings, she had caught a look of question on his face and, before he could follow the question with personal approach, had moved away from his vicinity as she now turned her eyes from him to the presiding officer's handsome mahogany desk behind which Vice President Calhoun glowered—his way of looking at everyone these days—but listened. In the section reserved for gentlemen of the press, Mr. Francis Blair of Virginia, whose new Democratic paper, *The Globe,* was having sensational popularity, sharpened his lead pencils and his ears.

Elizabeth turned her head; and Lily Foxe was wearing her most intelligent expression—also a small hat with a trailing feather—she had a way with such things—and a jacket she must have sat up nights to fashion. Elizabeth thought, "Lily Foxe has no better brain than mine, no better education. I can listen, too." So she folded her gloved hands in her lilac taffeta lap and prepared to do so. She did hope, in the unseasonable stuffy warmth of the room—had the architects never considered that people still must breathe in these marble halls?—that the dress would not crush or lose its freshness. Her latest from Rachel Bridport; and it was such a lovely day outside, the buds on the trees swelling. . . .

Now, then!

Senator Clay's speech was on the tariff. A person could not have lived in Washington three months without knowing that this was one of the most vexatious questions before Congress. It was dividing the country into factions even more than abolitionist societies and slavery, but along the same lines, because the northern states wanted the duties kept high to protect their manufactures, and the southern states didn't want imports taxed at all. In South Carolina the state legislature had passed a law saying the tariff would not be collected at the port of Charleston. That, of course, was open defiance, showing how high feeling ran. That was why Vice President Calhoun and others glowered. And what would President Jackson do if South Carolina carried out her threat? Would he use force, the army, to compel obedience to the national government? Nobody thought it would really come to that, but many shuddered at the possibility. Would it mean a civil war?

Somebody had to do something to relieve the situation; and here came Mr. Henry Clay—again. Elizabeth recalled that his persuasion and smooth oratory had settled a dispute over the admission of Missouri as a state. That had had to do with slavery and had seemed very silly to most of the people living there because nearly all of them owned slaves. Her recollections were hazy, her mind at the time having been occupied with a young man from North Carolina. . . .

Dear God, must she remember and remember . . . forever?

She stiffened in her chair and doubled her concentration. Mr. Clay that other time had sponsored, if he had not invented, the Missouri Compromise, and now he had worked out one on the tariff. A compromise, as far as she could see, consisted in letting everything stay just as it was and promising everybody something that would make everything all right presently. Missouri had been allowed to continue slavery; and now the states that wanted high protective tariff would still be protected by import duties for a while, anyhow. If the southern states would collect the taxes this year and turn them into the national revenue, if they would not raise a rumpus over them, next year the duties would be less and the next year even more so. In ten years or so they might be removed altogether. Or, did he say they would be?

It was really very warm. The air was heavy with mixed perfumes and less agreeable odors. A buzz-fly settled on the nearest skylight and made as much noise as a captive bumblebee. Mr. Clay's mellow tones and persuasive oratory were more soothing than exciting—to a mere listener. Mr. Clay, she noted, was not as homely a man in action as when he was still. That elongated upper lip was shortened when he smiled; but presently his face was more animated than that of any other in the chamber, except possibly Mr. Webster, now scowling to equal Mr. Calhoun. Under her layers of cloth and whalebone, she felt the dampness of perspiration. This was going to be a long, long speech.

Long enough. Fortunately, when it was done, others had begun to register protest against tedium. When Mr. Clay sat down, Mr.

Webster stood up, and fired a question that was sudden and loud as a cannon shot. Mr. Clay answered him, smiling more sweetly than ever; and then questions popped like exploding cartridges here and there and about; but presently, thanks be, a recess was voted and debate postponed.

Everyone in the gallery rose with a shake and a rustle and hurried to the stairway. There Elizabeth was glad to stand another minute, at Lily Foxe's direction, and enjoy the improved circulation of air. But not too long. A press of people piled up behind her and Lily; so they went on down and reached the foot of the stairs just as Mr. Clay himself emerged from the Senate chamber.

"Mrs. Ashley!" He came forward, with hand outstretched. "Spring has surely come to the Potomac."

That was the new lilac taffeta and it felt more like summer than spring to her, but she took the compliment as intended and offered one of her own.

"My first speech in the Senate, Mr. Senator." She could have said her first full-blown oration anywhere. Back home, in Boonslick, even at Fourth of July celebrations and political rallies, women were supposedly busy with their own concerns and did not hover about the speaker's platform. "I'm sorry Mrs. Clay was not present to hear you."

The Clays were in residence in Washington that year. This, gossip said, was a barometer reading of the Senator's rising or falling presidential hopes.

"Mrs. Clay rehearsed me on the speech only yesterday evening," he informed Elizabeth. "And that reminds me. We have just received from our farm at Lexington some Kentucky hams. Lucretia is planning for the near future a supper of ham and spring greens and other things suitable. She asked me to assemble guests able to judge the flavor of the meat . . . and the gravy. We should be very happy if you and Mr. Ashley will honor us."

It was on excitement such as this, she sometimes thought, that she lived these days. Mr. Clay had graciously ridden home to his tea in the Ashley carriage. Poke had swelled fit to burst at the display and her pride had been almost as great—not to be dashed certainly by the way in which Ashley received her news of the afternoon and the Clay invitation.

"Now, what," he asked, half-irritably, "except that Senator Clay is always counting votes, distinguishes a Kentucky ham especially? And how much do you remember, really, about Kentucky?"

"Not a great deal," she confessed, determined to keep her good humor. "Cousins and visiting and all-day picnics—and ham. Much like Missouri, and all very nice except for one thing."

"What was that?"

"Lessons. I had an English governess. Did I ever tell you about Miss Sullivan? She was good on the classics, but her specialty was deportment."

"I can see it must have been."

Elizabeth smiled at him across the supper table in their apartment. Unless they were entertaining, Ashley preferred his meals in private. Much as she regretted the custom—dark questions rose still to trouble her during such sessions—she could do nothing but accept it.

"You never look lovelier than you do in one of those fluffs you call wrappers," Ashley had once said, "but that's my secret and I'll keep it."

"Did your governess accompany you to Missouri?" he asked now.

"Mercy, no. At the first hint, she packed up and started back to England."

Ashley laughed, but the next minute his expression had soured again.

"We will accept the Clay invitation," he said. They could do nothing else. "But I'm not eligible to membership in the Kentucky circle. I didn't stop off there on my way to Missouri."

Elizabeth said carefully, "You seem a little out of humor this evening. Is it with Kentucky or Mr. Clay?"

"The Senator purely," Ashley assured her. "You, having been born there, are sufficient defense of Kentucky." He made a wry face and his features were so designed that it was a very wry one. "That bill of Clay's is going to keep us in session right up to the inauguration. If you ask me, it's a bid for notice on Clay's part. We had a good enough bill in the House, covering the situation and all ready for the vote. In a couple of weeks we could have been on our way home. Now we'll be here another month."

Elizabeth wondered at his fuming impatience. Had some business here or at home gone badly? She wished she knew, but hesitated to ask. This was the nearest he had ever come to discussing politics with her. Whatever he expected of their marriage it was not that kind of companionship.

"The great compromiser," he went on, acidly. "Compromise is a bookish term for fence-straddling. The trouble with that is, there are still two sides to the fence. A man of convictions makes his choice and plants himself firmly on one side or the other. Your

131

compromiser half the time is afraid to jump down for fear he will be wrong. He had better be wrong and make a stand."

Years afterward Elizabeth recalled his sharp words. At the time she was only acutely conscious of a lack of real information and reproached herself as well as Ashley with that lack. It was ridiculous that she knew so little of what went on beneath the pomp of Washington. If Ashley would not keep her informed, there were other sources. That supplement Mr. Blair published to his paper, for example, edited especially for Washingtonians. She would have to read it in secret, of course; and God knew there was too much of that already between her and Ashley. Still . . .

"Enough of politics," he said, sure enough, in the next breath. "How is the music coming?"

"Indifferently well," she told him. "I got on better with Mr. Seidensticher. What I really need, though, is to increase my special repertory. I think, while we are in St. Louis, I'll coax Mr. Sublette to teach me some of the songs he does for the children."

Ashley laughed.

"Bill Sublette's songs would embellish any repertory," he granted. "I might recommend in preference to them a voyageur's chanson. Did you ever talk to my Captain La Barge? The father, not the son, who's a steamboat man. Joe La Barge used to hire my boatmen for me. . . ."

Another second and Ashley was a thousand miles away—or more— far up the Missouri, probably. Very probably. This time she ventured close to a question.

"Mr. A., I do believe you are homesick for Missouri."

"I am," he said, with a return of vehemence. "All this taradiddle— but you like it, don't you?"

She liked it perilously well; but, if he did not . . .

"What you've got, my girl," he said, "is a touch of capital fever. You'll be cured of it, I trust, presently, because, I warn you, don't go plotting a career here for me."

"Why, Mr. A., nothing was farther from my mind, although I have heard it said, and I believe it, that you can have or be anything you really want."

"I can never be Senator from Missouri, for two reasons."

"What are they, please?"

"Both places are too well filled. Senator Benton is rooted like an oak. Only a hurricane could dislodge him. Dr. Linn is a young man and looks in excellent health. He'll outlive me by forty years, I'd say."

But . . . how could he be sure? To be a senator's lady . . . no doubt Ashley was right. She had contracted capital fever.

By contrast, then, to the general excitement of this gay first season, the supper party at the Clay residence had a nostalgic Boonslick flavor. Simple, folksy—the Clays were like that when one came to know them.

Mrs. Clay, a woman who bore her years and her responsibilities with a grace and dignity worth studying, on extending a definite invitation had called on the Ashleys. Elizabeth had conceived at once a great admiration for her. To be so sweet, through lines of sadness—Mr. Clay had already begun a long career of being denied the presidency—to be so strong and so lovely! Returning the call, she had felt inspired to ask whether she might not be of help in preparing the feast. Once she had been thought proficient in such things.

"Why, my dear!" Lucretia Clay said. "Of course, you can. I didn't know— Have you some special dish, perhaps?"

When the day came, Elizabeth was at the Clay address from early morning, busy as a hive of bees. She would not have believed how happy it would make her to wrap herself in a borrowed apron, to "mess around," as Pommie would have said, with eggs and spices. When Susanna arrived in the late afternoon with her good dress, she had to scramble to be ready in time for the party. "Putting on her other face," Mr. Clay called it.

He was right, of course; but, thanks to her happy exertions, it was a flushed and pretty face and she was instantly the center of an admiring circle. Since that circle was made up, as usual, of notables, including Congressman Letcher of Kentucky and the other Kentucky Senator, Mr. Bibb, and her good friend Justice McKinley of the Supreme Court, who had lately bought land near Louisville, and, for variation, Mr. Edward Everett of Massachusetts, presented by Mr. Clay as "one of more reasonable New Englanders, meriting a taste of southern conviviality," and others of equal importance, the day just for that would have been memorable; but there was more to come. Just before supper was served, Mrs. Clay called her away to meet two latecomers.

"Libby, I want you to know our good friends, the Crittendens of Frankfort. John, Maria, this is our Mrs. Ashley."

It was one of those occasions when time forgets to run on.

"I am sure I've heard the name often," Elizabeth said, acknowledging the presentation.

Though she could not say exactly in what connection. Later Congressman Letcher, who was the Crittendens' neighbor in Frankfort, and others who knew and loved John Crittenden well were happy to enlighten her. It appeared that he had already served a short term in the United States Senate—that was when James Monroe was President and before Dr. Moss had moved his family to Missouri. His record had been brilliant for a newcomer, but family and financial obligations had forced his return to Frankfort. Since then he had been content to serve Kentucky there—as Speaker of the House in the state legislature and now as Secretary of State for the commonwealth. It went without saying that he could return to Washington at any time in one capacity or another—whenever he was willing. An able lawyer, an outstanding fine man, a . . .

The information was interesting but quite apart from Elizabeth's sharp and instant sense of recognition. The most charming gentleman, she thought, that she had met in Washington or might ever meet there—or elsewhere, but could not define his charm exactly. He was not handsome. Like Mr. Clay, he was beanpole thin, though more pliable and certainly of quicker movement than the older statesman. He seemed young to have reached his political eminence, much younger than Mr. Clay, at least ten years younger than Ashley. His dark hair was only lightly touched with gray. His features were contradictory—rocky cheekbones and a prominent nose, then dark eyes of melting warmth and a mouth made whimsical by a thin upper lip, which was in turn given the lie by a full lower one. Here Elizabeth lost her way. What impressed her, what struck her as new and different and, at the same time, vaguely familiar was some inner quality which she would not venture to name until she knew him better, if, happily, she should come to know him better.

Of Mrs. Crittenden, whom Mrs. Clay called Maria, she was not so sure; but their first meeting was brief, broken off by the call to the supper table, where Elizabeth found herself seated between John Crittenden and her now good friend, and trusted champion, Justice McKinley.

"I understand Washington is new to you, Mrs. Ashley," Crittenden said, making conversation. "Do you like being here?"

Almost exactly Ashley's words at their first meeting: "Do you like living in Boone County?" And her answer had surprised him. Now . . .

"Yes," she said. "Very much. Do you mean you don't like Washington, Mr. Crittenden?"

"We miss you, John," Mrs. Clay put in. "We'd be glad to have you and Maria back here—to stay."

"Why, thank you, ma'am. You've shown me a valid reason for returning."

The gallantry was a flower laid in Elizabeth's hand, delicately, with a bow, a touch of knight-in-armor homage.

"Are you here on business, Mr. Crittenden?" she asked quickly, making talk in her turn now.

Justice McKinley answered for him.

"John is arguing a case in the Supreme Court this week, my dear."

"Hadn't you heard?" Crittenden added. "Henry Clay and I are fellow gallows cheaters."

"Oh!" Elizabeth said. "What a thing to say!"

"Very exact description," the Justice observed. "It has been said, and I'm sure with reason, that no man was ever hanged whom either defended."

"You are making fun of my ignorance," Elizabeth protested. "Oh, I should like— Do ladies ever . . . ?"

"They do, ma'am; and I, for one, find them highly distracting. But this is not a criminal case. A civil suit, dry as dust. You'd find it most tedious."

"I'm sure I wouldn't, Mr. Crittenden."

"I am sure you would," Justice McKinley declared. "I expect to have trouble myself keeping awake through the hearing. However, my dear, if you would care to brighten our dusty room with your presence some day, I'll look over the docket and select something of real interest."

Elizabeth thanked him and said she would be much obliged, but she was disappointed in not getting to hear Mr. Crittenden. She did hope that some day she might enjoy that privilege.

"Now that will do for him," the Justice growled. "Leave him to Mrs. Clay and his dinner. He looks hungry. And you give your attention to me."

After supper Crittenden again took charge, but now with a delightfully human and material motive. Taking her arm, he guided her purposefully around the long table into the presence of his wife.

"Lucretia Clay tells me," he explained, "that you made those delicious pies we've just been eating. Come right along with me and tell Maria how you do it."

"Mercy, Mr. C.," Mrs. Crittenden said, "you can't ask Mrs. Ashley to do that. For all you know, she has built a reputation on those pies."

"Not here in Washington," Elizabeth said.

Strange that she should find formidable in Mrs. Crittenden the very qualities that she admired in Mrs. Clay. Here was another woman of dignity and assurance and quiet poise, utterly devoted to a distinguished husband. Maybe it was the wifely devotion, surely not the husband, that drew a response of envy from the gay, the charming, the beautiful Mrs. Ashley and turned her slightly captious. Plain, she pronounced Maria Crittenden, whereas she was in truth a handsome woman, with clear brown eyes, good skin and a pleasantly wide, smiling mouth. A little oblivious of high fashion in her dress, as one might be who rose above such vanities. . . .

"Why not in Washington?" she asked Elizabeth. Then, without waiting to be answered, "Will you forgive me for saying so, but you seem young to be the Mrs. Ashley I've been hearing so much about." What in Heaven's name had she been hearing? "So young, so free, so detached— Tell me, have you no family?"

Nobody in Washington had ever put the question just that way to Elizabeth.

"Two daughters," she said, glad to be able to claim them. "One seven-year-old and one three. They are at home with my parents."

"Where is home, Mrs. Ashley?" That was Mr. Crittenden again. Elizabeth hesitated. Where, indeed?

"I was speaking of Boone County, Missouri, where my people live."

"And where you learned to make pies? I see. Boone County—would that be near Howard County? I ask because years ago some land office man sold me several hundred acres there on speculation. I came near to following my wildly spent dollars, to see the land of promise for myself."

Here was coincidence. Crittenden must have bought his land at about the same time that had seen the Mosses moving on to Missouri. Or when a young man named Wilcox, on finishing school, had thought newly settled territory would have a great need of doctors. Why not of lawyers? What had held Mr. Crittenden in Kentucky? It was marriage, Elizabeth suspected, and later found she was right in her guess. For some reason, she was happy to learn from the same source that the wife in the case was not the estimable Maria, who, like Elizabeth, had been a later choice. This was almost the only bond of similarity between them. Maria Crittenden had no quibbles and qualms about her position with regard to her husband.

"Why do you inquire about this land you've never seen?" she asked Crittenden. "I've never heard you mention it before."

"Sundry tax bills I get from there," he answered. "I always pay them—ultimately—but am not sure why."

"Well, mercy!" she said then. "Why don't you take the problem to Mr. Ashley? From what I hear, he is an authority on land values. Do go and rejoin the gentlemen, dear. I want to talk to Mrs. Ashley about her children."

"I'd rather you discussed pies," Crittenden insisted. "Babies seem to me much less remarkable."

Driving home with Ashley well on toward midnight, Elizabeth surprised herself with a sharp sigh. She covered it deftly, she thought, with an evasion.

"I like the Crittendens so much," she said dreamily. "Don't you?"

"Yes," Ashley agreed, "I do. Mrs. Crittenden is a fine woman, I imagine."

Even he reserved some opposing opinion, but it was not of Mrs. Crittenden that Elizabeth was thinking. Mr. John Jordan Crittenden of Kentucky—of whom did he remind her? A little of Daniel, a little of her father—nothing much of either, but something. A most interesting man—the most interesting . . .

"Justice McKinley says Mr. Crittenden is a great lawyer," she said.

"I can swear he's a good card player. Outside of Senator Clay, the best hand at whist I've yet encountered."

"Is he better at it than you?" Elizabeth asked.

"No, ma'am." In the darkness she could picture the gleam in his eyes. "But nearly as good. A person wonders . . ." he did not finish; but Elizabeth could see that he was following a thought through his own mind. If she kept still, he might reveal what it was. If she asked, he would turn the conversation aside. Must a woman be a Maria Crittenden to have her husband's full confidence?

"The trouble with Kentucky," he went on presently, but talking to himself more than to her, "is the same thing that's wrong with Virginia. Its best citizens give too much time to politics. While they're saving the nation, everything at home goes to ruin. Senator Clay, I hear, owns some of the richest grazing land in the Blue Grass; but it won't run itself. His wife does the managing when she's at home, where she had rather be than here. The same problem took Crittenden away from Washington. He was in the Senate— young, but with rare prospects of advancement. His law practice, however, languished and his farm went to weeds. He had to go home, to support his family. Holding a state office doesn't interfere. His land is near Frankfort and his law business thereabouts. He prospers so long as he stays near enough to keep an eye on both, but— Well, he's better off to do just that. His wife sees that, if he doesn't always. A woman of rare good sense." But he fidgeted on the carriage cushions, recalling her. "Heigh-ho!" he said. "It's springtime in Missouri, too. I wish I were there. Don't you?"

"Yes, of course," Elizabeth said. But did she, really? Her children, her parents? Yes. But Missouri?

If her consent was half-hearted, that could not have appeared, for the next day Ashley made her his first gift of jewelry. His many presents so far had kept away from that. On her hands she wore only her wedding band. She was too young, too lovely to require heathenish ornamentation, he argued. Even now . . .

"It may be years before you'll want to wear this," he said. "But I knew you admired it and I thought you might like to own it."

It was a chain of delicate filagree medallions, set each with a translucent emerald, a larger stone centering in the pendant. A goldsmith from Boston had displayed the piece, with others, in the hotel parlors. The color of the stones, more than anything else, had caught Elizabeth's fancy. They had a natural affinity for the elusive lights in her eyes, the shimmer of her hair.

"But, if I am not to wear the necklace, why give it to me?" she asked.

"Say I turned a dishonest penny," Ashley mocked.

"I don't believe that," she said; and she did not.

"Then say I like to be the one to make your eyes shine, my dear."

He wanted her eyes to shine like emeralds? Because of emeralds? Then, so they should. What else was there?

That was the spring of 1833. Presently, with the tariff bill disposed of in Congress, the Ashleys said good-bye to Washington and went back to Missouri, where Elizabeth found her worst doubts justified. The warm welcome of her parents, the wild, tender welcome of her children—how they had grown!—could not armor her against the painful associations of Boonslick, the inquiring eyes of old friends and neighbors.

"The girls look well," she said to her father and her mother one day, "and I know they are happy, living here; but presently they are going to have a position in society and perhaps we ought to do something more to fit them for it. Miss Mary, how would you like to spend the winter in St. Louis? We would put Mary Jane in school there, to stay this time. It would be good for sister Mary, too. She ought to see more of the world now. Papa will enjoy hobnobbing with Uncle Farrar. Well?"

She had no difficulty in obtaining her parents' consent, nor Ashley's. Ashley was delighted that she had thought of using the big house so well. The rest of the summer, then, and the early autumn went better. She was busy buying clothes for her little girls, settling Mary Jane in school, chaperoning her shy young sister to parties, snaring beaus for her—and laying her own plans for the winter. This season she meant not to be hampered by doubts or diffidence. Washington should see a really gay, a brilliant, a dashing Mrs. Ashley. She had buried the past finally and forever, Elizabeth Wilcox with it.

She was sure of that until she saw a portrait made of her that winter. A British artist, named Robert Sabre, set up a studio in Washington shortly after the Ashleys' return; and, oh, because it was fun to do, because he was an unusual person, and because many other fashionable ladies did the same, Elizabeth allowed him to paint her. It was all very proper. Sabre sketched her in various poses and in various places—the hotel suite or the litter of his attic studio, but always with someone in attendance—Ashley or Lily Foxe or Susanna. His methods were interesting. He talked continually as he worked and at such a rate that she hardly knew what he did with brush or pencil and so need not have been too astounded at the final result.

He talked very well. He had been everywhere—India, Egypt, China, Australia, everywhere except America. This was his first visit to the Western Hemisphere. He had painted in Italy, France, Switzerland. Vagabondage, a poverty of everything except experience, and a contemptuous disregard for what he called things were part, perhaps all, of his picturesqueness. His sack coats and loose trousers of coarse woolen, his cosmopolitan assortment of footwear, his open-collared shirts—he would not submit to the imprisonment of buckram and black satin—his habit of wearing no hat on a shock of rough, light brown hair, all created a sensation; and further acquaintance brought no decline in anyone's interest.

"We should, perhaps, get up a testimonial," Ashley said, "thanking England for this diversion." He despised Sabre. Why? Because he painted for a precarious living? There spoke American barbarity.

The man was virile and to spare. Tall, rangy, his bones emphasized by abstemious living, he reminded Elizabeth faintly of Ambrose Bohannon. Except in speech. When he talked, everything shone with the inimitable polish of the highborn, well-schooled Britisher.

"Hearing him," Elizabeth said to her husband, "is like reading a book."

"Much better," Ashley said. "More fascinating?"

"Oh!" Elizabeth fretted. "I'm not one of the sillies. I'm not charmed by him."

The way she said charmed turned up the corners of Ashley's mouth.

"I am glad to hear it," he said. "Who engaged him to do your portrait?"

"Why, nobody. That is, he asked if he might try. He's doing a number that way—to get the work. Nobody is under obligation to buy his paintings."

"Hmm!" Ashley said.

Lily Foxe had brought him to Elizabeth. Lily, Elizabeth knew, would derive some profit from any sales the painter should make. By performing all sorts of services to the shifting population of Washington, Lily now earned, over a year, a sum exceeding her husband's legitimate salary. She would rent houses, she would purchase carpeting and draperies and furniture for those houses at attractive prices. She would arrange parties, order the food and the flowers and the extra servants, for newcomers strange to the capital's ways. All on a commission. So far Elizabeth had done no business through her, but she recognized a Foxe proposition when she encountered it.

"I see no harm in sitting for him," Elizabeth said to Ashley, "and you seemed to raise no objection."

"I haven't any now," Ashley said. "His loose way of doing business is, no doubt, part of being an artist. So long as you are not charmed by him or he by you—"

Elizabeth would not have taken her oath on the last stipulation; but, again, where was the harm? A woman whose reason for being was her power of fascination should overlook no field of practice. The "artist fellow," as Ashley called him, was far less dull than many another to whom she was equally kind. As to Ashley's objections, if any, they came late. He had been present that first afternoon, when Lily, using her sly approach, asked if she might bring a stranger to tea. Not willingly present and not continuously. He liked Lily Foxe less and less as time went on, but he was curious about the stranger. Then, before anyone knew what was happening, Sabre had out his sketchbook. Did they mind if he worked as they talked? His hands had the habit of being busy.

"But in this?" Elizabeth protested. She had not bothered to dress for Lily, meaning that she had not made a *grande toilette*. She wore, not one of her "fluffs," but the next thing to it by her present standards. It was the vogue just then, a part of the passionate interest in tariff and home manufactures, for ladies to use cotton textiles wher-

ever possible. Elizabeth's at-home frock was of New England gingham, of excellent quality and modishly made, but hardly a thing by
which a lady high in the world of fashion would want to be known.
Susanna had arranged her hair becomingly. She wore then a high
braided bun on top of her head, with curls forward of her ears. She
had tied her favorite double ruche of lace about her slender throat
and kept a light shawl handy, because the day was chilly and the
mantel fire not just adequate; but the entire effect was the extreme
of simplicity.

"Charming," Sabre said, in his bold, direct way. "If I want to paint
a creation, I can always arrange for a dressmaker's showing."

If she had had any idea of the purpose already shaping in his
thought . . . but she could be wrong about that. He might not have
known his own intention at the time. They fell to talking. Presently
about Boonslick. It was the name of the place. Daniel Boone, like
Pocahontas, to a foreigner was a legend; and any suggested connection with him provoked curiosity. A touch of spite colored Elizabeth's chatter as obligingly she shaped her tales to satisfy this interest.
She told of a duel with axes in the square at Boonville, of the ferryman there who had to build new landings every year but always
had driftwood for timber, of the monument ordered for the grave
of a first settler and how the brawling river had washed away the
graveyard before the stone could be placed, so that it was good finally
only for another settler's steprock. She told of wagon trains moving
west, of Captain Sublette's mule trains coming home; and Sabre
stopped her.

"For all that," he said, "I have only to open a book. Washington
Irving or any other traveler. Tell me about your life in that amazing
country, your home, your people. What, for example, is a steprock?"

Still with a high spice of humor, she told then of her father, how
he was by training and gift an able physician but was more interested in his acres and horses and distillery than in his profession,
of her sharp-spoken lady mother who had once lived on the James
River in Virginia and had been kissed by Lord Cornwallis. She
told how these, and others like them, dreamed of making a new
and richer Virginia in this far land and how near they had come
to doing so and yet how far also they were from their mark. She
told of picnics and barbecues and Fourth of July and itinerant preach-
ers, of Pomegranate, their cook, of Barcie Harris and Barcie's
father, of Colonel Gentry and the little town of Columbia, how
the settlers there, disappointed finally in their hopes of commercial
prosperity, had decided that all along they had meant the town to

be the seat of learning and culture. All was told in light mockery; but Boonslick came alive for her, as well as for the stranger—the folds of hills, the green valleys, the flowering prairie, the tawny river and gravelly creeks, the dear, friendly people. She rattled on, led by hungry fascination on the Briton's homely features; and his pencil raced to keep up with the lights and shadows over her face.

"And out of all that, you!" he said at last, resting.

"And Mr. Ashley," she reminded him.

"No," he contradicted. "I beg your pardon, but I'm afraid not. He could live there, he could call the place home, be devoted to it and yet remain an outsider, while another, from equally far away, could gather it all to him and be part of the land, as if he had never known any other. I know."

How did he know? She had said nothing of a young man named Wilcox.

"You were happy there," Sabre said.

"I'm happier here," she insisted.

"I doubt that," he said.

If she had only known, if she had dreamed . . .

"What do you do with the sketches you accumulate?" Ashley asked that day, as Sabre tied up his portfolio.

"Some of them," he acknowledged, "are no good—waste. Some are useful. Some we keep, for our private store."

This was the beginning of a lively and busy winter season. That it was especially busy for Robert Sabre was proved by the exhibition he held of his work when spring came. He rented a house for the purpose, Lily Foxe helping him find one on I Street, near Pennsylvania Avenue. Elizabeth went with Lily to the first showing, open only to patrons and high officialdom. That was enough.

Naturally Elizabeth's curiosity was centered in her own portrait. Would it be a gratifying climax to two winters' effort to be as charming as the new social circle that had opened to receive her? Would she be proud of it, hung high on a wall, for everyone to see? She hoped, but she couldn't be sure. Perversely Robert Sabre would seldom allow her to look at his work after a sitting. He would put her off, saying she might not like the painting in the rough and her disappointment would be death to his inspiration.

"Are you inspired?" she had asked him one day.

"If I am not," he answered grimly, "I never shall be."

And now, at last! With equal perversity, Lily, who had helped with the placing of the pictures, started off at the opposite end of the

142

show. The work, even to Elizabeth's impatience, was impressive. There were many portraits, the most notable being one of General Winfield Scott, later purchased by Congress, and those of Daniel Webster and John C. Calhoun, purchased by subscription in their respective states—to the profit of the artist and Lily Foxe. He had painted other ladies of the capital—very flatteringly. Now, surely . . .

No, there was another room to be done first. It held samples of work Sabre had brought to Washington with him. Impressive but hardly of burning interest. After that, there was a grouping of more casual sketches, presenting odd corners of the capital—a gambling house and oyster bar near the Capitol, with a too recognizable figure coming out the door, the slough that was most of Pennsylvania Avenue on a muddy day, Thomas Jefferson's avenue of poplars, all tattered and torn, the north door of the President's House, market day in Georgetown Heights. All diabolically clever, but . . .

"I think you are purposely leading me all around," Elizabeth charged.

She was certain of the maneuver when she saw her picture. It hung in a small parlor to the left of the entrance hall. They could have begun right there. It was not a large painting, nothing like as imposing as those of the statesmen, and thank Heaven for that. It was conspicuous enough. If other work was grouped in the same room, Elizabeth did not see it. One look, and she wanted to drop through the floor, carrying the portrait with her.

"How dared he?" she said. "How did he dare?"

"You don't like it?" Lily cooed.

"I . . ." Elizabeth choked. Tears sparkled in her eyes but anger burned them away. "This is not . . . I thought . . ."

Her formal sittings in Sabre's studio and lately at the hotel had been in the latest Bridport creation, a dreamy frock of corn-yellow silk, with clouds of Mechlin lace. She had worn her emeralds. She had looked a queen—a young queen, but regal enough.

"You know this isn't the picture he was working on," she said when she could speak. "What became of that?"

"He burned it," Lily told her. "Just last week. In a towering temper. Then, of course, he had to work like fury to get this ready."

Those sketches he had made that first afternoon at the National, of her in her country gingham, prattling of Boonslick!

"My dear," Lily said, "control yourself. What if Robert should come in? He would be crushed."

"My feelings, I suppose, don't count," Elizabeth said.

"Don't be an idiot, darling. It's lovely, really."

But that was what hurt—the exquisite beauty of the woman in the portrait—a young creature, imperishably young, slender, winsome, appealing, laughter on her face fighting a threat of sorrow, a cloudy something in the wide, eloquent eyes, petulance tugging at the sweet, full mouth, the costume in its simplicity taking nothing from the woman's radiant charm. But all of this indescribably bitter to the taste of the woman who looked on. How had Sabre dared? How had he known?

A brass plate under the painting labeled it "The Honorable Mrs. William Henry Ashley." That was a lie. Mrs. Ashley stood before the picture in lustrous silk and a wide-brimmed Leghorn hat—thank Heaven for that hat!—and nobody, among her friends or her few enemies, would have thought she could possibly have sat for that painting. They would say, "Really? Well, she may have looked like that once, but she doesn't now. Beautiful still, of course, but in a different way."

"You like it?" Elizabeth said to Lily Foxe.

"It's the best thing in the whole exhibit," Lily declared.

Was it truly?

"I'm sorry," Elizabeth said, choking. "I suppose I'm not the one to say. If you will excuse me now, I think I've seen enough. I have the beginnings of a headache. No, don't come with me. I am sure you meant to stay on."

"You're leaving without speaking to Robert?"

"Give him a message from me, if you will. Say I shall be obliged if he will call on me at my hotel at his earliest leisure."

What she would say to him she hardly knew, but the painting must come down. She would not have people murmuring over it, laughing, coming to her, perhaps, with questions. Pulling the brim of her hat down over her face, she hurried away, thankful for meeting nobody who recognized her. Her narrowest escape was from Ashley himself in the entrance hall. Blinded now by tears, Elizabeth did not see him; and he, talking to another visitor, missed her. Lily Foxe saw the near encounter, held her breath until she was sure Elizabeth was gone, then shrugged her shoulders and retreated.

"You deceived me!" Elizabeth accused Sabre the next morning at the hotel. She was splendid in full costume then. "You know I would never have consented to your hanging that picture."

"I suppose it was a sort of deception," Sabre granted. "I didn't know it would displease you so. Will you tell me why it does?"

"No," she said. "If you were clever enough to do the painting, you

144

know why I dislike it. The woman you drew and want to show to the world no longer exists."

"My dear girl," Sabre said, startled, "that's where you're wrong. In our parlance, she's been painted over considerably, but she's still there."

No. She was gone. That was what hurt.

"Mr. Sabre, I didn't ask you here to discuss my character but to do business. I want to buy the portrait."

"You?"

"Does that surprise you?" she asked. "I assure you I can."

She had a little money. How much exactly, she couldn't say. After Daniel's death, she had put the disposal of their Columbia property into her father's hands. When she married Ashley, Dr. Moss had tried to give her an accounting, but she had refused to listen. Would he take the money, to please her? He could use it for some improvement on his farm. Perhaps Miss Mary would like to revisit Virginia. There were Elizabeth's brothers to be educated. With gentle obstinacy Dr. Moss had said no to every suggestion.

"I know you've no need for the money now, Betsy. I hope you never will have; but, if a time should come when you'd like to have it, why, there it will be. God knows and you know I'm no financier; but I will try to put it where it will be safe and gather a little interest. It belongs to you and the girls and it shall be yours on demand. At any time."

Out of the past, on another occasion, she heard the same gentle voice protesting, "All that for a hat, daughter?" She brushed the warning aside. If it took every cent of the money, she would use it to buy the portrait. She could think of no other way to hide it from public view. She would give it to her father. It was suitable only for one of his pure, doting affection. He would hang it—where? In the great room of the double log house? No. In his office study where he kept his books and boots and lancets, where only those should see it who were allowed to see those other things that were his alone.

"I am sorry," Sabre said. "I seem destined to give offense where none is or has been intended. The portrait is not for sale."

She could not believe him now and said so.

"I'm sorry," he repeated. He, too, looked as if he had slept badly through the night just ended. "I wish it could be for the reason you suspect. I wish I could afford to keep it myself—for what solace it might give when this time past is only an old man's memory. The truth is, I can't afford even that. I've gone deeply into debt here in your country. And now I must leave sooner than I expected. You see, I've given displeasure elsewhere, too."

She forgot her confused anger for a second. Who, besides herself?

"In not just the same way," he explained. "This is a general offense. Those impromptu sketches and water colors I made of the town. They're too good, it seems. And too many of us Britons have visited your shores and done the same sort of thing. We've a way of pointing out flaws, of caricaturing what often we secretly admire or even envy."

But that was what he had done in her case. Not a caricature, perhaps, but equally presumptuous—satirical, judging.

"A committee of resident congressmen," Sabre said, "waited on our ambassador, one of them claiming he recognized himself in an unbecoming environment; and the upshot was that I am to be allowed to keep the exhibition open the remainder of the week, making what profit I can, on condition that as soon as possible afterward I ship out."

Almost Elizabeth said, "I'm sorry." Out of the habit of politeness. She was not sorry. It served the man right. And yet, her conscience squirmed. His face was haggard. Restlessly he walked over to a stand in the corner of the room, and his sack coat rose up in the middle of his back as if overnight he had developed a hump. He picked up an ornament and laid it down. He turned again to her.

"You see, I was in no position to turn down an offer for the picture." He smiled then on the edge of a yawn. "It was a handsome offer."

"You sold my portrait?" She was horrified. "But who . . . ?"

Except for two reasons, she would have known at once it was Ashley; but it was not his way to put down money for something he did not want; and she was sure he would not like this painting any better than she did it if he saw it. She still did not know that he had seen it. The other reason was just money. Not Ashley money, everybody's. The nation was in a state of financial unrest. It stemmed from the refusal of the Jackson administration to renew the charter of the great national bank at Philadelphia, established by Alexander Hamilton, in which since Hamilton's time all of the money collected by the federal government had been deposited. It was the Jacksonian theory that for one bank to hold so much money gave it and the government too much power over the nation's business. So the bank had been destroyed by the lapse of its charter and the withdrawal of the government deposits, which had then been distributed among various state banks in favor with the administration. The ultimate result nobody could foresee, but the immediate one was wild confusion. Nobody knew whose money was worth anything, unless it was gold or silver, called Benton's Mint Drops because the Senator went about with a sack of coins, preaching specie payment. "Old Bullion," people called Benton now.

How did Elizabeth know all this? Not from William Ashley. For all that he let on to her, his money still flowed in some magic, inexhaustible stream. She had only to wish for something—sometimes not even that was needed. However, if he was not concerned about money right now, he was the only one in the nation. The most indulged wife had only to keep her ears open in public to go home and have frightening dreams. Still . . .

"I am not at liberty to name the purchaser," Sabre said. "I will tell you this much. He is a great admirer of yours—poor devil!"

That settled it. It was not Ashley. Nobody had ever called him a poor devil. Still, it could be nobody else. But why?

He came in just then; and she made a show of affectionate welcome, taking his hat and turning her cheek for a kiss.

"I am so glad you're here," she said. "Mr. Sabre called to say goodbye. He's leaving at the end of the week. Did you know?"

"I heard," Ashley said.

Such a fuss about a picture! It disappeared. If Ashley had bought it, he said nothing to Elizabeth about it and she chose not to ask. The whole subject had best be forgotten; as it was, in the whirl of another Washington season. Robert Sabre, too, was all but forgotten. He must have done very well, after all. At least, Lily Foxe returned to the capital with a new wardrobe which she had not fashioned for herself. There was a striped silk pelisse, quilted; there was a visiting dress of dark red moiré, the full skirt pleated into the waistband. There was an air of accomplishment about Lily's dark, secretive self. Could it be true that Mr. Van Buren might be the next President?

Sitting in the parlor of the Ashley suite one late winter afternoon, Elizabeth looked up to find her husband studying her absorbedly.

"Mercy, Mr. A., how you startled me! I didn't hear you come in."

"I'm sorry, my dear. Will this atone?"

A jeweler's box slipped over her shoulder into her lap. She recognized the crest embossed on green velveteen.

"What in the world?" she said. "Christmas is over."

"New Year's Day just ahead," he reminded her. "Open it."

Her bracelets! Hers, because they matched the emerald necklace.

"You shouldn't have!" she said, softly gloating.

At least, that was how Ashley read her bemused expression. He

147

was pleased, then disturbed by it. Ought he to tell her specifically why he had bought the bracelets? Under a continued show of lavishness, he, too, was guarding his expenditures these days. The money situation was bad. The bank of which he was a director in St. Louis teetered on the brink of a most uncertain future. Only one thing was in his favor. Money unrest made land more valuable—good, solid land; and that made the sound basis of his fortune. Land—even the government, anxious to know how much public land was now at its disposal, was behind a movement to clear old titles, validate old claims. He would be a richer man than ever once that business was cleared up; and, of course, that was his reason for being in Washington.

His work there was now all but finished. This would be his last term in Congress, though Elizabeth did not know. The bracelets were to make the telling easier, but still he delayed. A little premature to fret her, if she chose to be annoyed. Anyhow, he had had to buy the bracelets. When the jeweler opened his display, that Foxe woman had reached for them with her velvet eyes. He wouldn't have supposed she had their price, but a man never knew. He had bought them at once, and a pair of drop earrings to match, to be reserved for another occasion.

Libby—his beautiful, spoiled darling! How would she take it when he told her he was about to whisk her away to that baronial castle he had dreamed all these years of building? Not a minute too soon for the rescue, he felt. Damn that artist and his painting! That had shown him what was happening to Elizabeth. It had been fun to spoil her, but now . . .

He drew up a chair beside her, opened the bracelet, and snapped it on her wrist. He would have knelt beside her, except that he had never gone on his knees to anyone; and now it would seem ludicrous. The more so because he might find it difficult to rise with grace from such a posture. Advancing age was something to which he had given little thought until lately. Now, a twinge here, a stiffness there began to sound a warning. All the more reason for him to step out of the national picture and begin to realize certain dreams of living. He could not afford delay.

He thought of that, as he held his wife's small, firm hand; and he thought, too, what a lovely hand it was, how delicately and perfectly joined to wrist and arm bones. A lady's hand and arm—the prettiest he had ever seen. The prettiest lady in the land, he thought still, the sweetest wife. She did not love him with the wild abandon of a girl. She never had. There had been a time when he had fretted over that, as there had been a time when, without warning, she would draw away; but gradually there had been less and less withdrawing, and finally none. Duty, increasing respect and deepening regard, a natural tendency to add affection to liking, had built up another sort of love. She turned to him in any difficulty; she relied on him. She was wholly his now. He couldn't be mistaken in that. Some men with wives so beautiful, and popular, were uneasy. He was not. The nearest he had come to that sort of vexation was in the case of that artist. Fortunately, however, in some way the man had offended Libby, too; and that was all there was to that.

Still holding her hand in one of his, with the other he turned the bracelet, so that a chain, which was part of the design, lay on top.

"Bracelets— Do you suppose they are a sort of fancified fetters?"

She laughed at the notion but did not deny it.

"Caesar leading Cleopatra in chains?" she said lightly. "But a woman without such fetters is a sorry spectacle, don't you think?"

"I do, indeed; but I didn't know you did."

She drew her hand away then; but it was only to take up the second bracelet and fasten it on her arm, then hold both up to her own admiration.

"You are too generous," she said, as she had said many times before. "You think of almost everything before the wish takes shape in my mind."

"Almost?" he said. "Where have I missed?"

"It would be monstrous to suggest anything right now."

"Out with it," he commanded, never dreaming that she could name the one thing he could not and would not give her. "You'll never have me more at your mercy."

"Well—" still she hesitated and he should have been warned— "ever since our second season here, I've had in mind, I've wished that we could take a house in Washington."

The one thing—absolutely the one thing. Harsh denial all but burst from him. Control had never been harder.

"Instead of the hotel?" he temporized; but she saw his agitation.

"There!" she said. "I knew I shouldn't mention it."

"But I thought you liked the hotel. You're free to go and come. No housekeeping worries."

"I know. It's perfect in many ways, but . . . I don't mind keeping house. Really. It need not be a large house."

"A small one wouldn't satisfy you—or me." He tried to laugh.

"Oh, but I mean it. A small house, nicely furnished but simple. It would be a place where we could entertain."

He had it. It was that Kentucky crowd she had got in with. At first, following the supper at the Clays', he had been glad. They were real folks, her kind and his, much better for her than that giddy set with which she whirled in company with Lily Foxe. But this house idea—

"It would be better for your dyspepsia," she coaxed; and he winced. It annoyed him to have her note that his old trouble was upon him with renewed force. It was all but impossible not to have dyspepsia in Washington. Late hours, rich food: *"The Virginia mutton is exceptional this evening, Mr. Ashley. Do pass your plate. . . . Help yourself and your lady to some of that juicy mongrel goose at your end of the table. Or would you prefer a bit of kidney?"* But the terrapin was the worst. There were more ways of cooking terrapin than there were shellbacks in the Chesapeake sloughs, each way more indigestible than the one before. Still, he did not like to be reminded of his dyspepsia, least of all by his superbly healthy young wife. She would be at great pains, he teased, establishing her reputation for a good table. Only the other day someone had mentioned those pies she had baked for Mrs. Clay. Then he recalled who had spoken of them and studied Elizabeth's face. She was still admiring her bracelets.

"Representatives in Congress seldom bother with houses," he told her. "Their tenure of office is brief and can be snapped off too easily." He went on swiftly, before she could say that he was secure in his place as long as he had a mind to keep it. "Some senators prefer a hotel. The Crittendens are in rooms."

Modest ones at that. A matter of taste possibly, but more probably a matter of means. John Jordan Crittenden, against his wife's better judgment and, it might be, his own, had returned to Washington to fill out the unexpired term of his good friend, Senator Bibb. Chances were, he'd be elected to a full term in 1836.

"The Crittendens are no sign," Elizabeth said. "Mrs. Crittenden lives here only by sufferance. She almost never goes out, never entertains."

Ah! Estimable woman, Mrs. Crittenden. Intelligent, pleasant, a great sense of duty . . . but would he want her for a wife? No. He objected to women who ruled, no matter how gently or wisely. Now, how . . .

"I know what you're thinking," Elizabeth said. "With that great house in St. Louis standing empty most of the year, another one here would be extravagant."

He sighed. Elizabeth had never liked the St. Louis house, never been happy there. At first she had seemed almost frightened. Later a restlessness possessed her. She showed herself at her worst there, if she had a worst. She would fill every vase with flowers from the garden, then, before the blossoms drooped, order them all emptied. She moved the furniture about, replaced some, but was never pleased with the results. She paraded her beautiful gowns at balls and receptions. To smaller groups she chattered merrily of Washington and its great folk. She sang her gay songs at the piano, enchanting every male present —Sublette with the dust of the trail dry in his throat, Campbell, his eyes weary of figures on an accounting sheet, Dr. Farrar, who had always a soft heart for a pretty woman, even that stern man of affairs, James Tower Sweringen—but chilling all the women. She couldn't help it. A wayward demon drove her.

"If we, if you," she said now, "could lease that house, with the rental we could take a house here. The maintenance would be less than our hotel bills. For the little time we spend in St. Louis each year, a small place would do. No?"

Without meaning to, he must have shaken his head in the negative. No, in St. Louis or here or anywhere, a small house would not do for him. She sighed now, and, not too hopefully, brought out her final argument.

"We could have the girls here with us. Mamma does not mind the care of them, but she is not too strong just now."

That was true. The winter Dr. and Mrs. Moss had spent in St. Louis had not been a happy experiment. Miss Mary had been feverishly excited at the prospect of urban life, of seeing people, her kind of people, but had discovered that years spent in the dull serenity of Boone County had unfitted her for existence less tranquil. Now, except for bright summers spent with Elizabeth at a lakeside resort, the children lived in Boone County with, of all things, a governess.

"Washington would be such an advantage for them," Elizabeth pleaded.

Ashley was not so sure. What the move would accomplish would be to offer Washington a new and delightful picture of the Honorable Mrs. William Ashley. His Libby never looked so charming as she did with her two girls. She was a sweet, devoted mother; but . . . his thoughts paused and doubled back. Just whom did she want to impress with a hidden virtue? The Crittendens? No. She had had the idea of a house before she knew them. Nevertheless, for the first time since their marriage, jealousy laid discomforting hold on his emotions.

Was it the first time? There had been her devotion to her first husband, the memory bravely masked, but too slowly relinquished.

There had been the fleeting episode of that British painter. Now what? Some frustration on his own part, some defeat. He had said to himself that she was wholly his. Had she ever been that? Would she ever be? On impulse, he unfastened the bracelets, and hated it because there was a barely visible tremor in his hands as he did so.

"You needn't wear them if you don't like them," he said.

"But I adore them." Her eyes questioned him. "I am sorry I spoke of the house, since it does not seem practical right now."

Not now or next year or ever, and he should have said so, because her graceful withdrawal did not mean abandonment of her wish; but he lacked the heart to deliver a final, crushing "No!" That did not mean that he, on his part, had abandoned his plan or purpose. Give up his lifetime dream of retiring like a feudal lord to his own proud acres—land which he had now been twenty years in acquiring? No woman, no man, not even his sweet Libby could persuade him to that.

Still he waited to tell her.

CHAPTER FIVE

Bitter Waters

WHITE SULPHUR SPRINGS in the flush of early summer. The White Sulphur, high on the James River and Kanawha Turnpike; and even the weather favored the Ashleys in a roundabout and potentially arduous journey homeward. It rained at night or ahead of them just enough to turn the dust of the well-traveled road into a soft brown carpet, which sometimes adhered to the wheels of the carriage and gave Poke extra work on the horses' coats, but was never really mud. They rolled down the avenue of trees at the Springs in excellent style, Poke cajoling the horses, assuring them that they could rest now for a long week—rest from climbing, on this stage of the journey —nothing to do but eat and roll. Susanna up front beside him, in charge of Elizabeth's personal portmanteau, said, "Hmp!" She hated mountains going up or down. Twice in every year Elizabeth had to reason with her.

"Susanna, you can't travel from east to west or west to east in this nation without striking mountains somewhere. Sit still and nothing will happen. What if, like your mammy, you had to do them on foot?"

"Miss Libby, on foot is the bes' way." Susanna was struggling hard with niceties of speech right now. "And when Mammy got there, dar she was!"

"You don't have to travel with us, Susanna. I can arrange for another maid." So she could have, but she would have hated to do so.

"Miss Libby, I goes where you does and stays where you stay—wherever dat is."

Other journeys, as far as the Ohio and steamboats, they had used a hired coach and post horses, changed at every halt. This time, on a whim, Ashley had decreed that they would travel in their own carriage, following the James River through Tidewater Virginia. It would be a long journey and the carriage would suffer, but a coach builder in St. Louis could repair the damage. They would stop frequently to rest the horses.

Elizabeth was enchanted. In a week they had a dozen invitations for visits along the way; and they must, of course, stop at Dover on the James to see her mother's home and her people. And Mr. Ashley's sisters? Didn't they live in that part of Virginia? He would want to see them? What? Oh! Oh, yes. Yes. He agreed to everything. Just so they reached home before summer was over. He had business in St. Louis, if she recalled.

It had been a happy journey, through a smiling country set with smiling, friendly people. Elizabeth still glowed with the pleasant warmth of it. Dover had seemed smaller, something less impressive than her mother remembered; but the uncles and aunts and cousins were sweet, protecting her against a chill she took from her encounter with the Ashley women—Sister Martha and Sister Nancy. The former a spinster and the latter a widow, they lived together on a plantation in Powhatan County, which Sister Martha in person managed, doing the actual work of an overseer, while Sister Nancy ran the house. The plantation was smaller than a New Madrid grant in Missouri, but it was land; and they were gentry—women with handsome, dark eyes, a bit dowdy in dress, a little rusty in their middle years, fiercely proud of "Brother," and equally suspicious of "Brother's" lady. Brother, they agreed, had done well. He was a man of consequence. He had made money, but there'd be mighty little of it left when "she" got through.

But now White Sulphur. Mountain laurel, blushing pink on encircling wooded hills, the valley fresh in new green. White buildings peeping out under dark trees. A savor of wood smoke on clear air, and something more, not yet definable. Rocking chairs suddenly still on a long veranda and their host hurrying, with swinging coattails, to welcome them. Knowing who they were without being told. Just knowing. That was a landlord's business. Poke saying to the boys at the horses' heads, "Don' need to hold 'em. Dey'll stan'."

"Mr. Ashley, Mrs. Ashley, glad to see you. We've been expecting you. Ah, before you step down, may I say I have reserved choice rooms for you in the main building, which some prefer because of its convenience, but also a cottage, in case you would prefer privacy and less noise, though of a cheerful sort. There is dancing every night but Sunday in the main lodge."

"The cottage by all means," Ashley said, "if it is comfortable."

"Exceedingly so, sir. A two bedroom cottage in Virginia Row? With its own veranda and all conveniences furnished. Most families choose a cottage, but occasionally a lady complains of loneliness."

"I won't be lonely," Elizabeth assured him.

"Ah? Ah . . . no, madame, I am sure you will not."

"I mean," she said, as Ashley laughed, "I have lived in wilderness country and so— Mr. Nestle, what is that odd, salty smell in the air?"

"Do you notice it? Madame has sharp senses. That, madame, is the fragrance of our health-giving waters. I will send a pitcher to the cottage."

She might have known, but she wouldn't believe it.

A Greek temple, a pillared shrine rising above a marble-lined octagonal pool, from which rose a Stygian stench. Or, it would have been a stench except for what an earlier visitor had called a strong infusion of fashion.

"You do not take the waters, Mrs. Ashley?"

"No. We have an agreement in our household. Mr. Ashley drinks the waters and I do the strolling and the dancing."

"Now, what are you up to, Mr. A.?"

"This morning, my dear, I am making a tour of the waters."

"You mean—there are more springs—besides this one?"

He laughed at her. He was in exceptional spirits these days. The waters? Possibly. More probably some new scheme was hatching in his active brain or some old scheme was prospering. She knew him well enough to recognize that; but what the scheme might be, or in what field of endeavor, she couldn't say. Partly because she gave the matter little thought. For four years now, she had schooled herself to give first attention to the brightness of new possessions, new adventures, and a minimum of consideration to small annoyances that might increase in importance if encouraged. The schooling had not been arduous. The brightness had been very bright and she avid to enjoy it; but now it had become habit to fend off unpleasantness. Was she to allow mineral waters and any association they had with things past to spoil her holiday?

"Have you been here three days," Ashley mocked, "and nobody has invited you to make the tour? There are, indeed, other springs—Red Sulphur, Green Sulphur—"

"Ugh!" she said, shuddering.

"Hot Springs," Ashley continued. "Warm Springs. It is a pleasant drive, I am told. Will you join me? The horses are rested now and should have exercise."

"Thank you, no. If you discover a Sweet Springs, you might mark the location and I shall drive there with a basket of jugs and bottles. What is called sweet water here still seems to me to have too much flavor. As for the rest, take a saddle horse, if you prefer riding. Poke

155

can walk the carriage horses for their exercise—and his. He has need of some activity other than throwing dice with the other grooms and coachmen." Though he increased his political acquaintance mightily by those methods.

"How will you amuse yourself?" Ashley asked.

"I?" she said. "Well, I shall have to make the morning pilgrimage to the Shrine, I suppose, just to give notice that I am still here and able to be abroad. I shall walk to the dining room for my dinner and back to the cottage, then remove my shoes, to dust them, and my dress likewise. After that, Susanna and I have a task of mending. This combination of rusticity and high fashion is ruinous to one's wardrobe. The ballroom floor has splinters and my slippers prove it. The woodland paths are delightful, though dusty at times; and the briars, although the brush has been cleared, know when a lady is passing. Why do you look at me so?" she finished, disturbed by something in his scrutiny.

"Am I looking at you—so?" Ashley asked. "How? I am, as always, your devoted and obedient husband."

"I grant the devotion," she said, "but, obedient? To whom, please?"

To nobody but himself. It was a good self. That alone saved the situation. She turned her cheek for his good-bye kiss and sent him off on a tour of the waters.

The damnable, elegant, treacherous, putrid waters!

It was their last night at the White Sulphur. Tomorrow they would proceed over the turnpike towards Parkersburg and the Ohio, steamboats, and finally home. Home? Sadness tugged at her heart beginning with the first dance. "Money Musk" on a Negro's violin could sound a lament. She bowed, she smiled, she passed, she promenaded. She waltzed. Mr. John Tyler of the James River and Richmond was a marvelous leader of a cotillion and equally good at the waltz.

"We shall miss you," he said.

"I hope you will," she conceded.

"Washington will hardly be the same without the Ashleys."

Washington without— What did he mean?

"You must not let your husband bury you too deeply in the fastnesses of Missouri."

She counted her steps carefully, her heart in sudden dire panic.

"Though, of course, I wish him well in his race for Governor."

The violins screeched, the piano sounded like a tin tub being thumped. His race for Governor . . . and this was how she learned of it? She murmured that she and Mr. Ashley were obliged to Mr. Tyler for his good wishes. She finished the dance. She sank gracefully into her chair among the chaperons and opened her fan. Bury her? She wanted to die.

"Where," a fat voice near by asked—it had to be fat, coming from that expanded creature—"shall you live when your husband is Governor of Missouri? I am ashamed to say I don't know the name of the state capital."

Who except a Missourian would know? How should she answer? Why had some warning not come to her of this before now? What had she talked about with these women before the dancing began? She could not remember.

"You seem very sure that Mr. Ashley will be elected," she managed.

"I supposed there could be no doubt of that," the woman answered.

Probably there was none. Mr. Robert Letcher of Frankfort, Kentucky, close friend and neighbor of the Crittendens, bowed before her, claiming her for a quadrille. She was tempted to beg off, to retire right then for the evening, if Mr. Letcher would be good enough to look for Mr. Ashley, who was probably in the cardroom. Before she could shape her speech, Letcher drew her to her feet.

"The first time I've had the honor or the privilege," he said. "Come."

And then, as they took their places on the floor, he murmured for her ear alone, "Smile! Did that old—did—? Was something said back yonder to offend you?"

The Honorable Robert Letcher was one of the most likable men in the Kentucky representation. In refreshing contrast to most other men, he boasted of a lowly origin, declared that, when he was first seated in the Kentucky legislature, most of his pride came from finding himself inside walls for which he had helped to make and lay the brick. A man of means now and of position, he had a lovely wife in Frankfort whom he reverently called "The Queen"; and the homage he paid her he was likely to transfer in a measure to any other lady he admired. Elizabeth smiled at the form of his question.

"No," she said. "Not really. She was bidding me farewell to Washington, with too much satisfaction, perhaps."

He did not answer at once. When he did, his tone was sympathetic, not surprised. So, he, too, knew!

"Tell me," he began; but the music called them into the maze of a dance figure. "Tell me," he repeated, as they promenaded.

"Later," she said, glad that the dance was lively, that it took her

157

breath and colored her cheeks. Everybody in this room knew what she did not. Why? Why had Ashley kept the truth from her? Habitually, he did not discuss projected acts with anybody, male or female; but this seemed more deliberate concealment. He must have known that she would be broken-hearted at the tidings. He did know. That was why he had not spoken. Not that her heartache would dissuade him from his intentions. For a man of his size he could stand with more rock firmness than any other she had encountered.

I wanted you to look at a man who gets everything he wants.

The dance was over.

"It's a mild night," Letcher said. "Would you risk your good name and stroll with me outside?"

"A fig for my good name," she said. "What of yours?"

"Mine was won or lost a long time ago. Come."

Outside a light breeze stirred the trees and caressed her hot cheeks without cooling them. Here, where nobody could see, tears burned in her eyes.

"How is it," she asked before Letcher could question her, "that those women know what nobody is supposed to have heard?"

"After four years in Washington you ask me that?" Letcher countered. "My dear, I didn't give out the news, I swear. I had it, I'll tell you that, in a letter from John Crittenden, which I haven't shared with a soul but meant to do so with you, because he sent you a message."

Momentarily her turmoil subsided, then doubled. People like the Crittendens . . . never to see them again?

"John said in effect, 'I hear from reliable sources in Missouri that Mr. Ashley will be named as a candidate for Governor of that state, whether with or without his consent, my informant neglected to say. I presume that means the Ashleys will not return to Washington this winter. Congress will lose an able Representative in Mr. Ashley and the society of the Capital lose its most charming lady. Mrs. Ashley is a favorite with all who know her. Please tell her for me—' but I will give you the letter. John has his own way of saying things. What is it? Have I blundered now?"

"No," she said quickly, "no."

She had hardly heard what he said. She had been thinking, "This lovely holiday, in this gay place—it was a sop to my hurt. He brought me here, knowing . . ." and then the breeze, flower and pine laden, had blown a whiff of sulphur her way; and everything came out cruelly clear. Even the roundabout journey through Virginia had not been purely to pleasure her. Ashley had wanted to visit the Springs, to compare them with those on land he owned in Missouri. That Chouteau Grant?

Of course, that was it. In four years of Washington, as Letcher had reminded her, she had gleaned from chance conversation, from a line here and there in newspapers, some idea now of Ashley's work in Congress. It had to do with public works, with public lands. Lands— How could she have been so blind? That wretched Indian grant! She supposed the title to it now was clear. That was why he was returning, with his maidservant and manservant, his wife, his horses, and his carriage.

"Mr. Letcher, I'm sorry. I meant this last evening to be so gay, but I find I can't feel anything but sad. I don't want to dance any more. Will you place a chair for me on the veranda and see if you can find my husband?"

Couldn't he see—or could he?—that her world was falling apart?

"I'd rather—" he said, and then, "Have you the next dance spoken for? Mr. Tyler? Good. He is probably looking for you now. While you're dancing, I'll try the cardroom and call Mr. Ashley out, even if he is winning."

Talk probably, to cover his perception of her suffering. He kept it up until they reached the doors of the ballroom. She swallowed her tears and smiled, but the bright lights hurt her eyes. The many-colored silks and jewels of the ladies were unreal as tinsel. Through a swimming haze she saw Mr. John Tyler of Virginia walking toward her, in the company of another gentleman. She blinked away the haze; and the second gentleman was Mr. Van Buren, the Vice President, the heir apparent, as everyone now called him, in seeming certainty that he would be elected to the presidency in the fall.

Wouldn't that be a day for Lily Foxe? She blinked again, fluttered her fan, and spread a more determined smile over helpless fury.

And now the dancing was over, at least for her. Back in the ball-room the musicians scraped away at "Sir Roger de Coverley" for the final reel. The night breeze carried a thin strain of the rhythmic measures to the Ashley cottage in Virginia Row. What Elizabeth could not hear she could supply from memory, having danced so often to the tune. And now, never again? Never again in such gay, light-hearted, important company? Oh, preposterous!

She waited impatiently while the boy who had lighted her and Ashley to the cottage touched a taper to shaded candles on the rough mantel above a cold hearthstone; and yet, when he was gone, what would she say? How would she begin? Her throat ached, as the tumult of her feelings—humiliation, chagrin, anger, alarm—crowded upward, demanding release.

"Shall I light de fiah?" the boy asked.

"Thank you, no." She marveled at her clear, firm tone, a tremble under the words not showing. "It's warm enough. Our people will see the light here and be along."

A dim light, but visible; and she was thankful for the dimness. She would try not to clamor like a fishwife; but, oh, God, it would have been good to do just that! Ashley gave the boy a coin and put him out the door. She clasped her hands tightly together. Now!

"Letcher said you had a headache. I'm sorry, my dear."

"You know it wasn't that. You know why I couldn't finish the dancing." The tremolo was there now. She flung her hands wide. "Why didn't you tell me?"

"Tell you what?" It was his way to move cautiously.

"You know," she said. "Why didn't you tell me that you had no idea of returning to Washington? Does it seem fair? I feel such a fool."

"Would you have enjoyed this visit more if you had known it was not to be repeated?" he asked.

He had her cornered already. What could she answer? That she would not have come? How would the fun of the past few weeks have looked, seen through tears? Frustration did not reduce her fury.

"I had thought," he said, "the time to tell you would be when you were at home, with your own dear ones about you. I wonder if you know—but no matter. It's this governor business, I suppose. You won't believe that that is almost as recent news to me as to those tattletales who've been at you? My friends arranged that for me in my absence. I've only just heard."

"Don't tell me," she cried, "that you've a letter in your pocket. Mr. Letcher has one in his pocket. Mr. Van Buren had a dispatch. I don't know what the ladies carry in their bosoms or their reticules, but everyone had the news, except me."

"And took pains to deliver it, each in his or her own way?" Ashley mocked. "Those are your dear friends to whom you hate to say good-bye? They've waited a long time to even the score with you. You've given them few openings, my dear. Yes, I had a letter on my way here —so recently that I knew I could carry the answer in person as fast as send it by post. And, of course, even if I consent to run, there is still the election."

But that was what she had said. He had still to be elected.

"Don't you want to be Governor?" she asked.

"I want it very much." Harshness grated in his deep tones. "I'd like to go down on the records as a governor of Missouri. I've tried for it before, but something or somebody stood in my way. Even now, I could be defeated. I've been away too long. I've lost touch."

"Mr. Ashley, you amaze me." She had to hurt him, if she could. "I always understood that you could have anything you really wanted."

"You understood wrong." The harshness was more noticeable. "The governorship of Missouri is only one of several things denied me. Would you care to hear about the others? One is the abiding love of a desirable woman. Once—a long time ago—I had that in my grasp; but I was young and so busy with other matters that it slipped from me. Since then—" he drew up his shoulders in a shrug and made a wry face.

"Mr. Ashley—"

"Let me finish. The other thing I've been denied is a family. A man's achievements dwindle when there is nobody of his blood to carry on his name."

"Mr. Ashley, I'm sure I've known my wifely duty. I have never—"

"I didn't say you had denied me any of these things. You've been wholly sweet and dear as a wife—warmly affectionate, tender; but then," his eyes flashed again, "I've never denied you much, either, have I?"

In the dim light the silk that was her dress shimmered. The deep, rich lace of its flouncing was soft to her touch. Her smooth, perfumed flesh was even softer. It was true that he had given her much, but to give so much and then ruthlessly to snatch it away! Her anger stiffened.

"There is a thing more precious to you than those others you have mentioned," she said. "Don't think I don't know what it is. You are not returning to Missouri, just to be chosen its Governor. You did not serve in Congress for that honor or purely to serve the nation. It was to serve some secret purpose of your own—to help manipulate laws that would give into your hand a piece of property that you coveted, which was never altogether yours until, perhaps, just lately— some conglomerate mass of earth and stone and water and trees."

"Libby!"

She had struck fire now.

"You didn't bring me to White Sulphur for my pleasure," she charged. "It was to compare the putrid waters here with the foul ones on that land. All my grown life, it seems to me, I've heard of those reeking springs. You don't know—"

"It's you who don't know what you're saying," he countered.

"Libby, I'm taking you home before it is too late. Libby," she had hurt as well as angered him, because he spoke pleadingly now, "once you said—to my surprise—that you liked the simple, beautiful way of life on your father's farm."

He remembered that. But, then, so did she.

"A person can't go back," she told him. "Nobody can turn life around like that—not even you." The idea of him, with his ideas of grandeur, talking about simple ways of living!

"I can try," he said.

Well, she hadn't supposed she could turn him from his purpose.

"Suppose I say I won't go?" she demanded. "To that wild land you own? If I had ever dreamed— You couldn't have deceived me more cruelly. I can't bear the thought of it. I won't endure it. I won't."

"What will you do?" he asked.

It was then that she began to hate William Ashley—only then. She had deceived neither herself nor him with any pretense of ardent love; but, from the first weeks of marriage, when she had had to school herself not to shrink away or show other signs of repulsion, she had come gradually to a substitute warmth of affection—at least a liking and a trust. This had been made possible only by a remolding of her whole personality, if not her character. This she had done, she thought, with Ashley's encouragement. Certainly he had provided the means. Now to ask her to toss all that aside, to go with him into exile, and that on the very ground . . .

"Oh, Daniel, Daniel! I called them putrid waters to you, too!"

But Elizabeth Wilcox would have made a heaven out of any land her husband walked. Elizabeth Ashley called for a special environment. Surely life and William Ashley had played her a cruel trick. And now to be taunted with her helplessness!

"I don't know," she said drearily to Ashley's question. "I don't know."

A footfall sounded on the path outside the cottage. She raised her head.

"Susanna," she said. "When she comes in, please send her to me in yonder. She will want to pack this dress for the journey."

With that, on legs that wobbled treacherously, she went into the second and smaller room of the cottage, and closed the door behind her. With finality. Let William Ashley now choose between the Chouteau Grant and her!

As anyone, including Elizabeth herself, might have anticipated, he chose the land. That night and later he made no attempt to intrude upon the seclusion into which Elizabeth now retreated. Publicly, when occasion demanded, she took her place by his side. Privately she kept to herself. On the journey westward the state in which the Ashleys traveled made seclusion easy to achieve. In St. Louis the mansion on the mound offered no difficulty, each room being provided with a lock and key. Not that Ashley ever rattled a knob to see whether her pride still held.

It held, but this was a miserable way to live. Elizabeth Ashley might be a gay and frivolous creature, but she was neither cold nor hard. That much of Elizabeth Wilcox, willy-nilly, lived on in her. Not that she conceded then or ever that there was justice in William Ashley's new demands. She still thought he had practised cruel deceit in allowing her to arrange her life on one set of terms and then asking for a complete reversal. And that for the most selfish of reasons. Because he wanted to play the feudal lord on a patch of wilderness. Nevertheless, it was impossible that hot anger and tempests of tears should go on forever. They supported her for most of the journey home. Then came a numbness that was like creeping paralysis. It terrified her when she realized it. Poor, bright Elizabeth Ashley! Must she say good-bye to her now, too? What would be left?

It was hard to meet her father's kiss, his gently probing eyes.

"Betsy girl! Was it a tiresome journey? You look fagged, for you."

It was hard to meet the warm welcome of her children, aged ten and six now, Mary Jane more the exquisite sprite than ever, Anna Marie with the disturbing look of her father in her broad brow and handsome eyes.

"Mamma, are you truly going to live with us always now? Will we go to school in St. Louis again?"

"Yes, darlings, yes."

She held them close, gathering comfort and more hurt from their rejoicing. St. Louis, by all means. It was like making a last stand on a line of defense to give special effort now to the complexities of keeping the great mansion there, to entertainment of old and new friends —the Sweringens, who were a family now, the delightful Farrar crew, the John O'Fallons, the Peter Lindells, who lived near by, Mr. Beverly Allen, the attorney, Joseph La Barge, the old keelboat man, and his son who captained a steamboat, those perennial bachelors and exact opposites, Robert Campbell and William Sublette. The house glittered with lights every evening. Elizabeth wore her pretty dresses one after another and entertained the guests with intimate reports on names high on the national calendar—her heart near to breaking as she chattered—or at the piano, airing her repertory and, on more intimate evenings, adding to it chansons by Captain La Barge or camp ballads, hastily amended, by William Sublette. She had never been more dazzling or more charming. Only Ashley seemed those days to lack something of old lustre.

Missouri kept its old custom of holding state elections in early August. Counting the votes went slowly. It was a day toward the middle of the month when Robert Campbell brought her the final news on the selection of a new governor. From the tall windows of the front parlor she saw him ride up to the house alone, his long face more sombre than usual; and she was in the hall when James opened the door for him.

"Is Mrs. Ashley in?" Campbell asked, then saw her.

He gave his hat and crop to James, came over to her, took her arm and led her back into the parlor, closing the hall door behind them.

"Mrs. Ashley," he said then, with enough solemnity to suggest any disaster, "the General's not going to make it."

"You can't mean," she said, shock piercing the numbness that possessed her, "that he is going to lose the election?"

"Ma'am, he has lost it."

"But I thought . . ."

"Yes, ma'am. We were all sure at first; but for days now we've watched his margin of victory diminish; and now, ma'am, it is gone. After all he has done, it seems incredible. He has earned ten times over any honor that Missouri could give him, but—"

But men forgot. Some did not know. Some who did know his achievements would think he had been sufficiently rewarded. He was a rich man and, therefore, open to suspicion and resentment. It might be simply that, as Ashley himself said, he had lost touch. But what a blow for him now! What a blow! Campbell took her arm again and led her to a chair.

"Are you ill, ma'am?" he fumed. "I shouldn't have come at you with bad news so suddenly."

"I'm all right," she assured him. There was just this shock. William Ashley a loser instead of a winner? "How is he receiving the news?"

"As always, Mrs. Ashley, calmly, with now and then a sharp comment, but no other show of grief. I was with him in 1824, ma'am, when the savages and the great river all but wiped out his fortune. He took that in the same way—only a glitter in his eyes at the repeated crushing blows; so, how can a person be sure? However, that was a dozen years ago. He was a younger . . . not that he is old now . . . but that's why I came to you, Mrs. Ashley, so that you could be prepared. You know, of course, that you mean more to him than a dozen elections."

That was what Mr. Campbell thought. How little those who claimed to know William Ashley really did know! She clasped and unclasped her hands against what was becoming a heavy pain in her breast, some of it fright now. All this—Campbell's solemnity and the tidings—had an ominous import.

"I will do what I can," she promised. "We had planned a supper party for this evening, as you know, to celebrate the election, thinking victory would be a certainty by then. I will make no change in the plans until I talk with Mr. Ashley. He may want to have the party, as if the news were the best."

"Right you are!" Campbell said admiringly. "That's exactly what he would do, I think. Then, we can count on you to keep up the appearance of good cheer?"

She could promise that. It would be the easiest part of her trial.

Regardless of the state of her feelings, Campbell went off immensely reassured. Ashley had his dinner in town, as he did more frequently than not these days. He came home in the late afternoon, escorted this time by James Sweringen as well as Robert Campbell. Elizabeth, having sent Poke and the carriage for the girls at school, was waiting there to receive him.

Ashley was surprised. The sudden spark in his eyes was that rather than pleasure.

"Madame," he said, "have you been informed of our overthrow? It seems we are not going to have to accommodate ourselves to the crudities of the new governor's mansion in Jefferson City."

"I heard," she said. "William, I am truly sorry."

The first time she had ever called him by his given name. Again a spark flashed in his eyes, and died.

"Why, my dear," he said lightly, "I believe you are sorry."

Supper was exceedingly, even excessively gay. The table extended through two rooms. Everyone who called—and there were a number —and all those originally invited sat down; and any of the guests wore a longer face than Ashley's own. He rallied them on their gloom.

"A person would think," he said, "that each of you had been repudiated instead of me. And, of course, that's how it is. Your idea, gentlemen, remember, to elect me to this office, not mine. I was on my way home to simple retirement."

"He would have made an excellent governor," James Sweringen said to Elizabeth. "We were expecting much from him and would have rallied around him to give Missouri four years, at least, of progress and advancement. These are muddled times, young lady, and grow more so; but I won't trouble you with all that. Is General Ashley serious about retiring?"

"Why don't you ask him?" Elizabeth asked. "I, too, should like to hear the answer."

"I will," Sweringen said, and did. "What's this, sir, about retirement? You can't be serious."

Ashley did not answer at once. Elizabeth thought, watching him, "He has taken a blow. To his pride, at least. And Mr. Campbell is right. He is an old man." That had never been so clear before. "The way he holds to his wine glass—to keep his hand from trembling, or the trembling from being seen."

Ashley caught her looking at him and the glitter in his eyes flared up in that elusive way again.

"I was never more serious," he answered, still holding fast to the glass. "I meant to announce my intentions later, but this is as good a time as any. Gentlemen, ladies, my friends, I have been a candidate for public office for the last time. Retirement has been in my mind for years. It has been my dream, as it is of many others like me, to spend my declining years in peace and quiet on land of my own, of my own selection. Some of you know my choice—a beautiful wild tract on the Missouri River in the Boonslick country, known as the Chouteau Grant. Well—" his tone changed, "one thing I have helped to accomplish in Washington in five years of trying is to end ridiculous, wasteful litigation on so-called dubious land titles. Early this year Mr. Chouteau's title to this tract was finally cleared and I was able to complete the purchase. A year from now I shall be happy to entertain any or all of you in my new home."

Silence greeted his announcement. How many besides Elizabeth of those present remembered another occasion when this land had been the subject of discussion?

"Leave St. Louis?" someone said.

"No, madame. Not entirely. We will keep our town home here." For how long, Elizabeth wondered. "Mrs. Ashley and I have two daughters to educate. She will be here most of the time, I fancy. I, too, occasionally, but not so often."

Elizabeth looked across the table into the quizzical eyes of her uncle, Dr. Farrar.

"Did you know about this?" he asked.

"Yes," she said, "I have known for some time."

How she would have behaved had this been her first warning was open to question. The numbness was on her again, but fright continued. The day and its events carried a threat she could not read.

"And will you be happy to return to the scenes of your youth?" Anne Farrar asked next.

"If it is Mr. Ashley's choice, it is mine, too," she answered. "If his health and peace of mind require the change, I have no objections."

Then it seemed that the house emptied itself of guests very rapidly and she was alone with this abnegation and the cause of it; and still the abnegation was not complete. She moved a candlestick back from the edge of her piano, frowning. The piano was a heavy piece for this white and ivory and gold parlor. With her toe she pushed a footstool out of the way and that was all. In spite of the people who had been there, the room was in its usual chaste, elegant order. That was what ailed this house. There was never enough disorder, the first visible sign of warm, impulsive living. She clasped her hands, then forced them apart and dropped them against the folds of her skirt. She raised her head—position number one of a lady standing at rest. Would he speak first? Would he, please, speak first?

"A very pretty gown, my dear," Ashley said at last. "Very becoming. Have I seen it before?"

"Do you remember?" It was *gros de Naples* silk, silver stripes on warm tones of red. "I had it when we were first married. I . . . I had a fit of stitching last week and altered it to suit the present fashion."

"Very nice," he said again. "Did you feel that it might be necessary to practise economy now?"

"I didn't know," she said. "I never know."

"Then I'll tell you. It is not necessary. I promised you when I married you that you and all your dear ones should live in comfort and luxury all your days and I am a man of my word."

Did he imply that she was not true to her spoken promises? From some depth in her, too little explored, perhaps, hot, heroic words rushed up to her throat—and stuck there. They would have said that she would rather sit at a stone hearth and wear homespun—but would she? Had she ever been overly fond of homespun?

"And that was a pretty speech you made at the table," he went on, harshly now, his feelings, too, rising, "about changing your place of residence to suit my health and desires; but that will not be necessary, either."

"I meant what I said," she insisted, wanting, above all, not to quarrel any more and yet not able to have her way even about this. "I have my reasons for disliking that special piece of land; but, if it is your purpose to have a home just there, why, I will live there, too. I will do all I can to make it a good and a comfortable home."

"You have a gift," he said, "for making a sour speech sound sweet. No. You have a perfect excuse for staying away in the children and their schooling."

"That is over winter," she reminded him. "When summer comes—"

"You will prefer a vacation in a cooler climate—the northern lakes or the sea. The girls will soon be of an age to find such places as appealing as they are to you."

Of what use was it to talk further? It was as if each of them swung an iron-shod whip about his own head and shoulders. She felt suddenly ill.

"You will make what arrangements you will," she said wearily. "I've told you my willingness. There is just one thing more. I am truly sorry you were not elected Governor. It is hard to be denied a dear wish. I know. Good night."

She lifted her skirts and went up the long stairs, holding her head high. She would not look back and down. Once she had done that and melted with sorrowful tenderness over a lonely man. Now she doubted that the man deserved better than loneliness. And the numbness encasing her hardened.

Beneath the hardness, however, there remained a softness that could feel. She opened the door of her bedroom reluctantly, wishing fleetingly that it could have been the simple "girls' room" in the house in Boone County which she had shared with her sister Mary—and Barcie Harris when she came visiting. This room she found oppressive now with its heavy richness—mahogany bed and chests and chairs and footstools, Staffordshire basins and jugs, red curtains, deeply fringed. She had opened the door against a push of unwillingness, then was relieved to find Susanna there, laying out her nightdress.

"You goin' to bed soon tonight," Susanna said. "I thought mebbe you would. My, my what a day! You wish I wouldn' talk about it?"

"Goodness, no," Elizabeth told her. "Do talk, please. Anything but— Go on and talk."

"Yas'm. What a day! Miss Libby, you gonna like goin' back up-country to stay?"

"Oh, I don't mind. Anyhow, that's a time off. A house would have to be built. I don't believe there's anything of the sort there now."

"No'm. Ain' anybody live thar since de Injuns. All wild land—catamounts, snakes, painters."

"And springs," Elizabeth said. "Don't forget the springs."

"Miss Libby, do you like spring watah? Bitter watah?"

"No. I abominate it. I always will."

"Yas'm. Me, too. Poke says——"

"Never mind what Poke says. I'll hear that some other time."

"Yas'm. You will, I reckon. Sure enough."

CHAPTER SIX

"I, William Henry Ashley . . ."

CAPTAIN BILL PORTER, son of the original Boonville ferryman, turned his new boat upstream after the Boonville crossing, to set Elizabeth down on the Ashley landing.

"No trouble at all," he assured her. "Told your pa I would. It's a mean road overland from town. I do considerable business for General Ashley. Got some boxes and barrels aboard now with his name on them. Glad to oblige, ma'am."

Glad to show off his steam-powered craft, too, she thought; and was there something more? Yes. His clear eyes took in her black bombazine skirt, her sealskin sacque and muff, her velvet bonnet, her fine cloth shoes with their leather toe-caps, and said plainly, "So, you're Doc Moss's gal, eh?" Afterward in town he would tell how he had had her aboard his boat that day. "Come up from St. Louis, for a look at the new house, I take it, and to visit her folks. Her ma's ailing, I hear. I carried her—and her trunks—to the landing."

Elizabeth thanked him for his kindness and left him to his conjectures. Her reasons for returning to Boonslick she would unfold to her father presently and to him only. There could have been another, but William Ashley desired her confidence less than ever now, if he had ever wanted it. It had been her father who, at her request, had told her when the house Ashley was building here was finished. His letter was in her handbag now. The house was done, he said. He and Miss Mary, at Ashley's request, were settled there comfortably. Then, less explicitly but just as clearly, he had urged Elizabeth, if it was in her mind to come and see for herself, to do so without delay. This, of course, was none of Captain Porter's business. She was grateful to him for taking her on up the river and sparing her the Boonville landing, where she might have met a dozen people with curiosity equal to his; but there the matter ended.

"I reckon you don't remember me, ma'am," he said presently, not to be diverted by her polite maneuvers. "I was hardly more than a boy when you used to visit in Boonville."

"I remember you very well," Elizabeth said quickly. "No, I suppose it was your father. My— Dr. Wilcox thought highly of him."

"No more so, ma'am, than my pa thought of your—of Dr. Wilcox. Still says he was one of the finest God ever cut off before his time was out. Excuse me for speaking of it, ma'am. General Ashley's a fine man, too, when you come to know him. We're highly proud to have him living here now."

Had he voted accordingly in the 1836 election, Elizabeth wondered. Probably he had not. *"Don't know much about this Ashley except what I hear. Did all right in Washington, they say, but he won't declare for any party now. Calls himself an Independent. Man can be too durned independent, if you ask me. St. Louis rich man. Land speculator. Wife's a Boonslick gal, but she don't show herself around here much."*

"First time you've been here since the house was built, ain't it?" Captain Porter arrived at more direct inquiry.

Well, she must learn to endure this now, Elizabeth thought. Nowhere was there a tribunal more likely to sit in judgment over her and her deeds and misdeeds than right here.

"I have two girls in school in St. Louis," she answered, and could read immediately Captain Porter's unspoken reply.

"We've got good schools here, good enough for most folks. Right here in Boonville, fancier ones over in Fayette; and what is wrong with the Seminary in Columbia, ma'am?"

But the next minute, and from then on, he was busy with his river. Whatever else he had to communicate was given sideways as he studied shoreline and current.

"Little river coming in there on the left is the La Mine. Partly it runs through Ashley property and partly it's boundary. Pretty little stream, but uncertain. Can't always get a boat of size far enough up it to do any good. So—landing's on the Missouri. The General probably wanted it that way, anyhow. It's just ahead now. If you keep your eyes over the trees, you can sight the house, though you can see more of the river from the house than you can see of the house from the river. Sets high, but back. All you'll see is roof and the flag. Yes, ma'am, a flag. Every day unless it's storming. Great patriot, the General."

Yes, indeed. She'd be the last one to deny it. Looking where the captain pointed, she saw the flag flying above a patch of dark roof, but nearer—and a more welcome sight—Poke waiting on the rough, new landing.

The Negro's face was one wide, rapturous grin of welcome.

"Miss Libby," he gloated, wrestling her trunks ashore and counting each one, "you're fixin' to stay!"

He meant no reproach, but the reproach was there. He looked up, to meet Elizabeth's silent appeal and changed his tone at once to a grumbling complaint over the freight he now helped the Captain stack beside the trunks.

"Can't make hit in one load. Too much of a pull fo' de hosses. I'll come down fo' mos' of hit later." He ventured another look at Elizabeth, her fine shoes against the rough planks of the wharf, the dirt road opening through the scraggly willows of the shore, the conveyance waiting to carry her up the hill. It was a brand-new carry-all wagon, but a far cry from a carriage. "Miss Libby, yore pa say you won' min' ridin' de wagon. He'd a come hisself in de buggy, 'cep' he don't like to leave Miss Mary alone dat long jes' now."

Good Poke! In his old uniform of clean jeans and jumper, as expert as ever at observing the decencies. But—no word of Ashley? Did he or did he not know of her coming? She, too, looked at the road, her shoes, the wagon, and, feeling resolution beginning to wither, covered all with a bright smile.

"The wagon will do splendidly," she said, then turned to thank Captain Porter again for his excellent care. She hoped she would see him soon and often. Probably she would since, as Poke had guessed, she was staying here now. Her girls would be along as soon as school was over, she told him. She would look to him to see to their safe arrival.

"Now go home and spread your report," she thought, as she waved her handkerchief at the backing boat.

"Miss Libby, you gonna be warm enough?" Poke asked as they took the road.

"Yes, I am dressed warmly, Poke. Why? Did I shiver?"

"Seemed like you did, Miss Libby. Weather stays col' fo' March."

The weather had nothing to do with her shivers. The horses pulled against a rising grade that hardly matched her rising unwillingness; and yet, here was a thing she had felt she must do. Taking her cue from Poke, she talked to cover her unrest.

"You're thinner," she said, "than when we lived in Washington."

"Yas'm. Don' live so soft now. Miss Libby, I ain' complainin', but I sho' am glad I ain' nevah gone up river wid de Gin'ral. You recollec' de gemmun what did git dey start dat way? Ain' a fat man amongst 'em, an' I knows why now."

172

"I suppose they had to work to live in camp in the mountains," Libby said.

"Miss Libby, we works yere jes' ez hard. We done a heap a'ready, but seems lak dey's always mo'."

"I should say you have done a heap," Elizabeth said. "To clear the land and build a house in a little over a year. And this road—"

"You make note o' de road, Miss Libby? An' de lil trees?"

It was a remarkable road for one newly cut through timber. The timber near the shore was sparse, the willow growth of flood land, but became heavier as they climbed; and not a stump blocked the wagon's progress. The soil was soft alluvial clay and sand, then looser, browner, richer clay, but still soft. The roadbed had been packed and tamped to near boulevard smoothness. Simple living, indeed! Along both edges young cedar trees had been planted. They were already several feet high and their symmetry was downright incongruous against the wild growth behind them.

"Where did they come from?" Libby marveled.

Poke sighed.

"We rassle 'em out o' de rocks. We take a stick wid us fo' measure. Ef we bring one back shorter dan de stick, de Gin'ral th'ows it on de bresh heap. He say he ain' no min' to wait fo' sprouts to grow into a hedge fence. He wan' trees and he wan' 'em right now. Miss Libby, you know what dey say 'bout movin' cedah trees?"

She knew. They grew where God willed and birds sowed them. If man uprooted one and set it elsewhere, to suit his fancy, either the tree died; or, if it grew in the new spot, when it was tall enough to cast a shadow over his grave, the man died. But Ashley wanted trees and immediately. A driving man and now a driven one. This time, when she shivered, she did not bother to conceal it.

"It's just a saying, Poke, because they don't take to transplanting."

"Yas'm," Poke agreed, not happily. "Dat's what de Gin'ral say. Say ef he stop fo' all things lak dat, he'd still be stuck fas' on a po' lil hill farm in Verginny."

The black man sighed, with obvious import. Elizabeth shivered again. As she did so, the sun found a hole in massed clouds overhead and shone down on the wagon, the road, the marshaled cedar trees and—abruptly—the new house.

She had not known what to expect in the way of a mansion this time, but certainly it was not what she saw—a Virginia farmhouse of the better type, generous in proportion without being massive, four-square but with its own special grace, two stories high, not counting the elevation of the roof, which sloped to a railed enclosure,

173

hiding the flagstaff. The walls were of soft pink brick. A portico sheltered the door. The grounds about the house had been cleared of rubble, and made smooth, ready for grass and flowers.

He was a poor boy, but he knew folks who were rich. . . .

"Poke," Elizabeth said, "it's a beautiful house."

"Yas'm," Poke agreed, "hit's right nice—when de sun shine. Yere's yore pa."

There he was—the lines of his face a little deeper, his hair more gray, but his eyes as fondly proud as ever—at Ashley's door, not his own. This was just one of several things gone wrong; but, before she could dwell on that, his strong arms were helping her down from the wagon.

"Betsy, girl!"

"I came," she said into his ear, "as soon as I could, after your letter."

"My child, I didn't mean to frighten you."

She clung to him.

"Everything," she said, "frightens me now—just everything."

And yet, when finally the two of them sat alone together before a log fire in the living room of this house, talk between them was at first fragmentary, touching lightly the subjects that burned in Elizabeth's consciousness, as if too brusque an approach might start a general conflagration.

"You are more anxious about Ashley's health than Mamma's," she guessed.

Miss Mary was resting in bed, so that she would have strength to take supper at the general table. She looked, Elizabeth thought, only a little frailer than when Dr. Moss had brought her recently to St. Louis, ostensibly to visit Elizabeth, but really for the sake of Dr. Farrar's opinion on her health. She kept her sharp tongue. Elizabeth could smile over her greeting:

"I don't know as I like you in black. Fashionable, no doubt; but you look your age. Do you care for that?"

Ashley was still away, somewhere on his land. He had not known that Dr. Moss had summoned Elizabeth, nor of her impending arrival until that was an accomplished certainty. Dr. Moss had now sent word to him that she was here.

"Say I am concerned," Dr. Moss said now, "rather than anxious. So far, I have not been able to diagnose satisfactorily the fever that drives him."

But now, with Elizabeth present, he would be able to decide. Silently she studied the fire. She might be grateful, she thought, for her father's judgment. Certainly there was a fever. It seemed incredible that in such a place, against difficulties at which Poke had only hinted, this house could have come to such real completion. Heavy logs burned in the wide mouth of the chimney with a minimum of fuss, dropping hot embers into a thick bed of gray ash, their smoke drawn smoothly upward. The room was at once finer and rougher than the great room she remembered from Boone County, the chimney stones more expertly piled, the walls plastered over all supporting beams, the floor of boards hewn at a mill, planed smooth and polished to a glow. There was no mahogany, but also no splint-bottomed hickory. Everything was made of walnut, simple and comfortable and sturdy. For other decoration there were mementoes of the Far West, kept under wrappings until now—Indian spears she had never seen, a feathered war bonnet, a deerhide stretched to show its painted legend, rattles, other barbarities she could not name. Her fine cloth shoes rested in the winter fur of a grizzly bear. She read all these things as signs of another love, long neglected; and the thought completed a humbling she had already forced upon her spirit.

She looked at her white hands against the lustrous black bombazine that had served well for traveling and wished that she could have changed into something simpler and brighter or at least have unpacked a scrap of needlework, but she had not wanted to take a minute from this talk with her father. However, now that she had his undivided attention, what should she say? How could she discuss with him the issue that smoldered between her and Ashley? She chose finally an oblique approach.

"I hate it so that you and Miss Mary should have been uprooted and moved over here!"

"Betsy, we were not uprooted. Ashley invited us."

"That's what I hate most," she said. "Did you have to come?"

"Yes, dear, we did. Betsy, if this is to be a confessional, let's have it a full one. I extended myself rather, years ago when I bought land in Boone County. There it was, beautiful, full of promise. Twenty-five hundred acres had a sound. Of course, it was more than I could care for. I never drew a profit from it that equaled the reach of my boundaries—distillery, horses, cattle, with medical practice thrown in. I would have done better to settle on one pursuit."

Elizabeth's heart sank. This was what she had dreaded to hear. *You and yours shall live in comfort always.* A promise kept too literally.

"You loved it so," she said. "You were so happy there."

"We all were happy," her father agreed. "Even Miss Mary had some joy in the place, no matter how she scolded. We raised a family creditably, but now—"

More than creditably. The boys were settled in careers at law or in medicine, Josiah in Columbia still, Oliver and James looking to the new West. Young Mary was in Columbia, too, teaching in a school for very young children; but she was promised now to a gentleman from the deep South, a Judge Logan Hunton of New Orleans, with interests in the new republic of Texas. Educating such a family was a costly business.

"I had so much rather," Elizabeth said, "you would have used that money of mine, if you needed it."

"No," the doctor said. "I have a sentiment about that money. Some day— I must give you an accounting presently. Don't let me forget. But now, dear, with all you have to distress you besides, do put Miss Mary and me off your mind. We do very well here, really. Our debt to Ashley is not large. I may even discharge it presently. I may draw more profit from my Boone County farm leasing it to another than I ever earned living on it myself. Meanwhile, I have everything here that I had there—horses, cows on some of the finest grazing land in Missouri, as much medicine as I care to engage in, and no responsibility. Miss Mary is content. And now we have you— if you mean to stay."

"I mean to stay," Elizabeth said, "if I am allowed to."

"Child," her father said, "has it come to that now? Betsy, I must tell you, I never approved of this marriage, even when it seemed a providential turn for you to take. You were not suited—"

"Ashley and I?" Elizabeth said. "We were admirably suited. Ambitious, vain, willful, self-sufficient—"

"Nobody," the doctor said, "is self-sufficient, Betsy, nobody."

"I wonder," she murmured. "At any rate, I was very happy for a while—happier than I ever thought I could be again. I liked being the rich Mrs. Ashley, and all that went with it. I loved Washington. Everything about it thrilled me. I can't believe now that I shall never return."

"Betsy, marriage must be more than that—to anyone. Even without true love, there must be a sharing."

"Sharing," she said softly. "Yes, that's it. There was none of that with us. In Washington any newsboy knew as well as I what Ashley did there. I never heard him mention an accomplishment or a plan. This land, over which he has gone into a doting frenzy—I knew he had some sort of title to it. He and Daniel had words over it before—you know. But what was a piece of land more or less to Ashley, I thought. How could I know that he meant to make this his home—and mine?" She struck her hands together in some baffled, helpless anger. "I still think he deceived me cruelly. I have not forgiven him. I never shall."

"Then why are you here, Betsy?"

"Because I can't bear to let things go on as they are. It's a monstrous way for two proud, decent people to live. We must settle our differences, if not in fact, then at least in outward seeming. I will not have his name or mine smirched by scandalous gossip. So, I thought . . ."

Her father waited.

"Ashley will not yield about this place and his plan for living here," she said. "Then I must appear to. When we were first married and things looked difficult, I made a pretense of accepting everything as it came; and so I found peace with myself and him and our life together. It wasn't always easy. It will be harder now, but—"

"Ashley won't be fooled by pretense," her father warned, "and you will be practising deceit."

"No more than I did then or always to a certain extent. And the reward will be—well, just a kind of peace. Oh, I know it's a forlorn hope, but can you suggest anything better that I might try?"

"No," her father said. "No; and my heart aches for both of you."

Shadows were darkening outside and candles were being lighted inside the house when William Ashley returned. Elizabeth, hearing him almost before he set foot across the doorsill, stood up, not trembling, more stirred than shaking. Again her hands were white against black, her face pale. Firelight ruddied her hair. She, too, had lost now a roundness that had come to her in the years of soft, happy living, and was thin as a reed again. Ashley halted at the threshold of the room, his eyes burning, his lips tight. Her heart turned. She thought, "He has aged terribly. Every time I see him, more years appear. He is ill." She went over to him and put her hands on his shoulders so that he would have had to be rigid indeed not to make the simple motion of putting his arms about her. She'd have none of this "madame" stuff now. She laid her cheek, pale but warm from the fire, against his, then turned her face and kissed him, suppressing a rising shiver. His skin was dry and dead as parchment. He was ill.

"Well, William?"

He held her, with no reassuring warmth, and looked past her at her father.

"Am I benefitting from a family conspiracy?" he asked.

"Only a promise," Elizabeth said quickly. "I asked to be told when the house was ready. Well, aren't you glad to see me?"

For another full minute his arms were like hinged wood about her; and then they tightened and he who could say things both bitter and sweet with fire and grace had only first words at his command.

"Yes," he said. "Yes!"

The house was built on high ground with a sweep of the Missouri River in view from its front windows and its doorstep, also a small part of the sparkling River La Mine, where it joined the big river; but the bluffs westward went on climbing, reaching their summit in the high mound which had first caught William Ashley's fancy. A wilder, lonelier spot it would be hard to imagine; but to Ashley it was never that. He knew the mound for what it was, a place of council for the chieftains of the forest people who had first held the land. To him their shadows still moved about the clearing.

It was the gift of their Manitou to them. Its height above all the surrounding country made them safe from attack by their enemies. They could look down the river of the Missouri past where the white man's towns of Franklin and Boonville would later come into being. They could look up the river past the flint hills that would forever be known as Arrowrock—another white man's landing now. Attack from the river side was impossible. War canoes could be seen too far away. On the land side the forest trails were few and steep and their own.

Moreover, on this high place Manitou had caused the winds to drop a burden of deep, powder-fine soil that yielded to their rude tools and gave them corn and pumpkins in abundance at harvest time. So, here the Grand Osage had built their main village and tilled the ground after a fashion, and buried their dead—as evidenced by the lesser mounds scattered all about—and held council. Later, when the movement of peoples, as steady and irrepressible as the movement of ocean tides, had carried them on southward and westward, they had deeded the ground to a white man who had dealt fairly with them:

"As thou hast since a long time . . . always been good to us . . . take thou on the River Lamine that quantity of land which may suit thee . . . and none can take it from thee, neither today nor ever. Thou mayst remain there and thy bones shall never be troubled. Thou askest a paper. . . ."

William Ashley had paid gold into the hand of that white man for the gift of land, and patiently striven with local and national government to clear the title; and yet, when he stood on the great chief's mound, he could feel that he was the one to whom the great chief, perhaps even the great Manitou, had made the lordly grant. In his mind he could look up the river to the wild waters and the snow-topped ridges of barrier mountains and down the river to a city growing where two great rivers met; and the far mountains above and the city below were of his kingdom, by right of conquest. Standing on the high and lonely mountain, he was a great white chieftain.

"I, William Henry Ashley . . ."

Usually he felt that. Not today with such complete fullness and certainty. It was a blustering, neuralgic day nearly a week after Elizabeth's arrival at the new place. It was a fine day for a man to remain indoors, casting up his accounts, putting plans on paper, writing letters, discharging debts, especially when he had only to turn his head an inch and see the prettiest woman this side of Heaven sitting in a low chair at the far end of the hearth with a bit of fine sewing in her hands. It was a year for wearing broad, flat collars of net or crisp organdie, embroidered to each one's fancy, over dark daytime dress; and Elizabeth Ashley seemed bent on having a new one for each day in the week.

But it was this very apparition that had driven him out of the house. This was and was not his Libby. If she had fretted, if she had sulked, if he had caught the glimmer of a single tear, he could have been sharp with her and asked, "Why did you come? I didn't urge it." But she did none of those things. She went about the house calmly, even happily; or it seemed so. She directed the placing of furniture. She fussed pleasantly over curtains. She planned for the arrival of the children in May. Susanna, whom she had left with them in St. Louis, would fume; but the girls themselves, she was sure, would be very happy. If Susanna fussed too much, she could return to Boone County and her mother. Pomegranate, the Moss's fat cook, had refused to stir from her hearthstone. She had heard that in the Ashley kitchen cooking was done on an iron stove and she would not risk her reputation on any such contraption.

Libby laughed over Pomegranate and went out to the kitchen herself to study the stove, and burned her fingers and several puddings, but turned up finally triumphant with one of those feathery, melting pies that made such a sensation whenever she favored chosen people with them. Nothing for Ashley to eat—sweet, rich, with a fillip of spicy tartness—nothing for him to eat; and yet, half-angrily

179

he had eaten his share, and even more angrily suffered hellishly afterward. In such ways she busied herself; then, flushed, breathless, she would settle down in a chair by the fire with a bit of stitching and be all the tranquil, contented matron.

Except that he knew she was no such thing. How did he know? He could not say exactly. If she was playing a part, she played it well. Still he knew. The day after her coming, in his surprise at her surrender of a position she had taken—and he had insisted on her keeping until she wearied of it—he had thought he would get out of storage that painting he had bought of her in Washington. Furious at the thought of another man's discovering what he had always known, he had bought the painting, thinking, "This is my Libby. This is the girl, the woman, I love." For he realized now, if he had not before, that she was the great love of his heart. His feeling for her was more abiding and more compelling than the sweet urgency of young romance, much more potent than his appreciation of the St. Louis heiress who had so handsomely and capably graced his fine mansion in that city. Libby was everything—beauty, fire, sweetness and delight.

She was his great, true love. When he had first seen that Britisher's portrait of her, his conscience had recoiled. He had thought, "What have I done? This is the way she was, not the way she is." And, while that had not determined him to leave Washington, since his purpose all along had been to leave, it did strengthen his determination. He had bought the painting, because he felt it should not be in any other's keeping; but, now that he was ready to take it from its packing and hang it in the hall of this new home, to make it part of a tender reconciliation, he was afraid to uncover it. He remembered a near smile on the face. Suppose that smile should mock him now? Suppose it said to him, as Libby's demure placidity said daily, "Well, sir, was this what you wanted?"

Damn it, no! It was not what he wanted. He wanted those deep, elusive eyes to shine—as they had shone for him and did not shine now. False as the glitter might have been in those gay Washington days, putting an enamel over a loveliness that called for no such treatment, she had loved it all, and him for giving it to her. There had been moments, bought very cheaply, after all— Well, he'd give the world if he could live them over.

Would he really give so much as that?

Yesterday the twice-a-week mail had brought Libby a letter from Washington and that Foxe woman. Libby had concealed it quickly, but he had seen. He had asked about Lily. Was she riding high these days—though the world crashed? It had all but crashed the year before. The country had gone through its worst time financially since the bitter embargo days before the second war with England. Only men and business rooted securely had survived; but how was Lily?

"Oh," Elizabeth said, with a pout, "putting on airs, of course. Strutting proudly. Quite the leader of capital society these days."

"Would you like to dethrone her?"

For a second a veil was lifted. Libby's eyes brightened, her lips parted. Then just as quickly the radiance passed and the veil was dropped.

"Not particularly," she said. "Besides, how could I—now?"

"I was just thinking," he said.

"Pooh!" Elizabeth declared. "I'm glad I'm not there to see her."

But was she glad? Ashley went on thinking. In that same mailbag he had had a letter from Beverly Allen, the St. Louis attorney, asking whether he would consider offering his name again that year as a candidate for election to Congress. Missouri had two representatives there now and people from St. Louis and roundabout would like to show their appreciation of all Ashley had done for the state. Anyhow, the business panic of the year before had undermined the popularity of the Democratic party. This year, 1838, and on to the presidential election of 1840, the opposition was likely to win most contests. The Whig battle cry would be reform and internal improvement. How did he feel about it?

That was the question to which he hoped he might find a clear answer out on the bluffs this dreary, windy morning. It seemed to him that the bluster of the day had been assembled to match his own unrest. The tumbled clouds were like his bed when he'd got up from a near-sleepless night. The sigh of the wind was his melancholy. The shifting gusts were the arguments that pulled him this way and that.

For himself he had no desire to return to Washington. When he had closed his accounts there two years before this, his decision had been made, his purpose was clear. He would spend the rest of his life in well-earned retirement, devoting all his energies to improving and developing this wild, beautiful land, overlooking his River of the Missouri. This had seemed to him so right and so glorious and so satisfying a way to end his days that he had not supposed anything or anyone could have shaken his purpose. But now, with the work only well begun, to make a woman's eyes shine again for him, he would abandon all of it.

It would come to that finally. A man, it seemed, could have room in his heart for two great loves; but he could not serve them both fairly and equally. At least, he, William Ashley, could not. He was not one to work with a divided purpose. If he took Libby back to Washington, he would say good-bye to his La Mine barony.

And he knew that was what he would do. It was not indecision that had made him toss through a restless night. It was protest against the way he knew he would turn. It was not to seek an answer to his doubt that he had walked over the spine of the river bluffs this cheerless morning, it was to say good-bye. Oh, the land would still be his. Dr. Moss would stay on, keeping the house and developing farm and pasture land. He might, in time, be willing to supervise the opening of a health resort at the springs. A doctor's name would give prestige to such a venture.

Wretched as he was—and he was worn down with a misery of unwillingness—Ashley had to smile. There was a topic which he and Libby had sidestepped since her return as if it were a coiled snake. *Putrid waters*—he could still hear how she said that. He wasn't sure what made her aversion so strong. It was deeper than just physical distaste. It might have been some survival of devotion to her first husband, who had had some plan for purchasing just the springs area and opening a spa.

Well, that was beside the point. Some day the resort would be built and it would make money—a lot of money. Enough, perhaps, to maintain Elizabeth Ashley in Washington; and that, he had cause to know, was a good, round sum. Every year the dear girl had some new idea. "Could we have a house? It would be so pleasant to entertain our friends in our own home."

Ashley's face twisted in amusement and in pain. His heart continued heavy. He climbed to the top of the high mound and stood there as motionless as a white pine a few yards away. He had a feeling that this actually was the last time he would stand there, looking up and down the river. That was absurd. He would write to Beverly Allen at once, but several weeks might pass before he had the attorney's reply. Then, at the worst, if his name was entered in the political race, he would have what was left of the spring. The campaign would not be fully active before summer. And yet, the feeling of farewell persisted.

The words of the Indian grant—they had always put a spell upon him—went through his mind: *"Thou mayst remain there and thy bones shall never be troubled."* Thy bones— Had he ever set down in writing that here was the place where he wished to be buried? He was afraid he had not. Well he must do so at once. That much surely he could claim for himself forever. Hot upon his return to the house, even before the letter to Allen—well, he must go now. He couldn't stand here mooning all day. But not a word to Libby of his plans until all was settled. He could live a month in anticipation of her surprise.

He turned, and a splash of rain cut across his face. He looked up at the sky in startled protest. He had not considered that possibility when he had set out on foot after breakfast. It had been a windy sky, but that was the worst. Now, in what seemed to him a few minutes, the picture had changed. The tumbled clouds had melted together into a gray oneness.

More rain fell on his upturned face. His protest now was sharp impatience. A half-mile of rough walking lay between him and the house. On the fairly bald top of the bluffs no other shelter offered. He would be drenched before he got halfway home.

But there was no help for it. The rain came down harder. He pulled his coat tightly about him, scrunched his head down into the collar, settled his hat closely above his ears and set out.

The rain came on relentlessly. It made a gray curtain finally, blotting out the river to one side and the forested slopes to the other. He tried to run, stumbled, and caught himself up firmly. Nothing to be gained if he broke a bone out here, and nobody knowing where to look for him. Just plod along now, keep his bearings and his footing. This loose top soil was slippery when only a little wet.

Twice he did slip, but went down easily enough. The second time he got to his feet, the house was in view just ahead, within shouting distance if he had had any breath with which to call. He was wet through by then, of course, as much from below as from above. The only time he had ever been more thoroughly drenched was years ago when a boat had capsized under him on the upper river.

But finally . . .

"Gin'ral Ashley, suh, whah you been?"

"Ah . . . Poke! G-get me to my room, boy. Dry clothes . . . whiskey . . . my room . . . before anybody sees me."

The house reeked of camphor, of hot grease and turpentine, of whiskey, taken plain in a small medicine glass, in a mug hot with sugar and lemon, beaten up with eggs for nourishment as well as warmth; and it might as well have been poured out on the ground for all the good it did the sick man. On the third afternoon, when Elizabeth was in the outside kitchen whipping up another futile eggnog, Poke rode off the place on the swiftest horse from the barn. At once her hands, not too obedient servants these days, stopped their movement; and she was ready with a question when her father, who had sent Poke to town, appeared at the kitchen door.

"He's worse?"

"No," Dr. Moss said. He, too, was pale and tired. "No worse, but no better. I can't conquer that chill. Burning with fever outside, but complaining always of feeling cold. I'm very anxious about him, Betsy."

"Papa, what's to become of us? What shall we do?"

"Betsy, Betsy!" Her father shook his head. "But I know what you mean. Ashley, I think, has asked himself the same question. Poke's gone to fetch a lawyer and now your husband wants to talk to you. Never mind the eggnog. You can serve it later. Mr. Thompkins will enjoy it if Ashley doesn't."

"Does he know how ill he is?"

"If he does, he won't admit it. Insists this is just a deep cold. He's had the same kind before. Well, that could be; but— Betsy, I know you're frightened."

Only once before had she been so frightened as she was now— that dreadful winter with Daniel away in Jefferson City. It was as if— She looked up at the beams of the kitchen fearfully. It would be only fitting that they should snap and let the roof down on her. That was how things looked to her generally, all threatening collapse and ruin, and she helpless under the heap.

"Betsy, Betsy!" her father said again. "Smile now and run along. Poke and the lawyer will be back directly. Smile—surely I don't need to tell you to pretend to be cheerful."

Surely he did not; but in the space between the kitchen and the house she stopped a minute to fill her lungs with warm, fresh air, to swallow, if she could, some of the day's sunshine. Such a beautiful day, so filled with promise, a meadowlark near by whistling for spring to come on. It was high time.

Then, into the house with its reek of illness, its warm, close atmosphere. Into the room where Ashley lay, wrapped in blankets, propped high on pillows, his eyes closed, his chin slack. She tiptoed to the bed.

"William?" she whispered.

He was not asleep. He opened his eyes at once. His hand groped for hers; and she caught it and held it, though her first impulse was to let it fall back on the cover. It was so cold and inert—Ashley's hand!

"Sit down," he said, and she drew up a chair.

Then, as his eyes glazed over, she thought he had lost consciousness again, but the lapse was only temporary.

"My sweet Libby!" She had to lower her head to make out his words. "Did you no service by marrying you."

"William, please. You've given me everything."

"Yes. What I mean—"

And a little later,

"You've no feeling for land, have you?"

What should she say to that?

"I think women seldom do feel as strongly about it as men. We depend more on people."

"Right. Depend on people. Good people. Beverly Allen, Sweringen, Campbells. Good friends," he sank again, and rallied. "All in land . . . property. Only sure thing. Keep it and it will keep you. Hold it. Don't sell."

Now it was not a ceiling that threatened to fall on her. It was land —high land and low land. It was houses, large and small—nobody knew how many.

"Libby . . . sweet . . ."

Her father and the Boonville lawyer waited at the door.

Ashley rallied strongly for the business with the lawyer.

"Mind you," he said, "this is my father-in-law's idea—a precaution."

Benjamin Thompkins agreed respectfully, laid his portfolio on the table that Dr. Moss cleared for him and untied its strings. He was considered a promising lawyer, although he had hardly promised himself service to the Honorable William Henry Ashley. He cleared his throat but was still afflicted with hoarseness as he said that he understood the document involved was a will. He had brought foolscap with preliminary inscription.

Yes, Ashley agreed testily; but first there was a paper. In the upper drawer of the desk by the wall. Would the lawyer cast his eyes over it and say whether its instructions were clear and legal and binding? Written in his own hand, signed, but without witnesses—

Thompkins found the paper. Casting his eyes over it, he discovered that under it lay an unsealed letter, directed to Beverly Allen, Esq., Attorney-at-law. As for the paper, it lifted even his hair a little, used as he was to the vagaries of people in similar crises. The Honorable William Henry Ashley had laid out instructions for his burial, explicit as to location, including surveyor's signs and symbols, just as explicit for the placement of his remains: "facing East, feet toward the river."

Really, some might question that the sick man was of sound mind, sufficiently to draw a will.

"Well?" Ashley demanded. "Is it binding?"

"Why, I think so."

"Damn it, can you lawyers never say a plain yes or no? I want no doubts."

Thompkins abandoned legal barricades.

"There is no doubt," he said. "Your heirs will certainly be obliged to follow your instructions."

"Including my stipulation that, no matter what happens to the rest of the land, that acre including the Indian mound cannot be sold?"

Mr. Thompkins had some doubt about that, but thought it best to yield to the other's insistence. He would add his signature to attest Ashley's writing and name on the paper.

"Good!" Ashley said. "At least, you know of the paper's existence. Put it where you found it and get on to the will—while I am in the notion."

He meant while his strength lasted. If he was able to sign his name to the document it would be a marvel. Thompkins settled himself with his prepared foolscap at the desk, where pen and ink were at his hand.

"I might suggest," he offered, "that, if you would be willing to give me in broad detail the general terms of the testament, I could write them out, arranging all in proper sequence, and save you the strain of dictating. I would then read you the document before you signed it."

Ashley agreed impatiently. The terms were simple—the bulk of his estate to his wife.

"Are there exceptions?" Thompkins prompted. "Other heirs or claimants?"

Yes, two. He wished to continue during their lifetimes the money allowance he had made for some years past to his two sisters: Mrs. Nancy Steger, widow, and Miss Martha Ashley, spinster, of Powhatan County, Virginia. Beyond that, in common they were to receive half-interest in the La Mine property known as the Chouteau Grant. If or when it was ever sold—as a whole or in part—their share to be paid in cash out of the proceeds.

Thompkins summed up the items on his fingers. Provision for two sisters as specified, the residue of the estate to the widow—

"My wife," Ashley rasped. "My beloved wife, Elizabeth Ashley."

"Yes, sir. I understand."

Thompkins turned to the desk and began scratching. He wrote

186

furiously fast against time, the hard breathing of the sick man prodding him. It was a short will. He could not have been at it more than ten minutes. In the same urgent haste, he pushed back from the desk, stood up and began reading:

"I, William Henry Ashley . . ."

His own voice called his attention to the utter silence in the room. He looked at the bed, and with a sigh laid the foolscap down.

Here was a state of things, he thought. A man of untold wealth dying so! That piece of paper in the desk, written in his own hand, signed and witnessed, disposed of his mortal remains and one acre of ground. As for the rest, litigation would come of it some day, no matter how fairly and honorably his heirs carried out the dead man's wishes. "The bulk of my estate to my beloved wife"—the way he had said that!

The silence in the room became a near vacuum. The lawyer put aside speculation for present reality, and tiptoed away to summon the family.

Part Three

Lady Crittenden

CHAPTER ONE

Beautiful Lady, All Alone

THE RECEPTION was a social triumph, as brilliant an affair of the sort as any in which Elizabeth Ashley had ever participated.

"Dear Mr. Gautier," she said in ordering it, "let us have everything of the choicest and best. I want it a day to be remembered."

By Anna Marie, by her young husband, by those of the Washington set who came to wish the young couple well. And herself, Elizabeth Ashley? Yes, by her, too. Anna Marie was opening a fascinating new chapter in her life. Elizabeth Ashley—E. Ashley, she wrote it now—was closing another in hers.

A baker's dozen of years had passed since William Ashley's death. In many ways they had been full, satisfying years.

"You're rich, Libby," Miss Mary had said, when the shock of Ashley's going and the near barbaric splendor of his funeral were over. "Very rich, they tell me. And young still—thirty-four. What will you do now?"

"The girls first," Elizabeth answered.

Duty had been ballast she needed just then. Sudden control over the Ashley fortune and independence, without something to anchor her, might have sent her soaring into realms of untold folly. But there were the children. She had been a devoted mother, with, however, no real sacrifice of self. Their care, their young problems had been just distracting enough. She had needed ballast, distraction and time. Time to heal the scars of her second marriage, to realize its compensating benefits and to re-establish her own personal balance. Schooling the girls had challenged her hungry mind; happy, young companionship had revived her even more hungry heart; and travel— the Lakes, the seashore, New York, New Orleans, Saratoga, but never White Sulphur—a season in Washington when it could be arranged; had broadened her vistas as well as theirs. The flowering of her daughters into maturity had gone along with her own development into ripe, gracious womanhood, the more charming and refreshing, possibly, because it came late, rather than early.

But now she had gone as far as she could with her children. *"Dear*

Daniel, are you proud of them? And me? Mr. Ashley, have I done well?" At seventeen, five years after Ashley's death, Mary Jane had fallen in love with Andrew McKinley, son of Justice McKinley of the Supreme Court, who by then had made Louisville, Kentucky, his permanent home. Startled as Elizabeth had been by the sudden romance, she had no thought of raising any objection, and after that had given double attention to her younger daughter, Anna Marie, always more of a problem than shy-seeming, sweet Mary Jane. Anna Marie's exuberant, nearly hoydenish good health was a threat to desirable femininity, and her avid, unmasked enjoyment of all the pleasures the world had to offer was a constant pricking of Elizabeth's conscience. However, by virtue of special schools, by emphasis on the right contacts everywhere and in Washington particularly, where the two for some years past had spent every winter season, Elizabeth had brought out Anna Marie handsomely. Now Anna Marie also had a husband, of irreproachable status, Mr. Edward Carrington Cabell, of the Richmond Cabells, his father a judge of the Virginia Court of Appeals. Young Cabell himself represented the new state of Florida in Congress.

"Dear Mrs. Ashley," one guest after another said to her during the reception, "it must be gratifying to you to think of both your girls so well placed in marriage—happily, too, we trust?"

The afterthought, rising to a question, betraying envy mixed with admiration, delighted Elizabeth. Yes, indeed, she said, smiling, to every inquiry. Yes, indeed, to those who expressed regret that it was only a reception they attended, not the wedding itself. Yes, Elizabeth agreed, she had been disappointed herself in that; but her friends must remember that she and the girls still called St. Louis home. They had a large house there and even more extensive family connections, all clamoring to see Anna Marie's young man. But she had insisted from the first that, when she and the Cabells returned to Washington, another reception must take place there. She owed as much to Anna Marie, to young Cabell and to herself, in view of her many friends in the capital.

Privately, she had intended this to be the really grand flourish; and it was all of that. Gautier, Washington's caterer, had surpassed all previous records with a towering bride's cake, with fanciful lesser pastries, and ices in metallic holders shaped like wedding bells. Champagne corks popped and crystal rang. Every corner and every niche was filled with flowers—roses and masses of camellias. Camellias were the flower in Washington during the 1850's, but never were more displayed at one time or in one place than in the ballroom of the National Hotel that December evening in 1851.

"Sent to me express from New Orleans," Elizabeth said, knowing that all would be a-buzz to know whether she had ordered them or were they a gift from her sister and brother-in-law, the Judge Huntons, or had that sugar baron, Mr. Hobbs, who showed her so much attention both in New Orleans and in Washington, made one of his grand gestures? The camellias were from Mr. Hobbs, but Elizabeth was not saying.

All the late afternoon and early evening important people came and went. She had screened the guest list and sifted it and still five hundred invitations on crested vellum paper had gone out and most of them had been honored by some form of acceptance. Sweet Mrs. Fillmore, the President's mother, had stood beside Elizabeth in the receiving line for a few minutes. The Cabinet, the High Courts, the Senate, the House—especially the Southern element, which ruled Washington socially and, for the time being, politically—most of the foreign embassies and legations were represented. Mr. Webster, the Secretary of State, came. So did the aging and feeble Mr. Clay, leaning on the arm of his good friend, Mr. John Jordan Crittenden of Kentucky, now Mr. Attorney-General, if you please.

Poor Mr. Clay! He showed the ravages of time and successive bitter disappointments. He had so wanted to be elected President and now would never be. But he remained the courtly gentleman. Standing before Elizabeth and the bridal couple, he released Crittenden's arm, to make his bows unaided.

"As you know, my dear," he said to Elizabeth, "I always honor the prettiest girl at any party so," then kissed her, instead of Anna Marie.

Funny as the incident was, pathetic also, it would have been embarrassing had not Mr. Crittenden stepped into the breach. He kissed Anna Marie on both cheeks to make amends, and all passed over with laughter.

"The sweetest gentleman in this whole city," Anna Marie declared.

"Well, well!" young Cabell objected.

Elizabeth said nothing, her mind taken up by the band of crepe on the Attorney-General's coat sleeve. It was hard to establish an image of John Jordan Crittenden bereft of his devoted Maria.

All in all, the reception was a most satisfying affair. If only Lily Foxe had been there to see! Poor Lily—the Whigs being back in power and the Democrats out, she not only shared her husband's political eclipse but had the care of him besides. Charley Foxe's failing health might never permit his return to Washington. Elizabeth, liking and disliking Lily in the same proportions as formerly, missed her when she was away, especially at a time like this. Anna Marie had never looked so handsome, her rich coloring subdued by the silver brocade of her Bridport second-day dress. Young Cabell, very conscious of his new honors as a bridegroom, also of his political prestige, representing a new and important Southern state, and a little impressed, too, Elizabeth hoped, with being son-in-law to the rich and beautiful Mrs. Ashley, was as solemn as an owl; but it became him at his years. She herself looked far from her worst, in self-striped pale green silk with falls of creamy Mechlin lace and her emeralds.

A wonderful party, really. There came a time when the press of people made flowers seem too flimsy a barricade for safety; and then, more quickly than the crowd had gathered, it began to fall apart. There were straggling knots of people instead of a steady coming and going. The rising tide of talk and laughter ebbed in little waves. The music of stringed instruments, muted behind a screen of greenery, sounded too loud and clear and distracting. Empty glasses accumulated faster than quiet servants could gather them. Here and there a rose or a camellia drooped; and Elizabeth, the habit of guidance strong upon her, put her arm around her tall daughter and said,

"Now, dear. Let's not just be standing here when everybody else has gone. I've made your excuses. You can leave at any time quite properly."

Anna Marie caught her breath and looked first at her grave young husband, then her mother for reassurance.

"So beautiful!" she said. "And it's all over."

Elizabeth's arm tightened.

"Silly girl! It's just today that's gone. After this, there's tomorrow, and the day after and all the new year, you know."

But she understood what Anna Marie meant, and felt closer to her than she had in all the years when, as people said, she and her younger daughter had been "everything to each other." Anna Marie, not naturally of a sentimental turn, would have, if happy in marriage, new and gentler attitudes now. She had taken sudden fright at the swift passing of happy hours.

Oh, but she was too young for that! Much too young. Now it was Elizabeth who looked to Cabell for help. Surely he could find something to say.

Edward Carrington Cabell, it seemed, was struggling with a speech. Oh, confound the fellow! Had he contracted that disease already? In Elizabeth's experience, only one congressman had failed to form the habit. His name—pshaw, it was her name, too. She had worn it so long that she could hardly realize ever having been known by another. E. Ashley . . .

Young Cabell cleared his throat.

"Dear Mrs. Ashley, you have been most generous to Anna Marie and to me. We do appreciate your kindness."

"My dear fellow," she interrupted, "you are sweet to say so."

She was not going to listen to a speech now. She was tired. A nagging ache had set in between her knees and her ankles. It annoyed her. She, who had danced many an evening away right through its formal closing figures and into smaller parlors and the fading darkness!

But Cabell would have his say.

"I am sure you did it all for us."

"You were never more mistaken," she told him. "I love all this."

"What Mr. Cabell means, Mamma," Anna Marie interpreted—she must warn the girl about that—"is that we hate to go away and leave you—at Christmas, especially. Won't you change your mind and come with us?"

They were leaving for Richmond early in the morning, to spend the holidays with Judge Cabell, who was ailing. This Elizabeth had said in forty ways to more than forty people all evening.

"No, dear, of course not. You go right on and have a happy holiday and don't give me a thought."

"You're sure you won't be lonely?"

"My dear, I'm never lonely."

"But what will you do?"

"I haven't had time to think," Elizabeth said. "I've invitations upstairs that I have never opened. I may spend Christmas Day with friends in Baltimore. I may—pshaw, you'll be back before New Year's Day. You must, you know, be here for the President's reception."

"As if we'd be missed in that mob!" Anna Marie said.

"You would be missed," Elizabeth assured her, "and you must not let it happen—this year, above all. Cabell . . ."

Her son-in-law was clearing his throat again.

"Mrs. Ashley, we will be back in good time for the New Year's levee, of course. When we do return . . . ah . . . well, we've never discussed living arrangements. I do hope you will consent to share our quarters, wherever they are. You must always feel that you have a home with us."

Or vice versa, perhaps? Now, really, that was too bad of her. Just because this was Washington, it didn't follow that a man could not say exactly what he meant—no more and no less.

"How charming of you, sir!" she answered. "I shall remember. Now run along, both of you. Here's Susanna with Anna Marie's cape." God bless Susanna! Able to time even an appearance like this. "Take good care of my child, Susanna; and you, Cabell, do remember me most affectionately to your father. He and I are old sweethearts, you know."

Cabell's face was worth the daring of that sally.

"Now, Mamma!" Anna Marie complained. "I shall be all week trying to explain what an angel you are, really."

"Don't attempt it," Elizabeth begged. "Let the Judge explain for me. He will be most happy to do so, I'm sure. Run along, do!"

They left, Susanna masking a smile, Anna Marie looking back with a puzzled frown, Cabell still shocked; and a queer thing happened. Quite suddenly Elizabeth was alone. Utterly, irretrievably, completely alone. It was an odd sensation. Not only everyone, but everything was gone. All was hollow; and there she was, doing what she never did under such circumstances, what she would not permit Anna Marie to do. She was just standing there. As realization came to her, the manager of the hotel appeared.

"Mrs. Ashley, I hope everything was to your taste today?"

Elizabeth roused herself.

"Everything was lovely," she assured him, "perfect."

"I think myself," he agreed, now that she had spoken, "that I have seldom seen an affair go off so smoothly. But you must be tired now. If you wish to withdraw, I shall be glad to send a collation to your rooms. I'm sure you have taken no refreshment all evening."

"Why, thank you," she said, grateful both for his offer and his reminder that she ought by now to have disappeared. "If you will be so good. A little later, when I have rested."

It was her intention when she reached her rooms to get out of her formal silks at once into something soft and comfortable, and relax. Lie down, perhaps, and really rest. It had been a long time since she had so indulged herself; but now she would be neglecting nothing urgent. There was nothing she even needed to think about immediately. She would rest. Perhaps that was all she would do over Christmas, not accept any invitations, not see anybody, just keep to herself —like somebody taking a cure.

The very thought was reviving.

"Susanna!" she called gaily as she opened her door.

And then she remembered. Susanna wasn't there. She had sent Susanna with Anna Marie to Richmond, to get the bride off to a proper start with her husband's connections.

No Susanna. Oh, dear! That made things more difficult, took most of the feathers out of her idea of resting. She closed the door behind her and, with a stifled laugh at her own expense—it was not the first time that a generous impulse had betrayed her—and without bothering to touch a fastening to her elaborate dress, sank down on the nearest convenient chair.

It had to be convenient as well as near. Not every chair accommodated a lady's dress of the 1850's. The one she chose was low, with a good spread and a mere suggestion of arms extending only half the depth of the cushioned seat. Even so, crinoline and a multiplication of petticoats and nine yards of taffeta, topped by a bodice cruelly tight and boned for firmness under the concealment of rich lace, did not, without skill on the part of the wearer, permit immediate relaxation. Elizabeth Ashley had that skill. She eased herself softly over the seat until her back met the tall narrow back of the chair and she could rest her elbows on the half-arms, allowing her hands and wrists to droop gracefully and easily over her lap. At the point of letting go, a twinge, shooting up her left leg from ankle past her knee, made her wince and stiffen; but, while she counted twenty, both pain and accompanying grimace passed. She allowed her head and shoulders now to drop back against the support of the chair and sighed—the nearest she could come to a full, deep exhalation.

She closed her eyes. Oh, she was tired! For a while weariness, just pure bone weariness, washed over her. Not unpleasantly. There was a physical satisfaction in resting when one was completely fatigued, and there was other satisfaction. Imperceptibly weariness became contemplation.

Weddings. Anna Marie's. Between St. Louis and Washington it was two weddings, rather than one. Enough fuss and feathers to wear out a platoon of mothers, but she had enjoyed all of it. The kinfolk flocking to St. Louis for the occasion, some of them curious to see how she would stage such an affair and eager then to brag about their part in the show, some curious to see the husband she had secured for Anna Marie, all of them, she was afraid, avid to see what the years were doing to her, Elizabeth Ashley. Was she beginning finally to fade or wither a little?

She did hope that all the dears had gone home satisfied; and what a blessing it was that she had kept the big house going! It was an expense, an extravagance, considering how little of each year she spent in St. Louis. A short while back she had been on the point of releasing the property for rental or sale. The smaller house on Locust Street was adequate for her needs. But about then a spark from a steamboat had set the St. Louis waterfront on fire; and, before it could be checked, had burned out the very heart of the town. She was still involved in a discussion as how best to rebuild her downtown property. Most of her advisers recommended that she build with a view to leasing to the growing businesses of the city. The initial cost would be heavy, but she would get it all back eventually. Eventually. Men were strange about money. They would turn green over the cost of a ball gown, then lay out thousands on brick and stone and a future possibility. Well, this was just one of many matters to be decided later. Naturally she had not been able to give much thought to such things with a wedding on her hands.

What a wedding it had been! So many people, so many near, dear people that she had had to parcel out her time sparingly to get to see them all. She had not been able to manage a half-hour alone with either of her children or their husbands, to say nothing of her father.

Dear papa! She loved him better, she was certain, than any other being on earth. There was between them still a perfect understanding; but sometimes a year would go by without their seeing each other. Since Miss Mary's death, within a year of Ashley's, he had no fixed home. Her business agents had instructions to keep a guardian eye on him. "Let my father draw on my account for anything he needs. . . . If he has not gone South, please see that he gets off before cold weather sets in." His half-brother, Uncle Farrar, was gone now, too, caught in the cholera epidemic of 1848, and that had seemed to add to Dr. Moss's restlessness. He liked best to visit his daughter Mary in New Orleans or his granddaughter, Elizabeth's older child, Mary Jane McKinley, in Kentucky. Sometimes his visit and Elizabeth's in one place or the other would be simultaneous and they would have time together. That she did not see him oftener would have grieved her more, if it had not been true that, when she did see him, she knew instantly that she was still and forever his dearest, his Betsy.

He never came to Washington. But then, she had no home there really. She spent part of each year by choice at the capital; but, for such seasonal sojourns, rooms at the National seemed still the best arrangement. Now, perhaps— No, probably not now. Probably not ever. If each year multiplied her connections, it also made more divergent ties. And anyhow, her father would not make his home in Washington under any circumstances. By now it was probably too late for him to achieve a sense of home in a new environment. If, after Daniel Wilcox's death, she had married in Boone County and lived on there . . . if, after Ashley's death, she had stayed on in the new place . . . no, her father didn't like that house any better than she did, William Ashley from his burial mound keeping ghostly watch over everything.

Besides, all these surmises and explorations involved a girl named Elizabeth Moss, not a woman named E. Ashley. She sighed again, and her thoughts now were of today. She thought of the people who had bowed before her, filled her ears with sweet compliment, some of it sincerely meant. Senator Stephen Douglas of Illinois, who, after an impoverished boyhood had risen to wealth through Chicago real estate, railroads and marriage to a Southern lady. Daniel Webster of Massachusetts, as gallant a lady's man as ever. Too gallant, to too many ladies, but illuminating any gathering he attended. Adela Cutts, daughter of an obscure government clerk but also the grand-niece of Dolly Madison, proud and spirited and much courted, but waiting dangerously long to make a choice of husbands. Senator Jefferson Davis from Mississippi, limping still from the wound he'd got in Mexico, and his beautiful young wife, whose barbed tongue reminded Elizabeth of her mother's sharp speech. Varina Howell Davis was likely to have a brilliant career in the capital, being much admired by men and much envied by women, both for her handsome, charming and gifted husband and for her own beauty and wit. Elizabeth envied her, and Adela Cutts, for that matter, only their youth and the long, full years ahead. Mr. Clay and Mr. Crittenden.

John Jordan Crittenden. He had risen since her first acquaintance with him. In 1848, when the Whigs elected Zachary Taylor, he could have had the party's nomination for the presidency; but, out of regard for his old friend, Mr. Clay, he had refused to allow his name to be considered. As Anna Marie had said, he was more than ever the charming gentleman, still in the full vigor of manhood. The years ahead might still bring him name and fame.

John Jordan Crittenden. Was he lonely, as her dear children had suggested she might be? No, not a man with his list of friends. Not here. He had taken a house this season with Senators Toombs and Alexander Stephens of Georgia—two who might be counted on to keep any friend's days and nights from being dull. No, for all his band of crepe, John Jordan Crittenden had not worn the look of a lonely man that evening. Subdued below his usual run of high spirits, but very alive and alert. Well, of course. This was his city, too.

Washington . . . She stirred and opened her eyes. The early

winter dusk had turned to dark while she rested. Only a pale glow of light from a gas lamp on the street below illumined her parlor. On impulse, she sat up, and then, as easily as she had placed herself in the chair, slipped out of it and stood up. Carefully she made her way through the shadowy obstacles of chairs and tables to the brightest window and stood there, looking down on Pennsylvania Avenue.

Washington in midwinter of 1851. The dear, dear, changing and unchanging picture! To her left, the Capitol, its classic outline marred again by scaffolding. Work had begun on new wings to be added. As the nation grew, so must its government offices; and the bare trees of winter exposed all the skeletons of that growth.

Building went on in all directions. Down the Avenue, where Thomas Jefferson's unhappy poplars had been replaced by elms, which might in their turn some day go down before the axe, and in areas to either side, dark masses of stone and granite now housed special functions and departments of governing a people that multiplied and a country that stretched from sea to sea. Some day each phase of government might have its own stone or marble palace.

Houses, too, multiplied. People who had once wondered what could be made of such a slough of a townsite now fretted for fear that it would presently lose its arboreal charm. At Fourteenth Street, a great, barnlike hotel, operated by an enterprising man named Willard, was threatening the traditional supremacy of the old National and Brown's across the way. Beyond the White House and its sacred environs, in Georgetown Heights, where once she had happily and proudly and fashionably attended Farmers' Market in company of Mrs. Clay and other ladies of note, where legislators whose names were now history had once gone fishing and hunting for relaxation, great, elegant homes were rising. Mr. Calhoun had been among the first to build out that way. Now almost everyone of means or with hope of permanency was following his example. If things had gone for her as once she had hoped they might, she could have been one of those elect.

Pshaw! A person could lose himself in a swamp of ifs, once he tried to relive the past. She had done well enough. She was here, was she not—in the place she liked best to be of all the world? Her eyes swept the panorama again—more and more lights pricking the darkness—on the Potomac the riding lights of boats at anchor, a battleship or two, a private yacht, small sailing boats, a clumsy, waddling ferryboat. On the canal a light moved, suggesting a child's toy pulled by a string. From the direction of the railway depot, a hoarse steam whistle split the silence. A train of cars arriving or departing. A person could travel west or north or south that way—a dusty, fatiguing business if one went very far, but expeditious certainly. Her lips parted in ecstasy as she watched and listened and perceived. Standing at her narrow window, she felt the city's very heartbeat, and hers warm and close against it.

Why, if she had been able to see only the scrap of Pennsylvania Avenue just below, the view would have breadth and scope. A carriage drew up at that moment before the hotel entrance. The footman on guard hurried to the curb to open the door. A gentleman in a caped coat stepped out, then turned, tall hat in hand, to assist his companion to alight. His hair shone white in the light of the gas lamps. The lady wore silver slippers, a voluminous wrap of red velvet, and a jeweled comb in her hair. Bother! They disappeared too swiftly under the National's new door canopy for her to recognize them surely. She could, however, have come within three names of being sure.

On the other hand, the episode reminded her that the supper hour was at hand. Her promised collation would be arriving, and she must not be found in the dark. Just that would be enough to start a rumor: "Mrs. Ashley is feeling the loss of her daughter. She spends too much time alone, brooding. What can we do to keep her from pining?"

Well, she couldn't allow that. She must have a light at once. She turned from the window and, again guarding against her full skirts' overturning light obstacles in her path, made her way to the mantel, beside which hung a wrought-iron wall bracket, holding Lucifer matches. She hesitated before striking one, then chose an oil lamp on a small stand near by. It was a pretty lamp, with a china base and a china globular shade about its glass chimney, both base and globe ornamented with painted sprigs of violets. She had done the flowers herself during a season when china painting was all the rage. Many of the furnishings in the room, particularly the ornaments, were her own. When she was away and other patrons used these rooms, the hotel boxed and stored her belongings until she sent word that she was returning; and there they all were in place when she arrived. It gave her a nice, settled feeling to find them waiting.

She lighted the lamp, adjusted the wick and the shade, blew out the match and returned it to the waste pocket in the wall bracket. There, that was better. The room, a little crowded, as a hotel sitting room nearly always was, looked cosier with soft illumination. Now, what should she do in order to appear busy? In foreknowledge of the answer, she wrinkled her nose. She ought to look over her mail. Some of it cried aloud for answering and for days she had given the matter no attention. Her desk was full . . . ah-h! On the top shelf, above the pigeonholes, between a silver comfit dish and a silver candlestick, lay a fresh packet that must have arrived that afternoon. It was such a packet that whoever had thoughtfully placed it there for her had knotted a string about it to keep any of the items from escaping.

Elizabeth closed her eyes, hoping that, when she opened them, the packet would have disappeared. There had been a time, she well remembered, when her hands had reached out eagerly for letters. That had been when someone else had removed the burrs from her nuts, leaving her only the tender kernels to enjoy. Now she had to take burrs and all; and, she had long since learned that husks were out of all proportion to the goodies they surrounded.

To prove her contention, when she received mail, she always began by sorting it. On a lower level of the desk lay now four neat piles of correspondence. The first was letters, just letters, from friends and kinfolk, awaiting her pleasure and convenience. The second was invitations. These were both fair-sized stacks at present, but she could reduce them in a few hours, and very pleasantly, tomorrow or the day after. The third pile would probably throw her into a headache when she tackled it, being composed of communications from various business agents. It was the smallest pile of the four, because the letters usually were brief: "We have today placed to your credit . . . We regret to inform you . . . I enclose . . ." etc. If she had only been able to tell from the outside how the text would begin, she could have made still another classification: money as opposed to advice. There was one agent in particular, and he the most important of all—Mr. James Tower Sweringen of St. Louis—who could be counted on to deliver a minimum of one well-meant sermon per annum. "My dear lady, with your best interests at heart . . . " Ah, dear! She thought she saw in the unopened packet atop the desk the special blue-white stationery he favored. Now, if that letter did not contain a money draft or a statement of credit, Heaven help her! For the fourth pile of mail was bills. Naturally and quite justifiably, she felt, it was the greatest pile.

How Mr. Sweringen would regard the matter, if he knew—and in time he must know—was open to question. Money had a vexatious way of coming late for a person's immediate requirements. She remembered one horrible occasion when she and Anna Marie had been held virtual prisoner in rooms at Irving House in New York, while they waited on a money draft, past due, she writing daily and frantically to Mr. Sweringen for succor. Mr. Hugh Campbell of Philadelphia had come finally to her rescue, being nearer and within reach of the telegraph, but it had been a hideous experience. Mr. Sweringen had apologized afterward, blaming the mails for the delay; but she would always be sure he had meant to teach her a lesson. Men could be tiresome that way. Now, if Mr. Sweringen chose to be difficult about these wedding bills, how would she handle him?

The blue-white edge of paper in the unopened packet of mail tormented her until she could think of nothing else. Finally she took down the bundle and cut the string. The mail scattered over the table of the desk and, gathering the pieces, she thought, "I will sort all of it before reading any," and began to do so. Two invitations checked the movement of her hands, but firmly she laid them on their proper pile. A letter stopped her next. Oh, dear! Young Bernie Farrar writing from Charlottesville, reminding her that he had asked if he might spend his midwinter vacation with her in Washington instead of remaining at school, the journey home being still too long for a short holiday. She had meant to answer his plea at once, telling him, by all means, to come right along. He knew he was always welcome. She must write now, at once. . . .

No. A glance at her calendar told her she was too late. Bernie's holiday would have begun before her letter could reach him. What he had to say now, bless his heart, was that he realized why he had not heard from her. She had been too busy to write; so he was coming on, anyhow. He would arrive on such and such a day—well, she was glad. She loved having her young cousins with her. They were so alive, so full of zestful curiosity about everything that went on. Bernie would be present for the New Year's levee, the return of Congress—

Hm! His mother might not approve. Partly that would be maternal jealousy, partly a growing attitude of question toward Elizabeth on the part of her relatives, because she had such a good time living, making her money serve her instead of her serving the money. What ever did people mean by suggesting that she was alone in the world? Never had a woman been more surrounded by solicitous people. She began a pout, then smiled. Dear Aunt Farrar, way off yonder, widowed, sensing her remoteness, fearful always for the welfare of the sons she had mothered—she must write to Aunt Farrar first thing in the morning, to reassure her. She must try to tell her what drew her sons—first young Dr. John and now fun-loving Bernie—to the capital. It was no preference for her, E. Ashley; it was other excitement, and all of it to their advantage, really.

Still smiling, now indulgently—the boys did enjoy visiting her—she laid that letter on its pile and went on with her sorting. When she had finished, the heaps were higher but in the same general ratio. And now at last, Mr. Sweringen. She held his letter under flattened palms on the desk and turned her eyes upward in silent petition—just for what favor might be granted her in this hour. Unfortunately, this brought into range two portraits on the wall above the desk. One was of herself, a black and white reduction of that fifteen-year-old painting— Heavens, she had forgotten the artist's name. The original portrait she had given to the Huntons in New Orleans, then had had this print made because the children wanted it and it was a suitable companion piece to the second portrait—an enlargement from a miniature of William Ashley. The latter was not a good likeness. It emphasized the sharpness of his long chin and his prominent nose. It masked the kindness that she knew had lurked behind the firmness of his thin-lipped mouth. But it was only too good of his eyes. Some days they seemed to follow her every movement when she was in the room. Right now, from the shadows, they glowed at her in a kind of mischief:

"My sweet Libby! Did you no service. . . ."

She bridled, then with a gesture of impatience broke the seal of the letter under her hands and unfolded the pages. It was a long letter, but—

"Coincident with this, I am depositing with W. W. Corcoran and Company the sum of one thousand dollars. . . ."

She could breathe again. That pile of bills—a very leaning tower of Pisa—could be reduced considerably if she paid off her Washington obligations. She wanted to be right at the pleasant task, but discretion told her to wait on that, too, until morning. She wanted to make no mistakes in addition or subtraction. Corcoran and Company was indulgent with small errors—Mr. Corcoran was a true Irish gentleman—but, whether anyone believed it of her or not, she had considerable pride about being right in her sums.

More cheerfully she braced herself for the remainder of the letter, which must be, and was, the anticipated homily: "While I know that you have been at considerable expense . . . with your best interests at heart . . . there is a satisfaction in not allowing one's obligations to run ahead of collections. . . ."

Bless the man! He was very patient, really; and she must often have been a trial to him, especially this past year, when things had seemed fairly to outrun even her sense of discretion. She must do better now and she would. Tomorrow morning, ahead of letters and invitations, she would settle the Washington bills, and report immediately her balance there, if any, also the sum of her obligations elsewhere and what would be needed to cover them. All this must be out of the way before the New Year, after which she meant to surprise all her financial agents with her proper conduct of affairs. She would not only give her collections and rentals time to establish safe balances for her; she might even have enough over to permit her making a modest quarterly allowance to each of her daughters. This had been her firm intention ever since Mary Jane had married young Andrew McKinley. Even before that. She did not want her girls to have to ask their husbands for everything they wanted or needed. She wanted each to have funds of her own. Why? She just wanted it that way.

But this was not the time to mention such a wish to Mr. Sweringen. The bills and credits first. Tomorrow morning without fail. Heavens, yes, before young Bernie Farrar burst upon the scene. There'd be little business done with him buzzing around.

A knock on her door made her jump. Not Bernie already? No, of course not. That collation . . . and she was beginning, in truth, to feel a little hungry.

"Who is it?" she called.

"Me, Miss Libby."

"Poke? Come in. The door's unlocked."

Poke came in. Her gratification expanded to include him. Good Poke! Like Susanna, a constant source of satisfaction. He did her credit even in the smallest ways. His appearance, for example. At the time of Ashley's death, when the most worn of that gentleman's broadcloths had been fitted to equip Poke with livery suitable to a house in mourning, she had known what disposal to make of the rest. She had stored everything in camphor-impregnated chests against the future. The supply was still far from exhausted.

"Don't you dare fatten now!" she had admonished Poke.

And he had not. Today, in his sober blacks, enlivened by a cream-colored waistcoat with brass buttons, he looked the absolute in the way of trustworthy gentility. With all that, he was still Dr. Moss's boy, Poke.

"Miss Libby, you leave yore do' unlock' lak dat?"

"Now, Poke! This is the National Hotel, and nobody . . ."

"Yas'm. You 'member dat time yore watch got stole? 'At pretty lil Swiss lady watch?"

"That was Saratoga," Libby reminded him, "where everybody came and went."

"Sa'toga or Washin'ton, ain' much diffunce. We got thieves yere, too. Dey's lak bedbugs. You gotta . . ."

Libby changed the subject.

"Are those more flowers?" she asked, knowing that the long bundle, well-wrapped in paper, in Poke's hands could be nothing else.

"Yas'm." Poke's grin touched both ears. "An' a telegraph, too."

He handed Elizabeth the message. It was from Mr. Hobbs of New Orleans. Urgent business was bringing him to Washington before Congress reconvened— Mercy, with Young Bernie Farrar on her hands! Bernie would furnish the family with a morsel. She made a face at the telegram. She had nothing really against Mr. Hobbs, a rich and lavish gentleman, except that she could never think of him apart from his money; and right now, too much reckoning of money had left a metallic taste in her mouth.

She looked up; and Poke had laid back the wrappings from the flowers—a sheaf of pale yellow roses.

"Mr. Senator Toombs's boy brung 'em," Poke reported, "wid a note."

The note had been written by Mr. Crittenden. It said—and most appealingly—that three derelicts from Bachelors' Hall, bereft in one way or another of sweet companionship, would consider the day illumined in gold if Mrs. Ashley would grant them the radiance of her presence at a supper party they were arranging for the evening. Toombs's boy would carry her reply.

She looked up from the note to Poke, standing there with his arms full of roses, waiting. She had no doubt that he knew what was in the note. To cover her pleased surprise at the attention offered her, again she turned the subject.

"I was reading a letter from St. Louis when you came in," she said.

"Yas'm." Poke's face clouded with disappointment, and some apprehension.

"A good letter, Poke, from Mr. Sweringen, with news that might interest you. Mr. Ashley's man, James, wants to purchase his freedom."

"He do?" A blast of scorn. "You gonna let um go, Miss Libby?"

"Surely, if that's what he wants."

"Might as well. Man widout propah 'tachment."

"Naturally not for me, Poke. But it set me to thinking. Poke, I wouldn't want to keep anyone against his own will. Have you ever thought . . . ?"

"Miss Libby!" This was pure horror. "Mist' Sweringen ain' say you cain' keep me now?"

"Heavens, no, Poke. He wouldn't dream of doing that."

"Well, den. Miss Libby, you jes' kinda ove'come wid things, ain' you? You wanna bresh it off now, ef you kin. I'll fotch a pitchah o' watah fo' dese posies whilst you write a note to dose gemmun sayin' you'll be glad to take suppah wid 'em. Do you good, Miss Libby. I tole um downstairs not to bothah wid' a tray fo' you. You'd likely be goin' out presently."

Speechless, Elizabeth watched him leave with the roses. With some difficulty, then, she extracted a sheet of stationery and a pen and the inkwell from her barricaded desk and thanked Mr. Crittenden, Mr. Toombs and Mr. Stephens for their gift of roses, saying she would be most happy to join their party and would be ready when they called. She was signing her name when Poke came back with the flowers in water. He set them carefully on a stand and lit two burners of the chandelier in the center of the room.

"Miss Libby," he offered, extinguishing the taper, "ef you needs a gal place o' Susan, I knows one." She was sure that he knew a number. "Aberlitionists," he concluded, "ain' tuk ovah yere yit awhile."

"Thank you, Poke, not tonight." Smiling, she handed him the note. "I won't bother to change this evening. I'll just freshen up a bit."

"Yas'm. I—I'll be back direckly. I'll lock up and put out de lights. Don' you bothah, Miss Libby."

And his black shadow would preserve all the proprieties surrounding her name, tonight and always, she knew. On the way to her bedroom, she stooped to sniff the roses, then straightened to take a good look at herself—a woman most blessed by Heaven—in a gold-framed mirror on the nearest wall.

On the whole what she saw was not unpleasing. She hardly looked her years. A fair forty, perhaps, but a very fair one. Not a thread of gray in her shining hair, its natural wave just rippling the fashionable smooth coiffure. She had added some weight—a pound for each year of the past ten, perhaps. Enough to plump out what could have been wrinkles or hollows. Her complexion was creamy, smooth, her eyes were still bright. Not so wide or so deep as once they had been; but that scrawny girl could never have worn her favorite deep décolletage; and the gold chain with the emeralds had always looked too heavy, while now . . .

On impulse, she unfastened its clasp and laid the necklace aside. The earrings next, and the bracelets. She snipped off a rosebud and tucked it into her chignon. Another she fastened in the lace on her breast. There! Did she imagine it, or was there a transfiguration? A simple velvet band and brooch now for her throat—behind her someone mocked at her whimsy.

"My sweet Libby! Did you no service . . ."

Hush now, General Ashley. You, out yonder on that lonely Indian mound, laid with your face toward a meandering river—your feet, too, for that matter, so that, come Judgment Day, you can just get up and follow where it leads—hush now, and let your lady be!

CHAPTER TWO

Mr. Attorney-General

ANNA MARIE WAS IN TEARS. The whole suite was in an uproar.

"Poor Edward!" Anna Marie sobbed. "As if he didn't feel bad enough about losing his seat in Congress!"

Elizabeth put the tip of her tongue between her teeth and held it—gently. If Cabell weren't always so cocksure of himself, so certain that he was in the right that nobody could tell him otherwise, he might not have lost the recent election. Mr. Crittenden and others had warned him that the voters who had honored him with their trust lived in Florida the year around and he wasn't spending enough time among them. It wasn't enough to have canvassed the state once or twice in the past, to make himself known. It had to be done every time there was an election. Folks forgot. But no. This time Cabell had had to take himself out to Missouri, setting himself up as her—E. Ashley's—legal adviser, his purpose being to set her finances in order, obtain a complete accounting, settle all debts and claims, turn over certain valueless property—

Valueless property—dear Heaven grant her patience now!

"You don't like him, really," Anna Marie sobbed.

Elizabeth released her tongue briefly, then caught it again. About to remind Anna Marie that it was she in the first place who had selected the young man as the most likely of the suitors who offered, she had to admit to herself that liking had not influenced her choice. Edward Carrington Cabell was a most estimable young man, a gentleman and a gentleman's son. He was proving a devoted husband and father, and Anna Marie justly was loyal to him; but, as for herself, Elizabeth Ashley, right now she wished she had never heard tell of him.

"He didn't ask to take charge of your business," Anna Marie said.

Elizabeth could hold her tongue no longer.

"No?" she demanded. "Surely I didn't think of it myself."

Anna Marie's tears came in a fresh outburst.

"You were more than willing," she charged.

Yes. Very probably. And why not? The way Cabell came to have his residence in Florida was that his father had sent him down there to take charge of property the family had bought.

His father had sent him . . . his own father . . . oh, dear!

Still, educated both in law and in engineering, he had done very well in Florida, developing several plantations with upward of two hundred hands working them. He had canvassed the state from end to end and got himself elected to Congress.

Once, twice, even a third time, with a steadily narrowing majority; and now he had been turned out. It was all very well for people to say that the defeat of the Whig party in 1852 was general and national, that the South was going to be represented from now on by Andrew Jackson's more forthright disciples, the Democrats. Cabell himself might talk big about his return to Florida, of the work he meant to do on the plantations, now that he was free of other obligations, of a railroad he was going to lay out. The fact remained. Temporarily he was out of a job.

As for helping Elizabeth, well, whatever Cabell's impact on Florida, his work for her in Missouri had been little short of disastrous. With an enthusiasm which she had at the time admired and only now began to question, he had set about his task of reducing her tangled affairs to order. His plan had been to gather information on her various and scattered sources of income, together with a similar summary of outstanding obligations and claims, into one large accounting. Upon this bewilderment he would then turn the light of his legal acumen and fresh, wholly disinterested, viewpoint; and the result would be an absolutely clean sheet tomorrow or the next day at the latest. The first of the year certainly. Out of a great need for somebody's assistance, she had signed a power of attorney.

Oh, dear! The nearer Cabell had come to doing all he promised, the more out of pocket she was. He had made collections, spreading bitterness everywhere by his persistence. Then, with equal gusto and a fine sense of moral rectitude, she had no doubt, he had begun on her debts. He had done an equally thorough job at that. Only a few notes remained, neatly packaged and described on the exposed cover; but what she was going to live on during the next few months, not even Cabell could rightly say. He had cleared her books the way a grass fire clears a prairie.

But the worst feature of all, worse than the offense Cabell's operations had given, the thing that made her ache with dismay and helplessness, was that he had sold some of her land in Boonslick. For a mere pittance. The sum obtained had vanished like a raindrop in

July. Deeds of sale were all she had left of a thousand acres. It made her ill to read them.

"I don't understand your attitude," Cabell said when she reproached him with this transaction.

Indeed? Obviously, Ashley's eyes from the wall did not haunt him. *"All in land. . . . Keep it and it will keep you. . . . Hold it. Don't sell."*

"Worthless hill country," Cabell said. "The tenants' rent hardly covered taxes."

But now it was gone—just gone. Her alarm was deep and real.

"Worthless," obtusely Cabell kept repeating. "You had a report on it from that Mr. Freeman of Boonville."

"That Mr. Freeman" was Barcie Harris's husband. He and Barcie had attended Ashley's funeral and called on Elizabeth afterward. The ever-widening gulf between Elizabeth and Barcie had put more of a constraint upon their meeting than if they had been utter strangers; but Mr. Freeman had been bold enough to say that, if he could ever be of service to Elizabeth in the way of business or friendship, he would be proud to have her call upon him; and Barcie had added wistfully, "It's been a long time, Libby."

She had seen the Freemans again at the time of her mother's death, and after that had maintained a desultory correspondence with one or the other. If she wanted an agent to buy or sell for her, why in Heaven's name hadn't she employed Mr. Freeman? As long ago as 1840 he had taken up with her an offer for part of the La Mine tract— that part with the springs. She had been too timid, still too overawed by her possessions and how she had come by them, to consider selling; but the sum offered had been magnificent in comparison with the miserable amount Edward Cabell had obtained for a thousand acres. Afterward, just recently, when, to be honest, she herself had entertained the thought of selling a farm or two—but only at a good profit— Freeman had been honest enough to advise against it. Right now the discovery of gold in California had sent everybody in such a mad rush for the Pacific Coast that property in the Midwest had declined severely in price. That had been all of Mr. Freeman's derogatory report.

What would he think of her now, if he knew? Of course, he did know. The sale had been recorded in Boonville. One of these days even Ashley's sisters in Virginia would hear about it and add their inquiry. Ashley's sisters. They had seemed content all this while with her continuance of the allowance Ashley had made them during his lifetime. An annual acknowledgment of the receipt of the money was all she heard from them, but she had always an uneasy feeling that some day she would hear more. Let them discover that she had converted Ashley land into money—much or little money—and that would bring them out of hiding.

These and other ghosts haunted her, but none so terribly or so constantly as those bits of paper which were the deeds of sale.

"The worst of it is," she said now to Anna Marie, "I have no place to turn in my distress, nobody to help me. All my friends have taken offense. The Campbells are barely polite. Mr. Sweringen was downright cold when I was in St. Louis in June, and I haven't had a line from him since."

She was genuinely sorry that her trust in Cabell had turned out so badly. The worst feature of her years of independence had been the lack of some one person able and willing to handle her rather complex finances. Help she had in abundance and too much advice, really, but nowhere ever that one dependable person. She had had high hopes of Cabell. He had seemed so capable and forthright. Now —well, now she'd have to go back to handling everything herself, placate Mr. Sweringen and the others somehow, unless . . . unless . . .

After Ashley's death, with a comfortable living assured her as long as she lived, she had vowed there was one thing she would never try again—marriage. Now here she was, contemplating it very seriously. At any time in the past fourteen years such a course had been open to her. It still was possible. There was Mr. Hobbs, for instance. Lately he had become assiduously attentive. Oddly, the more attentive he was, the more something in her withdrew. It might be his wealth. His fortune made hers seem a mere competence, and she liked being "the wealthy Mrs. Ashley." But what really dimmed Mr. Hobbs's prospects now was the fact that in the last year another gentleman had come forward, one whom she had known for years, without dreaming that ever— Well, she dreamed now, and so absorbedly, that presently, when she looked up, Anna Marie had dried her tears and was studying her, Elizabeth, with a steadiness of contemplation that Elizabeth recognized.

Bless the girl! Often Elizabeth had thought that, except for her resemblance to Daniel Wilcox, Anna Marie could have been Ashley's own daughter. She had probably put Cabell up to offering his services as Elizabeth's attorney in charge of her business; and she was, in spite of copious tears, by no means ready to relinquish that handhold on fortune.

"Mamma," she said, "don't you think you have been hasty in dismissing Edward? He has had hardly time to show you what he could do." Mercy! Two years of such service and his mother-in-law would be a pauper. "He feels that you need someone." Did he really? "You don't even know, he thinks, how rich you are."

No! True enough. But now Cabell knew—and Anna Marie? Things had come to a pretty pass when she mistrusted her own child.

"Just now," Anna Marie continued, with a smoothness that Elizabeth herself had taught her, "if you are temporarily a little short, until things pick up again or for as long as you like, Edward and I would be proud to have you share our home in Florida."

Florida? What was there in her destiny, Elizabeth wondered, that eternally opened the abyss of wilderness life at her feet? Florida— swamps, snakes, Indians . . . she would resist exile there to the last ditch, but pleasantly, if possible.

"Darling," she said, "that's most kind of you and Cabell. I treasure your offer. However, from all I've heard, I think I would probably not be happy in Florida. I don't exactly like the prospect for you and little Ashley Cabell. You must manage to spend most of the year on the coast and . . . we'll see. We'll see. Now, no more tears. A swollen nose never endeared a woman to any husband. Use cold water and— Oh, my!" She glanced at the face of an enameled watch pinned among her laces. "I must dress now. I have an afternoon engagement."

"Mamma," Anna Marie said petulantly, not liking to be put aside, and especially not in this fashion, "you have more engagements still than any other woman alive. Who is it this time?"

"I am taking tea, dear, with Mr. Crittenden."

"Mamma, again? Really, people are beginning to talk."

"In Washington," Elizabeth said gaily, "I should be more concerned if people stopped talking. Don't worry, child. About me, after all these years, the talk is not slanderous, only speculative. Susanna! Where is the girl? With the baby, I suppose. You know, Anna Marie, when you do leave for Florida, you'll have to provide another nurse. I can't do without Susanna permanently. Susanna— Oh, there you are! Susanna, the plum-colored silk with the black velvet jacket, and no other wrap, I think. It's a very mild day for November."

A mild, sunny day, summer taking a last fling before winter swooped down. The trees, except the oaks, had lost their leaves, but here and there in a sheltered corner of a garden late roses bloomed. Everybody who could walk or ride was out. The benches behind the iron fence of the President's Park were all occupied—dignified statesmen reading their newspapers, visiting, or coaxing squirrels with nut meats.

"Poor fellows," Crittenden said. "No pretty ladies to go riding with."

With Poke's connivance, he had hired a carriage for the afternoon. Since Ashley's death, Elizabeth had not kept one except in St. Louis. People who charged her with extravagance should credit her with that economy. Really, living in so many places as she did, and with travel so much improved, a carriage of her own would have been a nuisance. She did, however, have an open account with a livery man, who always managed to have on demand what she wanted. On Poke's demand, that is. Poke personally selected landau, barouche, or closed buggy, and then drove her where she wanted to go. He drove the open carriage now. This was a help to sociability, because he needed little direction. It also added something to propriety, but probably increased speculation, which, of course, took nothing from the zest of the afternoon's engagement.

Elizabeth smiled at Poke's correct back, at Mr. C.'s compliment, and then turned thoughtful. To this day she was not sure that she understood fully the special charm that was John Jordan Crittenden's. So many things entered into it. A sweetness that was a boy's, when a boy was sweet, which was a frank, natural essence that no daughter of Eve could possess. A fresh, unspoiled faith in the rightness of everything, at least, a certainty that right must always prevail; and one didn't look for that in a man who had made a high name for himself in criminal as well as civil law, and who was still reputed to be the best whist player in the capital. It was, she concluded not for the first time, a great inward kindliness, so evident to all, that even now almost everyone they met still called him John. Sam Houston, in wide-brimmed hat and panther-skin waistcoat, riding his tall, cream-colored horse as if the streets of Washington were the Great Plains, Jefferson Davis and Mrs. Davis, turning from a street demonstration of a sewing machine, the Honorable Mr. James Seddon of Richmond and his beautiful, brown-eyed bride, Mr. Caleb Cushing of Massachusetts—all greeted them in the same way:

"Evening, Mrs. Ashley. Well, John?"

Only the ladies said Mr. Crittenden or Mr. Attorney-General. Elizabeth studied the side view of Crittenden's face while he talked with Mr. Cushing and was impressed by the fact that, for all his easy friendliness, his features were as clear-cut, his profile was as strong as the New Englander's. What should one make of that?

"Mr. Crittenden," she said, as they drove on, wanting now all of his attention for herself, "this is my first opportunity to thank you for making an opening in your law office in Frankfort for my son-in-law, Andrew McKinley. I am sure there are many closer to you than he is to claim your kindness."

Her ruse worked at least to the extent of causing Crittenden to turn her way, with a smile so warm and so suddenly intense that it fairly confused her.

"I didn't make the opening," he said, "though I would have done more than that at your request and for the Judge's son. As things are turning out, I have much the best of the bargain. Young McKinley is a fine fellow, a credit to his late father. I wish I could be as sure that he will prosper according to his abilities. We practise much law in Kentucky; but payment is slow, the people down there not being drilled to recompense service which seems so friendly and personal. Have you ever visited Frankfort?"

"No," she answered, still confused, and amazed at herself for being so, "only in Louisville and Maysville. My father has relatives in both places. I was born near Maysville."

"Were you, indeed? But you will come to Frankfort now?"

"Why, yes, I suppose so. The children—"

"We'd be proud to have you, ma'am. We'd roll out a carpet for you to walk upon. I mean it. We like nothing better than to make glad welcome for those we love and honor." He smiled again, wholly for her, then turned away, to look at something she could not see, to study some problem rising in his own mind. "You've never been there," he meditated. "How, then, can I make you see? It's a quiet town, old, a little poky except when we have important company or the legislature's meeting. A little poky even then, compared to some places. We think a lot and talk a lot, and go visiting and such— and get along with a minimum of doing."

Elizabeth laughed.

"I know," she said. "The pushing folk moved on west. Peace and peaceable folk stayed where they were."

"That's our choice," Crittenden agreed, "when we can have it. We can't always." His face darkened and he spoke now with fierce vehemence. "I love every stick and stone of Kentucky in general and Frankfort in particular."

It was a very passion of loyalty, a little disturbing to hear.

"Mr. Crittenden," Elizabeth said softly, "I will not be distracted from finishing the speech I set out to make. My children—Andrew

215

McKinley and my little Mary Jane—are very happy in your town. Andrew feels that it is a privilege to serve a legal apprenticeship in your office; and I think he's right."

"Do you truly?"

"I do, indeed."

"Why, thank you, ma'am. That's a mighty pretty speech from a beautiful lady, most gratifying to a dusty old lawyer's weary ears."

He seemed to her anything but a dusty old lawyer. He had lived a while, but so had she. He was not old. A good ten years younger than Ashley, he had seemed a young man when they had met first. A man in his middle sixties, possibly, but even so, not old. That way he had of brushing back his hair with his hand—heavy hair, now frankly gray, but the brow smooth and the dark eyes clear. Confusion swept over her again—warm, incredibly sweet.

"You—" she began gropingly, then thought he had forgotten her. He was not old, but he could be tired. His work as Attorney-General must be trying. Every year times and conditions grew more troubled until nobody knew just what would be the end of all the differences. These were now chiefly over slavery. Twice recently a motion had all but reached the floor of Congress to free all slaves in the District of Columbia, to set an example to the nation.

Slavery . . . what had been custom when the nation was born, then a bone of contention as it grew, was now an increasing bitterness on men's tongues, a bitterness that had passed beyond most men's personal feelings, because it had come to apply to industry, to profits and losses, to tariff, to territorial expansion. Ugly words like civil war and revolution and uglier personal epithets crept into public speeches and had to be expunged from the record later. A terrible righteousness spread over the northern half of the country, and its expression made the fairest-minded Southerners stiffen their jaws and hurl back defiance. It did more. Surveyors' lines between states, parallels, became something heavier and blacker than marks on a map. Beyond the Missouri River, where Kansas had now enough settlers to justify its being made into a territory, organized government was made impossible because men argued and even fought over whether people could or could not take their slaves with them when they moved there from Missouri. In St. Louis on her latest visit the feeling had been, if possible, more heated than here in Washington, though, of course, it was in Washington that the issue would finally be settled.

Not a dusty old lawyer. John Jordan Crittenden, Attorney-General of the United States of America, a loyal, devoted citizen, these things heavy on his heart and in his mind. How could she distract him, since, when such a man asked a lady out to tea, distraction was surely what he sought? She sighed.

"Was that you," he asked incredulously, "making that mournful sound?"

Had she sounded doleful? She said she was sorry, but she, too, had her troubles.

"You?" He was more unbelieving than ever. "What kind of troubles?"

Should she tell him? Yes, perhaps that was the very thing.

"Money troubles."

He laughed. He screwed his features into a mockery of grave consideration. He gave up the disguise and snorted, then shouted his laughter.

"That," he said, "is, I am sure, as charming an absurdity as you ever uttered."

It might be absurd, but it was also painfully true. Then, would she care to tell him the whole story? She pondered that a while. It was not a confession she would make to many people, but Mr. Crittenden was not many people. He was one apart. Poke, uninstructed, had headed the carriage toward a road that skirted the Potomac. It was an old road, newly discovered by the growing population of the capital, and so, frequented just enough for a minimum of respectability. Other carriages this bright day had turned into it. At wide intervals some had drawn to a halt. Their own wheels turned slowly.

"There is time for a stroll," Crittenden suggested. "Would you like that? There seems to be no dust."

That for her plum-colored silk, the braided black velvet jacket and the small bonnet to match, set back on her bright hair. A most considerate man.

"You forget," she said, "that I grew up in a place where mostly there were no roads, sometimes not even paths."

But she had not worn crinoline in those days. They did not abandon the carriage until they found a place where a wide, well-beaten stretch of ground bordered the river.

"I'd be honored by your confidence," Crittenden urged, "but I should want to hear everything, beginning with the land where there were no roads."

Yes, of course, if she told him anything, she must tell it all; and she wanted more and more to do just that. Finally she tossed discretion, the schooling of years of social practice aside, and began.

She touched lightly on the Boonslick era, wondering at her timidity, until a pain that she had not felt in years thrust at her. A house, a green and smiling countryside, dear, almost forgotten faces, sweet simple ways of living came back to her. Daniel . . . she hurried on.

"Anna Marie looks like her father," she said. "I've often wished that she could have been a son."

Quickly then to her life with William Ashley—expanded horizons, because he was a man who recognized no boundaries. St. Louis, Washington, the glimmer of silk and jewels and . . .

"When I first knew you," Crittenden reminded her.

"Do you remember?" Elizabeth asked.

"I remember perfectly."

"I admired Mrs. Crittenden so much," Elizabeth evaded, "but . . . she didn't altogether approve of me, did she?"

"You do my Maria an injustice," Crittenden said. "She was never harshly critical of anyone, certainly not of you. The best and the worst she ever said was that a woman with so much beauty and so much love of life, endowed with wealth, besides, was carrying too much water in her pail. She was fearful of your future; but she wished you only happiness, I am sure."

Elizabeth was not so sure. A good woman, but—

"Tell me more of General Ashley," Crittenden said. "He was a man too little credited with his great accomplishments."

But not in his own mind, Elizabeth felt. What would he have thought of the mess she was in now? So sure himself always!

"Not always," Crittenden said. "A man of decision, but, like the rest of us, harassed at times by doubt. He was only human."

Only human in the final judgment. Elizabeth saw herself standing by the window of the house at La Mine, a house empty before it was filled, watching a funeral cortege make its way over the rise of a hill overlooking a river—his river, Ashley's river, by right of conquest. It was a long procession she watched. The two Joseph La Barges, father and son, had made a record trip up the Missouri from St. Louis in young Captain Joseph's steamboat, the *Boonville,* carrying the mourners. The burial day was bleak with wind and rain; and Dr. Moss had urged Elizabeth to remain in the house with her mother, to watch from there. She stood by the window, her tears running unchecked; and Miss Mary, sharp-tongued to her last word, chided her.

"A person would think you'd lost another sweetheart."

"It is for him," Elizabeth said. "For all he had and all he did, he lived and died alone."

She had turned from the window then, knowing she must leave the house as soon as she could decently, that she must live far from the sight of that stark mound.

"It was after Ashley's death, I take it," Crittenden prompted, "that money became troublesome."

This it was to be a good lawyer—to have the right question ready for the right opening. With a lighter touch she outlined the difficulties that had accumulated, and was amazed to find many of them smoothing out as she talked. Her descriptions of James Tower Sweringen and other worthies who guarded her capital had Crittenden in stitches. This, he declared, was what power over finance did to men—turned them sour. Now, he, sadly lacking in such abilities, could laugh at her adventures in credit and debit. Did she know anyone in her circle, he inquired, who did not live more on his expectations than on what he had in hand? As to lawsuits, they were indigenous to property. The sons-in-law? He knew and loved young McKinley as one of his own sons. Cabell—it was well that young man had lost his seat in Congress and a little of his self-confidence early. He would serve himself, his state, his country, and her better when he returned to Washington.

"You laugh," Elizabeth complained, smiling herself as she spoke, "but I have reached the place where I take fright at a piece of paper and a pen, not knowing what may happen once I set my signature down: E. Ashley."

For a long minute Crittenden said nothing to that. Then—

"Would it help if you signed E. Crittenden, instead?"

Apparently it made no difference how much people, herself included, speculated on a possibility. When it became reality, when it was put into words, there would be a shock of surprise. She struggled for dignity in her answer; but when she gave it, with utmost sincerity, she told a falsehood.

"Mr. Crittenden . . . I never thought . . ."

"I assure you," he said, "it's been in my mind and heart a long while."

In the carriage, on the way back to town and tea, he added ruefully, "I know I have very little to offer you."

Did he really believe that? Mr. John Jordan Crittenden, Senator Crittenden, Mr. Attorney-General—and, many believed, not yet at the peak of his attainments? They passed the White House.

"You have everything you need to make you happy, without me— wealth, beauty. You are still a young woman. . . ."

There was only one thing she stood to lose by marriage—her independence. To give over now being the rich, the beautiful, the queenly Mrs. Ashley? To change her identity as well as her name again? Let nobody try to tell her that she could do one without the other. On the other hand . . .

"*A woman without fetters is a sorry spectacle. . . .*"

"I am thinking of you," she insisted.

Of him? Yes, of him. Bachelors' Hall, the happy existence he and Senator Toombs and "Little Ellick" Stephens had there would be destroyed. John Crittenden, Bob Toombs, Alec Stephens—they made a rare combination. They gave gay parties to which everyone sought an invitation. They entertained their male cronies at cards, sometimes from Friday to Monday, without a break. Many a course in national lawmaking was charted at those sessions.

A poor, one-armed, one-legged way to live, John Crittenden said now. Anyhow, Fate had already broken the combination. Alec Stephens was of those thrown out of office by the count of votes in the recent election; and Mrs. Toombs, after two winters away from Washington, was returning next year.

They were late for their tea. Gautier's was crowded, but no place in Washington could be so full that there would not be a choice table for Mr. Crittenden. And his lady. Seated there, to one side of the room, but in full view of a score of people who knew them well, Crittenden recklessly covered Elizabeth's hand with his and said,

"We have discussed the case now from all angles except one. My dearest, I love you with all my heart. Will you marry me?"

Elizabeth shook her head at him.

"You forget . . . I know what it is to love like that."

"My dear, I am sure you do. That was in your eyes when we first met. It glows there still. Otherwise—"

Otherwise she would have meant nothing to him, he meant. Dear Heaven, what had she done to deserve this devotion?

"The question, dear lady," Crittenden persisted, "calls for a simple yes or no."

Only one answer was possible. That answer, as Crittenden had suggested, had been in the making since the first hour of their acquaintance. Only the fact that neither had dreamed this present hour could come to be, had prevented recognition.

"Then it must be yes," Elizabeth said, lightly but through a mist of sudden tears, "if only to save my reputation."

To be again the center of another's thoughts and tenderest feeling, and that other John Jordan Crittenden! He wanted the marriage to take place at once. Toombs and Stephens would move out of their house and give immediate possession. But Elizabeth would hear to no such haste. The decencies must be respected. Crittenden must notify his children and more intimate friends and she must do the same before public announcement was made of their plans. However, when urged to set her own time, she yielded briefly to consideration of her personal advancement. With the coming in of a new President, Crittenden would be resigning his Cabinet post; and, while nobody thought he would be long out of office, she wanted to be known, however briefly, as Mrs. Attorney-General. In Washington, once a Cabinet lady always a Cabinet lady. Of that much she had best be sure.

She mentioned February. Reluctantly Crittenden agreed, but exacted a last promise. She must be influenced by no outcry on the part of her family.

"But there will be none," she said.

She was wrong. In her family circle, some—Cabell among them, but only in Anna Marie's behalf—questioned her right to hand over herself and her fortune, especially the latter, into a "stranger's" keeping. Among her Washington acquaintance she encountered many a raised eyebrow and acid-flavored felicitation. The latter she recognized as envy, the former she viewed sorrowfully as avarice; but both assured her that her decision had been a wise one.

On the whole, however, her friends and Crittenden's were most generous. Lily Foxe, a widow now too, wrote from New York begging for an invitation to the wedding. General Winfield Scott spoke for the privilege of "giving the bride away." Through January Elizabeth's hotel suite bloomed with flowers sent by those who wished both her and Crittenden long life and happiness together. All this, added to her own new serenity and enhanced confidence, made it possible for her to silence most objectors, even Cabell, who maintained his attitude of disapproval longest. Finally only a few could stir doubt in her. One of these was William Henry Ashley. In fourteen years of widowhood, Elizabeth had never been more conscious of his attitude of remonstrance.

"*Libby, Libby, what are you up to now?*"

"Nothing," she insisted. "It is true, I need help—protection. Surely there is nobody better able to give me that."

"*No better legal counsel certainly. Practically speaking, however—*"

"I am lonely. I shall be more so. The children gone and . . . Mr.

Crittenden is a dear fellow. I am very fond of him and he of me. He loves Washington, too, as much as I do."

"Suppose it should turn out not to be Washington? You will find Frankfort more tedious than he admits."

"I don't expect to be there long enough to weary of the place."

"So, that's it. I know the house you've got your eye on now. Libby, Libby . . ."

She went over and turned his picture to the wall, lacking at the last second courage to take it down, as she knew she must do presently.

CHAPTER THREE

At Home in Frankfort, Kentucky

THERE HAD BEEN thunder in the air all day. A storm warning, everyone said, apprehensive under bright sunshine. It was a still day. A person could hardly believe it was early November, except that the autumn had been queer all through. Any breeze there was stirred the leaves high in the treetops but hardly touched the picnickers on Elkhorn Creek. At four o'clock in the afternoon John Crittenden, with the ease of an old-hand at such diplomacy, stepped into the circle of women near the covered baskets, put his arm through his wife's, listened appreciatively and patiently until the last scrap of chatter died down, and then said softly,

"Ladies, Mrs. Crittenden—" into her ear a quick whisper: "My dearest"—"don't you think it might be a good idea to begin packing up? No hurry now. It's just that we can't carry everybody and everything in one load and it might be well to be under cover by dark."

"Oh, pshaw!" the ladies said, but began at once to scurry around, gathering each her own property and her own children. "There are so many things to talk about, so much to hear! You folks have been away practically all summer. We've only begun to get acquainted. Still, if you think . . ."

"I do," Crittenden said, his voice rich with satisfaction in what he took to be pure friendliness, which Elizabeth, too, knew to be friendliness but also, as the ladies said, mixed with much still-unsatisfied curiosity about her. "I do think we had better be going. As for the visiting, we've the winter ahead of us, and our door opens as easily as ever. I hope you'll come early and often."

Now, in the cool, shadowed darkness of the old house, the tension of the gathering storm was even more perceptible. Candle flames lay this way and that without any other sign of wind, and had to be snuffed out. The wicks of kerosene lamps were turned low. Mr. Crittenden was still away. He had insisted on going back to the picnic grounds with Poke and Andrew McKinley, to make sure that all stragglers had been collected. Children, he explained to Elizabeth, forgetting that she had been brought up in an atmosphere of barbecued pig and fried chicken and pies in a basket, would wander off and get lost. Somebody had to make the final tally.

As twilight deepened, the first true thunder began far off and rolled downhill toward the river and the town. A noisy, brawling stream, the Kentucky, when in a passion. Fed by countless creeks and branches, it could come to a boil in no time at all.

"Listen!" Elizabeth said to Mary Jane McKinley, who watched and waited with her, "I wonder what can be keeping your father."

It was Crittenden's wish that she speak of him so to her children; and he, in turn, sometimes with a barely perceptible wink, said "your mother" of her to his brood. A good man's virtue, she had discovered, expressed itself in small ways and great and she had married now a truly good man.

"Bes' I evah did know," Poke said, " 'cep' one—yore paw."

Elizabeth thought Crittenden's humanity surpassed even that of her father. Outwardly she accepted the maternal emphasis for the tribute she knew it was meant to be; but in her own mind she had not quite decided whether she liked it or not. Crittenden's two youngest sons, the bequest of the handsome Maria whom she had known, were engaging, open-natured youths, and she had taken them on and they her quite easily; but it was harder to achieve concord with several mature women and three bearded men who went back to a marriage so remote now that it was almost beyond her imagination's reach. The three older sons seemed in ways more mature than John Crittenden himself. However, if it added to her status as queen of this remarkable household for her husband to name her the mother of Major George Crittenden of the United States Army, of the present American consul at Liverpool, and of an established Louisville merchant, she would bear the honor gracefully or die trying.

"He's just talking," Mary Jane said now in answer to her surmise. "He'll be along. Surely, Mamma, you're not afraid of a thunderstorm."

"No," Elizabeth said. "No, of course not."

It was the house, perhaps . . .

No perhaps about it. It was the house and the town. New fears, new doubts had been aroused in her by both.

It was late April of their wedding year, 1853, when Crittenden handed her down to the wooden platform of the Frankfort railway depot, saying, "Welcome home, my darling. Welcome home at last!" In Washington, he had offered to stay on after the inauguration to

show the new Attorney-General the ways of his office; and President
Pierce had gratefully accepted this service. After that, the journey
west had been slow because they had stopped in a half-dozen places
to allow old friends the privilege of entertaining John Jordan Crittenden and his new wife—the gay, the beautiful Mrs. Ashley of
Washington society. How many friends Crittenden had everywhere!
They had been wined and dined and feted in every way imaginable;
and it had been an exhilarating adventure, in no way interrupting
Crittenden's devoted attention to her. After each rousing reception
he had turned from the crowd to her and said, "It's you, my darling.
They'd never go on like this just for me. You make everybody and
everything shine."

But Frankfort was sharply different. It was a little town, tucked
into the elbow of the tumbling river. A little town and old—so
mossy old that it was as much like something the river might have
deposited as anything man could have built, so little that everybody
literally knew everybody else and claimed priority of kinship for
that reason. It was the custom, when any beloved citizen had been
away for a few weeks or a year, for the whole town to gather at the
depot to meet him on his return; and the whole town was present that
April evening. Before Elizabeth could respond to Crittenden's welcome, she was seized by the Robert Letchers, and Crittenden by a
dozen others.

Mr. Orlando Brown, a neighbor, made a speech of greeting. It
was nothing short of biographical in scope. Crittenden replied at
length, managing to seem to include every citizen present. He, of
course, was prepared for what happened; Elizabeth was not. Tired
and dusty and warm, she had to make a public bow. Never had her
training—to spread smiles over any depth of inward turmoil—served
her better.

At long last they set out for the house—in a mass and on foot.
Since the house was only a few squares away, that was logical,
but again, to Elizabeth, unforeseen. Her fine kid shoes were too
thin for walking. She tossed them away, cut and scarred, the next
morning.

All in all, it was a weird, noisy hymeneal procession, she and the
Letchers leading, Crittenden with the Browns following, and then
the mob. Glad as she was to see the Letchers again—Mr. Letcher
had gained weight in pounds and importance, serving Kentucky as
Governor and the United States as Minister to Mexico since their
last meeting; and Mrs. Letcher was the most gracious woman alive—
Elizabeth had unreasonably counted on something like privacy in

this homecoming. Privacy, she learned later, was hard to come by in Frankfort.

Crittenden, on the other hand, was radiant over the whole business. Several times he halted the procession to call out something to a member of the crowd, to greet a building, perhaps. In the home block he stopped to put his hand lovingly on a locust tree.

"Still here, old fellow?" he said.

And then the house. If only she could have seen it for the first time alone. No, perhaps it was better that at first shock she should have been aware of watching eyes. Crittenden had tried to prepare her.

"Just a house," he said. "Nothing great or special. It holds us all; or, when it doesn't, we move outdoors."

He had been very amusing in his report—too amusing. The house, he had said, stood on the corner and was flush with the street. That enabled them to get their news of the day firsthand. The Capitol being quite near, passers-by would stop at the Crittenden house and shout in through the front windows what went on over there, so that subscribing to a local newspaper was a mere flourish. Evenings, when the breeze blew up cool from the river, the Crittenden parlor was the front sidewalk. Immediately after supper Crittenden and the "missus"—that would be Elizabeth now—would move out to the doorstep. The children—whoever was at home at the time—would take their places on the carriage block at the curb. This was another sort of throne, a two-tiered, semi-circular block of marble, half of the base of a column from the original Capitol, which had burned to the ground while Crittenden was serving his first term in the state legislature. Passers-by in the evening would be invited to sit and chat a while, and all did so. When space on the steps or the carriage block was gone, chairs were handed out the front windows. Every fair evening through the summer the front walk was filled. Here was held the official Frankfort council on births, marriages, tobacco fairs, Bourbon whiskey and a nation's struggles. It all sounded such fun that she had not stopped to look behind the screen of jest; and now here she stood, face to face with reality.

It seemed such a small house for so much to have come out of it. Old—older even than the town. Low—the front steps were two, bringing the whole structure down to the level of the sidewalk. Well, of course, if people were going to shout through the windows! The door promised better. Its classic lines, however, were now obscured by people. The McKinleys waited there to receive her, flanked by two strange young men and two women almost as old as she was, whom she was now to call "daughters." In a rush of relief she went forward to embrace Mary Jane and Andrew McKinley and to meet the others.

But that merely postponed her test. The time came when she had to make her first comment. John Crittenden had finally disengaged himself from his friends and stood beside her, waiting. Everybody within earshot waited. She fastened her eyes on the graceful, hospitable door.

"The most beautiful I ever saw," she said. "I think you must have painted it fresh—just for me."

"Bless you," Crittenden said. With relief? "I'm sure you're right. Even the doorknob's been shined something extra, seems to me. I'll bet nobody has been let in or out this way for a week."

Then, sensing her need and desire, he took her hand and turned to face the crowd.

"Thank you, dear people," he said, in that way of his that searched one's heart, "for this warm welcome. I do hope you all will drop by for a little refreshment—later."

Only he could have dismissed so many without rousing rancor. The people laughed and cheered, but went away. However, only when the last one had disappeared, all turning at least once to look again and wave, had he led Elizabeth inside. And there again everything waited on her words.

"Yours," Crittenden said, somewhat anxiously. "Yours, to do with as you see fit."

"But," Elizabeth answered, "it's all very lovely as it is."

The interior was, for one thing, larger than the exterior had promised. A broad central stairway gave instantly a feeling of space, a sense of unexplored heights and depths. Otherwise the house followed no set plan. In the beginning it had been built to be lived in, then built on to several times, to make room for children and stepchildren and company. In the years she served the house as its mistress, Elizabeth never saw the time when visitors could not be put up suitably somewhere in it.

It was still an old house. There was no denying that. But old in the way of hardwood mellowed more by use than the application of polishing cloths, of silver worn down to the obscurement of its engraving, of glass and china reduced to oddments and hardly a complete dozen of anything.

"Carpets worn to a thread," Crittenden said a day or two later, seeing the place, he thought, with her eyes. "Have to get new ones, I reckon."

But the lustre of old mahognay and walnut and floors entirely bare of carpeting were aged things that Elizabeth knew and comprehended. She smiled and said there was no hurry about replacements. Summer was hardly the season to tear a house to pieces. Besides they had other, more pressing business to dispatch right now.

And she was glad of that. What had oppressed her on that first evening was not so much a matter of physical images as their power over John Crittenden. Mr. Crittenden of Frankfort, and especially of this old house, was not the Mr. Attorney-General whom she had known and married in Washington. Her hold on him was not the same. Here she shared him with too many—both the living and the dead. Did nobody else hear the echoes in this house that she heard?

Fortunately, she thought, her business had kept them in St. Louis most of that first summer. There, as she had been sure he would do, Crittenden had made friends with everyone. He had settled several troublesome land suits out of court, by the art of persuasion chiefly, Mr. Sweringen said. It also happened that St. Louis was passing through a time of high prosperity. They had rented the big Ashley house and sold a near-by block of land to a sugar refinery for a sum which, now re-invested, had added thousands to Elizabeth's annual income.

"It can now be said with justice," Crittenden said gaily on their way back to Frankfort, "that I married a rich widow."

He was very gay about the money. She was to spend all of it, he said, as she chose. The house, for example. He hoped she would not be sentimental about that. She had his permission to throw out everything that had outlived its usefulness.

"Everything?" she queried. "You know you wouldn't like that."

Away from the house she had been better able to decide what to do about it and Frankfort. If she had her way, the Crittendens would live there very little. It was a fair certainty that when the state legislature met in midwinter Crittenden would be returned to the United States Senate. All Kentucky, or most of it, favored that. There was just this winter to be got through somehow; then it would be Washington once more.

"Mr. and Mrs. John Jordan Crittenden have returned and taken up their residence—"

Now, there was a spur to planning!

Standing at the window of the old house that November night, she reproached herself with what must by now seem neglect. She could occupy herself very well this generally unprofitable winter doing a few absolutely needful things in this place. The draperies were about to fall apart. And then, through the rumbling of the gathering storm, a sound outside claimed her full attention.

"Mamma," Mary Jane said now, "do come away from the window. That lightning's sharp."

Elizabeth turned to her daughter, then back to the dark glass.

"Listen!" she said again. "Don't you hear . . . no, not thunder. It sounds like a horse—someone riding this way."

"Now, Mamma!" Mary Jane said.

But she, too, went to the window and laid her ear against the glass. Her small, delicate face was grave. After all, Andrew McKinley, too, was out there in the mysterious dark; and there was urgency in the beat of hoofs on the macadam, the sound growing louder and louder, until the rider pulled up at the Crittenden mounting block.

Seconds later the crash of the door knocker sounded through the house, followed by quick footsteps in the hall. A servant opened the door.

"No, sah. No, he ain' jes' yit," Elizabeth heard the woman say. "He will be back direckly."

With a reassuring pat, Elizabeth pushed Mary Jane back into her chair and went toward the hall. As she did so, a vagrant scrap of the past came up and around her. She was a girl opening a door on a stormy night to a stranger, her mother calling from the fireside: "Well, Libby? Ask the gentleman in."

The stranger tonight was another gentleman, but a sorry figure compared to that other of long ago. He had ridden through rain and then dust. The dust had made a coating over his clothes and grimed his face. That and pallor and eyes hollow with anxiety made him look a very spectre.

"I am Mrs. Crittenden," Elizabeth said, repelled but pitying. "You are looking for my husband?"

The spectre sighed, swayed, and recovered his balance.

"Your servant, ma'am." He managed the semblance of a bow. "I . . . yes, ma'am. I've ridden hard from Louisville to see him. You are expecting him soon?"

"Any minute," Elizabeth said. "Do come in and sit down."

The stranger protested that he was hardly fit to do that. He would wait in the hall.

"Nonsense!" Elizabeth said, but set a chair for him there. He was truly not a parlor specimen. "Mr. Crittenden would be incensed if we kept anyone standing who is tired and in trouble."

"Thank you, ma'am. The tiredness wouldn't matter. As for trouble . . . I will wait, thank you."

229

But he could not sit just yet. Mary Jane had appeared at the hall door.

"Don't I know you, sir?" she said. "You mentioned Louisville. The Ward house comes to my mind, but you are not a Ward?"

"A friend," the stranger said. "God knows they need friends now."

At that moment Crittenden's calm drawl came from outside.

"Somebody's left his horse out here untied. Whoa, there, boy! Got him, Poke? Good! Hold him, will you, till I find out who's here?"

The stranger, looking as if Heaven had opened, gave a sigh of pure exhaustion and folded up on the chair.

That was how the famous and infamous Ward case attached itself to the record of John Jordan Crittenden. It was not fair to blame his residence or the town of Frankfort for that. If he had been a thousand miles away, he still would have heard the call and answered it.

The Wards were a prominent Louisville and Kentucky family, the name going back to the early history of the state. The present head of the family, Mr. Robert Ward, was immensely wealthy, owning lands and business in Kentucky and plantations in the deep South. He and his sons, however, were not generally liked by their fellow Kentuckians. Perhaps with justice, perhaps only because less favorably situated folk expected Wards to behave that way, they had the reputation of being hot-headed and arrogant. But they were in deep and real trouble now. Matthew Ward, the eldest son, had shot and killed a man and was at this very hour in jail for doing so.

His victim was the principal of a boys' high school in Louisville, a man highly thought of, his name—Butler—also prominent in the state. It seemed that the evening before this, the youngest Ward boy, Willie, had come home, weeping and disheveled, to say that he had been severely beaten by the schoolmaster and, what seemed to him worse, called a liar before the whole school. Mr. and Mrs. Robert Ward happened to be away from home; and it was to Matthew, the acting head of the family, that the boy told his story. Willie's offense, then and later, seemed small. He had had some chestnuts in his pocket, and, when another boy begged for some, had shared them. This, Willie declared, had happened during the freedom of a period for recess; but the chestnuts in the hands of the second boy had come to light during a recitation hour. Asked where he had got the nuts, the ungrateful youngster had said, "Willie Ward gave them to me." Whereupon, Mr. Butler, without further questioning, had turned upon Willie, had refused to listen to his defense, had called him a liar and beaten him with a stick—publicly. At least, that was how Willie told the story.

Matthew Ward would have gone back to the school at once with Willie, but it was now evening, the school dismissed, the principal probably away. So he waited until morning. In the night the elder Wards returned home, but still Matthew insisted that he was the one to demand an explanation from Mr. Butler. Reluctantly the parents let him go, along with Willie, who was to get his books, and with a second brother, Robert, Junior, whose support anxious Mrs. Ward had felt Matthew might need. Matthew had laughed at her fears. He declared he anticipated no trouble. Mr. Butler was a gentleman. All would be settled soon and satisfactorily, he was sure. Still, Robert made a third in the party.

School was in session. Because Willie had been called out of his name and flogged before the assembly, Matthew was inspired to interrogate Mr. Butler under the same circumstances. Mr. Butler refused to answer his inquiry, said he had no apology or excuses to make. Whereupon Matthew told him he was a coward and a scoundrel and Butler struck him in the face twice for that, knocking him—he was of slight build—against the schoolroom wall. Then and then only it appeared that Matthew on leaving home had dropped a loaded pistol into his coat pocket. He fired the gun. Butler fell; and a few hours later, at his home, he had died.

Crittenden heard the story through without question or comment. "Where is Matthew Ward now?" he asked finally.

"In jail, sir—young Robert, too—a filthy, common jail."

Crittenden put up his hand.

"The law," he said, "makes no allowances for name or station. Did the Wards send you here to me?"

"No, sir. I—I went to the house when I heard what had happened. I was there when Matt gave himself up. You were the first one the Wards named in their need. Mr. Ward wrote a letter that I was to carry to you, but he tore it up. He said to his wife that, in view of your public responsibilities, this was hardly a thing to hang about your neck at present. Mrs. Ward, most unwillingly, finally agreed with him. Then, knowing how they both felt, I took it upon myself to come on, anyhow. I've told you their side of the story, of course; but I must say also that in Louisville public feeling runs the other way. Because of the gun in Matt's pocket, people are saying he went to the school, meaning to kill Butler for flogging his brother. Murder in the first degree will be the charge."

Elizabeth's heart was lead. No lawyer, she still could see how the case was exactly the sort that might, as Mr. Ward had said, hang about a good man's neck and drag him down. She could not look anything but stunned when Crittenden turned to her to ask whether they could accommodate a guest overnight.

However, the stranger would not stop. Storm, fatigue, high water notwithstanding, he must ride back that night. He ate a little cold chicken, with cold buttered bread, he drank a glass of port and then, on a borrowed horse, rode away.

"May I tell the Wards that I have seen you, sir?" he asked.

"To be sure," Crittenden answered. "Please offer them my sincere sympathy for their difficulty. You may also tell Mr. Ward that I shall be in Louisville next week and from time to time through the winter. If he wants to see me, he can do so there or here."

"Mr. Crittenden?" Elizabeth said in dismay when the house was still again, except for the rolling thunder.

"Now, now, my dear! Come along to bed. You're tired. So am I . . ."

"But . . ." she hardly knew how to word her protest.

"Sweetheart," Crittenden said earnestly and, she had to admit, persuasively, "I have known Matthew Ward all his life, his father all my own. Would you or anyone else think better of me for denying them my support, if they ask for it?"

He was hardly more reassuring to Robert Letcher the next morning. The Letcher house stood on the opposite face of the same square on which the Crittendens lived. It was Letcher's custom when he rose in the morning to stand on his rear porch and bellow forth an invitation for one or the other of his neighbors to join him at breakfast. This day he appeared instead at the Crittenden front door. Elizabeth met him in the hall. He shook his head at her.

"Is John up?" he asked, as casually as possible.

"Yes, of course. We're at breakfast. You'll have coffee with us?"

"And a platter of middlin' and grits," Letcher replied, "or what you have and, thank you, ma'am."

"Good. I'll see about it at once." Passing the dining room, she called, "Mr. C., look who's here."

All the time that she gave orders at the door of the kitchen, Letcher's appetite being what one might have expected from one his weight, she prayed that he might find the right argument to turn Crittenden aside from appearing as the champion of an aristocratic hothead who thought himself above the dictates of the law; but, when she returned to the dining room she knew that this favor had not been granted. Letcher had a newspaper spread before him and was reading from an editor's ironic comment.

"'A Ward has been insulted,'" he quoted. "'A Ward has been whipped. Therefore the stain must be erased with blood.'"

"You, too, Robert?" Crittenden said quietly.

Letcher folded his paper and put it away.

"I suppose you'll take the case and disregard the consequences."

"Not necessarily," Crittenden said. "I can hardly engage myself as attorney for the defense."

"Rats!" Letcher replied fittingly.

"Robert, suppose it were your son?"

Elizabeth went on into the room. Letcher held her chair for her.

"Madame," he said, "I suppose you know by now that you married a stubborn, sentimental old fool. If I had been in the country at the time, I would have advised against it."

It was agreed, silently and in spoken word, between Elizabeth and Crittenden's anxious friends that there was nothing really they could do to deter him from whatever line of action he might choose to follow, perhaps had already chosen. They had no arguments of any force to bring to bear on the situation, every plea turning on personal gain, which meant less to Crittenden than to any man Elizabeth had ever known. They could only hope and pray that the Wards would stand by their decision not to involve him and that he, with his own sense of dignity, might continue to remain aloof.

It was a slender hope, on which Elizabeth, for one, never put much dependence. It was a Louisville lawyer who asked for a change of venue and obtained the removal of Matt Ward to Elizabethtown in Hardin County, Robert having been freed, pending the trial; but she fancied she saw Crittenden's hand in the maneuver. Sedulously she accompanied him on every trip he made to Louisville and there kept him busy helping her choose draperies and carpets, but she could not account for his every minute. However, autumn and early winter passed without Crittenden's name being linked publicly to the case.

Christmas came and went, the house so full that a person could hardly see the new furnishings. Dr. Moss paid his Betsy a long-postponed visit. It was a glad reunion; or it would have been, if Elizabeth had only known whether it was the civil war in Nebraska Territory or the Ward case that threw her husband frequently into a deep study, from which he would rouse to a consciousness of his immediate surroundings—and of her—with a start and a snort. In her heart she did know what it was that absorbed him. Matthew Ward still languished in jail in Elizabethtown. Four lawyers were on his case now, but the best they had been able to do was to secure two postponements of the trial. Nobody believed that Ward would escape conviction and punishment. Nobody, apparently, wanted him to get off—except, possibly, John Jordan Crittenden.

In January, Major George Crittenden came home on leave.

"Madame Mother," he said, with an apologetic twinkle in his eye— he had much of his father's charm, becomingly crisped by army drill, "how deep is Father into this Ward case?"

"I don't just know," Elizabeth said, glad to talk to someone with a right to hear how things stood. "I think Andrew McKinley is doing some work on it—writing briefs, or whatever it is called, making a record of witnesses, evidence and all that. I asked him outright and he only blushed and stammered . . . so that's what I think."

"If he takes the case," George said, "you know why, don't you? It won't be because he's able to save a guilty man from punishment, though that is what most people will think and say. No, Father's reasoning will be, 'Here's a man'—any man, you know, not just a friend—'here's a man in peril of his life. I couldn't face God or my fellowman if I didn't go to his help.' That's Father."

Yes, that was John Jordan Crittenden.

"I don't know whether you've ever known anyone just like him," George said.

She had known one other—a young man of vigor and promise, gone to an early death because his profession bade him serve the poor in their filthy hovels.

"Once set on his course," George continued, "he'll make any sacrifice; and there will be sacrifice, dear lady. For the first time, Father will experience public censure. That won't deter him, but it will hurt. You couldn't lure him away for a while, could you? You are the only one who could—possibly."

The suggestion implied a compliment—when she had leisure to examine it. George spoke for the Crittenden "children."

"I've hoped and prayed," Elizabeth said now, "that something would come up."

Later in the month she thought something had developed. The Kentucky legislature in session at Frankfort, as a matter of routine business, returned Crittenden to the United States Senate. It was a rather anticipatory election, Elizabeth learned to her dismay. The vacancy he was to fill would not occur until the following year; but the yawning expanse of time between now and then could have been filled most profitably away from Kentucky. An association was being formed to provide a national memorial to Henry Clay, and letters poured in, begging Crittenden to head it. His chief duty would be appearing at fund-raising rallies over the nation—from Maine to Indiana to Georgia. It was opportunity at its shining best. Edward Everett of Massachusetts wrote a special letter to Elizabeth urging her support.

"Don't let him refuse on any account. People everywhere will come to know him. This could be a splendid prelude to his nomination for the presidency in 1856. The Whig party, some think, has already breathed its last; but, with him to lead it, it might revive and win the election. Don't let him refuse or suggest delay. There's no time to be lost. Party organization plans are already under way."

But when Elizabeth went to Crittenden—there was no barrier to such an approach in this marriage—he shook his head.

"Later, my dear. If they will wait a while." They wouldn't, of course. "At present I am fully occupied."

Then he showed her a letter he had written to Robert Ward, offering, since Ward still refrained from making the request, to undertake the defense of Ward's son.

"Well, there we are at last," Letcher said, when he heard. "Only now I don't know whether to pray for you to win or lose."

"Spare the Almighty your unworthy petitions," Crittenden told him. "I intend to win."

He could easily have lost. Never, he admitted afterward, had he taken a case where his chance for victory seemed slighter. The trial was set finally for April; and he spent the interim studying Andrew McKinley's reports, hoping to glean some small bit that he could put to good use. What success he had he didn't say. He declared that, to the day when he took his chair at the law's table in the Hardin County courtroom, he didn't know exactly how he would build his defense.

The chances were, however, that almost immediately he began to perceive. The familiar picture—the jury box, the judge on his high bench, the reporters below, the clerk of the court at his desk, the dust raised by spectators, who gathered before ever a jury was chosen—all these things, so dull or lifeless to another, were tonic to him. He drew a sheaf of papers toward him and studied them as if he had not already committed every word on them to memory, all the time keeping ears and eyes alert to the routine business of getting the trial under way.

These things Elizabeth saw through the eyes of Andrew McKinley. Mary Jane was expecting another baby and twice during the eight days of the trial her husband made the long journey from Elizabethtown to Frankfort by horse and railroad to see that all was well with her. And to bring Elizabeth letters from Crittenden. He always wrote to her when he was away, even for only a few days, and insisted that she write to him as faithfully and frequently, telling him how she was and what she was doing. His letters, even these in the stress of the trial, were chatty reports, telling her about his boarding place and the people he saw, ending always with a personal message:

> I miss you, my dearest. If I were to say how much, this would read like a love letter and you might say, "What a silly man!" Do you think of me so—ever?
> Write to me at once and at length on this and other less important matters.
>
> As ever, your devoted husband . . .

"I wish you could be there—to see and hear him," Andrew McKinley said to Elizabeth, his eyes bright with excitement. "For my part, just to sit by, to watch and listen, to hand him what he asks for, to do an errand, is worth all the criminal law I ever read. I knew he was good; but— Won't you change your mind and come? Mary's doing all right. You'd feel differently, if you could be there."

How could she feel differently? A great man spending himself so!

She said to Andrew McKinley, "I still wish he had not touched the case; but now I couldn't bear to witness his failure, if he should lose it."

At the same time she thought, "Win or lose, if this is the end, what shall I do?" The mossy old house, the quiet town made a pleasant retreat when a person was weary and sought rest; but . . . to live there always—year in, year out?

"I warned you, my dear," a voice mocked from the past. "I warned you!"

In the end, Crittenden having named the day when he thought the case would go to the jury, she went with the Letchers to hear him make his plea. They drove, taking two days for the journey and changing horses at their overnight stop. Still, arriving just before the opening of court, they had difficulty putting up their rig and more difficulty obtaining places in the crowded courtroom.

"Don't put anyone out for us," Elizabeth told the sergeant-at-arms.

"No, ma'am. I'll set three chairs," he said.

This made the party conspicuous, but not unfavorably so. Elizabeth heard her name being passed from bench to bench and saw eyes, shy and bold, turned her way, some of the curiosity being about her, but the second glances being for her dress, which looked simple but was not, being a matter of convent embroidery on muslin, which she had been to some pains to keep looking fresh and crisp.

She heard Crittenden examine one witness—a Mr. Sturgus, an assistant instructor in the school, who had witnessed the shooting. Sturgus, the Commonwealth's most important witness for prosecution, had already given his testimony; but Crittenden asked to have him recalled for additional questioning. That no objection was raised indicated the confidence of the Commonwealth's attorney in his argument for conviction of the prisoner.

Sturgus was a gawky young man, with a bold, truculent manner of speech and an unruly forelock. Both seemed emphasized by Crittenden's quiet urbanity and perfect courtesy. He began his examination by thanking the witness for his patience in consenting to undergo the ordeal of questioning a second time. The courtesy seemed farfetched, since the witness had no choice and was perfectly willing, anyhow, to come back to the stand, having ever since the unfortunate shooting rather enjoyed the notoriety consequent to his participation in the affair.

"Mr. Sturgus, you have testified that you were present on the morning of November sixth, when the defendant and his brothers called at the school? Were you in the room with Mr. Butler when they entered?"

"No, sir. I was in the next room, but—"

"Had Mr. Butler instructed you to come to his assistance if a Ward called?"

"No, sir. When I knew who was there, I just went in."

"Why? Did you anticipate trouble?"

"I— Yes, sir, I did—sort of."

"Why?"

"I knew the Wards—Matt Ward, in particular. They're a high-handed—"

The attorney for the Commonwealth objected, perhaps because the violent answer called attention to the prisoner on trial, whose slight physique was now accentuated by five months of living behind bars. The Judge instructed the witness to answer questions without flourishes and Mr. Crittenden please not to lead the witness on. Mr. Crittenden bowed and resumed.

"Mr. Sturgus, much has been made of the fact that Matthew Ward that morning carried a loaded pistol in his pocket. Did you, when you entered the schoolroom, have anything in your hands?"

"Yes, sir—a small stick."

"A small stick. A cane, perhaps? Such as is used for chastising unruly boys?"

"Yes, sir."

"Can you produce that stick?"

Sturgus could easily. He had been brandishing it about Elizabethtown the past two days. It was the stick which had been used for punishing Willie Ward. Crittenden established that in court. It looked a heavy cane for that use. Elizabeth felt its weight on her own inviolate shoulders. To a Kentucky jury it might almost better have been a smoking pistol, but Crittenden was not through.

"Mr. Sturgus, you were present in the schoolroom when the interview between Mr. Butler and Matthew Ward became violent. Did you at any time that morning make a threatening motion with that cane?"

"No, sir; but I would have if—"

The Commonwealth's attorney was already on his feet, loudly objecting. Again the Court sustained him. Again Crittenden bowed and presently released the witness. He had made his point—a small one, but possibly potent. Whatever Matthew Ward's intent had been in going to the school, those in charge there had anticipated trouble.

A half-hour's recess was granted, to enable the lawyers of the opposing sides to make ready their summaries and final speeches to the jury. Letcher led his ladies outside. Elizabeth, faint with the exhaustion of oxygen in the crowded room and under the stress of her own emotions, was glad of his strong arm. She saw now why Andrew McKinley had wanted her to be present. Nobody of any sensitivity could have sat through a half-hour of such court procedure and not known why a man and a lawyer and a friend had taken this case. The isolation of the prisoner, his complete dependence on someone's interpretation of the law, on the reaction of the stony-faced jury—it seemed that to her—wrung her heart. The Letchers had packed a hamper of lunch, but she couldn't swallow a morsel. She asked, instead, for a sip of cold water. While it was being fetched from the town well, Andrew McKinley brought her a note from Crittenden.

"My dear," he had written, "thank you for coming. With you present, I am twice the man I could be otherwise."

She held the note in her hands during the prosecution's violent harangue to the jury, which shocked her to her toes with its bloodthirsty vindictiveness, then more tightly during Crittenden's long, carefully worked out reply. It was, folks said, one of the noteworthy speeches of his career. No doubt they were right. She worried a little about the serenity of his opening, then forgot to worry and listened.

He began with a direct address to the jury, explaining in the simplest words his belief as to why a man on trial for his life or liberty enjoyed in all civilized nations the privilege of having his case heard by a jury of his equals. The twelve men named to this duty were the medium through which the harsh technicalities of the law were translated into human judgment.

"You are a jury of Kentuckians," he said. "The accused is before you in a house of Kentucky justice. All vengeance must cease to pursue him at this threshold. This is his sanctuary. I expect you to do your duty manfully and firmly; and I expect you to do it—notwithstanding all that has been said to the contrary—mercifully."

With the same simplicity and forthrightness he retold the story of the alleged crime. Each person present shared the family scene on the evening when Willie Ward came home with his tale of injustice and abuse. Everyone understood his turning to the older brother and asking him to go see Mr. Butler, to have things made right.

He showed the two young men and the boy on their way to the school the following morning. The most of twenty-four hours had passed, allowing first heat to cool to better judgment. They left home, assuring their parents that they anticipated no trouble. Mr. Butler was a gentleman and so forth. On the way Willie had spoken of Sturgus. He would be there—with his stick. The older brothers had laughed at Willie. If Sturgus took a hand, the second brother was to come to Matthew's rescue. A little later they had passed a woman in the new Bloomer costume and their talk was of that.

The jury relaxed, smiling furtively.

Did they seem criminals on their way to a deed of premeditated violence, Crittenden asked. No. It was a fine day—

Elizabeth remembered it well. Unseasonably warm for November, thunder in the air.

He did not try to avoid the matter of the pistol in Matt Ward's pocket. He made use of it. The prosecution had gone so far as to charge, without proof or supporting evidence, that murder had been in Matthew's heart when he had bought the pistol. Now, now! Crittenden again appealed to the jurymen as Kentuckians. How many of them on occasion had gone to town and, without murder in their hearts, bought a gun? Did that act lay them open to suspicion forever afterward? How many of them habitually took advantage of their constitutional right to bear arms, particularly if they thought some such protection might be needed. A man might buy a pistol with intent to murder, with no intent, or simply to have one in case of need. It could be argued that Matt Ward had slipped the pistol into his pocket at the last minute before leaving home, anticipating some need to defend himself against attack, but nothing more.

And so he went on, missing no detail of evidence. Witnesses had been called, schoolboys chiefly, who swore that through the interview at the school Matt Ward had kept his hand in his coat pocket on the gun, his right hand. Crittenden reminded the jury that he had stood up to address them less than a half-hour before. How many could say where either of his hands had been when he did so? How many jurymen knew where their own hands had been a half-hour before this, to say nothing of a scene four months old?

He demolished the prosecution's case brick by brick. It had been established by a physician that Butler's arm had been raised when the bullet entered his body. Butler on his deathbed had said, "He gave me the lie. I struck him and then he shot me." Butler was a powerful man, fond of exercising his arms with a blacksmith's hammer. He had seized Matthew Ward by his cravat, forced him back against the wall of the room and struck him twice in the face. Sturgus was behind Butler with a stick. Another assistant had laid hold of tongs at the fireplace. Crittenden gave the jurors Blackstone's definition of justifiable homicide—killing in self-defense, when a man found himself in sudden peril of death or great bodily harm. "A man," Blackstone said, "must retreat to a *wall*, or some other impediment he cannot pass." The jury was electrified. By Godfrey, there Matt Ward was against a wall, like Blackstone said.

When people spoke of the beauty of the speech, many recalled Crittenden's final plea for mercy, which was eloquent, his apology to the jurors for taking up so much of their time, his simple restating of his reasons for volunteering his services in the defense of the son of his friend; but Elizabeth, and the jury, it was probable, remembered his reading of the law. The twelve men filed out in a near vacuum of silence and returned almost immediately with a verdict of acquittal.

Again Elizabeth stumbled, leaving the courtroom, and caught at Letcher's arm. Letcher had suggested that they wait outside for Crittenden to join them.

"Now, what do you think of your husband?" he asked, his own eyes moist.

Elizabeth was not sure. It was a little—it was a great deal—like falling in love again. Pleasure, pride, but gnawing anxiety as well. The case was over, gloriously won; but the consequences were still to be reckoned.

The first of these was physical exhaustion. In the carriage, on the way home, it seemed to her that Matt Ward after five months in prison was not nearly so pale or hollow-eyed as Kentucky's foremost lawyer. She would get him to bed as soon as they reached Frankfort, but it would take a month or more of rest to repair the ravages of this trial.

"Your friends, Kentucky, this sort of thing," she said in futile protest, "will be the death of you if you don't watch out. Do you always go on like this?"

Later, when a partisan mob in Louisville stoned the Ward residence, to show that the participators had not been "lawed" out of their outrage, and circulated a petition demanding that the Wards leave town, never to return, when the same angry folk petitioned the Kentucky legislature to ask for Crittenden's resignation from the Senate, when Crittenden spent hours composing a letter for publication, defending a stand which, he thought, was the only stand he could have made and then, white-faced, tore the letter up and made no further effort to justify himself, she suffered all over again in his behalf.

And a little in her own. Could a man so sensitive, so delicately balanced in his sense of right and wrong, so steadfast in his loyalties, be anything finally but a martyr?

CHAPTER FOUR

Again, the Capital City

THAT WAS NOT TO SAY that ambition would not revive once Elizabeth Crittenden breathed the air of Washington again. The city had never seemed to her so gay. After another taste of exile, she opened her arms and her heart to its click-clack, its rush of coming and going, its tempests, its plots and counterplots. There were new names, new faces, but enough old, familiar ones to enable her to settle herself rapidly in place.

"How could I bear to stay away so long?" she asked herself.

Lily Foxe was back. She had opened an *atelier*. She had taken an old house and made it over into a combination studio, shop and residence. In the back rooms sewing women slaved. In the parlors, which were, frankly, display rooms, hung in lush silks and velvets and heavy lace, Lily entertained her friends. The *décor* changed constantly because all of it was for sale. All—the chairs her guests sat upon, the china cups from which they drank their tea, the jewel-like chandeliers over their heads—for sale, and at a figure! Oddly, the price schedule had added to the volume of Lily's business. Expensive things were the vogue, as they had never been before. Mrs. Foxe, widow, had done well for herself. Unaided? Who knew?

"A little longer away," Lily said, in challenge to Elizabeth's delight, "might have been too long. As you see, Washington changes overnight."

Not too much, Elizabeth thought. She could still follow the pattern. What Lily meant, of course, was that she, Elizabeth, had changed. So she had. She had left Washington forty-nine years old and come back fifty-one. Strange that two years could mean so much more at one time in a person's life than at another. Still the beautiful Mrs. Ash— she caught herself in time. The beautiful, the queenly Mrs. Crittenden. More queenly than ever. Plumper . . .

"Have you ever attended a Kentucky burgoo?" she asked, going right to the point with Lily, which was the only way to handle her in combat.

"No!" Lily repudiated the very idea. "But I can see you have."

"Forty this past summer," Elizabeth admitted, and from that went into a spirited description—the gathering in a shaded grove, the barrel of lemonade, the smaller casks of something stronger, the roasting pit, the simmering iron pot, the hampers packed with pies and cakes, the bowls and jars and jugs, the speech-making, literally from stumps, the exchange of family gossip and receipts and quilt patterns, the games in the late afternoon, the tired, crying babies, the adult young unwilling to leave even when dark gathered, song and laughter drifting down the road under the moon, bed at last: "Gosh, doesn't this feel good?" But even bone weariness replete with every sort of satisfaction.

"Horrors!" Lily Foxe said.

Elizabeth laughed, but accepted her criticism. She was plumper, a little too plump now. She must take up the matter with Rachel Bridport at once. She had already arranged to spend a week with the Hugh Campbells in Philadelphia. Clothes were so lovely now, and the best she had were wrong in ways only a woman of pride in self could know. Lily, of course, would say, "Still that Philadelphia dressmaker? Couldn't you do better here?" No, Elizabeth could not. Rachel Bridport had been her chief reliance for so long that she would be afraid to change. Bridport knew her. Bridport would study her special problem and her heirloom laces and arrive at the right answer. No tulle, no fluffy net, no garlands of rosebuds now. No delicate flower tints probably. Jewel tones, rather, in silk and velvet. She loved velvet. Her hand made an old, stroking motion as she laughed her defiance of Lily Foxe.

So, she was a trifle plump now? Well, at her years—and Lily's—better that than to be gaunt. She would be wearing décolletage charmingly when Lily was pulling lace fichus high about her ears. Lily, however, did very well still. There was that same smooth smartness about her which had always distinguished her. Her dark hair, for one reason or another, was still a shining black; her tough olive complexion was clear. A person had to know her well and look at her closely to discover that her eyes had narrowed and that there was something drawn about her mouth. When she was really old, she would dry up like a witch.

Now it was John Jordan Crittenden who, wonderful to relate, expressed disapproval of her—he who hardly ever disparaged any woman.

"She is hard," he said. "I dislike hard women. And I would never trust her."

No, Elizabeth did not trust her, either. She never had trusted her fully, but she still had use for Lily. From no one else could she have obtained so quickly such expert analysis of the changes in Washington society. Soon the two of them were deep in discussion of all the important personages on the scene.

"But, pshaw," Lily said enviously, "you will be right in with the leaders from the very start, you in your position."

Elizabeth examined the grounds in the bottom of her Sèvres cup. Certainly, as Mrs. John Jordan Crittenden, she had position. Few in Washington were so well entrenched. Still—

"And, as I said when I first met you," Lily continued, "how fortunate that you were born on the right side of the Mason and Dixon line. Oh, I mean it, my dear," as Elizabeth looked up startled. "We should declare 'Dixie' our new national anthem. Some people think that, if there should come a division of the states, Washington will be the capital of the Southern federation; and that might be a wise solution, better than all this bickering—two friendly federations. We might get on as neighbors where apparently we cannot do so under one government."

"Lily," Elizabeth said, before she thought, "never, never talk like that before Mr. Crittenden. He calls any talk of separation seditious."

He went further than that. He would not willingly tolerate a discussion of slavery. What were his words? "A fire bell at midnight." The way he said them prickled a person's scalp.

"Really?" Lily's eyebrows tilted. "You surprise me. Is that the feeling generally in Kentucky?"

"I've no authority to speak for Kentucky." Elizabeth knew her tongue had betrayed her. She must be more careful than ever now. "Nor for Mr. Crittenden. It's the light talk he hates, I think, taking these things all very seriously himself." At the same time she thought, "Will it help his advancement that I am well connected in the South?"

"Well, you can't stop people from talking," Lily said; but in another minute she had turned the conversation. "I suppose you'll be taking a house now."

"We are considering it," Elizabeth answered.

That was a mild misstatement. It was a suite at the National again; and, heigh-ho, that was where the Crittendens were likely to remain, for a while at least. For one thing, they needed to estimate more carefully this matter of cost. Returning from a long period of simpler, plainer, if abundant, living in the rearward part of the country, Elizabeth as well as Crittenden had been shocked by soaring costs. People talked about that, to avoid quarreling over other matters. Senator

244

Toombs and Mrs. Toombs, who had ample means, were an example. "Twenty thousand dollars last year," Toombs told Crittenden. "That's what it came to; and damned if I know what it went for—except to feed the poor. It is a good thing cotton is up."

Still, those who cared about prestige and leadership did manage a house. The Jefferson Davises, for instance. Mr. Davis was rounding out four highly successful years as Secretary of War under President Pierce when the Crittendens returned to Washington, and nobody doubted that his wife's entertaining had smoothed many a rough spot in the road for him. Varina Davis's Sunday evening suppers—the guests limited to six—and her larger "At Homes" were select affairs to which everybody sought an invitation. Mrs. Davis in antique brocade or her equally favored white net over wide hoops, with a Canton shawl about her bare shoulders and a camellia in her dark hair, was as lovely as a cameo carving and her hospitality elegant to match. But she was a Natchez belle, to money as well as manner born. Mr. Davis on his part was a successful Mississippi planter and helped by a millionaire older brother, who, it was said, largely financed Jefferson's political career. Jefferson Davis was coming to be considered the most brilliant defender and one of the most outspoken champions of states' rights and other Southern interests. If he went out of the Cabinet with the inauguration of a new president, like Crittenden, he would certainly come back as Senator.

There were others—the Clement Clays of Alabama, the Aikens of South Carolina, the Douglases of Illinois. Senator Douglas, after several years of conspicuous mourning over the loss of his first wife, had married the handsome, well-connected, but impoverished, Adela Cutts; and, if ever a glittering moth had emerged from a chrysalis, there was an example.

All these changes made Washington more tremendously exciting than ever, but even Elizabeth could see how easy it would be to step overboard into deep debt. Of course, if Mr. Crittenden could or would collect some legal fees he had outstanding, with that and her income, they wouldn't need cotton plantations or Illinois railroads behind them. However, Mr. Crittenden, though excellent in his management of her affairs, was strangely indifferent about the money end of his own work. The Ward case was an example of that, too. She had thought that the wealthy Mr. Ward, out of gratitude for Crittenden's volunteered service in behalf of his son, would have been just as quick to volunteer a handsome payment. No. Looking at the case from all angles, he had decided that money should not be allowed to sully the record of such chivalry and had sent, instead, a magnificent silver service to Frankfort. The tray fairly obscured the mahogany sideboard in the old house. Mr. Crittenden had read Mr. Ward's engraved words of tribute on the tray and then turned from it himself, vaguely discomfited.

"More state than I am well accustomed to," he said to Elizabeth.

"I know a dining room where such a service would not be inappropriate," she had said outright to him then; and he had smiled at her and bowed. Now . . .

"We're in no hurry to see about a house," she said to Lily. "Mr. Crittenden is exceedingly occupied at present."

"So I hear," Lily said, with her slanting smile, and then added, too casually, "I saw a friend of yours this morning. Mr. Hobbs?"

Elizabeth jumped. Her thoughts had certainly not turned that way —or had they?

"Does he still come to Washington?" she asked.

"A man with sugar and cotton to sell? Certainly. Not so often perhaps, and he doesn't stay as long, but he comes. I think he took your marriage to another very hard. Have you ever regretted your choice?"

"No," Elizabeth said promptly. "Why in the world would I?"

"No reason," Lily said. "I just wondered."

"Your friend, Mrs. Foxe," Crittenden said with deep chuckles when Elizabeth told him of the visit. "Why do you continue to see her?"

"To learn something of the evil abroad in the land," Elizabeth told him, "since from you I hear only of the good."

Crittenden laughed again, and then surprised her with a sigh.

"Where are we dining tonight?" he asked. "I take it for granted we are not having a quiet evening here."

"Good heavens, Mr. C.!" Elizabeth said. "Have you forgotten? We're dining at the White House."

"Not again," he protested. "It can't be our turn so soon."

Well, if it was not their turn, they had been asked for a better reason. Nobody in official Washington had welcomed the Crittendens back more cordially than President Pierce. Mr. Pierce, a Democrat from New Hampshire, had sailed a troubled course through his administration. When he pleased his Southern friends, he displeased those in the North who had supported him; and almost as often it was the other way around.

"I like Mr. Pierce," Crittenden said. Whom did he not like? "But I'm of no use to him politically."

No? Well, why not? Party issues were very confused. Mr. Pierce

246

called himself a Democrat; Crittenden still called himself a Whig. In the elections of 1856 he worked hard, and fruitlessly, trying to re-elect his old friend, Millard Fillmore, to the presidency. He might have accomplished more, many people said, if he had used his influence to mold the policies of the other party, to which most of his friends belonged. The result of the elections was the naming of another compromise Democrat, Mr. James Buchanan of Pennsylvania, Minister to England at the time. Mr. Buchanan had nowhere near the respect of his partisans that Crittenden could have commanded; but the worst of all was the choice of vice president. That office had gone to another Kentuckian, a Mr. John Breckenridge of Lexington. "That upstart," Elizabeth called him privately, to the intense merriment of her husband, who saw through her rancor. Young Breckenridge, he informed her, was a man of excellent antecedents and considerable personal ability.

"That upstart," Elizabeth called him still. Ah, well, if Mr. Breckenridge was a younger man than Crittenden and rising, Mr. Buchanan was older. She had by no means given up her idea that Crittenden could still attain the highest office in the land. Not she or many another. Meanwhile, nobody discounted his influence or his pleasant ability to smooth ruffled tempers.

"Come now," she said to him this evening. "You know you enjoy a party as much as the next one. Who knows? You may have the charming Mrs. Clay of Alabama next to you again tonight." And when Crittenden, as much of a gallant as ever, seemed to brighten at the prospect, she added maliciously, "She thinks you are just about the sweetest old gentleman she ever knew."

"Does she, indeed?" Crittenden retorted. "Is her admiration of you along the same lines?"

Well, Mrs. Clay and others of the newer crowd had a way at times of suggesting that Elizabeth's headdress might better be a lace cap than brilliants in the net over her chignon. Nevertheless, both with the younger set coming up who looked to the best sources for guidance, and with the older set going out who needed support and loyalty, the Crittendens were popular. No gathering of importance was complete without them, and they both did enjoy going about.

As gay a time in Washington as Elizabeth had ever known, as, possibly, Washington had ever known or might ever know. With an undertow that was both a worry and a challenge. On occasion even John Crittenden's urbanity gave way under strain. Once he locked horns with the formidable Mr. Seward of New York. Crittenden had objected to certain erasures on a public document and Seward spoke

247

slightingly of "county courtroom practice." This brought an angry protest from Crittenden; and Seward apologized, saying he had meant to cast no reflections upon Mr. Crittenden, "whom he placed at the head of his profession."

"Well, for that I thank the Honorable Senator," Crittenden replied, still angrily. Then he added regretfully or, perhaps, just wearily, "I do not wish to continue this debate. I've had my time in that. My purpose is not to be a partisan. It is my only ambition to be a patriot. In the little of life that is left to me there is no hope of preferment, just a simple desire to serve my country."

The two gentlemen then shook hands, but the story went the rounds of Washington, each narrator coloring the part of it that impressed him. Why had John Jordan Crittenden no hope of preferment? Who had ever denied his patriotism or his ability to serve his country?

Elizabeth, proud of his spirited reply, depressed by his denial of personal ambition, asked herself the same questions. Surely it had all been just a manner of speaking.

Then came the Brooks-Sumner affair. Crittenden was present in the Senate chamber that awful day when Preston Brooks of South Carolina, armed with a cane, beat Senator Sumner of Massachusetts into insensibility for making a speech which, Brooks maintained, vilified his state and one of his relatives. The first Elizabeth knew of this was Crittenden's return to the hotel, white-faced and shaking. He ate no supper. He would not read his paper. He snorted at the bold type and threw the sheet across the room. He went to bed finally, but could not sleep; and Elizabeth summoned a physician, who gave him a sedative. Crittenden slept after that, but did not rest.

"He struck to kill," she heard him say over and over. "He struck to kill."

The following morning, to ward off another call for the doctor, he took some breakfast, then sat down at his desk, asking Elizabeth to refuse admission to any caller. At noon he went to the Capitol, bowed still by the shock he had endured, and spoke his mind. The deed of violence he had witnessed seemed to him a desecration and he said so. Here was the rule of unreason, not reason. He hoped he might never see such a thing repeated. It shamed all men present.

Then he went home and slept, while Washington buzzed—with partisan warmth, with admiration for Crittenden and some pity. Did he think that the growing differences in the nation would be settled any other way than by violence? All evening Elizabeth turned away anxious inquirers from various factions, Senator Toombs among them.

"He took this thing hard, Duchess," he said. "How is he now?"

When Elizabeth said he was still asleep and must not be disturbed, he shook his head ruefully.

"The rod that chasteneth," he said. "He blistered all our backs today, ma'am. I don't know that it will do any good, but we love him for it."

They loved him, but would they uphold him in an hour of crisis? Elizabeth knew now what stand Crittenden would make in national politics. It would be against violence—a beautiful, honorable stand; but it called for staunch support; and it might be too late to make that stand. She turned a troubled ear herself now to even the most trivial political chatter.

Some incidents, like the Brooks-Sumner affair, were easy to interpret; others were only vaguely disturbing. Coming home one late afternoon from a *soirée,* in which the capital ladies had been entertained by Mr. Thackeray, the British novelist—and what a pleasant man he was, compared to Mr. Dickens!—she found Crittenden visiting with a stranger—a tall man in an ill-fitting suit, dusty gaiter boots and an every-which-way necktie. He had the ugliest mouth and the highest forehead she had ever seen. Receding dark hair made it a regular dome.

"Do I interrupt?" she asked, ready to escape if Crittenden made the least sign. But he seemed relieved to see her.

"I thought you'd be along," he said, kissing her cheek with an affection he never troubled to hide and then presenting the visitor, a Mr. Lincoln of Springfield, Illinois. "Indeed, you don't interrupt. Mr. Lincoln and I were comparing families. Another Kentuckian, my dear."

"I thought you said Illinois," Elizabeth reminded him.

"It is Illinois now, Mrs. Crittenden," Mr. Lincoln said. "But I was born in Kentucky. That was a long time ago, however. My wife is more truly a Kentuckian than I am."

He had a curious way of speaking—a slow speech that was not quite a drawl, an intonation not harsh enough for a Yankee but not soft enough for a Southerner. His eyes reminded her of someone she knew; but he was so oddly different from anyone she could recall that she could not define the likeness.

"Mrs. Lincoln is a Todd," Crittenden supplied.

"One of ours?" Elizabeth asked, Frankfort being full of Todds.

Crittenden's estimable Maria had been a Widow Todd when Crittenden married her.

"Well," Crittenden said, pleased by her manner of asking, "all Kentucky Todds are more or less related. Mrs. Lincoln was Mary Todd of Louisville."

"Oh!" Elizabeth said. "I may have known her. I have visited there often, Mr. Lincoln." She was laying herself out to be charming to this gawky stranger. Why? Well, habit; and in Washington it was not safe to do otherwise. You could never judge a man's significance by his appearance. "Ask her if she remembers Mrs. Ashley or Mrs. McKinley, my daughter."

"I will, ma'am. I surely will."

Those eyes. Deep-set, seeming darker than they were for that reason, eyes more eloquent than speech could be. Where . . .

"And now," she said, "may I order some refreshment? Mr. Crittenden enjoys a mild toddy usually at this hour, Mr. Lincoln, after a long day in committee. He enjoys it more if he has company."

"Thank you, ma'am, no. I've taken up too much of the Senator's time as it is. I'll be going. I—excuse me, ma'am, if I seem to stare at you in a way I shouldn't. It's your pretty clothes. I promised Mary I'd notice what folks were wearing here; but, till you came in just now, I'd clean forgot. You will forgive me, ma'am. That's the prettiest silk dress I ever saw and I want to tell Mrs. Lincoln about it."

"Mercy!" Elizabeth said. "And I've just discovered that nothing I have is fit to be seen. Just tell her she can't have a skirt too wide, the more breadths of material the better. As to hair—no, that may change before you get back to her."

They had a laugh over fashion; and then Mr. Lincoln, with a return of awkwardness which must have been due to diffidence, really said good-bye.

"Mr. Crittenden, it has been a pleasure to talk with you and I thank you for the privilege. I can tell plainly what you'd not be unkind enough to say to me. At least, you'd not enjoy saying it. You are not going to give me your support. I'm sorry about that. I think we agree more than we disagree, but I see your reasons. I'll never hold them against you. Times like these a man has to find his own wisdom or what he hopes may be that. I—I just promised my friends I'd see a few people. You were the first on my list."

"Lawyer from Springfield, Illinois," Crittenden repeated, and gave Elizabeth what information he had. It wasn't much. "Has a case on before the Appellate Court. I knew him slightly when he was a member of the House back in—1846, I think. He served only one term; so it would appear he does better at law than politics, but that's never a cure." He had dropped into his chair and closed his eyes. He opened them now, to wink at her; and she tried to smile responsively, but felt troubled, just the same. "Has his eye on Douglas's seat in the Senate," Crittenden told her.

"Oh, no!" she said. "Not possibly. And what in the world did he expect you to do about that?"

"We hold a couple of beliefs in common," Crittenden answered. "He wanted a word of endorsement from me to friends in the Illinois legislature, if I would give it. I hated to deny his request, which was not extraordinary; but recommending him meant that I was against the re-election of Douglas. He and I have had our differences, as everybody knows; but—" he paused, to shake á threatening finger at Elizabeth. "Now don't you ask me to go through it all with you."

Elizabeth laughed spontaneously enough at his pretended ferocity, but almost immediately perplexity, at least, returned.

"You wouldn't think of taking a man like Mr. Lincoln seriously?" she coaxed.

"I don't know," Crittenden answered. "If I were Stephen Douglas, I might. Heigh-ho, what do you hear from the children?"

Sure enough, when the time came for Senator Douglas to seek re-election, he barely won the race. Adela Cutts Douglas made a funny story out of the hard campaigning that preceded the taking of a vote. For a year to come, she entertained dinner guests with the tale; but she wouldn't have thought it funny if Douglas had lost his place in the Senate.

Adela Douglas was tall. In spite of hoops, she managed a creditable mimicry of the gawky backwoods lawyer who had dared to debate public issues with her gifted husband. People shrieked at her performance. Elizabeth at first laughed with the others. Then one night, after dinner in the Douglas home, she thought, "This isn't funny, really. This could be another warning of some sort."

1858 was a year of phenomena, which those of a superstitious turn of mind did interpret as warnings of wrath to come. There was a comet. There were hailstorms late into the winter. And earthquakes. Elizabeth, her eyes on a crystal chandelier which Senator Douglas had given his lady in celebration of his hard-won victory, thought, "Suppose a quake should lay hold of this house now, and send that glass bauble crashing!" What made her think of such a thing? She had never been a person of tremors and superstitions. Surely she didn't want a thing like that to happen.

And yet, on this night she was beset by a sense of unreality that took in this fine house and all the people under its roof, especially the pretty, silken ladies in the front parlor. Each year one newcomer, at least, added herself to the charmed circle. This year it was Mrs. James Chesnut, wife of the new Senator from South Carolina. As yet, she understood little of the importance of, say Senator Douglas's re-election; but every so often she said something, just to call attention to herself. This time it was,

"Mercy! Let us be thankful things turned out as they did."

"If they had not," Mrs. Clement Clay informed her, "we wouldn't be here tonight; and who knows . . . ?"

Pretty, fashionable Mrs. Clay, who had made her bow in Washington under the protection of the Crittendens, riding in their carriage, asking what she must do or say if she drew a foreign ambassador for a dinner partner—one whose language she couldn't speak.

Pretty Mrs. Clement Clay. Pretty little Mrs. Chesnut, for that matter. Handsome, clever Adela Douglas. Varina Davis, with her hair like raven's wings, so proud of her distinguished husband! What of Mary Todd Lincoln, meanwhile? What were her thoughts this night? Was she bitterly disappointed in her husband's defeat? Did it seem to her final? Probably not, since she was a woman and tenacious of her dreams.

Elizabeth stood up with sudden decision.

"For all our mercies let us be thankful," she said. "Now, how about some music?"

The strain of everything, she thought afterward, was beginning to tell on her, too. Mr. Crittenden wasn't the only one to feel it. She did what she could to conceal the anxieties that beset her—they were still quite small worries—but there were days when her temper had little of her usual, well-schooled serenity. Such a day was the one on which the Senate moved from its old chamber to the new north wing of the Capitol. She was captious and petulant even while Susanna helped her dress. It was an important day; but, then, she had lived through many another, smiling.

"There!" Susanna pinned a silk veil about Elizabeth's shining hair and said, "That will hold it till we get the dress on."

"We!" Elizabeth, on the point of repeating the syllable, in mocking rebuke, held her tongue. That irritated her further. Why couldn't she scold Susanna as freely as ever? Simply because Susanna, with the deftest hands in the capital, skilled as seamstress and hairdresser, was no longer strictly dependent on Elizabeth's patronage. These days she could easily have slipped away from Elizabeth and set herself up in any of a dozen cities, and made herself a good living, using the skill she had acquired while waiting on Elizabeth. That must not happen. Elizabeth needed her now; and, if the world should go to smash presently, she might need her even more. Susanna, in that case, might have to make a living for Elizabeth as well as herself.

Elizabeth made a face at the thought, creeping into this beautiful January morning, and then made another at the dress Susanna had lifted from the bed. Susanna drew back in her own reproof and displeasure.

"Miss Libby, you ought to be shamed o' yoreself, the way you look at this pretty dress. This—this fine lady's cloth . . ."

Elizabeth laughed.

"You sound like tomorrow morning's paper," she said. " 'Present in the Senate Gallery, as usual, when her husband speaks, was Mrs. John Jordan Crittenden, handsome in fawn-colored cashmere, with latticed bands of deep gold velvet.' Well, it will have to do, of course. I look horrid in gray. I dislike black except under lights, with lots of jewelry. I wonder what Mrs. Foxe will wear."

"I know," Susanna said. "She asked the color of your dress so she wouldn't clash with it. When I told her, she said she'd dig up something in brown. That will look nice, won't it?"

"Hm! We'll be a pair of autumn leaves. Once I was a lilac in flower and she in green; but you wouldn't know about that."

Susanna sucked in her lips. If there was anything Elizabeth knew that she did not, what could it be?

"I know," she said in a minute, "this is the prettiest dress Mrs. Bridport ever made for you."

"It's the most expensive, I'll swear to that," Elizabeth said ruefully.

Bills again, and there had been another money panic. Susanna settled the dress about her and fussed with the folds of the enormous skirt, to give it that new flat look in front, all the flare going to the sides and the rear.

"Still the prettiest lady in Washington," she cajoled, whisking the veil from Elizabeth's hair. Elizabeth laughed at her again, called her a goose. An important lady, perhaps, but certainly not the prettiest, not any more.

"I do well enough for a *grande dame*," she conceded, to smooth the anxiety on Susanna's dark face.

"And a grandmother," she could have added. She would be fifty-five on her next birthday. The parade of grandchildren, which had begun with an Ashley McKinley and then an Ashley Cabell, now included a John Crittenden McKinley and a Crittenden Cabell, she having made her peace a long time ago with Cabell, as with her other connections, and having even visited the Cabells in Tallahassee, on her way to spend a month with her sister Mary in New Orleans. The long ocean voyage had been tiresome but worth while. Cabell, chastened by time and family responsibilities, had talked to her seriously and respectfully. Florida, as Elizabeth had foreseen, did not agree with Anna Marie. And since the visit, Cabell had exchanged the family property there for plantations in Mississippi and Arkansas, which he could manage from St. Louis, where the family now made their home—at a certain expense to Elizabeth, but she much preferred having them there.

She had enjoyed the New Orleans holiday. She was fond of her sister Mary and her brother-in-law, Judge Hunton. She had visited them often, with her father and her children, when the girls were still children; but she had not been back since her marriage to Crittenden. She had wondered, not too anxiously, whether this return was wise. Would she have as gay a time as when she had still been the fascinating Mrs. Ashley and Mr. Hobbs her *beau gallant?* Mr. Hobbs, to her surprise, had entertained handsomely for her in his villa at Pass Christian; and he had been only one of many, Mrs. Crittenden being a person whose presence was spread over all society columns.

"Miss Libby, you are going to be late," Susanna warned now, holding out her bonnet.

Ah, the bonnet! That climaxed everything. A *grande dame* in her fifties, if she had the means and a good dressmaker, could find gowns to wear with pride and a certain becomingness—though they were not of lilac taffeta—but headgear of excitement was for youth. A proper old lady could tuck her white locks under a cap of lace and stay at home; but, if one's hair did not turn gray and one's heart still found life tasty, one let one's self imagine one could still wear—well, that bit of corded silk with velvet leaves and flowers, for example, in Susanna's hands.

Susanna set it down lightly and expertly.

"Can't you make it cover more?" Elizabeth complained. "It should have been darker, too."

Her whole costume was too light. Dark tones were easier. But what? Prune? There had been a time when she delighted in shades of purple. That was when purple had called attention to her youth. Now, like gray or black, it was a color of surrender. Wine-red? Deep, rich, but warm?

And Poke, his eyes bulging, stood inside the door. Fancy her ever being late to an appointment, with those two on guard!

"I wish I could hide in a corner and see and hear," Susanna said, buttoning Elizabeth's short kid gloves.

"I'll tell you all about it," Elizabeth promised, adding wickedly, "even Mr. Crittenden's speech, if you insist."

Susanna would not permit Mr. Crittenden to be taken lightly.

"I'll listen to all you remember to hear," she retorted.

"Well, I may skip some if it is too long," Elizabeth conceded. "Be sure you have his slippers and pipe ready when we come home."

Susanna's face was a thundercloud.

"Miss Libby, can't you ever forget that piece in the paper?"

No. The *Post's* account of President Buchanan's recent New Year's levee, his second while resident in the White House: "The Crittendens attended, Mrs. C., as usual, in yards and yards of priceless lace over satin, Mr. C., equally elegant, but looking as if he'd give anything to be at home in carpet slippers, smoking his pipe—an indulgence his lady is not likely to permit while she can keep moving."

"I don't intend to forget," Elizabeth said. "I'll find out yet who wrote that piece and bite the woman's head off, if it was Harriet Lane herself."

She was fairly sure it was not Miss Lane, the President's spinster niece and hostess. More probably it was one of those clever young things who ate Elizabeth's cake and drank her wine and flirted behind her rented palms.

"Miss Libby," Poke erased a smile and took a shawl from Susanna —for covering the cushions of the hired carriage, "anurr minute and we gonna be late, sho' nuff. Mis' Foxe waitin' downstairs."

"Then do let us be off," Libby said. "We can keep the Senate waiting, or the boy with the horses, but never Mrs. Foxe."

With a swirl and a swish—fine wool over crinoline and taffeta— and setting adrift about her a vapor of distilled French violets, she set off to play her part in still another show.

It was a good show—the last meeting of the Senate before it moved its business to a more spacious hall in the new north wing of the Capitol; and to John Jordan Crittenden, who, by right of seniority, was to make the farewell address in the old chamber. When Lily Foxe and Elizabeth arrived, visitors overflowed the lobby and all the stairways. Guards had to lead them to the space reserved for them in the Ladies' Gallery. They made a good entrance. The seats had been kept with such difficulty that spite as well as curiosity had been thoroughly aroused. A murmur followed Elizabeth and Lily, and was not hushed even after they sat down.

"That bonnet!" someone wailed.

The guard glared. As he did so, a page gave a message to the Vice President—"young Breckenridge"—who rose immediately.

"Gentlemen, we are about to receive—"

Hard upon the bellow of the sergeant-at-arms, the President entered.

"Looks dreadful, doesn't he?" Lily Foxe whispered.

Not much worse than he had at his inaugural, Elizabeth thought. She had been shocked then at the change in a man who had been that handsome Senator Buchanan from Pennsylvania when she was the young and dashing Mrs. Ashley. A muscular paralysis that drew his head to one side had been a peculiarity that one forgot in the charming company of the younger man. It was a painful affliction now. His high white stock was like a bandage. He had looked frightened at his inaugural. He was always gently uneasy these days. Pathetic, rather than dreadful.

But Elizabeth's concern was not for him today. She looked down in search of her husband and found him by the familiar shock of iron-gray hair. She was startled to see how silvery was its overcast now, seen from above. But he made his usual distinguished appearance. His broadcloth was as fine as her cashmere, his linen perfect, his neckwear fresh and in order. She had thought when she married him that one of her wifely duties might be keeping these elegancies in line, only to learn that he was in such respects as fastidious as she could ever be. Still, his hair had silvered ominously fast of late. His back, too, seemed to her just a little bowed. Nothing, however, dimmed the good will that beamed from his sensitive face turned now toward President Buchanan. He had no great admiration for Buchanan, just—bless the man—this good will!

Young Breckenridge opened the ceremonies. His words were bland, reasonably eloquent, shaped into elegant sentences; and nobody except the recording clerks and the reporters remembered anything he said. Everything and everybody waited on John Jordan Crittenden. What would he find to say today? That he would say it well was taken for granted, but what would be his message?

A hush enveloped the room as he stood up finally at his desk. He looked about at his fellow senators, he acknowledged the Vice President's introduction, he glanced down at a sheaf of papers on his desk; then, impatiently, he gave them a push and left them where they lay. He was going to speak extemporaneously—today? Apparently so.

Again his eyes swept over his friends, this time including those in the galleries as well as those on the floor. That winning, self-deprecatory smile by which men would always remember him, illumined his features. Well, the smile was all right, but now?

It seemed to Elizabeth that the hesitation with which he began to speak was perilously close to stumbling. He made an apologetic gesture and again he smiled, then went on more strongly, more smoothly. Still apologizing, however. Men who knew how long-winded he was habitually, he said, were going to be disappointed. He was not going to occupy anyone's time or weary anyone's ears with oratory. He knew why he had been chosen to make this address, this last address in this room of hallowed traditions. In point of time elapsed he had served here the greatest number of years. Forty-two years before this he had made his maiden speech in this room. In the period between then and the present, other duties, other offices had claimed him from time to time; but, with those duties discharged, it had been his proud privilege always to return to his place in the Senate. Witness the scars on his desk, on himself, for that matter.

The import of what followed was just that—import rather than so many spoken words. Where he could have taken time to call up with familiar anecdote those with whom he had served in this place, he contented himself with naming only a few—John Randolph, John Calhoun, Lewis Cass, Rufus King, Henry Clay, Thomas Hart Benton, Daniel Webster; but he pronounced each name slowly, reverently. It was a parade of giants. For a minute the men who occupied the desks he indicated looked puny in comparison and bowed their heads in acknowledgment.

A parade of giants; and, of them all, John Jordan Crittenden alone remained. Early in his address, a winch at work on the new Capitol dome screeched; and Elizabeth thought, "Oh, dear!" Then, either someone hurried with an order for the work to stop, or external noises ceased to matter. Men sat with bowed heads and women had out their handkerchiefs.

A parade—but not for pomp. It was a prelude to a prayer. These men whom he called back and their brothers—he could not begin to name them all—through the years, through and in spite of bitter disagreement and factional and sectional dispute, had together built a nation. That was their record of service. That was the tradition of this old hall, now too narrow, too small, too restricted to accommodate the senior legislators representing the several states.

"This has been the scene of the Great Past," he said. "The new chamber is to be the theatre of the future; and that future, I hope and believe, will not be dishonored by a comparison with what has gone before. The new chamber will have illustrations of great services rendered by great men and pure patriots. . . ."

"Oh!" Elizabeth thought, adding a personal codicil to Crittenden's solemn entreaty, "if time could only be moved up a year and a few months! If the elections could only be tomorrow or next day, while the spell of his words is still on men's hearts!"

"This body," he concluded, "the great preservative element of the government, will discharge—"

In the middle of the sentence he swayed. He had been standing too long. He was too much moved. A half-dozen men up front started to their feet. He recovered and smiled them down. A page handed him a glass of water.

Elizabeth did not hear his closing phrase. When he sat down, cheers and outcry ringing to the roof, she was still shaking; and Lily Foxe had both arms around her, comforting her. Lily Foxe!

Now, things, indeed, had come to a pretty pass. . . .

Elizabeth should have known then what to expect of John Jordan Crittenden, politically speaking. In her heart she did know. Still, in the elections of 1860, it did seem as if any prominent man almost could have been nominated for the presidency if he were willing to carry a banner. He was not a banner-waver? Perhaps not. There was only one flag for which he felt such devotion.

To her dying day she would remember that June afternoon in the Galt House in Louisville. She sat there in a public parlor with the Letchers, waiting for a telegram from Crittenden announcing the hour and means of his arrival from Indianapolis, where he had been engaged in the pleading of a civil suit—she had no idea over what. Crittenden had said it was important: "This time, my dear, we are sure of a fee." But only one thing was important now.

Outwardly, the occasion was purely social. Ole Bull, who was making a western tour, was playing a concert that evening in Louisville; and Crittenden himself had suggested that the Letchers, with Elizabeth, should meet him at the Galt House for a gala evening, either celebrating the successful conclusion of his case or consoling him for an absence from home which must drag out for another week.

It had seemed to Robert Letcher and other good friends an opportunity made to order. Elsewhere in the hotel the Orlando Browns waited, and throughout the town prominent Kentuckians buzzed over a gentle conspiracy to place Crittenden's name on the ballot for the presidency. They thought they had a party and a banner ready for him. It would do no good now to look longingly toward the Democratic party, to try to control that nomination. Things had gone too far for a peacemaker to have a following there. The even more radical Republicans had still less regard for compromise; and who in Kentucky had any leaning toward that party, anyhow? But there were good men and true over the nation who hoped that a way still could be found of preserving the Union. Given the right leader, one popular both in the North and the South, and a reasonable support in Congress, the trick might be turned.

It had seemed worth while to try. A border state man was the logical nominee, and who would have a better show at being elected than John Jordan Crittenden? At least, following every speech he made in the Senate on important legislation, letters poured in from all sides begging him to head a movement that would have as its sole object the preservation of the Union of States, as outlined by the Constitution. Of course, nobody knew whether the fervor of these entreaties would abide in men's hearts through an actual election. A convention of the new party was not certain so far. If enough enthusiasts were assembled to hold one, to choose a nominee, that nominee might merely be making a sacrificial gesture. Still, it had seemed worth trying.

Elizabeth wished that she could share the enthusiasm of Crittenden's friends and wondered at herself for not being able to do that. Had she, after all these years, taken leave of ambition? No. Was it the probable composition of the new party, a rag-tag mob of malcontents adding themselves to it, their adherence courted to swell the vote? No. It was Crittenden himself. She could not picture him in this time of bitterness, leading any party through a campaign. That no longer seemed a fitting climax to his record of service. That climax, when it came, would be sacrifice, she had no doubt, but with honor and no self-seeking. It was with great reluctance that she had given her sanction to the present well-meant conspiracy.

A supper, of banquet proportions, had been planned following the concert. When it was time for toasts, by general acclaim Crittenden's friends would inform him and the world that Kentucky was going to nominate him for the presidency on the Constitutional Union ticket. Kentucky would support him to the last man at the convention and at the polls in November. Everything was ready for that final act— everything except that John Jordan Crittenden was still in Indianapolis. The afternoon was passing and with it the hour for the arrival of the only train from that direction. If Crittenden was coming, it must be by other conveyance. There was still no word or sign.

"He is not coming. He is not coming," Elizabeth's heart told her over and over; and whether she was glad or sorry, she still could not say.

At long last, the door of the parlor opened, to admit the square, heavy figure of the violinist, half-obliterated by a sheaf of yellow roses—her roses, her color. She knew their meaning at once. She hardly waited for Mr. Bull to cross the room, to bow before her and hand her the roses and a note that went with them. The note unopened in her hand, she said to Letcher now what her heart had been saying to her,

"He's not coming," and then, "Mr. Bull, do, please, forgive us. We were looking for Mr. Crittenden, you see."

She presented the Letchers. Mr. Bull bowed, then turned back to Elizabeth, anxiety, a touch of bewilderment, too, on his broad face.

"He's got wind of something," Letcher surmised. "But, good Lord, what a way to do!"

"Mr. Bull?" Elizabeth said uncertainly. "Do you know . . . ?"

"It is in the letter, perhaps?" the violinist suggested.

It was and it was not in the letter.

"My dearest," Crittenden wrote, "I am fortunate in the messenger who will carry this word to you. I hope the time you spend in his company will cover my defalcation. Needless to say, he remembers you well from Washington, where, he tells me, you were among the first to make him happy to be in America. I leave it to your natural kindness to make his visit to Louisville equally pleasant. He tells me it will be his first visit to Kentucky."

And then at last,

"I am unavoidably detained here; and still, having made an engagement with you, I would have moved Heaven and earth to keep it, if I could have done so with any peace to my conscience. Please give my affectionate regards to the Letchers, to whom I am sending my personal apology by telegraph."

While she was still reading the letter, the Letchers' message was delivered, and a few minutes later Mr. Orlando Brown came in with a similar one.

"He doesn't want it, Bob," Mr. Brown said. "Won't have it. Adds something about serving us and the nation better in his present capacity. What do you suppose?"

"Dear Mr. Bull," Elizabeth said, "we are being very selfish, and impolite in consequence. When you have been so good . . . and condescending."

"Madame," the musician bowed, "Mr. Crittenden in permitting me to do him and you a service has explained that you would be disturbed by his letter. It is a sorrow of some sort?"

"No, Mr. Bull. A disappointment, only." Hardly a disappointment. Relief? More than that. Pride—a great and shining pride. She turned to Crittenden's crestfallen Frankfort neighbors. "We should have consulted him," she said. "He would have told us his wishes. He has told us over and over."

"Not a partisan, a patriot . . . in the little of life left to me, my simple desire to serve my country."

"He means it when he says he will serve you and the nation well," she assured Brown and Letcher, if, knowing Crittenden, they needed reassuring. "And now, if you will excuse me, I, too, should like to attend to some personal business. Mr. Bull, are you free now? I know you like to understand the people for whom you play. Would you enjoy a drive about Louisville? Nothing would give me more pleasure than to be your guide and informant. I think I am well qualified for the task. Mrs. Letcher, will you join us? Shall we leave the men to their dusty politics?"

CHAPTER FIVE

Not a Partisan, a Patriot

IT RAINED OFF AND ON all that November day. The house, Elizabeth said, smelled like a root cellar. Privately she told herself that if it should happen that she must finish her life here in Frankfort, she would do something in earnest now about that house. Tradition and keepsakes to the contrary. She would knock out more windows, widen doors. She would put fresh gay paper on the walls—if it could be made to stick—have all the wood trim painted white . . . in such humdrum ways a woman's deep devotion must prove itself.

In the front parlor Crittenden and Robert Letcher were playing dominoes. Large, black dominoes with large, white spots, easy to see. Two old men.

"I'm so glad you're here," she had said thankfully to Letcher when, as usual, he appeared right after breakfast. "Otherwise Mr. C. would be walking the floor or else have his nose down at his writing again."

"Writing what, for Heaven's sake?" Letcher roared. "What's the good of that now?"

She shook her head. Let Crittenden say if he would. All she knew was that there was no lack of spills these days for lighting fires.

"Some nostrum," she said, "to save an ailing country. Do me a favor, will you? Don't tell him you're sure it won't work."

Letcher lifted her hand and kissed it.

"Sorry, Duchess."

He turned then and bellowed toward the parlor.

"John, where are you? Came over to finish our game. So many folks kept popping in yesterday—"

Only the weather kept them from popping in today. In Frankfort, as in every other town in the nation, people waited in all forms of restlessness for the final outcome of the November balloting. Poke, as he had been every morning since election day, was uptown at the post office, ostensibly to fetch the mail, but with instructions also to stop by the printing office and the depot for the latest tabulations. If by any chance the final word was in, Elizabeth had told him to run like everything and reach the house before somebody else brought in the news. She, and she alone, wanted to tell Crittenden.

"Does it make any real difference," she had asked him once, "who is elected? I mean will it alter the general situation?"

Yes, Crittenden thought it would. Whichever way the wind blew, this was going to be a critical winter; but the election of Abraham Lincoln would touch off that much sooner the conflagration he dreaded.

About eleven-thirty Elizabeth heard a back door close and somebody raising a fuss about folks traipsing through the house all dripping wet. She hurried out into the hall.

Poke stood there, literally dripping. A more miserable Poke she had not seen since the wet and muddy days back in Missouri, when he'd had to stable and then fetch visitors' horses. Water poured from him and the mail pouch.

"Miss Libby," he said hoarsely, and shivered from top to toe, "hit look lak hit's Mistah Linkum."

It seemed to Elizabeth that it rained an unconscionable amount that fall and early winter. It rained that day in Frankfort; and in Washington, the day that Crittenden's compromise resolutions were to be passed upon in committee before being brought to the floor of the Senate for a vote, an early-morning fog dissolved just before noon into a chill drizzle.

"Mr. C.," she said, as she and the Senator were about to leave the hotel, "I wish I could be with you today, to add my prayers to yours. If there is any way I could be—"

He had worked so hard, so valiantly over the bill!

"It can be done," he said—to himself with pressed lips or to her, if she sat beside him. "It can be done."

He had written finally a good bill. All his experience as a legislator, as a pleader, had gone into it. It was simple, clear and complete. As a lawyer, he had armored it against future tampering. If it passed in Congress, it was to be submitted to the vote of the states as an amendment to the Constitution, and repeal was to be forbidden.

A good bill—he had done Elizabeth the honor of reading it to her. She asked a question here and there, not many.

"You are a critic," he said. "I didn't know—"

"Did I never tell you about my English governess?" she asked, striving for a light sally. "Or how, when we moved to Missouri and my mother thought I might grow up a savage, my father went right on with me in the classics? You would be amazed at what I used to know—but have long since forgotten."

She saw, if Crittenden did not, the one irreparable weakness in his compromise bill. It asked men to go back ten, twenty, even thirty years and do things all over again and do them differently. It was not probable that they could or would. Still, if the bill should pass, the sun might shine again.

Of the two issues that had split the country into sections, the bill avoided one—secession. There was no need as Crittenden saw it to write anything into the law about the right of a state to secede from the Union and so destroy that union; but the issue which had made men desire or think they desired to do this awful thing could be handled by legislation. Not one himself to uphold the morality of owning slaves, he viewed the unhappy custom as an economic fact and had shaped his bill to permit its natural extinction but not its abolition by edict. While this process went on, he asked for the restoration of the old Missouri Compromise line. He asked the people of the North to respect the property rights of slave owners and the slave owners to compensate fairly and equably for the return of their runaway people. In legal terms it begged men to hold their tempers and their hands.

A good bill, a valiant effort at peaceful settlement.

"I wish I could be there, to add my prayers to yours," Elizabeth said, but knew she could not. There was no provision for lady visitors in a committee room. All she could do was parade her finery, mask her anxious heart with a smiling face—and say her prayers hard wherever she spent the day.

"A new dress, isn't it?" Crittenden asked.

Yes. The red dress she'd been wanting. Did he think it was too bright?

"Not at all," he said. "Warm, cheerful, most becoming. What is the occasion, may I ask?"

"Surely," she told him. "A wedding. A Pryor grandchild. High noon, but I've plenty of time to set you down dry at the Capitol."

"Thank you, my dear. I was about to ask if you had ordered a carriage."

"My finery," she said, "wouldn't be very fine by the time I arrived, if I had not. Mud is boot deep everywhere."

"The first time I ever knew you to admit mud in Washington," he reminded her.

"The first time it ever seemed to matter," she said ruefully.

"I suppose all your friends will be there," Crittenden said during the short drive down the Avenue.

"And some of yours, no doubt, who could do better elsewhere.

Even the President, I understand, has promised to attend. But I'll be home early, I think. Shall I order supper served in our rooms?"

"That will be charming," he said abstractedly; and then, as the carriage pulled up under the Capitol steps, he added just as indifferently, "Well, kiss the bride for me."

Watching him disappear into the vaulted basement, Elizabeth thought, "Crusades are for the young—not for the old."

For the very, very young, and heedless. The house that sheltered her presently was as gay as the city was dreary, bright with camellias, roses and southern holly, Christmas being only a few days away. From the chatter a person would have thought it a Christmas like any other. Many of the guests were leaving the next day for quick journeys home to Pennsylvania, to New York or southward to Virginia, the Carolinas, even to Georgia and farther. Some had brought gifts to exchange. The only difference was a sort of spontaneous reluctance on the part of all to separate, once they had got together.

At half-past five the house was still packed solid with people. In just two places was there room to stick out one's elbows and breathe deeply—in the immediate vicinity of the bride and her young husband, and around the chair where the President sat enthroned. At exactly that hour a hubbub broke out in the hall which caused the President to ask, half-joking, whether the house was on fire

The excitement was over a telegram, of which the messenger apparently knew the contents; and he could not resist giving out the gist of them as he made his way through the crowd. A small silence followed the delivery of the message to the President He read it and turned white.

"Mr. President," his hostess said, "what is it, sir?"

"Madame," Mr. Buchanan answered, "I'll trouble you to have someone call my carriage. I must leave at once."

Rising excitement was barely held in check while he made his departure. It broke into shrill outcry the moment he was gone and presently everyone knew what had happened. South Carolina—at last—had voted to secede from the Union.

It seemed to Elizabeth then that everyone went a little mad. Faces turned pale, but eyes glittered. Smooth, well-modulated voices screamed. This it was to be young—to seize the excitement of the moment, the hour, to relish it, to think no further. Fear and distraction came with years, tearing one's heart to pieces, sending the bits here and there in futile pursuit of loved ones—hers to Mr. Crittenden at the other end of the Avenue, to her children in St. Louis, to her sister in New Orleans, her father there, too, wishing to avoid the rigors of a northern winter. Thanks to the telegraph, word would have reached these cities almost as soon as it was received here. Would the people in those places go mad, too? The excitement, the uproar would be great; but the chances were that not even Charleston, where the spark had been struck, would know quite the madness that prevailed in Washington.

It was another hour before she could extricate herself from the turmoil of this one house. What a wedding day for those children to have to remember! When Poke drove up to the carriage block, her own knees were so weak that she could hardly manage the low step, and did make an awkward business of her skirts, catching a hem on a protruding pin.

"Dis ol' ramshackle buggy!" Poke excused. "High time Mist' Brown buy hisself some new rigs."

It was dark now, but she could hear or thought she heard a shouting up and down the Avenue.

"Poke, I'm concerned about the Senator down at the Capitol."

"He's all right, Miss Libby," Poke assured her. "Dey's right smart o' folks in de street, but ev'ybody know Mist' John Jerden Crittendem. Dey'll make way fo' him."

"They will if they see him," Elizabeth said, "but maybe they won't. Most of them don't even see where they are going."

A person couldn't think. A person could only feel. Her feeling was alarm and an unsteadiness, as if she couldn't be sure, when she stood, of the ground under her. When they turned into the Avenue, mobs were forming, regardless of mud and puddles. The shouting she had heard was from vendors, hawking ribbon cockades. Now, how had they known in time to have these ready?

"You wears a blue one," Poke explained, "you's a gemmun f'om de Souf. Red, white, an' blue, an' you's a Yankee."

If it were only as simple as that!

"Poke—"

"I see you safe fust, Miss Libby. Den I'll look after Mist' Crittendem."

The first was almost more than he could accomplish. At Fourteenth Street, the crowd before the Willard Brothers' great hotel blocked passage in either direction, and Poke had to turn off from the Avenue again. Singing and shouting followed the carriage.

"Look lak dey gonna make a war cry outa dat 'I wisht I was in Dixie,'" Poke prophesied.

266

The rhythm lent itself admirably to the beat of hands or feet. A ribbon cockade, a flag, a song . . .

Sixth and Pennsylvania at last, and another mob before Browns' and the National, but divided. Poke rounded the corner skillfully, muttering to people to get out of his way, then with a subdued shout called her attention to Senator Crittenden approaching the hotel on foot, accompanied by Senator Toombs.

"I see them," Elizabeth said. "Get their attention if you can."

The carriage guard at the National accomplished that. He recognized her or Poke—the latter was more probable—and shouted her name with emphasis. The men heard and turned to the curb. It was the Georgia Senator's strong arm that helped her to alight and his strong back, together with the commands of the door man, that got them all across the sidewalk. As they went through the crowd, Elizabeth heard him admonish Poke.

"Take care of yourself now, boy."

"Yassir, Mist' Senator, I will."

At the door Elizabeth recoiled. Kegs of rum and whiskey had been tapped and flowing freely for some time. Men with cockades linked arms and marched through the lobby and public rooms, singing hoarsely. Crittenden's face—under the lights it was a dead white—flushed darkly, then went whiter than ever. He turned to Toombs.

"I thank you, Robert, for your support this day; and now you'll be wanting to get home to Mrs. Toombs. You could have gone in Mrs. Crittenden's carriage."

"I'll see you to your rooms, John, if you don't mind."

"It's not necessary."

"You'll not deny me the privilege, I hope."

Elizabeth knew then that the news about South Carolina had been a second, and a secondary, blow. Crittenden's compromise resolutions had failed to pass the test of a committee vote. Afterward Elizabeth learned that the loyal friends who had voted for the resolutions, Robert Toombs among them, had been only one too few to give Crittenden the majority he needed. Afterward Crittenden whipped up his courage and failing strength to make another stand, and another; but each time was only that much more too late.

Upstairs in the Crittenden suite, somewhere behind drawn curtains a window had been left a little way open. The singing and the outcry from the streets came up into the room.

"They sound jubilant enough," Crittenden said drily.

Toombs muttered something under his breath and took his leave.

"I'll call around again in the morning," he said, in doing so.

He did call the next morning and on many another day while he and Mrs. Toombs remained in Washington; but it was a winter of farewells. The excitement of South Carolina Day gave way to soberer thought with time, but the rift did not narrow. It widened. On New Year's Day Elizabeth wore the last of her Bridport gowns to the President's reception. It was black velvet this time, with Chantilly lace. Matthew Brady made her portrait in it; and she looked a handsome dowager, indeed. Still queenly, with a display of jewels. Still fair, with shining hair, but definitely a dowager now, making the best of things. She called the velvet gown her widow's weeds for the city of Washington, which would never, never be the same again. Daily, it seemed to her, someone she held dear kissed her hand or her cheek and said good-bye.

In late January Jefferson Davis stood up in the splendid new Senate chamber and made his speech of farewell. He sounded no note of jubilance. When he finished there was not a dry handkerchief upstairs or down; and Elizabeth knew at last where she had seen eyes like those of Mr. Lincoln—deep, sad eyes under a high, broad forehead.

Oh, preposterous! The elegant, the suave, the cultured Mr. Davis and the self-taught backwoods lawyer? But there it was.

In the evening the Davises, making the rounds of their Washington friends, called on the Crittendens; and Varina Davis at parting broke down.

"Dear Mrs. Crittenden, if in the past I have ever been unkind . . . my wicked sense of fun . . . my . . ."

Her beautiful brown eyes glistened with tears. Elizabeth put her arms around her and they made moan together. She and Varina Davis, who, some said, was all mind and ambition and no heart. Then the Davises, too, were gone.

"Our friends have all left," Elizabeth said. "Shall we go, too, now?"

"We may have no choice," Crittenden said, with a flash of old whimsy.

His term in the Senate would end with the current session of Congress. It was possible that Kentucky might name another to his place. Kentucky had elected a secessionist governor, Beriah Magoffin. It would kill Crittenden, Elizabeth thought, if Kentucky left the Union now.

She went with Crittenden to Boston then, on the invitation of his old friend, Edward Everett.

"Will you take your compromise resolutions before the people in a general referendum?" Everett wrote. "Surely the people are the ones to say."

Too late, too late! The visit left Crittenden as much depressed as uplifted. He spoke earnestly to the audience that Everett had assembled, but knew that those who came were too few. Regiments of Massachusetts militia drilled on the Boston Common all through his speaking.

Elizabeth had a horrid time. She had left Susanna in Washington, thinking that the tactful thing to do. The dress of 1861 required a maid's attendance. Her hair in cold New England went dead and limp. Horrid, horrid, horrid!

Back to Washington then and the dreary, heart-breaking struggle to save what could still be saved. Back to Washington, where General Winfield Scott from a wheeled chair directed the policing of the city, to make it safe for a President's inauguration. At the ceremony itself Stephen Douglas held Mr. Lincoln's hat. A short while later, breaking under the intolerable strain of everything, Douglas collapsed on the floor of the Senate. In a week he was dead and Adela Cutts was a widow. At the inaugural ball for the first time Elizabeth came face to face with Mary Todd Lincoln. In the Bridport velvet, with emeralds flashing and bright hair once more in order, there was no question as to who looked the queen and who the impostor; but much good that did anyone now.

"Mrs. Crittenden?" Mrs. Lincoln's tone was acid. "We meet at last."

So, there!

Home then, to save Kentucky! Home?

"This house seems to me gloomier and gloomier," Elizabeth wrote in confidence to Lily Foxe. "Come war or destruction, if I am to end my days here, I must brighten it, and you must help.

"And it does look as if I might end my days right here. Mr. C. today is addressing the two houses of the Kentucky legislature in the Capitol, urging neutrality. He has speaking engagements covering the state, sounding the same cry: 'Stand firm. Extend a hand in friendship to both sides,' he says. A perfect way to be torn in two, I think; and that is what is happening to him and to Kentucky. One son is with Beauregard to the south of us—the West Pointer, naturally. The other, all his training in the field of diplomacy, is with McClellan in Ohio.

269

"In Missouri, I hear, it is much the same, except that they have had fighting over there. The secessionist governor—have I ever told you?—danced at my wedding in Boonslick most of a century ago. He was a clerk in a country store, his name Claiborne Jackson. Of my family, my father and Andrew McKinley side with the Union. Judge Hunton has brought my sister Mary and their family up to St. Louis from New Orleans. A wise move probably, taken in good time. Cabell, bless him, is on some secret courier service between Missouri's Governor and Jefferson Davis. He'll get himself hanged, I shouldn't wonder.

"Woodford County, ours, has elected Mr. C. now to the House of Representatives for the special session of Congress called by Mr. Lincoln for midsummer. Sometimes it seems to me I am racing madly back the way I came. I would not accompany Mr. C. to Washington, I would stay right here or, better, join my children in St. Louis, except that Mr. C. is not fit to travel alone. He makes these speeches. He throws his heart into them, and comes out each time looking thinner and older. Yesterday I reckoned his age according to the Crittenden Bible. He is seventy-four, Lily, and the very ghost now of the man I married so proudly."

The letter was addressed to New York. In the rioting that accompanied the muster of militia to the defense of Washington, stones had been thrown through the windows of Lily Foxe's *atelier* and several thousand dollars' worth of draperies and upholstering had been ruined by the rain. At least, that was the claim that Lily left behind her when she closed the shop and retreated.

It was a dreary city to which the Crittendens returned in July. Before the month was out, gloom was intensified by a state of panic following the ridiculous, the pathetic, the disgraceful rout of the Union Army at Bull Run. A new general had been called to take command—the second since poor old General Scott had been forced to surrender to gout and old age. McClellan put the city under martial law and succeeded in giving the raw troops something of the semblance of a defending force; but he was a little man, all strut and swagger; and Elizabeth would not like him. He had just completed a successful campaign in the mountains of a place now called West Virginia. When Congress passed a law dividing the Old Dominion, John Jordan Crittenden swore in his exasperation. For one excited evening Elizabeth thought, "Now it has come. Now he will abandon this fiction of neutrality and follow his heart. We can be with friends again."

Only her heart hoped for this. The next morning Crittenden went back to his desk in the House, to do what he could still, against partisan bitterness and greed and madness. And Elizabeth went to call on Winfield Scott, as she did often these days.

The old warrior was always glad to see her, and she took comfort in her turn, hearing him rumble and grumble and watching his eyes blaze in futile but glorious anger over things in general. Those fellows over there, he would storm, waving a heavy arm toward the Virginia shore, why, he'd helped raise them—Lee, Johnston, Jackson, Hill, Longstreet, Beauregard. The cream of his old captains. The Union had to get along with siftings. This fellow McClellan— he knew all the rules, but was he a fighter? Or it might be McDowell who made him growl, or Halleck or Hooker or Pope. Five generals in succession commanded the Army of the Potomac while the Crittendens remained in Washington; and none seemed the answer to anybody's prayer.

Out West a young brigadier general named Grant electrified the country with several astounding victories—Forts Henry and Donelson on the Tennessee and Cumberland rivers, then Shiloh; and Kentucky was inside the Union, whether or no. Maybe some day General Grant would be called to take his turn at the command in the East. Who knew?

But it mattered comparatively little to Elizabeth what generals fought where. Campfires over the Potomac depressed her, whether the men about them wore blue coats or gray. Victories for the Confederate forces kept her packed and ready for flight. Victories for the North made her tremble for the security of her friends in the South— Varina Davis serving Sunday night supper in Richmond now, Mrs. Clay, Mrs. Chesnut and the rest.

How long, Elizabeth asked herself. How long? Little things as well as big made trouble for her now. The new Federal Congress emancipated slaves in the District of Columbia and Susanna disappeared. Poke remained. She would have joined the general panic if he had not. She did not worry about Susanna, who would have set herself up in business, perhaps right in Washington, or Baltimore. But she had to do with hired maids now. She had as many in a few years as Washington had generals.

Finally there was the planting of a tree. The Crittenden Peace Oak, Mr. William Smith, Superintendent of the National Botanical Gardens, called it—with ironclad gunboats shelling each other as near as Norfolk and Hampton Roads. His idea was to offer lasting tribute to John Jordan Crittenden, for Mr. Smith was of those who believed that, if the Crittenden compromise resolutions had been adopted, this unholy war could have been prevented. For the ceremony he asked Crittenden to supply a Kentucky acorn; and Crittenden, sheepish a little over the idea, but pleased, did so. In fact, fearing that one acorn might sprout in his pouch in transit, acorns being as unpredictable as most other things in life, he brought several.

The ceremony was simple. The audience was small. It included the Crittendens, with Poke respectful in the background, Mr. Smith and his gardeners, Mr. Blair, Senior, editor of the old *Congressional Globe*, and a few bystanders. Travelers still came to Washington, perhaps to see the new Capitol dome, with Freedom triumphant on its peak. It seemed to many ironic that the building should have reached full majesty just now. To others the fact was reassuring.

The place where the oak tree was to grow was on the Capitol grounds, facing Pennsylvania Avenue. The memorial plate was ready, attached to a stake. A scrap of iron fencing would protect the seedling until the tree had reached recognizable proportions. Mr. Smith made a few appropriate remarks, principally to tell the strangers standing about, what was going on. Mr. Blair added a word or several. He also, he said, had given his country a lifetime of devoted service. He had two sons. One was a member of Mr. Lincoln's wartime Cabinet, the other was in uniform with the Union forces in the West. No one of the three or all taken together had done or could do more than John Jordan Crittenden had done in good times and in bad. The tree would sprout and grow, he promised; and weary travelers, resting under its shade, would read its legend and be better citizens for that brief acquaintance with a man loved and honored by all who had known him in his day.

"And now, Mr. Crittenden," Mr. Smith said, "will you drop the acorn?"

Crittenden had no speech, either; or he had forgotten it. For a second, as his hands fumbled with the strings of his pouch, Elizabeth was afraid he had lost the acorn; but he produced it finally, smiling at some secret thought.

"I suppose," he said, "it makes no difference how I drop it. They fall any which way in the woods."

And some of them pigs ate, or squirrels. Some remained to sprout and grow. All subject to God's will and the snow and the rain and the sun. They were boys burying a dead bird, Elizabeth thought. The bit of fencing would do for a burial enclosure, the tablet for a stone. And this was the end of dreaming?

"After much running about," Lily Foxe wrote from New York, "I have found a place where I can buy some good things at remarkable prices for these times. Brussels carpeting at $1.00, $1.25 to $1.50 per yard. Tapestry Brussels at 87 cents—very pretty, but I cannot vouch for the colors. How would you like a Green Oak Brussels at $1.37 for your parlor? I often can pick up remnants. What colors do you fancy in a hall carpet?

"Much love to your gem of a husband," Lily finished by saying. Elizabeth crushed the paper in her hands. Much she cared about carpeting now, with death whispering in shadowed corners of the old house and the other women sorting over crepe veils. It might prove difficult, they said, to buy decent mourning now.

Elizabeth would have no part in that, either. "I can't," she said to herself. "I can't go through that again. I won't."

What would she do . . . afterward? In her writing desk, among other unanswered letters, was one from her agent in Cooper County, Missouri—Mr. Freeman, Barcie Harris's husband, reporting another defaulted payment on the part of the syndicate that had bought those springs on the Ashley land—Chouteau Springs. He counseled patience. The war, he said, had ruined resort business, as she would see if she were on the spot. Did she think she might find time to make that long-promised and repeatedly deferred visit to Boonslick? Mrs. Freeman joined him in hoping, etcetera, etcetera.

Or, there was St. Louis. Logan Hunton wrote from there that business was at a standstill, either ruined or marking time and waiting for a better day. He had taken a place in the country outside the city for his family; and he and Mary would be enchanted if the Crittendens would visit them this summer, after they had rested up from their journey home. How many times he had wished that Crittenden were in Lincoln's place! There would have been no Emancipation Proclamation, he was sure. How had they left things in Washington? Was the Union lost for all time?

It might be, Elizabeth thought, unless an oak tree sprout would save it. Then she raised her head, listening to a muffled footfall abovestairs. Whoever it was crossed a room and recrossed and then was quiet. She bowed her head again, and waited. She could not escape now. Not now, but presently.

"Dear Mother, you are so tired! You have watched so long! Let me take my turn now. Go somewhere and rest. Can't you, dear?"

No, she could not. She could come nearer to rest, sitting here in a chair, than lying helpless, flat on a bed. She sat stiffly in the center of the front parlor. She couldn't place herself near a window because—

well, there were all those people outside. They pretended just to be passing; but they passed and passed again, hoping to see a member of the family and get the latest word. Several times a day Thomas or Henry Crittenden or Ann Crittenden Coleman would open a side door and issue a bulletin: "Father had a quiet night, but is no better. We can pray, but we have no grounds for hope, really."

He was dying. Kentucky gathered now to do him reverence, to watch and wait with her, with his family. She could not go near a window because of the people. She would remember how most of Frankfort had again met them at the train when they had returned this past March. She would see his locust trees and remember how once more he had paused to touch them lovingly, glad to have been allowed to greet them again. She would see the carriage block; and she would wonder about herself, her part in all this.

The third time in her life for a day of reckoning . . .

Her musings were broken now by a footfall on the lower floor— a man's step, heavy for all his effort to walk lightly. A hurried step, driven by great urgency. The next minute George Crittenden, the eldest of the dying man's sons, appeared. Elizabeth started up in surprise, and Lily's letter fell to the floor. Punctiliously Brigadier General Crittenden of the Confederate Army stooped and picked it up and handed it to her before he kissed her cheek in respectful greeting.

He was in uniform, the first and only time she saw him in the long gray coat, weather-spotted but neat enough.

"How did you get here?" she asked. "We were afraid you couldn't, even if our message got through to you."

"I just came," he answered. "For our own lines, of course, I had a pass. As for the others, I simply showed my papers, told them who I was and that Father was dying. There was always someone who knew him and so let me through."

She could believe his story. The town was filled with people from all over the state and beyond. Had he noticed?

"Yes," he said. "I had more trouble getting through Frankfort than all the rest of Kentucky." He flushed then above his brown beard. "Shall I change my coat before I speak to him?"

"No, dear," she said. "He may know you—I hope he will—but the coat won't matter. You had better go on up now, don't you think?"

"Will you go with me, Madame Mother?" he waited to ask.

"No," she said. "It isn't good for too many to be in the room. Anyhow, he doesn't know me. He has forgotten I ever existed."

"Oh, no!" George said. "I can't believe that. He adored you."

"I am sure he did—for a while. Don't mind, George. I understand. It's a general forgetting."

After all, he had forgotten his Maria, too. It was a girl named Sally whom he remembered now. She had never known Sally.

George Crittenden lifted her hand and brushed it with his lips. "You were always very sweet and good to him," he said huskily. "We wondered sometimes at your patience."

Then he left her and went upstairs.

His father did know him. That grace was granted both men. The Senator was asleep, they told her afterward, and those who watched were afraid he might not waken to this earth again; but, when George took a chair close to the bed, it creaked under his weight and the sick man opened his eyes. Slowly perception brightened in them.

"George?" he said faintly, but clearly. "Well!"

He did not see the gray coat. His next words were paternal chiding, but dealt with another matter.

"I don't hold with this custom of whiskers," he said. "I like jowls shaven clean."

He closed his eyes, opened them again and asked where he was. At home, they told him, home in Frankfort.

"Home," he repeated. "That's good." His last murmur, before he lapsed finally into unconsciousness, must have been unintelligible, for there were many interpretations. He died at peace with his world, if the serenity of his face was any sign.

Daniel Webster had composed an epitaph for him years before this: "A great and good man. Great men are not difficult to find, but a great and a good man is rarely seen." Poke's simpler, "Mr. Crittendem's a good man, Miss Libby," said much the same thing.

CHAPTER SIX

Chouteau Water

ON A BRIGHT, mild October morning of the year 1864 Barcie Freeman and her daughter stood on the entrance porch of Barcie's home in Boonville, Missouri. The house was a square, solid structure of brick, of no particular style or grace, but substantial. The same thing might have been said of the two women, Barcie especially, a plump, rosy-cheeked matron, frankly near sixty, but of an appealing freshness for all that—perhaps because of it. Her daughter resembled her in coloring and general build, but seemed more vehement, less bonny. That, however, could have been due to temporary impatience. The two women were dressed alike in gray calico, with full gingham aprons tied around their waists. The aprons were rumpled at the hem; and that and broad kerchiefs covering their hair spoke of a cleaning job.

"Good heaven's, Ma!" Barcie's daughter protested. "What is it you're trying to do? You've turned the house inside out and upside down—as if you didn't always keep it as neat as a pin."

Barcie studied her hands, made a face at them, and rolled them up in her apron. Her eyes turned then toward the yard gate and the street, though it was much too early to look for Libby, who had written that she would take the train as far as it ran, which was Tipton, Missouri, fifteen miles to the south of Boonville, and hire a livery stable rig for the rest of the journey.

"I wanted the place to look nice," Barcie said softly, wistfully. "The first time she has visited me since we were girls together."

"Fifty years ago!" her daughter snorted.

"Forty, Letitia," Barcie protested. "Don't make it worse than it is."

"Forty, then," Letitia conceded. "You literal person! Why do you suppose she's coming now? You've asked her over and over and she always put you off or simply didn't answer. And now—now, when everything's hard to manage, no help, and things scarce generally— Why, if she wanted to come back to Boonslick, didn't she go to her own people in Columbia? Or open the Ashley house here?"

" 'Titia, that spooky place? It wouldn't be safe for her, so far away from everybody, what with bushwhackers and Quantrill raiders and other tramps. And there's nothing now in Columbia that she remembers. The old house burned to the ground the first year of the war. I know . . . she has a brother there; but people drift apart."

"Do they, really?" Letitia mocked. "Ma, Pa's worried. She never writes to him, except to ask why such and such a rent has not been collected. Now, if she means to pester him about Chouteau Springs and the rest of that land—"

"I don't think that's it," Barcie said. " 'Titia, I don't know why she's coming; but I am glad and proud that she has turned to me. With her father gone, too, maybe she feels closer to me than to anyone else. As I keep saying, we were girls together. That's a special relationship, I think. Oh, 'Titia, she was the loveliest thing alive as I remember her. There was a kind of glow about her. Looking at her, you didn't know whether to be glad or sorry. It was wonderful to be like that, but you were sort of afraid, too. 'Tish, I don't know how to say it."

"Don't try, Ma," Letitia gave up the argument. A glow transfigured Barcie Freeman, too, now. "I'll run along, dear, and leave you to your reunion. You've just time to spruce yourself up and get your hair out of curlers. Good luck, Ma! See you tomorrow, maybe."

At precisely noon, the rattle of wheels brought Barcie out on the porch again—this time in a gray silk dress and a dimity apron. A livery rig, scarred and patched and drawn by two aging horses, was approaching the gate. It seemed to Barcie, however, as she hurried down the walk, that even these crowbait animals held up their heads with some special pride. Either that or their driver handled them with extraordinary skill. No livery stable pick-me-up, she saw at once. A Negro in good black cloth, with a high hat—

"Whoa!" he said with authority to the team. "Whoa, thar!"

"Poke?" Barcie said faintly, then in shrill question, "Poke?"

The Negro eased himself down to the sidewalk, lifted his hat from a head considerably frosted, and grinned, to show every gold tooth he had.

"Yas'm," he said. "Hit's me, Miss Barcie. Hit's me—Poke." He put his head back into the carriage. "She knowed me," he jubilated. Then, "Miss Libby, we got yere. You ready to come out now? Better res' yore weight on me an' not trust dat step too far."

"Oh!" With a soft, anticipatory exhalation, Barcie Freeman went on to the gate, then stopped again as a slender foot in a kid boot groped for the dubious step. A voluminous skirt of heavy black silk, disciplined by exquisitely gloved hands, came next. One of the hands let got presently, to reach for Poke's waiting shoulder. Nobody could have seen clearly through the yards of crepe veil that hung down on all sides from a widow's bonnet.

"Libby!" Barcie's cry was compassion, mingled with awe and considerable gratification. "Libby!"

It was not with too much hope that Elizabeth, following Crittenden's death, returned to Missouri. She had a reason for coming. She had even a wish, but that was all. Elizabeth Crittenden in search of a place to call home, just that.

She had never been more than a transient in Frankfort, Kentucky. The town had belonged to John Jordan Crittenden and he to the town. So for a while she had shared in the mutual possession, no more. When he died, as surely of mortal wounds as any hero struck down on a battlefield, when they laid him to rest in the Frankfort cemetery, if she could have had her immediate wish, she would have turned away at once and disappeared from the scene.

She couldn't do that. At the graveside Crittenden's "children" had made a ring around her. At home they were gentle, respectful, solicitous. "If there is anything of Father's that you want to keep, you know you are welcome." She smiled and shook her head. What she wanted of John Jordan Crittenden now, what she had of his, they could neither give nor withhold.

That in his last hours he had seemed to forget her was, she knew well, only a temporary aberration. Once he had loved her, as he said, with all his heart. She had been his dearest wife. She would hold to that honor and bear his name proudly through all of life that remained, and ask no more.

But where? Where would she live with that and other memories?

Not in Washington. She would never go back there. The bitter years when she had stood by, with a smile on her face, and watched Crittenden and other good men—her own bright dreams, as well—being ground to dust by inexorable circumstance had spoiled the capital city for her for all time.

Missouri beckoned then. Barcie wrote, once more urging her to make the Freemans a visit. "It will be like old times, Libby. . . . I hope you will make it a long visit." "Why not?" Elizabeth thought. Boonslick might be the very thing. It was a sweet and peaceful land, peopled by kindly folk. Twice, to be sure, she had fled from it in abhorrence; but, with the turmoil of youth and its mad fervors past, she might find it the refuge she sought. She would not try Columbia. Nor Boonville—too near the Ashley mound; but there were other towns. She pictured herself settled back into a hickory rocker by a warm fire. Sweet image, if only—

This solution had seemed especially desirable after a visit to St. Louis and a last interview with James Tower Sweringen. Dear man —old and weary, too, now—how glad he had been to turn her affairs over to Andrew McKinley! The Ashley fortune had suffered some from the distresses of war, but a good deal of the property remained. With the coming of peace—if it did not come too late—the income would increase. Meanwhile she had enough to enable her to live modestly almost anywhere or better than that if she chose a modest place of abode.

She had the money from Daniel's estate in her keeping now—a sum so pleasing that she dared not name it in terms of thousands of dollars. A thousand dollars had always seemed to send her off into a fit of spending. If unbroken, Daniel's bequest would buy or build her a house in some clean, little town.

"Splendid!" Mr. Sweringen had said when she mentioned her plan to him; and, perversely, from then on hope had dwindled. Oh, wicked, wicked! A woman of her years, chastened supposedly by life; but there it was. This bright October morning, driving over from Tipton in a hired hack on an execrable road, she had been like someone viewing a familiar pattern of land from a thousand miles away. Was it possible that Boonslick would have none of her now?

At the Freemans' gate, Barcie's cry made her recoil.

"I can't," she thought. "I really can't." But a gentle hand took her by the elbow then and a gentle voice said in her ear, "An old friend, dearest. You will, of course, be kind to her—at any cost to yourself." Elizabeth Crittenden, at that, put back her veil and summoned a smile.

"Barcie," she said, "how good of you to want me!"

Being kind, being to Barcie what Barcie wanted her to be, carried Elizabeth Crittenden through the ordeal of the visit. She would not have believed that it could be such an ordeal. Going up the walk to the front door, hand in hand with Barcie, the uncompromising, square solidity of Barcie's house frowned her to a halt.

"Your home," she said gently. "I've never seen it before, you know."

"Well," Barcie said virtuously, "mine and Mr. Freeman's. It's not grand."

"Precious," Elizabeth said; and so it was—for Barcie.

Poke carried in her trunk before he went away to put up the livery rig where he could keep his eyes on it and the horses. Elizabeth held him with last-minute instructions and precautions until he grumbled and muttered and Barcie said finally, "He'll be all right, Libby. Why are you worried about him?"

"In a way," Elizabeth said, "he's all I have left. Susanna skipped out, you know."

"Dear, you're tired," Barcie said. "Come inside now. Mr. Freeman will be home to dinner any minute."

In the house Elizabeth tried to miss no detail of Barcie's prideful housekeeping—the lace over pink pincushion on the marble-topped dresser in the best bedroom, the hand-crocheted counterpane on the bed, the starched lace curtains.

"All so beautifully, lovingly clean!" she marveled. "Just what I would have expected of your house.

She laid aside her bonnet then with its yards of veiling and was startled this time by a cry of distress.

"Your hair!" Barcie wailed. "It's as lovely as ever. I still have to put mine up every night of the world. It makes my arms and my head ache; but, if I don't . . . Oh, Libby, you have changed and you have not changed."

It was Barcie who had not changed. Sweet, impulsive, natural, a little absurd as always. The girl, Elizabeth Moss, had known and loved her well. Elizabeth Crittenden could sometimes hardly remember Elizabeth Moss. What she did remember of those days was a roseate hue rather than simple fact.

"You're a fortunate woman, Barcie Freeman," she said, on the third day of her visit. This was after she had seen all of Barcie's home, her chickens and her ducks, and all of Barcie's family. "You chose well when you married Mr. Freeman." A solid, seamy man in his late sixties, devoted, stalwart, dependable and quite uninteresting. "You've lived right here always. Your family grew up and stayed here with you. You're quite surrounded with loving ones. Do you know how fortunate you are, Barcie?"

"Libby," Barcie said in her turn, "I've never asked about you. You know, I am dying to hear it all. I thought, maybe, you might want to tell me. But don't, if you'd rather not."

Elizabeth had no wish not to tell her everything. She simply did not know how to begin or how to shape her story. It was a strange story. Some would find her part in it a subject for censure, some for wonder. She would like to keep the wonder in Barcie's clear eyes; but, if she told it all— And then she thought, "How would I make her or anybody understand?"

Right then one of Barcie's grandsons brought her a letter, battered, damaged, almost unreadable after its travels across the nation, from Lily Foxe.

"Whom do you think I saw yesterday?" Lily wrote from New York. "A Virginia cousin of yours—a Miss Pleasants."

Light burst all around Elizabeth.

"A letter from another old friend," she said to Barcie. "I'll tell you about her—as soon as I see what she has to say."

Barcie shed a few jealous tears over Lily Foxe.

"It's only to be supposed," she sniffed, "that you would have other friends, but I thought . . ."

"None as nice as you," Elizabeth comforted. "You wouldn't care for Mrs. Foxe at all. But we have many things in common." Memories chiefly. "Barcie, it's this business of living. A short while ago I called you a fortunate woman. I meant it. But I, too, have been fortunate, though in a much different way. I was always a reaching person, Barcie. You know that. And in life the way that works out is this. A person sights a goal and sets out for it, and only when that progress has been made and it isn't possible to go back, realizes what that has done to one's own character. That has happened to me three times, Barcie, until now it is as if I had been three women instead of one, but have to reckon personally with the sum of them all. I have changed. I have changed almost beyond my own recognizing. My stay in your sweet home has shown me how much I have changed. I could not sit quietly among the beautiful, simple surroundings I knew and loved as a girl. For many years I have made my life out of knowing people—numbers of people. Well, New York's that kind of place. People come and go. I can have a home there and shall hope that, of the many I have known and loved, some will want to seek me out for an hour or a day or longer."

Her children could visit her in New York. That would be better than her visiting them. Her grandchildren would come—Ashley McKinley and Ashley Cabell, Crittenden Cabell and John Crittenden McKinley and the rest. So she would keep a legend alive.

She wrote to Lily to find rooms for her, modest rooms in a pleasant, convenient location.

"Do not be extravagant, Lily. I must live within my means. If I do not, who is to come to my rescue now?"

"And now, Mr. Freeman," she said at midday dinner, "if you can spare me the time, I'd like to settle with you about my land here."

Harvey Freeman sighed.

"I'm sorry the sale of Chouteau Springs didn't net you more," he said.

"Not the Springs," she told him. "I was glad to be rid of them, really." Glad now to have thought of a way of disposing of the rest of the Chouteau Grant. "I want to deed what remains of the La Mine tract," she said, "to my children, Mary Jane McKinley and Anna Marie Cabell."

"There's an entail," Freeman reminded her.

"I know—the acre with the grave. You'll know how to arrange that, you and Andrew McKinley, my elder son-in-law. He has charge now of all my property."

"I've corresponded with him," Freeman said, "and some with the other one."

"Cabell," Elizabeth said quickly. "He's a fine fellow, too; but you will find Mr. McKinley smoother, pleasanter to work with. He practised law with my late husband, Senator Crittenden, and learned much from him. The children will have all I own some day; but this I should like to give them now."

And good riddance, good riddance at last!

There remained finally only Poke. Independently he elected to stay on in Boonville. The next day, as he drove Elizabeth back to Tipton over the awful road, he told her why and how.

"Ef you coulda made up yore min' to be easy yere, Miss Libby, I'd a stood right by you all thoo, but I cain't go back East wid you. I's gittin' on, Miss Libby. I'll jes' stay right yere. I got a projeck. I been lookin' aroun' at dose springs. De hotel's run down, but de springs is dar, de pumps and pipes, too. Folks in town set sto' by dat watah. I gonna bargain wid dis Tipton livery stable man fo' one o' dese pore ol' hosses, gonna git me a cyart and some jugs an' I gonna peddle Chouteau watah. 'Chouteau Watah! Chouteau Watah!' " He raised his voice in a howling chant, to show her.

"Mercy!" Elizabeth said. She would pay for the horse and the cart, but, "Can you live on that?" she asked.

"No'm. 'Cose not. Jes give me a lil money in mah jeans. Gonna git me a patch o' groun' somewhere an' plant co'n an' taters an' sech. I'll make out."

And now, with no loving, anxious eyes to witness them, tears came to Elizabeth. She let them flow, unchecked.

"Poke," she said, "will you be happy?"

"No'm, I won'," he said. "I'd much ruther be ol' Doc' Moss's boy Poke or de Ashleys' man or Missus Crittendem's coachman; but I cain' pick mah ruthers now. I got to figger how to make out. I ain' gonna be happy any mo' dan you gonna be real happy; but we'll all bofe make out. Hit's lak dat dish yore Pa an' Doctah Daniel and Mist' Crittendem favored so, de one de Gin'ral couldn't tech—vinegah pie. Dis yere's de vinegah in our pie, Miss Libby. Cain' hab de sweet widout de tart, seems lak. An' now we got mos'ly de tart. But dey's some sweet lef'. Some day—some day, Miss Libby, mebbe you come back to Boonslick. An' I'll be yere, waitin'. . . ."

"Poke, I can't bear to leave you like this. Goodness knows—"

"You gonna leave me. I gonna see you safe on de cyars an' you go right on to New Yo'k an'— Say 'Howdy' to Mis' Foxe fo' me."

"Poke, you're sure you've got all your papers?"

"De to whom it may concern dat you'se to be notified do I git in trouble? I got it, Miss Libby, in Mist' Crittendem's wallet right nex' to me. Git along, hosses. Make lak you cin trot now an' bounce Miss Libby so she'll yell, 'stead o' setting dar spottin' her good silk veil. Giddap, dar!"

AUTHOR'S NOTE

THIS TIME I hardly know how or where to begin my acknowledgment of indebtedness. I think first of the heroine of the story, born Elizabeth Moss. I owe her my thanks just for being her own lively, exciting self, for living in such a way that anyone who heard of her must want to try to tell the tale. But I must thank her, too, for introducing me to a part of Missouri to which before this I had given only passing notice.

Boonslick—somewhere in the book I explained the term. It is a region lying on both shores of the Missouri River about midway of its meanderings across our state. Its boundaries are hazy. You can hardly state them without waving both arms. I sometimes think it is as much a legend as it is a place.

The name comes from a spring, now in Howard County, where Daniel Boone and his sons went yearly to boil down water for salt. United States Highway number 40 still follows closely the old Boone's Lick Trace. The Boones, you see, moved over into Missouri even before the Louisiana Purchase in 1804. They were followed by a sprinkling of other hardy American pioneers; but the region was not really opened for settlement until after the War of 1812, when, following the location of a fort or two farther upstream, the territorial government pronounced the land safe for habitation.

Immediately a wave of migration, chiefly from Virginia and the Carolinas, swept over Kentucky and Tennessee into this fair new land. The land was very fair—noble hills, forest-crowned, fertile valleys and flowering prairies. The settlers were, on the one hand, struggling upland farmers who hoped to make an easier living here, and on the other, landed gentry, educated usually for some profession, but with a love for broad acres and hospitable firesides, who hoped to find in Missouri a manner of life which had become difficult or even impossible on the more populated and often worn-out land back East. Whether few or many of these settlers had their dreams fulfilled is beside the point. They established homes and left to the land and their children an inheritance not to be measured in dollars. Today

Boonslick in Missouri stands for true neighborliness, open-handed hospitality, hardihood and integrity of character, and culture by its broadest definition.

As I said in the beginning, all this was unexplored territory to me, too, until I undertook to trace the legend of Elizabeth Moss. This young woman, known in printed biographies by various other names, in an era when most men outlived several wives, managed to survive three distinguished husbands. She flew high and she flew far but she was a Boonslick girl to begin with. So it was to Boonslick I turned for my best information about her and so discovered this part of Missouri.

On location I had the advantage of several superior guides. Charles van Ravenswaay, Director of the Missouri Historical Society, which houses its library and valuable collections in St. Louis, is a native of Boonville in Cooper County. He knows, besides, almost all there is to know about Missouri history; and he personally met and escorted me and my companion, my sister Adele, up hill and down dale over what we call in the story the La Mine Tract or the Chouteau Grant. We stood with him on the Ashley Mound and studied the long stretches of the Missouri River visible from there. We drank of the water of Chouteau Springs. Later I heard of his going back to grub on hands and knees in my behalf to trace the foundations of a house long since gone to ruin.

On the evening of our first exploration, Mr. van Ravenswaay's mother, Mrs. C. H. van Ravenswaay, was hostess to our family party at dinner over in Fayette in Howard County, where a Mrs. Clifford still produces on order samples of matchless Boonslick cookery. At this party—just to show how things happen in Boonslick—I also met Judge Roy D. Williams and his lady of Boonville. Judge Williams is descended from one of the earliest families of that section and is possessed of an inexhaustible store of anecdote, which he poured into my thirsty ears all evening; and the next day at the Cooper County courthouse, he opened every door except that of the jail for me. I am indebted to him and to the gentlemen in the land title office across the way for a firsthand view of authentic records. In this connection, I am also deeply indebted to Judge Williams' secretary, not only for the many letters she wrote me after my visit but chiefly for her glad permission to use her inimitable, authentic Missouri name—Barcie Harris —for one of my secondary characters. If Boonslick folk like you, they'll just give you anything.

Down the river a way, in Columbia in Boone County, my thanks are due to Miss Sarah Guitar, another name to conjure with in Boonslick, who keeps the records and the newspaper files of the State Historical Society in the University of Missouri library. She and her assistants helped me glean whatever information exists about Elizabeth Moss's first husband. Also with drawings of plats and my quoted references, Miss Guitar helped me locate the Moss homestead on Two-Mile Prairie. Over and above all the help, I am grateful for ever so brief a meeting with this charming guardian of Missouri archives.

In St. Louis, I owe much, as always, to the willing service of the library staff of the Missouri Historical Society. To Marjorie Douglas, Curator of the Museum. To Barbara Kell, the librarian, and her assistant, Ruth How, patient fetchers of books and bound periodicals. To Frances Biese for fine-combing the manuscript collections for obscure items of information. To Dana Jensen, who edits the Society's magazine with one hand and bakes Boonslick chocolate cakes with the other. To the janitors, too, who give me hearty welcome whenever I enter the building. By now I suspect I am part of the Museum.

Elsewhere in our town, I am indebted to Mr. J. O. Spreen of the St. Louis Chamber of Commerce, who has set up most of our historical markers, and to Dr. Wm. G. Swekosky, who makes a hobby of historic houses, for many pertinent facts, generously given, about William Ashley, the second husband.

For the Washington picture, on a visit there arranged by Dr. Jacks of Creighton University, who engaged me one summer to lecture on the historical novel at a literary workshop sponsored by the Catholic University of America, I made an all-out taxpayer nuisance of myself to the staff of the Library of Congress. There among other research bits, I went through the 28 volume collection of the John Jordan Crittenden papers, which, balanced with Elizabeth's own correspondence, on file in St. Louis, set up the third part of the story.

I cannot close this acknowledgment without another bow. This time in the direction of George Stevens, my good friend and editor. May he live forever! His help and guidance are inspired and inspiring.

The principal characters of the story bear real names, all on the historical record. The interpretation of character is, of course, my own, but made after much contemplation and study, and so true to me, at least. Minor characters are either inventions or composite or type portraits. A few lesser dates have been juggled, to condense or point up a drama that covered a long stretch of years. Generally, however, significant events and the personal history of the major characters follow the sequence of fact.

The story was in all its aspects a rare adventure to trace and to set down. I hope that will be a shared experience for those who read it.